C000298697

First Printed in the UK in 2022

ISBN Paperback 978-1-7399355-2-8

ISBM Hardback 978-1-7399355-3-5

The book was written using American English Grammar. The characters in this book are entirely fictional of the author's invention and any resemblance to actual persons living or dead is coincidental.

Book Cover Design & interior elements by Thea Margarand

Book Map design by Chaim Holtjer

Proofreading by Kim Campbell

This is for my mother who really wants me to write a nice
historical romance.
Sorry, Mum!

INTRODUCTION & TRIGGER WARNINGS

To my dear readers,

Thank you once again for your ongoing love and support, and for following me on my author journey this far. I sincerely hope you enjoy this book. I enjoyed every moment of writing it, but it was a labor of love. *Time Travel*. Oh boy, that's all I'll say.

This book was written for a teenage audience and adults to enjoy, but I would like to take a moment to warn you in advance about some mild sexual references, profanity, descriptions of violence, divorce, and descriptions of child loss, which may be triggering to some readers.

Phew, now that is taken care of, I hope you have a wonderful time reading this book, and get lost in the woods again with Win, Rowan, Luke, and the gang. As always I would like to take a moment to mention that all Indie authors thrive on reviews and ratings. Please take a second once you've finished heading over to the place you bought it and leave a review, or some stars so that others are more likely to find this book and love it too.

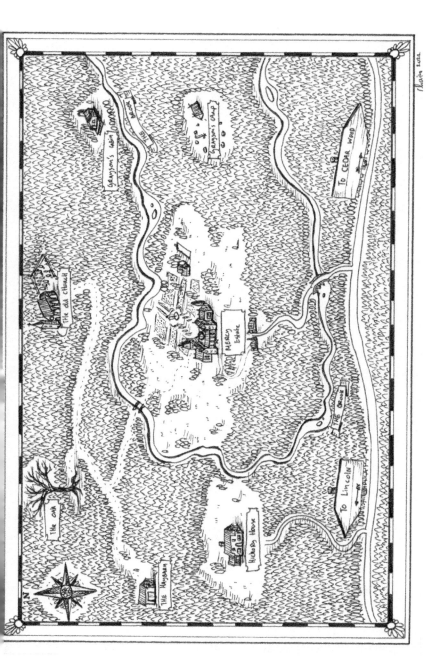

PROLOGUE

The burning hurt like hell. The scent of scorched flesh filled his nose; the searing, blistering pain threatened to engulf him as he rematerialized at his destination. Smoke rose from his charred clothing, amazingly intact after the journey, as he straightened and staggered to his feet, beating his arms. It hurt every damn time.

It wasn't often that he needed to make the trip. Jumping was something he avoided at all costs, knowing how much it hurt and how it chipped away at his life expectancy. Every jump cost him a year of life, gradually weakening him over time. He learned long ago that his last trip was coming, and once that day was over, maybe he'd grow into an old man and finally die.

But for now, he still had some years left in him, enough to do something good with this mess of existence. The man stretched, wincing as he uncurled from his knees. Tilting his dark head, he stepped out of the charred circle he'd arrived in, the sun blazing at his back. Underfoot, the soil was burnt, and he kicked it over with leaves, knowing his magic left an invisible trace in the air.

The question was, where had he arrived? He knew the time. That was certain. All he had to do was close his eyes and breathe through the flames, envision the timeline he needed to visit. Only back, never forward. If he could go forward, perhaps he could have fixed everything.

Why was it always down to him to fix the mistakes of his sisters? Plowing through the undergrowth, long, wet grass trailed across his heavy biker boots. He sniffed the air. It was morning, and slowly, the sun's orange glow peaked above the dense canopy. He trudged through vines and densely packed trees, recognizing the well-worn muddy path until it opened onto a place he knew well. Ahead lay an expansive, sprawling yard dotted with animal pens, and a great black-clad haybarn loomed in the distance. Mist circled the grassy field as he squinted, narrowing his gaze at a large wooden-clad farm-house, the cozy-looking kind, nestled in the woods, with a wrap-around porch and rocking chairs. A home built for a founding family, a place that had once been his home.

How many times had he waited here over the years? Squeezing his eyes shut, he forced away the image of the last time he'd been here, hidden among the trees. A yell from the haybarn made his dark eyes pop open and his breath hitch. Scrambling back to the safety of the trees, he watched as a farmhand—a young boy ran from the barn. Screaming.

"Help—please help!" Hurtling toward the house at break-neck speed, the boy didn't pause for breath till he clattered through the porch door. "She's dead...she's dead."

The stranger gritted his teeth. Without waiting for the house to wake in disruption, he ran across the yard, and with ice in his lungs, he threw open the barn door.

A shudder rolled over his entire body. The smell of damp hay clogged his nose. A young girl lay sprawled on the ground with dark hair tumbling over her face. With shaky fingers, he lifted her hair revealing wide, open eyes. Blood wept from the wound at her neck, pooling around her head, clinging to strands of dark hair. Carefully he backed away, shivering.

Mary Hickory was dead—but it wasn't right. If she was dead, then that meant somewhere.... Irritable and anxious, the man raked his hands through his wiry, dark hair.

Damn...she wasn't supposed to die this way.

"Father, stay in the house," a female voice made the hairs on his neck stand up. Familiarity sparked at the sound of that voice, though it was so much younger than the one he would come to know— forceful, commanding, and authoritative. Through the door, he spotted her running toward the barn, and he panicked, diving into an empty stall, hidden from view as she staggered inside.

Crouching on one knee, he knew this was a terrible plan. Just one glimpse of her made his heart rocket. Hitching up the hem of her nightgown, long golden hair trailing down her back, he watched as she swayed on the balls of her feet, gaping at the gruesome discovery on the ground. Louisa Hickory stumbled, and fell to her knees beside her dead sister. She let out a horrified scream.

Grimacing, he looked away as she wailed into her sister's chest, wishing he could go to her. She was so young, barely seventeen.

This wasn't *his* Louisa. He was about twenty years too early. She was not yet the woman he'd fall in love with. But she still had that steely look, that prim lip, defiant chin. The Louisa he loved was older, careworn, but courageous. He bit back a sob, something sorrowful igniting in his chest.

And she would die in his arms.

Louisa tensed, her shoulders stiffening as she lifted her chin. He froze as she let go of her sister's lifeless hand. Rigid, he swallowed, knowing she'd scream if she discovered him. Part of him almost wanted her to spot him. God, he wished he could warn her. He ached to tell her what he knew, seize her and take her away, and make sure nothing terrible would ever happen to her. Today would be the first of many terrible things in her life. Losing her sister Vivienne had been the first. Now Mary.

"Who's there?" She sniffed the air, and he edged back, pressing his spine into the slats of the horse's stall. She was a baby Therian, still so young, he couldn't tell if she'd yet made her change, but through the grooves in the wood, he saw her duck into a prowling stance, her eyes predatory, flicking back and forth as she got closer.

He almost grinned. She was his little fox, his soulmate. The thought coated his tongue, leaving a bitter taste, trying to forget the last time he'd held her. It should have been forever.

Her shoulders stiffened, attention drawn back to the house as someone called for her, and for a second, she appeared to forget what she thought she'd seen. A shadow, a memory. That was all he ever was. With a swish of long blonde hair, she ran.

Inside the house came terrible wailing and raised voices, and he knew that was his cue to leave. Forcing himself to move, he ran through the trees, panting.

"Shit..." he wheezed, clutching his chest. God, he was unfit. He bent double, his lungs cold and heaving. If Mary was dead, it meant something had crossed through the door, and he'd sensed the imbalance in his time.

Jumpers could tell when there'd been disruption with the line, sensing it eroding like waves beating a cliff edge. Time shifting, lines diverging. Propped up at a bar in Boston, the shift boiled in his blood like currants of electric crackling along a wire. It startled him out of his stupor.

Euelea needed him.

The forest darkened, and he scanned the mist curling through the trees. Magic left a trail, no matter how faint, like a threadbare strand of cotton unraveling before his eyes. Walking for a while, it grew brighter, violet, and pure, his sister's mark, and he wondered how she could be so stupid. Why had she never left?

An animal hunted her. The thing that crossed the door was close, and if he could spot her essence in the air, this *thing* would have no issues hunting her down.

The pines grew densely packed, and through the bleakness, he spied a small, dilapidated cabin, circled by a trickling brook. Smoke billowed from the stone stack chimney. Leaning heavily on a trunk, he hissed and wished he'd taken up that gym membership at the college—job perks he ignored. Leaves and twigs cracked under his heavy boots.

Dry-mouthed, he watched the door and contemplated knocking, wondering what her reaction would be. It had been a long, long time.

Luckily, he didn't need to wait to find out. The door clattered open, and a pretty young woman walked out with a bucket and pail under her arm. The corset stays hung loosely at her back. She looked like she'd rolled out of bed, half-dressed and sleepy-eyed. He released a breath caged in his chest. She looked the same as he remembered, young, unchanged by time, still lovely, golden-skinned and dark, with swathes of hair. The night Vecula bound them in their curse, from that moment, time and age didn't touch any of them.

Eternal youth and vitality. The curse of the Vargas.

Absorbed in her chores, she didn't see him as she waltzed to the brook, hitching up her skirts as she bent to fill her pail. Her dark, glossy hair tumbled down her back, and he gritted his teeth, knowing he was about to scare the hell out of her.

He crept closer, and his boot cracked a twig. "Ah, crap!"

The woman jerked, and two dark eyes that mirrored his locked on him. She screeched and tumbled backward, the pail spilling onto the mud.

He allowed himself a chuckle, imagining what she saw. A man big enough to fill a doorway, muscular with wiry, unruly dark hair that fell to his shoulders and arched, thick brows. The right brow was pierced with a silver bar. A man dressed in a tattered ACDC tee-shirt, with a dark long wool coat, ripped denim jeans, and boots he never bothered to lace. He resembled a grizzly bear, and apart from the gold flecks in his dark eyes, he had a rather strange feature that earned him his nickname.

The woman, his sister, cowered, eyes raking him top to bottom before she climbed to her feet. Then her lips twitched into an amazed, joyful smile. "My god....brother...." she gasped out. "Wolfric?"

He held out his palms in an open gesture. "Hey, babe."

She pelted across the shallow brook, sloshing water over her dress, and threw her arms around his neck, taking his face in her hands. It was an old face, though he looked no older than thirty. "Is it you? Brother...I thought you were dead."

"Nope, Euelea, I'm very much alive and kicking." She cringed at the use of her real name, her birth name, not the one she'd taken in Iceland—the last time they'd been together as a family.

She seized his large arms, craning her neck to look at him more closely. "How is this possible? I saw you die!"

"I don't have a lot of time to explain. Trust me when I say... it's been a ride. And it turns out I have a little gift—call it a present from Nassau. I call it the Phoenix flame. And I didn't know it existed until I woke up in a shallow grave and scared the shit out of the two men sent to bury me."

Brows, thin like brush strokes, drew together as she punched his arm harder than he expected. "Ow! What was that for?"

"You've been alive—all these years!" Her eyes were wet. "And you didn't come to find me? We thought you were dead...I saw..." She choked on emotion, grasping her throat, "I saw what that crowd did to you...."

He cocked a brow. "And yet...you two didn't wait long to see what happened. You were on the first ship out of there, bound for—" He waved his arms wide. "The brave new world."

Her nostrils flared angrily. "We were in danger...I never wanted to leave you behind. Vecula made me leave...."

"Ah, change the record, sis. It's been your mantra for longer than I care to remember."

At that, she huffed like a ten-year-old, and his chuckle rumbled, deep and rich, bestowing her with his smile. She jerked back at the sight of the two features he was infamous for, the two slightly elongated eye teeth got him his nickname as a child.

They weren't fangs, only long enough to catch your attention if you were unlucky enough to earn a grin out of him, which rarely happened these days—sharp enough to make you look, and question what you saw. Isaac gave him his name, Wolfric, and the real one he forgot long ago. Wolfric suited him and it stuck. He had a smile to scare small children. He was the biggest, the hairiest, and the most frightening.

His sister folded her arms. "Didn't you ever file those things off?"

He ran his tongue over the two sharp canines. It was good that he didn't have a job that required him to smile much. He only needed to glower at students over his coffee and mumble into his beard. "They grow back. I'm stuck with them—among other things."

She exhaled. "You left me. With her." Her tone was accusatory, sharp, and cold. He knew it was true, recalling the moment he'd awoke, half-frozen and starving in a pit deep in the Scandinavian woods. The two men burying him had screamed in terror, running frantically back to the village. Delirious and beaten, Wolfric staggered back to the hut, baffled that the crowds hadn't yet razed it.

Sensing his sisters had left, their trail long gone, he did the only rational thing he could think of. He rolled up his sleeves and held his forearm over a fire till the tattoo binding him to his family bubbled and melted along with his skin. The binding was undone, and Wolfric was free. Did he feel guilty about leaving his sister to her miserable fate? Maybe a little. Alone in the world, he struggled to understand how he was alive after being beaten to death by a crowd whipped to a frenzy with hatred and fear. He struggled to accept how he survived, yet Isaac...the best of them, lay headless in a cold grave.

"Look, I'm sorry, okay?" he grumbled. "I had a taste of freedom—at last. And I seized it by the balls. I did follow about twenty years after you left."

She bit her lip, pressing back tears. "It doesn't matter now. Vecula's dead." She glanced up at him, a thought coming to her, and it shocked enough to drain her complexion. "Gods...Vecula! She's dead, isn't she? She's not going to jump out and surprise me?"

Wolfric hated the questions that she was bound to ask. "Nope, *fortunately* for you, our big sister is well and truly dead."

Her face lightened, eyes sparkling with renewed hope. "What about Isaac? Is he...?"

It ached to think of his older brother—the gentle one, despite his size and what he was capable of. Isaac was powerful, strong, like an unmovable mountain, and yet he'd craved none of it. He'd loved whittling wood, something they teased him about endlessly. His death...he hadn't deserved a fate like that. "No," Wolfric muttered, swallowing a lump in his throat. "Unless he's playing a good game of hide and seek...he's gone."

"How did you find me here?"

He shook his head in amusement. "Your trail...your light. I can see it, remember? You aren't exactly hard to find, hiding out here. Which brings me to another point—why the hell are you still here?"

She lifted her chin. "I like it here. It's quiet and...." Her eyes traveled down his shirt. She wrinkled her nose, gaping at his worn jeans, his mud-splattered boots. "What on *earth* are you wearing?"

He fingered his shirt. "It's the fashion—where I come from."

"It's hideous."

"I like it."

"You'll stick out like a sore thumb here." Her dark chocolate eyes found him, and her initial annoyance seemed to have dissipated to his relief. She was the youngest, his baby sister, and he'd always been close with her. If they quarreled as children, it wouldn't be long till she sought him out to say sorry; thirteen years between them made no difference. "What are you...in your time? Why do you dress like that?"

He straightened his coat. "I'm a professor—at a college. And they don't care much how I dress, besides it's the weekend. Don't give me a hard time!"

She chuckled, but her smile soon wavered. "How long can you stay?"

Grumbling, he took her wrist, circling his fingers around her slim bones. "I'm not hanging around. I came here to warn you, and I don't have long. I'll have to go back—and soon."

"What are you talking about?"

Wolfric knew what was heading her way, and despite the serenity, the bubbling of the brook, and the gentle sway of the trees, she couldn't stay here. It was too quiet out here, the air thick with her magic, acting as a beacon. Birds scattered through the trees overhead, breaking their conversation, and shattering the peace of the woodland, cloaking the cabin on all sides.

Tension fizzled under his skin, and the itch to light up became a dull, groaning ache. He was about to be pulled back to his own time. Two hundred years into the future, the magic he used to walk through the centuries would only last an hour before he would catch fire like a lighted match and emerge the other end, smoking and charred. Euelea grabbed his wrist and rolled up his sleeve. She narrowed her eyes at the puckered skin where his family binding had been, the same place hers remained. Except now, there was something else tattooed over the top. It was a black outline of a bird...a falcon... a raven? She frowned.

"What is this?" she breathed out, running the pad of her thumb over the etching. Their eyes, so similar, locked.

"Evan..."

She jerked. "That's not my name. What is *this?*"

"A phoenix," he said. She blinked up at him, and he grinned, cocking his head. "I just keep on coming back."

Her throat bobbed, and he could tell what she thought as she stared unblinking down at the hideous remains of what had held them captive for centuries—locked to Vecula until death.

"You mean to tell me...this was all I had to do...to be free of her. All these years...."

He held her as she sobbed into his massive chest. "I'm sorry, babe. She was never as powerful as she made us believe."

"Why didn't you come back?" She looked up at him, watery-eyed and accusing. "We could have had a life together... as a family."

Stroking her hair, he planted a kiss on her forehead. "I needed to be alone. I got murdered and then woke up very much alive, pulled back from death by god knows what power. It's a lot to process...and I did show up eventually. About twenty years after you left. But I got a little side-tracked."

She scoffed. "By a woman? Was she a blonde by any chance?"

His grin slipped, a lump forming in his throat at her soft insult, hardly able to force out the words. Wolfric didn't talk about Louisa. And no other woman came close in the years he'd been alive. In his youth, he'd earned a terrible reputation as a womanizer and a cheat, but that ceased the day—the *second* he'd met Louisa. Wolfric exhaled out, "Try...the love of my life."

Her ire softened, and she touched his arm. "Oh, Wolfric. I'm sorry."

He shook his head, knowing she was distracting him. She'd want him to stay, and it broke his heart that he couldn't. "Listen...and listen carefully. Any moment now, I'm going to be sucked back. I can't stop it, and once I go back, I can't return, not for a long time."

"Why?" Her eyes shone with tears. "I've just got you back, and now you're leaving me?"

"When I make my last jump—it's over for me, my immortality. I don't have many jumps left but I had to make this one, and it *has* to count."

Struck by his selfishness, he realized he was the big brother, her protector, and wasn't that his role, to look out for her? And wasn't he done with this half-life? Living forever sucked, but knowing it could be over once he made the last jump was worse.

"Can't you go forward? See the future?"

He grimaced. "Not how it works, babe. I wish I could. I can only go back for a short time. Evan, you have to leave here, now!"

She pulled back, tutting. "Why? This is my home. And stop calling me that. It's not my name!"

"It will be, one day. Things are about to go wrong for you—badly wrong if you stay. Something is coming, a creature that crossed the door. He killed Mary Hickory—you remember *that* family, right?"

Her expression soured, his statement a sharp reminder of the curse she'd cast with Vecula, guilt written across her face. He had a feeling that regret lurked deep within her. Maybe that was the reason she'd hung around all this time. "I didn't want to hurt any of them. Vecula...." Guilt ate her soul. He could see it living there like a parasite latched to her innards. "I thought if I stayed here...maybe I could help them...be a part of their lives somehow?"

"I get that!" He gripped her shoulders urgently. "And one day—you will."

"Vecula..." she started, but he growled and cut her off.

"Yeah, yeah...Vecula made me do it, *blah, blah*. I get it!"

She withdrew as though she'd been stung, and he regretted being so hard on her.

"In my time, the one I came from, there has been a *momentous* fuck up. The Hickory family—the *current* ones sent something through the door, the very door that Vecula wanted to open the night you cursed that family. This thing came here and murdered Mary Hickory which was never supposed to happen! She never died that way the first time."

Euelea drew back, pacing frantically. "What killed her before?"

"She tried to force her calling in the woods, using the stone's light. But somehow, in the process—a hunter got to her. A hunter named Riley."

His sister's eyes widened, recognizing the name. "I know of that family."

He rolled his eyes, glowering with impatience. "Yeah, well, they've had a long-standing relationship with the Hickory's over the years...that family is responsible for killing—"

Breaking off, his throat clogged, sharply reminded of Louisa, choking and gasping for breath before she died.

"Brother..." She touched his arm, startling him out of his daze.

"Not a nice family...though the current one isn't so bad...I think he'll be useful." He waved his hands, frustrated he kept getting off track. "I have a plan—it's an insane, probably shitty plan, but you must remain alive if I'm going to pull it off. So you need to shift your ass!"

"Shift my ass?" she gasped at his crude tone, and he growled, frustrated. Wolfric was breaking his one rule, the one he'd sworn to live by. Don't interfere with the past. The Phoenix flame allowed him to jump back, as a watchful judge, an observer of time. Born from the heat of the sun, the phoenix was a witness of time passing, doomed to burn up and rise over, and over. The one rule was never get involved. Never change the past, even if it meant you lost the woman you loved. It was a sacrifice that sickened him to his core.

This was bigger. If he didn't warn his sister, then it was the end of everything. Wolfric considered it an extreme, nightmare inducing, exceptional circumstance.

"I don't have time to explain. You need to run! He's coming here, and he'll kill you—and I can't let that happen. You cannot die in *this* time! You need to live."

She took his arms, her face gaunt with terror, her neck muscles tensing. "Wolfric, I'm scared. Don't go, please!"

His heart broke. She was the baby of the family, and he hated to leave her. "I can't stay." Grasping her chin, he tilted her face up to look at him, and he smiled as kindly as he could, even though he could feel the pullback, the beginning of the burn. "Trust me, girl, you will have one hell of a life. And one day, you'll meet someone worth every bruise and year of hell trapped in this pitiful existence. You get to put stuff right, a shot at redemption. And you bring back someone who is the key to destroying what just came through that portal—a portal you helped open!"

She blinked rapidly. "I sent him here?"

"You and a bunch of idiot teenagers. You didn't know he'd land right here, where he needed to be!" He groaned and looked skyward, knowing he had mere seconds left, and there was no time to explain.

"I don't understand...."

Wolfic gritted out, "I know. And I can't do anymore, and I can't derail you. And all the good you do in the future... none of that will happen if you don't move your ass and get out of here!"

Maybe something in his expression sobered her. The urgency in his tone startled her into a nod, tears streaming down her face. "Will I ever see you again?"

He shrugged. "I hope so." Flames licked at his flesh, and he dropped to his knees, baring his teeth in agony. Euelea reared back in horror, her instinct to help him as she ran for the water pail. He waved her away as she darted closer, the flames licking at her golden skin. "It's okay, stay back... it's okay...promise me you'll stay alive!"

She sobbed and dropped the pail to her feet, where water trickled around her bare toes and seeped into the soil. "I promise."

He roared in pain as the flames curled and wove through his clothing, melting the skin till it bubbled. "Don't use magic, he'll find you....he can see the trail. If he catches you, stall him for as long as you can."

"I love you, Wolfric. Please find me again." She dropped to her knees, unable to tear her gaze away, and held out a hand, their fingertips touching.

"I love you too...k'a'ak'ate." He tried to smile, but he turned to ash, his flesh disintegrating, billowing into the air.

Goodbye... The use of their shared mother tongue made her cry harder. It was an old language, older than any known in history, a foundling language of a time never written or recorded. A life, a family ripped apart and stitched together by fear so long ago. Another plane, a different, terrifying existence long buried. A time of magic, fire, and elemental power.

She cried into her hands. "K'a'ak'ate." Flames engulfed his lower half, and he knew he was fading, and in those last moments, she chose to cry out. "Who is it? Who is coming?"

He wondered if she even heard his voice like a whisper on a breeze as he finally billowed away, dust on the air. But he'd tried, with his last breath, he'd managed to utter two words.

"A monster...."

ONE

An alarm sounded, loud and intrusive, right in Win's ear. She groaned, rolled under the covers, and with numb, sleepy fingers, she slid her phone shut. Silence engulfed the room, and she sighed and rolled into Grayson's back. She wound her arms around his waist, pressing her cheek into his shoulder. The motel room was small, snug, and condensated quickly. No matter how often they aired it, a faint aroma of staleness hung in the air.

Propped on her elbow, she gazed down at him, trailing her fingers down his scar, three long claw marks running from his ear, ending under his bottom lip.

He grumbled and squeezed her arm. "Do you want me to come with you?"

She smiled and kissed his bare shoulder. "No, I'm good."

"So you woke me up to tell me you don't need me to come with you?"

This made her chuckle, and she bit her lip. "Yeah...sorry."

"Attention seeker."

He snorted a short laugh and pulled her tighter around him. Outside, the wind howled against the glass of the motel window. The red neon sign rattled against the wooden walls, not thick or protective enough to exclude the icy draft that filtered under the door. Win hadn't liked the place much on the first night they'd arrived. It was cold, and the bathroom smelled moldy. The sheets were peppered with questionable stains.

But it became home, fast. Their little world. Win closed her eyes, resting her chin nicely on his arm, and started to drift off, lulled by the wind lashing outside and the smell of seaweed, salty air that crawled through the cracks. The motel was a run-down pit of a place, isolated at the ragged end of Rope's Point. It overlooked the ocean, surrounded by grassy dunes. No one came here for accommodation unless they were desperate, and any tourists preferred the quaint boutique hotels in the town. Apart from the odd hiker and those who frequented the strip club at the other end of the dirt track, they were alone.

When it was clear they didn't have much money to pay for living there, Win joked she could work in the club for a few hours, but Grayson struck up a deal with the owner, doing errands for money and rent. Far from bliss, but it was safe, somewhere she could hide and shift in relative seclusion.

Something she should be doing right now. Her second alarm went off with a loud beep, and she moaned against the scratchy pillow.

Grayson rolled in her direction, dragging the sheets with him. He yawned, massive arms reaching to pull her closer, and blinked in the dark. "I'll get up—go with you."

She ran her hand over his shoulder, finding the chain around his neck. "No, that's not fair. I'm fine by myself. Besides, it's freezing out there, and you can warm me up when I get back."

He managed a sleepy smile with his eyes closed. "Then you should go. Now before I change my mind."

Win grinned, stroking his blonde hair splayed on the pillow. "I'm going."

"Do it, then."

She laughed and poked his ribs, kissing his closed eyes. "I will—in a minute."

Grayson opened his eyes and grappled her in a tight hug. Breath hot against the arch of her neck, he grumbled, "Go now, or I won't let you go at all." It rumbled down her spine, and she shuddered in delight, wrapping her legs around his waist.

Win dissolved into giggles as he tickled her, wrestling her under the sheets. She squealed as he sat up and pulled her onto his lap. She kissed his grin. Suddenly the prospect of going outside was the last thing she wanted to do. "Fine—but I warn you, my feet will be cold."

Grayson made a noise in his throat as he kissed her. "I'm pretty used to you and your freezing extremities by now," he said against her mouth. Win wrapped her arms around his neck, sighing with contentment. As long as she looked at him, she didn't care about the peeling paint, the mold behind the bedside cabinets, or the weird smell in the bathroom. Grayson was a shield from the outside world, and this room was everything. In the last few weeks, they'd gotten to know one another very well, far more intimately than she could have imagined, and far quicker.

The alarm buzzed for the third time, the screen blurry and bright in the dark room. Smiling, she tossed back the covers and instantly recoiled as her bare feet touched the carpet. "Shit, it's freezing!" she whimpered, gathering her jeans and hoodie.

A reminder popped up on the screen, something she'd probably thumbed in months ago, and it was enough to make her smile slip and a knot tighten in her stomach—*Luke's 18th*.

She swallowed, ice washing over her skin. Taking a breath, she flicked the reminder away. As if sensing her tension, Grayson narrowed his eyes at her in the dark. "You okay?"

"I'm fine," she lied.

"Did you get a message?"

"No, it's fine. Just some Twitter notification. I don't know why I even have it on my phone."

Win effectually shut him down, he gazed at her in a way that demanded the truth, but she smiled sweetly and wriggled into her jeans.

No intrusions, not here, she told herself. She wasn't about to let the bubble they'd built pop with one beep of a phone. He watched her as she dressed and tossed her a pair of socks, which she gratefully shoved her feet inside. Catching his gaze, he blushed, rolled away, and she beamed in the dark, loving this little world, untouchable and theirs. Win was stupidly and hopelessly in love with him, and sometimes it was impossible to wipe the soppy grin off her face.

Unless something popped up to remind her of the real world. Like Luke's birthday.

There was little point in putting on anything else. The less clothing she took to the beach, the less accidentally blew away in the wind.

She'd lost countless shirts in the dark. If Grayson came with her, he usually spent half the time chasing her underwear down the beach as they got thrashed away in the breeze. Creeping to the door, she jerked as Grayson sat up abruptly.

"Be careful," he warned. He fixed her with his pale stare. "Keep to the dunes—"

"Yes, I know!" She waved him back. "Go back to sleep. I'll only be an hour."

"Half." His tone made her relent. She hopped across the room and kissed him.

"Okay, half-hour. Stop worrying!"

Before he could catch her, she was out the door, stuffing her feet into a pair of worn-out sneakers. Win tiptoed as she passed the motel office, creeping past the vending machine, which hummed loudly. Mrs. Tate was already up, vacuuming the reception area, so she ducked low to get past the window, unseen. Win avoided a few scattered lounge chairs as she ran across the untidy yard, carefully opening the back gate. This had become ritual, and she knew the gate well enough to guess how far she could open it before it squeaked in protest. Moments later, she slipped to the dunes, tugging her hoodie over her head.

In the distance, the lights of the sleepy fishing town flickered, and Win found a log to stash her clothes under, ducking low to the sand. Tears squeezed from her eyes as her body lengthened and stretched. Sharp claws tore through the flesh of her nail beds, and saliva gathered under her tongue as teeth erupted from her gums.

Panting through the pain, an almost unbearable sting, heat boiled beneath her flesh, coating her pale freckly skin with a soft, rosette-marked fur covering. The jaguar emerged, padding down to the beach, chasing a wave out into the bleak darkness, playfully darting in and out of the surf.

Win loved swimming in this form. She floated on the waves, choppier this morning and cold, but it cooled the heat bubbling under her skin. It bugged Grayson, and he was usually standing on the beach tearing out his hair with fear she'd sink, be dragged out, or suddenly shift back without warning.

Luke's 18th.

Win ducked under the water as if to wash the reminder away. A lump formed in her throat, and she wondered how he would celebrate today. Back then, they'd made plans and talked about his birthday and what they would do. The three of them. Ice struck her heart, and it hurt too much to think about them.

The night after they'd checked in, on her return from the bathroom, Grayson presented her with Luke's broken glasses, leaving them on her pillow for her to find. Locking eyes with him, she'd stuttered out a string of protests, but to her surprise, he wasn't angry.

"It's okay, Win. I know the guy has a thing for you."

Hearing those words made her want to vomit. How could she ever explain how she felt about Luke? "You aren't mad at me?" she'd asked, fingering the broken glass, the last piece of her friend, the boy who'd died in the woods.

"I'm not mad at you," Grayson said. "But is this why we're hiding? From him?"

Swallowing a ball in her throat, she'd half nodded, then said. "Ella—I've hurt her."

"But...Luke...you don't...you're not in love with him?" Grayson stumbled over his words like they were hard to say aloud.

Win took his face between her palms, staring at him soulful and honest. "No—not in that way. I love him like a brother."

It made her stomach churn, recalling the things he'd said that night and how it'd broken her to say no. She added a solemn, "Honestly, I had no idea," which made Grayson grunt in disbelief and made her feel like a prize fool. She should have seen it sooner.

"I didn't!"

"Well—okay," he relented. "I knew...I'm fairly sure your sister knew. I can't believe his girlfriend didn't guess."

I don't want you in my life right now...

"Ella...I've hurt her so badly," she admitted to Grayson while he studied her.

"You didn't do anything wrong," he reminded her. "It was him who finished it."

Win's eyes sparked tears. "*Because* of me!" Her voice was husky with unshed tears. "She doesn't want to speak to me."

"Won't you being gone just hurt her more?" Grayson asked aloud the very thing she'd dreaded hearing. Something that ate at her conscience on the hour. She swore she couldn't go a minute without reliving the look on her friend's face.

Win resurfaced, closed her eyes, and bobbed on the waves. Win had messaged Ella, and her guts swirled, remembering that day. Not long after they'd settled, Win couldn't stand not speaking to her friend and took the plunge. She'd thumbed a message, desperate to reach out, to see those little dots wobbling as Ella replied, the way they used to when they were amid a frantic text conversation, one always slightly quicker on the mark than the other.

I'm sorry, I miss you. Can we talk?

It had taken Win an hour of pacing and sweating before she sent the message, and the bitter disappointment came when her friend didn't reply.

The dots never budged. They didn't even jiggle, even though, under the message, there was one word to make Win's skin prickle. *Read.* Ella didn't want to talk to her.

Win let the negative thoughts of Ella, and the friendship she'd wrecked wash by her like a piece of driftwood, instead focusing on when they'd first arrived here in Rope's point. The first week of living in the motel room had been a delirious dream. With a flush, Win recalled how they hadn't left the room, only for food. When they surfaced, it was only to explore the town, eat, go to the library, or walk to the beach. For the first time in months, Win was at peace, alone and with Grayson, and it seemed nothing could intrude into their world.

But Win started to fret. She sent messages. The pull to home, to make contact was too hard to ignore. She called Rowan, but her sister was reserved and quiet, and Win could tell she was holding something back, but even the pinprick of guilt didn't make her want to leave. Despite Grayson's prodding, this wasn't forever. Win held fast. Rowan didn't beg Win to come home, and she thought it was best she stayed away.

The distance was good, for many reasons. Distance from Rowan. Distance from Luke. With a yelp, Win climbed to the surface, the saltwater stinging her eyes, her breath chugged as she waded back to the beach, her massive paws leaving an odd trail of footprints. She went for a long run through the dunes, finally settling on her paws and gazing out over the lights and the harbor. The fishing boats moored for the night bobbed on the waves, their hulls creaking and groaning on the water.

Puffing out air, Win ran the length of the beach, loneliness and guilt at her back, chasing her whenever she felt even the smallest amount of happiness. God, she missed them so much. She missed Luke, her heart utterly hollow without him, her best friend. She missed his sarcasm, his snarky comments, and his laugh. A little kernel of guilt nibbled away at her.

You walked away from him.... you ran away.

Time and distance from Luke was a good thing. Her head cleared, her vision sharpened, and she could think straight. Living confined, sharing space, butting heads daily, she hadn't realized how much he overwhelmed her. Win loved Luke to his bones. But not in the way he'd wanted. She hoped the distance had done the same for him.

The last night they'd been together, Luke died; or rather he went through his Calling. Linked by blood, Luke was powerless to stop the Therian mutation rampaging through his body, catching him up fast on something that should have happened gradually. It nearly destroyed him, but in the last moments, while he clung to his life, Win gave him her blood. It had been enough to power him across the final hurdle and turn him into an intimidating black wolf. Now they were linked, forever, whether she liked it or not.

Moping, Win stomped out of the waves, shaking off freezing water. Hurrying to the safety of the dunes, she shifted, her teeth clashing together as soaking and shivering; she scrambled back into her damp clothes. Rubbing her arms briskly, her cheeks flushed as she imagined the warm body in bed waiting for her, and she jogged the length of the beach.

Win stopped mid-step, her eyes narrowing, her brain trying to catch up to what she saw.

Laying on the beach, not far from the back gate of the motel, was a man on fire.

TWO

Win's sneakers slapped over wet sand, her breath like ice in her throat. "Hey!" she cried, her voice hoarse after the shift. *"Hey!"*

He thrashed on the ground, then, to her horror, stood, frantically patting his coat to expel the last of the flames. Exhaling loudly, he collapsed on the sand.

Win dropped to her knees beside him, gingerly taking his arm, wafting away plumes of smoke with her hand. Shaky and unsure of what she'd seen, she gave him a gentle nudge. "Are you okay?"

He looked up at her under a mass of thick, dark hair. He was enormous, and instinctively she drew back to her knees. It was early and dark and in the depths of winter. At this time of day, the beach was empty. What the hell was he doing out here?

The motel's neon light caught his face, and she bit back a gasp. Golden-skinned and dark-eyed, a silver bar pierced through his right brow. Tilting her head, she tried to guess his age. It was impossible to tell with all his hair, maybe early thirties? He coughed, loud and hacking, still smacking tiny flames on his coat. Smoke rose right under her nose.

"It's you," he said. Win rocked to the balls of her feet, a tingling sensation of familiarity creeping over her, but she couldn't place it. It was the eyes, pools of chocolate. She knew him from *somewhere.*

"Do I know you?" A gust of wind blew the red, tangled hair off her neck, still damp with salt water, and she folded her arms tight around her chest, suddenly aware of the stranger's eyes on her.

"Not yet."

Eyes widening, she eyed the distance to the motel gate, only a few yards, and she was fast. Her heart rocketed as he edged nearer. "Are you okay? You were kind of...."

"On fire, yeah." He stood abruptly, and she mirrored his stance. "It happens."

Win stared at his feet and the charred circle he stood in. The sand underfoot was blackened. "Who the hell are you?"

"I'm Wolfric," he introduced himself, his breath fogging in the air. "Wolfric Varga."

That name. Ice exploded up her spine. "Varga...as in Vecula Varga...you're..." Her eyes went saucer wide. "You're Evan's *brother?*"

"And you're Winifred. Winifred Louise Adler." He held out his palms in an open, honest gesture, almost as if he would go in for a hug.

Evan's brother? Win's skin prickled, and she shook her head in disbelief. Evan never said her brother was still alive and living in the next town! Win recalled the revealing conversation in her bedroom the night Evan's secret had been outed.

Wolfric cocked his head and gave her a slow smile. "I bet she never mentioned me, huh?"

"No!" Win scoffed, and when he chuckled, her spine stiffened. Her feet, like two slabs of driftwood, stepped backward. He caught her staring and snapped his jaw shut. What the hell were those *things* in his mouth?

"It's okay. I don't bite!"

"Are you...a...?" Win couldn't even bring herself to say the words out loud. Her vision spun. He laughed, guessing what she was thinking, catching her gaping at the teeth in his mouth.

"No. It's just a thing I have, like a birthmark." He dabbed at his teeth with his tongue. "Guess it's a little unnerving, huh? I can't believe I found you—so easily."

Win froze. "I don't understand. Evan never mentioned...does she know you're alive?"

He grumbled, and she saw there were still wisps of smoke curling off his beard. "Of course, she knows. My sister is good at keeping things close to her chest—but then you already know that, don't you?"

Yes, she did. Win admitted to feeling wary of Evan in the early days, her arrival on the scene a little too convenient. Evan lied her way into their home, into Rowan's life, but they'd come to trust her implicitly. And in the summer, Evan had given them the biggest gift. Their mother. Who took off and left the moment she got a whiff of freedom. It was a part of why Win left, their mother's rejection cut like a knife. And if Alice could run, Win saw no good reason to stick around.

"She..." Win choked on the words. "She dates my sister."

"I know, and I'm so happy for them," he said, though he didn't sound happy. "Rowan is far too good for her. However, this isn't why I'm here."

Win crossed her arms. "Why are you here?" She eyed the gate, her anxiety spiking. Grayson was barely yards away, she could scream, and he would hear her. "You said you were looking for me."

"And I found you." He seemed relieved. "I need to talk to you."

He took a wide step closer, and she shrank back, his bear-like size intimidating. He chuckled. "Oh, don't be afraid of me, Win. You know full well you could outrun me if you wanted. As much as you and your white knight are living the dream right now...." He didn't bother to disguise an eye roll as his gaze wandered over the shabby exterior of the motel. "You have to go home. It's where you're needed."

"What are you talking about?"

"You, Rowan, and my beloved sister made a goddamn mess of things. You sent a mutated Therian back to a time where he doesn't belong and will wreak havoc!"

"Spencer..." Win gasped, the mention of that name sending her reeling. "How do you know about him?"

"I know a lot of things. I've watched you for a while...you remind me of someone I knew once, and I have a bond with your family deeper than any curse. I've always tried to look out for you."

Bitterness swelled in her chest, and she fought the urge to spit out a vicious laugh. "Well, you did a shitty job. Where were you when Spencer Fraser tried to shoot my sister? Where were you weeks ago when he tried to kill me...and Luke?"

He groaned. "I said I tried...not much I can do without calling attention to myself. And I can't see the future. I don't know what's going to happen. I can only watch from the shadows and hope you don't screw it all up—which you did—royally."

Win glared, screwing up her nose. "Well, if you know so much, you'd know we had little choice. You'd know I'd never let Luke die."

He smiled, closed-lipped and melancholic, nodding to her wrist, where there was a noticeable bite mark under her clothes. Luke's mark. "Nice going, by the way. Blood magic...now you're stuck with the guy."

Win's face throbbed, the bite stinging as fresh as the night it happened. Under her jeans lurked another scar. Spencer's fangs had all but torn the flesh from her body. Two brothers, and two marks, forever imprinted on her skin. "I would do it again. I didn't have any other choice."

Something sparkled in his eyes, an air of mischief like he knew more than he let on. "You did good—and somehow, I don't think he minds."

She flushed at the memory and the conversation moments before Spencer dealt Luke the final killing blow. Her stomach washed around in fear, recalling aloud the words he'd said—things he couldn't take back.

"Win you saved him—and for the better. Though I know why you ran, who you ran from... *and* although it's as awkward as hell, you are stronger together. Unfortunately, Spencer is right where he shouldn't be!"

"Spencer was going to kill...It wasn't our fault!" Win argued, her temper flaring. Who the hell was this guy? Didn't he know what they went through that night?

"I know everything, Win. But it doesn't matter. You unknowingly sent him somewhere he doesn't belong, and right now, he's heading for Evan, and if he kills her...."

Win's insides crumpled, and she clutched her throat. "Oh my god."

Wolfric nodded, his expression somber. "We're going to need her, Win. We're going to need everyone."

"Everyone?"

"*Everyone.* He won't stop. He will never stop. Not till he uses Euelea—Evan—to get back here, and then he'll kill her, discard her as he did with your sister. Then guess where he'll go next?"

Win wrung her hands, her breathing slow and short. She tried not to picture Evan, alone and vulnerable in another time. Her chest thumped. "To us?"

Wolfric stepped closer, dark eyes glinting under the neon motel sign. "To *you.* You know why he wants to kill you, right?"

She didn't want to say it out loud. Win was seventeen years old, and dying wasn't on her agenda. It hadn't taken much to string the dots together. Spencer wanted her dead because her death equaled the end of the curse, the end of the Therian line. He wanted to continue on his own, a more powerful breed, a different type of Therian, mutated and lethal. Also, he was bat shit crazy.

Panicked, Win paced in front of him, and he watched, strangely intrigued, as she pelted back and forth. "I'm the end of the Therian line...the curse ends if I'm dead. But how can I fix this?" Win's sneakers made deep grooves in the sand. "I can only use the door—with blood. I don't even know how to summon the door. How can I find him?"

Wolfric crowded her space and placed a large hand on her shoulder, his thumb pressing into the nook between her clavicle and her shoulder. Her eyes ran the length of his massive, muscular arm, his eyes dark, a golden fleck swirling in the center. Shuddering under his weight, she was rendered immobile with fear, even though his expression was calm, unthreatening. "You should forget the door. You'd never find it if you needed it. It's useless."

"Then...how?" Evan was in trouble. Someone else she loved was in danger because of her.

"It's kind of why I'm here...."

Win tried to wriggle out of his grasp, but his hold was solid. Her feet sank further into the sand under his weight. "I don't get this...how do you know any of this?"

"I'm sorry. You'll soon understand. You need to wake up, pull on your big girl pants and go home. Fix this mess!"

Win struggled, her breath coming in short pants. Something stung under his thumb, and she half wondered if he was digging his thumbnail into her flesh. But the pain sliced across her shoulder, and it wasn't a sting—it was a burn. Her eyes filled up, and she panicked. "You're hurting me!"

"I know, and I'm sorry. But trust me, this will help you."

Win gasped, her knees buckled, and she fell, her spine arching as she hit the sand. Wolfric followed her down, his form hovering over her as he pressed his thumb harder into her skin, as though he could sink through to the other side of her shoulder. The pain was blinding, and her voice stuck. She kicked her legs. "Stop...please!"

Golden eyes met hers, filled with white light, and he bared his teeth. "Wait! Stop!" She yelled, thrashing her legs. The burn seeped through her flesh, into her lungs, and her eyes filled with pure light. "What are you *doing*?"

"Giving you a gift. Call it an early Christmas present." He winced in pain as he gritted out those words. "It'll be better in a minute."

Dark spots flooded her vision, and nausea swam in her gut as she prayed for the pain to subside. Her flesh smoked, a claggy tang right under her nose. Like a white bulb, a flash pierced across her irises, and her vision whited. Swirls of shapes and colors formed, and Win fought down bubbling sickness. Shapes misted into fragments, assembling a puzzle, and she was presented with a picture.

It was a tree. Win blinked and it focussed. A giant sprawling oak with long, clawing branches, devoid of life or leaves clinging to the arms. She was flooded with a sense of dread like nothing good could grow here.

Win tried to roll away, pressure from Wolfric's thumb searing into her skin, as the vision broke and another replaced it. Ahead, she saw the tree and a girl. Mary Hickory. Mary circled the tree, her tiny teeth jagged and sharp as she sang softly under her breath. Win shuddered upon recognizing the girl's sallow complexion, lank dark hair, and a thousand-yard stare.

"Casey..."

A name...it floated on the breeze. It sounded like Casey...or Maisey, at least that was what she could make out, but her ears were rushing, pounding with blood. Win tried to focus on Mary's words but they billowed away.

Relief flooded her as the vision crisped and fell away, and with a jolt, Win's eyes cleared as she blinked to the present, her back pressed into the wet sand while the dark stranger panted. Brows knitted, he glared at her. "What did you see?"

"You asshole! What the hell did you do to me?" Win couldn't fight the vomit rising up her throat, she rolled away and puked in the grass.

Wolfric fell back to his knees. "I'm sorry it had to come to this."

"What did you give me? What did you *do?*" she spat, her mouth bitter. Under her hoodie, her flesh seared, the pain throbbing and washing through her, an unbearable sting.

"Time," he breathed out, shuffling, exhausted to his feet. "I gave you time. Now you need to figure out how to use it."

Before she passed out, he smoothed the hair off her forehead and smiled as kindly as possible. "Come look me up, babe. I'm not hard to find. When you've got to grips with all your life bullshit—I'll explain everything—just don't leave it too long."

"Grayson," she whimpered, tears spilling out of the corners of her eyes. The golden light streamed around them, the wave dancing through the air. The scorch of the burn was working its way through her blood, disrupting every particle of her being.

Wolfric was a silhouette, a shape against the inky sky. She was tired of holding on, and his voice floated away with the crash of the waves. "I know cats have nine lives, but I just gave

33

you some extra. Come find me, Win—and for god's sake—go home to your family."

THREE

Luke groaned as he rolled awake, drenched in sweat. Blearily he opened his eyes, the glare of morning light streaming through the circular patterned drape. His long legs stuck out of his sleeping bag. Peeling himself off the floor, he scratched at the scruff on his jaw, taking in his surroundings. The floor he'd slept on suddenly felt like a bed of nails; his spine creaked in disapproval. His mouth tasted vile. It didn't matter what you slept on if you'd been drinking and fell into an intoxicated coma. The floor was comfortable until you woke up.

Gingerly he gazed to his right and spotted Cole's foot sticking out of his bed. Cole didn't move. Socks still on, face down in his pillow, his shaven-haired friend snored, and it rumbled around the room. Fluidly, Luke sat up, his joints cracking, and rolled his neck. "Cole...wake up!"

The door creaked open, and a blonde head poked around the crack. Cole's mother crept into the room and planted a cup of coffee beside her son's bed before giving him a shake. "Wake up, baby."

"Hey, Mrs. Ward." She hadn't noticed Luke sitting under the window, rolled in a sleeping bag till he cleared his throat, and she jerked in surprise. Luke grinned sleepily.

She laughed and clutched her chest. "You're here again? Aren't we making a habit of these late-night study sessions?"

Her joke brought a thin smile to his lips. There had been no studying, only drinking several cans of Miller's in Cole's backyard. She crossed the room and flung open the drapes, motes of dust floating in the sunlight. Luke squinted, horribly hungover.

She tossed him an amused smile. "If you keep this up, I'll have to make you up a bed in the spare room."

Luke stood too quickly for a guy who'd spent the night drinking, stretching out his massive arms. Mrs. Ward cracked a window, gazing back in his direction, craning her neck to look up at him. He was taller now. Luke grinned mischievously, turning on his boyish smile. "Maybe you could adopt me?"

She blushed and pinched his chin with a playful nip. "Don't tempt me. You're too cute." Luke loved her southern drawl, the Ward family having moved here from South Carolina a couple of years back.

Yes, I am, he thought, catching sight of his dark reflection in the round mirror nailed to the wall. Luke Fraser was a little more than cute these days; unfortunately, he knew it. Mrs. Ward eyed the trash can, brimming with empty cans, and made a face.

"You two are too young for midweek drinking—any kind of drinking!"

Luke ignored her. "Maybe I should set you up with my dad, and you can marry him and be my real mom?" His grin cracked his face, and she burst out laughing. Meanwhile, Cole stirred under the covers.

"As lovely as that sounds, I don't think I'm your dad's type. I'll get you a coffee."

She disappeared out the door, and Luke yawned. Cole sat in bed, scratching at the soft coating of fair fuzz on his head. "Morin'...uh. I feel like crap."

Luke found his hoodie on the floor; he shook it off and gave it an obligatory sniff. He smelled like sweat and stale beer. "You mind if I shower?"

Cole answered with a shrug and fell face down on his pillow with a hungover grunt. Luke snorted and headed for the shower room, not before checking his phone. Bleary-eyed, he stared at the screen.

Happy birthday, Luke. I'm bringing donuts.

It was from Ella. What the hell had he done to deserve this person in his life? Ella's loyalty mystified him. The night he'd broken up with her, he was sure she'd never want to see him again. But she'd showed up to lunch at school, sitting alongside him in the cafeteria, chatting as though the last few months hadn't happened. Like they'd never dated, never been more than friends. Luke admitted he was missing the *more* part of their friendship. A lot.

Wincing, he stepped under the hot spray of the shower, grabbing some of Cole's inexpensive shower gel that smelled like spice and pine needles. He hopped out and grabbed a towel, wrapping it around his waist.

Luke groaned, catching sight of his reflection in the dirty vanity. Stepping closer, he prodded at his face, the shadow forming, blue eyes dull with exhaustion, a different reflection to a month ago. His shoulders were thick with muscle, biceps doubled in size, and dark hair sprawled over his chest and ran under the towel at his waist.

He shuddered, pushing away the memory of his Calling, banishing the memory of the night in the woods. Every time he pictured Win's tear-streaked face, his blood ran hot, a permanent reminder that she was under his skin, her molecules fused with his, and a hollow feeling dragged in the pit of his stomach, knowing she was gone.

If she gave a crap, she would have been here.

Hurriedly, he slicked back his damp hair, rubbing it dry with a stale-smelling towel, and flung open the bathroom door. Mrs. Ward rounded the stairs, a coffee in her hands. She took one look at him, and the words "oh, my goodness," were out of her mouth before she could stop herself. Luke grinned, his blue eyes shining with mischief, knowing the woman had clocked every naked inch of him apart from the towel at his hips.

She shoved the coffee into his hand, stuttering, adorably pink-cheeked. "You'll be late if you don't get dressed."

Bashfully, she scrambled up an armload of dirty laundry outside Cole's door to distract herself, anything but look directly at him. Mortified, she tried to dodge him but bumped his chest, dropping Cole's underwear.

"It's my birthday today, you know."

"Oh, that's nice," she replied, taut, her eyes flicking to his chest, horrified and flushed at the same time. "Happy birthday!"

"Don't I get a birthday hug?"

Mrs. Ward went the color of the sun, and inwardly Luke cackled to himself. "Oh...well," she stuttered, edging past him in the hallway. "I'm not sure...."

"Dude!" Cole stood at his bedroom door, mouth agape. Luke laughed and scratched at his chest. Cole's gaze was fixed and narrow-eyed, and Mrs. Ward used Cole's appearance to escape downstairs.

"What the hell? Were you flirting with my mom?" Cole punched him in the shoulder and chuckled. "Not cool...not to mention gross."

"I was teasing. She's nice," Luke said, ignoring Cole's expression as he glugged the coffee, a hot explosion igniting in his chest. "You're lucky to have her."

Cole sprayed himself with deodorant, then pulled on a fresh shirt. "Still...you give off some intense vibes. It's weird—don't do it."

"Are you worried I'll seduce your mother?"

Cole laughed, though his eyes darkened at his friend. "I'm more worried she'd say yes."

Two months ago, he would have been having breakfast in the kitchen at the Adler's, fighting with Win over the shower or the last of the cereal. Arguing with Rowan when he'd left his dirty dishes in the sink or avoiding Ben as the older man attempted to strike up a conversation with him. He'd spend his days in school and his nights at work but would come home to fighting, backbiting, laughter, and undeniable warmth that made it easier to accept the life he'd left behind at Mercy. Jake's parenting style was cool, and detached, and Luke grew up aloof and alone. Unexpectedly thrust into a female-dominated home, enveloped by women who fussed over him and cared what or if he ate, was new and nice. Leaving it behind hurt more than he could've imagined.

And now he had this. In the last month, Cole became a friend, a drinking buddy, a teammate, and a confidant. He couldn't confide *that* much. Cole had no clue about Luke or Win's alter egos, but he was solid and easy to talk to—a friend.

Cole knew very little about why Win left, but after one boozy night in his yard, Luke emotionally confessed everything under the influence of too much alcohol. He poured out every last, icky, inappropriate, lustful detail hoping his new ally would chastise him, tell him how gross and weird he was. Cole never said much, only listened.

"And did she feel the same? About you?" he'd asked after Luke had revealed his miserable, shameful feelings for Win.

"No—she's in love with someone else." Saying it out loud tore at his guts. He stood more than a fair chance against

Grayson Riley these days. Grayson could have knocked him clean out a month ago—now Luke could probably render the guy unconscious with one good hit. Not that he ever daydreamed about that. Much.

"It's for the best, man. It can't happen, and you did the right thing leaving. Though why Ella is still on the scene blows my mind. But that does mean Ella's single—right?"

Luke had glared at him. "Cole...don't even...!"

"I'm kidding!" his friend reassured him. "She's in love with you, dude. She wouldn't look twice at me with you around. Jeez—you are *so* territorial."

Territorial didn't quite cut it. After Luke's Calling, he'd nearly lost his job at the bar—twice. His sudden primitive territorial vibe didn't stop with Win or Ella. Rowan was like his sister; he couldn't bear how men eyeballed her. It made his skin itch and his temper short. As far as Luke was concerned, she was *his* family, and he didn't want anyone sniffing her. Two bar brawls had got him into trouble and nearly cost him his job.

Luke hadn't seen Win in nearly four weeks. The night after he left, she'd disappeared, ran away to be with Grayson, and disintegrated his heart. Not only had she left without a word or a message, but Rowan unexpectedly quit the bar. His only link to his old life was severed. It hurt too much to even drive past the house.

Luke and Cole dressed and hurried outside, the streets wet and sludgy with snow. They had about fifteen minutes to get to school on time, and Cole looked pale and bleary-eyed. Luke flexed his shoulders, ready for a sprint, just as a black Mercedes pulled up alongside them. The door opened, and his father hopped out, leaning heavily against the vehicle. Jake Fraser, Luke's father, waved his gloved hand impatiently. The similarities between Jake and Luke were uncanny; both dark-haired, blue-eyed, and handsome. Jake wore a permanent downturned smile, an air about him as though he were irritated, annoyed, or bored. Usually, he was all three.

"You have to be in school in ten minutes." Luke jogged across the street and hopped in the passenger seat, raking a hand through his messy, black locks. Cole followed him, and Jake motioned for the boy to jump in the back.

"How'd you find me?"

Jake rolled his eyes and started the engine. "I followed the smell of hungover teenage boys."

Jake dove in the back and pulled out a fresh hoodie, stuffing it into his hands. Oblivious to the joke, Cole made a face and scrolled through his phone.

"If you're going to make a habit of sleeping out, you ought to make sure you have clean clothes," he said around gritted teeth, narrowing his eyes as he drove back through the snowy streets toward Cedar Wood. "Though I'd prefer you didn't do it at all."

Luke stared out the window, the wipers swishing as the car slowly rolled into town. Cedar Wood was firmly gripped by early winter. The streets were snarled with thick fluffy snow that fell nightly, leaving the roads wet, slippery, and impassable. It had started the night Luke made it through his Calling and, like his temperament and growth in the last four weeks, hadn't relented.

Jake peered at Cole in the rear-view mirror. "How are you, Cole?"

"Hungover," Cole answered with a snort and Luke groaned inwardly. Cole's bluntness took some getting used to, but Luke liked him. Cole didn't say much about that day in the woods, the day Spencer mauled him. He didn't complain about his injury, only forged on stoically, reinforcing how badly Luke felt about whining about his Calling.

Jake threw the car into the school lot, and Luke unstrapped and pulled the hoodie over his head. "Luke...I understand you're preoccupied. And you need to—let off steam. I'm hardly going to judge you for that. But I worry."

Luke stared at his father, stunned that they were having this conversation. Only a short while ago, it seemed they would never speak again. After Luke's Calling, his father welcomed him home, with no questions, no judgment, only offering consolation when it was sought out. And the emancipation Luke had fought for since the summer was a distant memory. Though they tolerated one another, Spencer's disappearance was a relief, the air between them lighter. His father was different, but he couldn't tell why.

Coming home hadn't been easy. Rowan called and told him Win had left with Grayson, and a steel coolness replaced the hurt. His broken heart iced over like a glacier.

"There's Ella with breakfast!" Cole joked as the car rolled to a stop.

A girl was sitting on the low brick wall. Small, dark, and pretty with her glossy dark hair piled up in a ponytail, Ella spotted the car and waved. She stood; her dark almond eyes lit up, and in the front seat, Jake groaned. Luke shot him a look. "What?"

"That girl—she's so adorable she breaks my heart."

Luke's brows rose in amusement. "Do you mean the dried-up prune in your chest? *That* heart?"

Jake scoffed, switching off the engine as the lot filled with cars. He was used to dealing with Luke's fragile temper and ignored the joke. "You liked her, I know you did, and she's a sweet girl. Seeing you off with other girls can't be easy for her."

"I'm not *with* other girls!" he argued, and in the back, Cole snorted.

"Yeah, he mostly hangs out with me. Thanks for the ride, Mr. Fraser!"

Cole threw open the door and jogged in Ella's direction, peeking in the box she held to her chest. Cole must've said something to make her laugh because she giggled, making her eyes crinkle. Sunshine beamed out of Ella's face, making Luke's chest swell. He ignored a brief stab of jealousy that he hadn't been the one to make her laugh.

Even after his confession, it still baffled Luke that Ella wanted to remain friends. She was there every day, helping him study, guiding him through his tests, tutoring him. She was content with the 'just friends' caveat he'd stamped on their relationship. Win made him swear he wouldn't change when she'd begged him not to leave. Luke kept his promises, even if she had fled only hours later.

Ella firmly planted Luke in the friend zone, making it clear it could work, despite the fact that sometimes she cast him some longing glances. Luke couldn't lose her too, and if she wanted a friendship, he swore he'd be the best friend she ever had. He wouldn't dare ask more of her, even if he yearned for her and missed her.

Relief came in the form of Cole, formally an outsider, he quickly became part of the crew, and the three had formed an unlikely friendship. Luke hadn't planned on Win ditching them all. But he asked himself what he expected after his confession?

Alone in the car with his father, he said, "I wouldn't hurt Ella like that."

Jake scratched his chin, nodding. "Well, then, great. It'd be good to see you dating a nice girl like her...I don't get why you can't start things up. Clearly, you're good for one another."

Luke grew hot and uncomfortable around the collar, trying to push away the memory of his confession, of his love for a girl who upped and vanished on them. "Dad..."

"But not that icy blonde you used to date. God, she reminded me of your stepmother...."

"Dad—Enough! I need to get to class!"

Jake smiled and hopped out of the car. Luke looked horrified as Jake held out his arms. "No hug goodbye?"

Luke stiffened as Jake folded his massive arms around him, then ruffled his hair. "Jeez, Dad, you're embarrassing...."

Hugging his father was like wrapping his arms around a bolder, cold and hard, with sharp edges. It surprised Luke, it wasn't always unwelcome. In the early days after his Calling, his father talking to him, his hand between his shoulder blades was enough to calm him down. He was a baby Therian, and it hadn't been easy. Luke struggled with pain at night, and he didn't want to phase, to become the wolf, even if he knew it would ease the unbearable itch under his skin.

Luke could roam free in the Mercy estate, unwatched and safe from prying eyes. He'd spot Rowan flying overhead, and feel so alone. They felt so far away, and he had no one to talk to about this crazy stuff. Ella listened, and Rowan called him occasionally, but the person he wanted or needed to share things with was gone.

Luke admitted the distance from Win was good. After a week of living away from Hickory, the fog cleared, the haze melted, and although he missed her, being away he could see straight. He was no longer saturated by her just *being* there. Her presence seeped into his bones. He couldn't think, couldn't breathe, and now, what love or lust he felt was slowly replaced with resentment. It made his skin crawl, remembering that night in the woods, how he'd confessed everything, emotionally vomiting everything he'd tried to hide and pretend he didn't feel. The feelings he harbored seemed to vanish as quickly as she had.

Jake gave him a wistful smile, patting his shoulder. "I'm not going out tonight—in case you were thinking of staying in for once."

Luke cocked a brow. "Why are you telling me?"

Jake cleared his throat awkwardly, flapping his arms against his coat. "Well, it is your birthday...I thought...we might...."

"Hang out?" Luke made a horrified face.

"Would that be so terrible?" He rummaged in his coat pocket and drew out his checkbook. Luke instantly recoiled at the sight of the dreaded leather book. How often had his father taken it out at birthdays and Christmas, when he had forgotten to buy him a gift? Too busy to make time, too preoccupied to make a last-minute dash to the store.

He scowled. "I don't want money!"

"It's your birthday. What else am I supposed to get you? You wrecked the damn car I bought."

Luke shuddered at the memory of the shiny, silver Volkswagen, beaten and battered and wrapped around an oak tree off the Boxford bridge. Luke had the car for precisely two days before trashing it. He'd been speeding, narrowly missed getting a ticket, or hospitalized. At the scene, Noah Chase was surprisingly lenient, marveling how Luke walked away without a scratch.

"If this is your backward way of asking me to spend my birthday with you— then fine. I'll be home."

"Great!" Jake looked abashed, uncertain, leaning heavily against the car's frame as his son glanced over his shoulder, keen to be off with his friends. "Luke, did you know...about Rowan?"

Luke flinched at her name. Hearing it aloud made him shiver, and a deep ache exploded in his chest. His throat went dry, suddenly alarmed. "No...what's wrong?"

"Oh, nothing, she's fine. Only I thought you should know—she has a job interview."

Luke balked. "Here?"

"Yes." Jake answered his thoughts, "I had a few drinks with Principal Geller last week."

"Oh?" Luke cocked a brow. Rowan working at school was enough to make his face break into a grin. He'd get to see her every day. "She'll have a fair shot, right?"

Jake frowned, pulling on his leather gloves. "Of course."

"Only I know how you feel about the family."

Jake laughed acidly. "What makes you think I have that kind of clout?"

"You *do* have that kind of clout. And I know Fraser incorporated is one of the governing bodies this year at school—plus, you blame her for Spencer."

His name floated between them, and Jake's smile dropped. "I would have preferred Spencer to be dealt with properly—lawfully. Not trapped in whatever hell that witch sent him."

"We don't know where he is, Dad. And if you recall, it was him or me. And Rowan chose me. She didn't have much choice at all."

"I thought you should know in case you ran into her. You get so riled up at the mere mention of Win or Rowan...." Jake's jaw clenched tight enough to cut glass, shoving his hands in his pockets.

Luke's eyes flashed, a dangerous, bright shade of blue. "*Riled* up?"

They ditched me...I'm alone...

Emotion clogged his throat, and he abruptly cast his eyes anywhere but at his father. Lately, he'd been welling up, random, unexpected bursts of melancholy, which bugged the shit out of him. He wondered if this was Win's influence, that somehow her personality traits bled with his, and now he couldn't even look at a stray, abandoned kitten without bursting into tears. Sometimes, he swore even his eyes looked sea green.

Jake backpedaled. "Forget it...didn't you say you had class?"

Luke threw him an even smile, tossing his bag over his shoulder. He left his father to stare after his retreating form; his feet flew as he ran across campus. As he jogged up the steps, past the library, he spotted Cole waiting for him on the low brick wall, kicking his legs. Ella perched next to him. They were talking but broke apart when they spotted him coming. Ella beamed and thrust a box of donuts under his nose, the sugary smell wafting out of the box.

"Happy birthday!"

Luke half smiled and took the box, tearing it open to reveal a gloopy array of pink and white donuts with 'Happy Birthday Loser' scribbled in bright pink icing sugar. Luke barked out a laugh, before stuffing one in his mouth.

"Your suggestion?" he threw at Cole as his friend hopped off the brick wall. Cole grinned and scratched his head.

"I made her write that," Cole said, bumping Ella's shoulder with his. "What did you have planned for the big night?"

"My dad wants to do something at home. Call it guilt for eighteen years of birthday fails!" Luke smiled at his father's thin attempt at bonding. "But feel free to come over and save me—hey, we could do a movie night?"

He directed the question at both of them, but a flash of pain crossed Ella's eyes. Movie nights had been Win's thing, the three of them hauled up on the couch with chips and popcorn, and the reminder stung.

Ella fell into step beside them. "At least he wants to spend time with you. That's progress!"

Luke side-eyed her, her long dark hair in a high ponytail, swished from side to side as she walked, her wide brown eyes searching his. She was lovely, more than ever, and he'd been an idiot. He was a deranged, love-sick moron who hadn't seen the jewel he'd possessed until he'd carelessly tossed it away. "Unless you guys have something wild planned for me?"

Ella snorted, hugging her books to her chest. "I'm not sure how much wilder an existence you need!"

"Yeah! Did you get that blonde's number, by the way? The one we met in the convenience store?" Cole said across Ella's head, and Luke shot him a death glare. *Shut up, moron*, he mouthed. Unfortunately, Ella missed nothing and bit her lip, her chin dropping. Cole mouthed a frantic apology over her head.

"Have you had any other messages?" Ella asked, and Luke's insides coiled, knowing from whom she meant. He shot her a sad look, and Ella sighed.

"No," he said. "Nothing. Have you?"

Ella looked at him sharply, but her expression softened in disappointment. "No. Not a thing."

"Have you tried calling her?"

"No," Ella replied, eyes downcast. "It's just—too hard."

Luke snorted. "And yet—here you are buying me donuts. Shouldn't you hate my guts?"

Their eyes locked as she swiped a donut from the box. "I bought them for me too. And no—never. I could never hate you."

"She didn't do anything wrong," Luke reminded her. Ella ignored him, taking a bite of the snack and then swallowing it. She cleared her throat.

"Yes, she did." Her eyes looked glossy and wet. "She walked away."

"From *me*—not you."

"From us both," Ella snapped, marking the end of the conversation. "So shut up about it."

Luke exchanged a glance over her head with Cole, who was giving him the 'enough' sign with a wave of his good hand. Luke let her walk a little way ahead, reaching out his fingers, inches from touching the end of her hair. He coiled his hand into a fist and shoved it in his pocket.

"Cole, you still on for practice tonight?" he asked, changing the subject.

Cole nodded and held up his hand. "I could do with getting some time in."

Luke opened his mouth to say he would drop him home after practice, but his jaw went oddly slack. Prickles of fear spiked on his neck, squeezing his eyes to clear the spot in his vision. Sometimes this happened, he'd get dizzy or hungry, and the need to phase at times was difficult to ignore, especially if he'd forgotten. A copper taste, tangy and hot filled his mouth, and he choked, spitting saliva out on the ground, bent double. "Shit..." he groaned, dropping to his knees.

"Hey..." Cole's feet shuffled to a halt. "Luke—you okay?"

Shapes misted his vision, white blobs of nothing, and nausea and taste of blood made his stomach swirl. His skin burned, beads of sweat gathered on his neck, and he saw flashes of gold brighter than the sun in his eyes for one startling moment. Temples pounding, darkness swept in, and he passed out, hearing the crack of his nose as he hit the ground.

"Luke!" Ella cried, grabbing his shoulders. Humiliated and instantly alert, Luke bounced to his feet, as blood sprayed from his nose. He blinked away throbbing pain in his sinuses.

Ella shrugged off her cardigan and held it to his face, drenched in blood in moments. "You just blacked out!"

"I'm fine." He waved her away, keenly aware of other students staring at him in horror. He stared at Ella's ruined white cardigan and shuddered, an image of the woodland clearing where he died running at him like a rushing tornado. "I'm fine."

"Dude, that was so embarrassing." Cole's cheeks were pink as he looked about, checking who'd witnessed his friend's epic fall. "Are you okay? Is it broken?"

Luke sniffed and winced. "I'm not sure." Though he doubted that would be an issue.

Shrugged off their concern, he wiped his bloodied face. "I need to clean up...." He handed the cardigan back to Ella, their gazes holding. She looked away dismally and took back her ruined garment.

"Hey!" a voice called from behind them. "Aren't you Luke Fraser?"

Luke groaned and looked around, waves of humiliation washing over him. He'd passed out and broken his nose in front of the whole school, holding a box of pink donuts. The sugary treats were scattered over the pavement. "Yeah," he answered, impatient and red-faced.

It was a guy he knew from one of his classes, young, blonde, waving his arms in Luke's direction. "I think you should see this?"

Luke eyed the guy, cocking a brow. "Unless it's life-changing, I'll pass. I need to fix my face."

Luke whirled in Ella's direction, staring at him, her bottom lip chewed so hard it was red. "Are you feeling okay?" She grabbed his arm, pulled him close, and lowered her voice to a whisper so Cole wouldn't hear. "Have you...managed to phase?"

"El—I'm fine!"

"You need to—regularly. You can't leave it."

Luke opened his mouth to tell her to stop nagging when the guy spoke again, desperate to get his attention. "Wait! Does your dad drive a black Mercedes?"

Luke's shoulders stiffened, turning his gaze back in the younger boy's direction. "Yeah, why?"

"Well...he just crashed his car into a stop sign out front!"

Luke's eyes bugged, and a cold wash of fear enveloped him. "What?"

The younger guy seemed relieved to have gotten his attention. "He blacked out at the wheel."

FOUR

"Something's wrong."

Rowan shot out of bed on wobbly legs. The room spun, and she grabbed a bedpost as sweat gathered on her temples. "Somethings wrong..."

A gentle pair of hands settled on her shoulders, and Rowan sucked in a breath, shaking as Evan eased her to the mattress. "Shush...it was a nightmare," she whispered, tucking a damp strand of hair behind Rowan's ear. "It was only a dream."

"No..." Rowan's eyes watered, and the room swayed, dotted with stars as she fought down nausea. In those moments before she woke, jolted out of the dream...she saw something. A shape cut against a black, inky sky.

A tree. Which considering where they lived should be normal. Trees surrounded them. But something about this one sparked dread in her heart. Something bad...forgotten...

She clutched at Evan's arm across her chest, fighting for her vision to clear, her girlfriend's cool breath on her face. "You had a nightmare, honey. It's not even light out yet. Go back to sleep."

Rowan, weighted to the bed by that dull, lagging feeling when you woke up abruptly, couldn't fight the need to close her eyes, and Evan stroking her head caused her to drift. Evan's fingertips sparked soft violet light, her eyelids drooped, and she went under.

Waking an hour or so later, Rowan was dry-mouthed and foggy-headed. Evan stood over the bed and presented her with coffee. Evan beamed. "Today is the big day!"

Groaning, Rowan sat up. Her temples and her eyeballs ached from lack of sleep. She took the coffee and sipped it. The liquid burned her gullet. "Great."

"Aren't you excited? Even a tiny bit?"

Evan's enthusiasm was infectious, and Rowan gave her a half-hearted smile and a weak thumbs up. Evan rolled her eyes, threw her arms around her neck, and gave her a long kiss. "Grump!"

"I'm tired...that dream...."

Evan frowned, sitting cross-legged opposite her on the bed. "It was only a dream. You're probably stressed about today. Why? What did you see?"

Rowan let out a slow, exhale, resisting the urge to giggle. "A tree."

"Well, that's just *terrifying*."

Rowan snorted and elbowed her in the waist. "It was a creepy tree."

Evan kissed her again and bounced off the bed with a mischievous look on her face. "C'mon. Get showered, and I'll do your hair all pretty. I hate to break it to you, but your mother picked you something to wear."

Rowan nearly spat out her coffee. "Is it awful?"

Evan cocked her head, thoughtful, and waves of dark hair tumbled across her shoulders. "It's nice. But I don't think she realizes yet that you don't like people picking your clothes—I'm lucky you're letting me do your hair."

Rowan sighed, imagining how excited Alice would have been picking an outfit, something pretty, conservative, and smart for a job interview. Rowan didn't own job interview clothes. She didn't possess anything remotely smart in her wardrobe, happy to spend most of her time in leggings, hoodies, or ripped jeans. Alice meant no harm, but Rowan hated being dressed by others. Spencer never outright told her what to wear, but he made suggestions. *Forthright* suggestions. Disappointed faces and troubled noises when she didn't do as he asked. It left a well of guilt pooling in her gut, so deep she would relent, change and do as he liked.

Rowan showered and endured Evan's pampering, closing her eyes as her deft fingers wove through her red, tangled mane, smoothing it into a pretty bun at the nape of her neck. Rowan gasped and admired herself in the mirror. "I look respectable—will I do?"

Evan wound her arms around her waist, staring across her shoulder in the mirror. "You are perfect. And you will be amazing today. They'll love you."

Rowan wandered downstairs, letting her fingers trail along the polished wood rail, the smell of burning eggs wafting under her nose. Alice rattled around the kitchen, ducking in and out of cupboards. She swore when she saw the eggs smoking in the pan. "Crap!"

Rowan made a face, pausing in the door to watch. It was still unreal. Her *being* here. In this kitchen. As though she'd never been gone a day. Rowan's heart tightened under her ribs, admiring her mother's slow and steady progress. The day after Rowan brought her out of the snow, Alice had taken baby steps; falcon hops toward becoming the shell of the woman they remembered. For the first two weeks, she'd hauled up in her bedroom, sitting cross-legged at the window, staring up at the sky in a way that made Rowan's gut ache. Ben took Win's room, letting Alice get acclimatized, but it surprised Rowan that her mother wanted him back in the bed before the week was out. She'd never looked at her father as a protector. He'd been absent during her teens, but somehow he understood

Alice better than anyone, sensed her moods, and she needed him on a deeper level than a blood bond could provide.

Cagily, Alice emerged from the bedroom, joining them in the family room, tentative and quiet as she huddled beside her husband, small and fragile. They watched movies, old shows, and she found her sense of humor and courage.

Eggs, even burnt eggs, were progress. "You didn't have to make me breakfast!"

Alice beamed. "Hey." She sniffed the pan. "I didn't do an amazing job. It's your big day! How do you feel?"

Rowan slunk into a chair, pulling up her knee and cradling it to her chest. Her throat was so dry she cracked out a bleak, "Nervous."

Alice's fingers reached to pat her hair but pulled back at the last moment, still wary about touching. "This is lovely," she referred to Rowan's updo. Rowan grabbed her mother's hand and kissed the back of it, even if she flinched. Rowan loved her mother, every inch of her, and was determined to get her back to the world. Over the last few weeks, her hair had grown out of the clumsy, choppy blonde bob, but she was still pale, with dark rings under her wide, pale eyes. Rowan wondered what kept her awake at night. Maybe she missed the sky? Rowan would too.

"Did you see what I picked for you to wear? Did you like it?"

Rowan smiled, swigging down some juice. "I loved it."

"You'll do fine. It's about time you got out of that bar."

It sounded strange, knowing her mother knew things, forced to watch them grow from afar, and yet she'd not been present. Alice presented her with a plate of clumpy eggs and burnt toast, and Rowan forced a smile and a weak thanks. She forced it down while her mother hovered around like a bird. It hit her stomach and rolled, nausea swept up her throat, and it took willpower to keep the food down. However, it wasn't the food that bothered her. Her temples throbbed, and she willed away the errant vision of the tree. When she glanced up, Alice was clutching the chair back with white knuckles.

"Mom...are you okay?"

Alice shook herself, batting her hand, and said airily, "Fine—just didn't sleep well."

Rowan eyed her, wary, and didn't believe a word she said. She checked her watch and darted for the stairs after breakfast.

An hour later, Evan pulled the truck into the Furlow's school lot. Unable to keep her excitement in, Evan squealed.

"It's only an interview—calm down," Rowan said.

"I know, but I'm just so excited for you!" Evan grabbed her hand and gave it an affectionate squeeze. "Do you have your resume?"

Rowan wafted the pink folder under her nose, containing one document her father helped write, over-embellished and exactly one page long. "Got it."

"Remember what Ben said—turn anything negative into a positive. Don't bite your nails, and make sure you smile—you are so pretty when you smile."

Rowan's face stretched into a fake grin, revealing teeth, and Evan punched her shoulder lightly.

She suddenly didn't want to leave the safe confines of the cab, it was warm, and the wipers swished gently, batting off fresh snow flakes. "Are you going to wait in the truck?"

"I need a walk. I'll see you at home," Evan said, handing over the keys. Rowan eyed her carefully as her girlfriend's smile slipped, and she blinked rapidly. For a brief second, she looked like she was in pain.

"Are you okay?"

Evan shook it off and plastered her smile back on. "I'm just nervous for you. Good luck!"

Rowan's skirt was too tight, and she could hardly walk in the shoes her mother picked. Evan planted a kiss on her lips and then shoved her out of the cab.

Her ankle cracked as she took her first step. She gritted her teeth but walked onward, head down, feeling like she was seventeen again. Letting a group of students go ahead, she paused on the stone steps, catching a fleeting glance at the back of Luke's head. Jolting, she pushed down a wave of sickness. He walked with Ella and the lanky guy with the shaved head. Seeing him hurt, she felt a sharp pang of guilt that she'd left the bar so abruptly, without so much as a goodbye or a send-off.

She loved Luke, he was Spencer's little brother, and she'd known him forever. Since the night of his Calling, he was drastically altered, and when she looked at him, she got flashes of someone else. His eyes changed color, and she wasn't sure if he even knew it, but sometimes...she swore he looked like her grandfather. Rowan couldn't explain it. It was something expressive in his face, in his mannerisms. It was old, soulful, grumpy, charming, and completely John. And oddly, sometimes, Win.

Maybe it wasn't odd at all? Luke was John's great nephew, and Iris was his grandmother. The blood link was weak, but it flowed, binding them together. He was territorial, annoying, and bad-tempered, and working with him on shift was unbearable. He blew up at customers if they so much as brushed her shirt. But he looked lost, like a pup who'd been abandoned. He missed Win.

Rowan walked into the building, then abruptly, her head swam, and without warning, the eggs she had for breakfast were about to make a comeback. She staggered to the nearest bathroom and threw up, gagging and spitting.

Rowan bent double over the toilet, dismayed as her breakfast disappeared down the bowl with a flush.

What the hell was that about?

She straightened, smoothing out her skirt, and wiped her mouth on her hand. Breathing hard, she exited the stall and then gazed at her reflection, her eyes still seeing stars. Thank god she had been early for this meeting. She shook off the tremble in her hands, gazing at herself in the girl's bathroom mirror, eyeing her pale complexion. Rouge curls had fallen from the carefully pinned-up do that Evan had spent most of the morning creating.

Huffing, Rowan shoved unruly curls back where they belonged, tucking strands behind her ears, and giving her cheeks a pinch. She couldn't remember the last time she'd worn makeup. With Evan, she didn't bother, preferring to be natural, effortless. Whereas with Spencer she'd worn it daily, knowing he enjoyed that she made an effort for him.

Get it together... you can do this. Perhaps it was pure nerves? She had been pacing all morning, wearing a frayed patch on the living room rug. Shakily, she wandered back into the crowded hallway, teaming with students. Ignoring any inquisitive glances, she made it to the school office and wrapped her knuckles on the glass door. A frazzled young woman with dark hair lifted her head and narrowed her eyes. "Yes?"

"Hi," Rowan uttered, her mouth suddenly dry. "I have an interview at nine am."

The lady stared at her over her wide glasses. "For the office assistant role? You're a little early. You can wait in the chair over there."

Rowan blew out air, and nodded, grateful to be out of the hall. Her mouth still tasted sour, and she wiped her lips, baffled at her sudden sickness. Normally in tip-top health, it wasn't like her to throw up. Her hand strayed to her abdomen, still swirling. She shrugged the feeling away, it passed as soon as it arrived. Nerves, it had to be.

Rowan waited, clicking her heels together, unaware she was doing it. *No place like home, no place like home...*

Though home wasn't the same place, it had been four weeks ago. Win was gone, her absence leaving a gaping void, and Rowan pined for her sister, aching to hear news of her. Dutifully, she'd done as her father advised. She'd given them space. But as days had trawled into weeks, things were becoming serious.

When Win left, they'd discussed how to handle things. Ben made phone calls, and once the school found Win was off with a long-term illness, it'd been difficult to shake them off. When the school threatened to get social workers involved if they couldn't visit Win at home, Ben panicked and called the only person he could think of. Uncle Willard.

The old, mysterious man had a history of erasing Hickory problems and making eyes turn in opposite directions. Family members vanishing in the Hickory family weren't unusual. The man had arranged fake burials and somehow swung death certificates for family members who simply disappeared, and over the years, there had been many. Luckily, Win had a long hospital record to back up her unexplained new 'illness.' But that was nearly four weeks ago, Win was close to racking up all her excused absences, and Rowan guessed the school would start asking questions again.

Now even Ben was fretting. Grayson called and kept them informed as he'd promised, but Win wasn't biting. A letter had arrived in the mail from the school secretary informing Ben that if Win didn't make an appearance soon, her absence would seriously derail any future with the school. She faced expulsion. Rowan messaged Grayson, begging him to bring Win home, but he'd replied with a simple. *I'll try.*

Rowan didn't want to push her parents, they were in a weird honeymoon stage, but sooner or later, someone would have to make a decision, step up and be a parent. Why did that have to fall on Rowan? She sighed, tapping her fingers on her knees. Ben needed to act, and she guessed why he hadn't. He was preoccupied with Alice. He wanted to be the good guy, give Win space and time.

A few minutes passed. The woman clicking away at her desk finally whirled in her chair, facing Rowan. "So, I'm Becky, the office manager, and I'll be interviewing you. Do you want a coffee or anything?"

Taken back, Rowan shook her head. "Water, please?"

"Sure," Becky said with a reluctant smile. "You look pale. Feeling okay?"

Rowan smiled, letting out a shaky breath. "Just nervous." At her admission, the tall, thin Becky snorted as she clicked over to the water cooler, filling a plastic cup and pressing it into Rowan's hand.

"It's an office assistant job in a school. It's hardly NASA."

Rowan's ego wilted, and her cheeks burned. Deflating inside, she ignored the cutting remark and reached for her resume in the folder she carried under her arm. Not NASA, maybe, but this meant more. This was the first time she'd tried...at anything.

Keeping her smile even, she handed the resume to Becky, who flipped it open. Rowan's stomach plummeted, recalling sitting in the office with her father while he dragged out any 'attributes' to add to the one-page report of her working life to date. It didn't make an enthralling read. Eventually, Becky glanced up, clicking her tongue, then bestowed her with a long, hard stare. "Maybe you can start by telling me about yourself? Any interesting hobbies?"

Rowan's tongue went sandpaper dry. "Well...okay. I'm Rowan Adler. I'm twenty-two...I worked at Hardy's in town...."

Her mind whirled endlessly, fighting for anything, any titbit she could think up, but instead, she went on an internal down spiral.

My ex-boyfriend shot me...My girlfriend is an ancient witch ...I have a habit of turning into a Golden Eagle. I'm cursed to be a Therian shifter, and I can't leave the state...my sister and I sent my ex-boyfriend to another time through a stone portal in the woods...My mom is human again, she was trapped as a falcon for ten years...my sister ran away with a guy whose mother was trying to kill us all....

"I like running," Rowan answered. "And yoga."

"That's where I recognize you," Becky said, tapping her pencil on the plastic coating of the file. "Hardy's! And it looks like you've been working there...."

"Since I was seventeen," Rowan filled in the gap, her lack of experience weighing heavily on her shoulders.

"And you never left? You must have liked it there."

"Oh, I love the place!" Rowan smiled genuinely. "But it's time to move on. I..." She was reluctant to reveal she had signed up for an adult community college, with Evan's encouragement. Somehow she didn't want to reveal her lack of good grades to this stranger.

"I needed a change," Rowan finished, and Becky lifted her chin, assessing her curtly with her dark eyes.

"It's a small role, but it can be quite busy. Lots of filing, typing, scheduling...does that sound enough for you? You might be bored. We don't have too many bar fights here."

Her smile, laced with cynicism, vanished the moment Rowan lifted her eyes, and she drew back in her chair. Rowan's temper frayed short, her eyes bright, flashing. She must have projected enough venom in her stare to unnerve Becky because she licked her dry lips and looked away.

"I like quiet," Rowan answered. "I'm going to be taking classes, and eventually, I want to move on to counseling. I had a rocky start in life and was stuck for a long time. But I know what I want now."

She heard her father's voice in her head. He had repeatedly warned her not to sell herself short, lift her chin, smile, and not keep looking at her hands. Coupled with Evan's love and encouragement, she felt a glow of positivity, knowing she'd done her best no matter what. She idly wondered what Win would think about this. Becky's eyes ducked to her resume again.

"It's Monday to Friday, and you'd be done by three...if you needed to take shifts at the bar."

Rowan fought the urge to roll her eyes. Instead, she chuckled. "My days hauling kegs are over. Those hours are perfect."

Becky plowed through more questions, asking about Rowan's background. Some personal things she expected were prying rather than it having any relevance to the job. Then, abruptly she crossed her legs and leaned forward on her knees in a conspiratorial way that made Rowan automatically inch closer.

"I hope you don't mind me asking...but isn't your sister a student here?"

Rowan's belly did a flip, and she nodded. "That's right."

"She needs to come back to school. She'll be risking getting kicked out if she doesn't. We've written to your father."

Rowan didn't think it was fair to bring this up in an interview, but this woman's entire approach was a little off the wall. Rowan smiled and rolled her eyes. "Win is having some difficulties at home. She was sick for a long time and struggled to fit into school life. I'm sure she'll be back soon."

Rowan evenly repeated what her father had already written as a reply to the school, stating that Win was sick, suffering from anxiety serious enough to keep her at home. Becky raised a dark brow.

"You realize that if it wasn't for your—*connections*—your dad would've been charged with neglect by now?"

Rowan's hands went hot, and the room spun enough to make her feel nauseous again. Becky was referring to Willard and wondered what he'd said or done to keep them away. Rowan licked her lips, struggling for words. "Uh, well...I...."

"When she does decide to come back to school, she can see the school counselor this time. Make sure she settles. In fact..." She scribbled some notes on her pad. "I'll have the counselor make arrangements for a home visit—see if we can't coax her back in. Otherwise, we may have to take this further."

"I don't think...."

"I'll call your father...but back to you...."

"She's had a tough time!" Rowan interjected, fueled by the need to protect her sister. Rowan admitted she'd been tough on Win, especially regarding Grayson. "She's...gone through a lot of...changes."

Becky made a face. "Sounds like it runs in the family. Good thing you have friends in high places."

Fuck you, Becky. Rowan gritted her teeth and did her best to project calm as she listened to more of the role. Finally, the woman stopped, checked her watch as though she was bored, and met Rowan's gaze. In her handbag, Rowan's phone buzzed. She ignored it, but then it started up relentlessly, and she scolded herself for not switching the damn thing off.

Becky noticed and nodded to her bag. "You need to get that?"

Rowan flushed down her neck. "Uh...no...."

The phone buzzed again, and she groaned.

Becky leaned back, giving her an odd smile. "Aren't you popular?"

She tried to laugh it off, but it buzzed and buzzed. Rowan was mystified, everyone who might need her knew she was here, and her skin tingled with apprehension. A young man stuck his head around the door and called to Becky that she was needed outside urgently. Groaning, Becky rose. "I won't be a moment—you can check your phone while I'm out."

Rowan ground her teeth, grabbed up the phone, and saw Evan's number, and her skin washed cold. Seconds later, Becky rounded the corner with an apologetic look. "Rowan—I'm so sorry, but we might have to reschedule. Some *idiot* just ran into a stop sign out front. Can we call you?"

Rowan didn't need an excuse to leave. She nodded grimly, waiting till Becky walked her into the hall before she snatched her phone out of her bag.

"Rowan..." Evan's voice trembled on the other end of the line, making panic explode in her chest.

"What's wrong?"

"It's your mother...she collapsed....and...."

Rowan choked on her breath, the very words she dreaded about to come out of Evan's mouth. "She says...something is wrong with Win."

FIVE

The truck's thick tires sloshed through gray sludge as Rowan threw the vehicle into the driveway. Within moments, she'd flung open the door and sprung up the porch steps, her feet almost skidding on the polished wooden floor. "Evan?" she called. "Dad?"

Evan emerged from the kitchen, a dishcloth in her hands which she dumped the second she spotted Rowan in the hall, rushing for her. "How did it go?" she asked, polite despite the rushed, stressful conversation they'd shared. Rowan rolled her eyes.

"Never mind that... what happened?"

Evan gripped her hands and let out a shaky breath, pushing dark, glossy hair off her shoulder with a shrug of her shoulders. "After you left, she got sick, then blacked out—we got her upstairs, but she's unsettled. She's been upset since you left."

"Unsettled?"

Evan made a face, hating to be the bearer of bad news, running her thumbs up Rowan's arms. "Let's go up together."

Sickly, Rowan nodded, took Evan's hand, and followed the dark-haired woman up the stairs. Not long after Win ran away, Evan nearly left, pushed away by Rowan's temper. Evan forged a place in her heart, wedged herself to her soul, and no matter what, no matter how Rowan argued and pushed her away, Evan clung on, loving her despite her anger. It took time, lots of nights talking it out, but Rowan forgave her betrayal and the lies she'd told over the summer. Rowan couldn't bear the thought of losing her.

In the bedroom, the one her parents shared, drawers and cupboards clattered.

Even a month later, it was still so odd to think of the room as the one her parents—plural, slept in. Alice came home and, like a disruptive tornado, stormed back into their lives. Though smaller than her daughters, Alice Adler made up for it in strength and stealth. Alice could appear out of nowhere, her footsteps so quiet, that even Rowan's hearing didn't pick it up.

Rowan eased open the door with her fingertips, she was met with a confusing sight. Alice was dressed. And not in her father's pajamas. She wore jeans that hugged her figure and a sweater swiped from her own closet.

"Whoa, Mom!" Rowan found herself laughing, but the smaller blonde lady snapped her head in their direction. In a chair in the corner, Ben sagged, elbows on knees. "You actually have a pair of legs."

Ben's head snapped up, his eyes creasing as he looked at Rowan in expectation. "How did it go?"

Rowan rolled her eyes. "I need to work on my interview skills. I don't think she liked me."

"Then she's an idiot," he said, and Rowan's cheeks flushed, even though she didn't want to admit a compliment from him could make her soar.

Alice had thrown on a pair of faded jeans, and Rowan was sure they were Win's. The strawberry blonde hair Evan chopped into a bob hung neatly at her shoulders. Therian hair grew back fast, and the older woman quickly tied it into a scruffy bun at her neck.

"Are you going somewhere?" Rowan cocked a brow, and Alice stared at her sharply, her chest rising and falling rapidly.

"Something is wrong," Alice said, and Ben groaned. Red-eyed, she whirled in his direction. "And *he* isn't listening to me!"

Worry stirred in the pit of Rowan's belly. "What do you mean?"

Alice clattered in a drawer and pulled out some socks. "I need to find her. We need to go, now!"

Ben stood, his dark hair greyer than she'd ever seen, and he rubbed his eyes under his glasses. "She thinks something is wrong with Win."

Alice flung her hands in the air and fell to the edge of the bed. "I'm telling you...something is wrong. I felt...."

Rowan knelt by her feet, peering up into her mother's pale face, her wide blue eyes framed with pale lashes. "What happened, Mom? Did you...?" She wanted to say out loud what she'd felt, her dream last night. Alice met her gaze, her lips trembling.

"You felt it, too."

"I threw up," Rowan admitted, blushing. "But it was just nerves."

Evan joined them in the room, arms crossed and a pensive look on her face. Rowan caught her with a glare. "Do you know anything?"

Evan blanched, hurt at Rowan's instant mistrust, and the redhead immediately regretted it. "Of course not," she said, lowering her eyes. "Only Alice has been frantic since you left."

"We need to go and get Win, now!" Alice urged, shaking her head. "She's been gone too long, and I don't like it."

"We know Win is okay!" Ben sat beside his wife on the bed, grasping her hand. "Grayson messages regularly, and I trust him...and Win...."

Rowan's shoulders stiffened at her father's complacency, and half wondered if he would ever really change. When Rowan went through her Calling and became a difficult and challenging teenager, Ben was too happy to drop her on John Hickory's doorstep. Driving out of her life for five years, he allowed himself to hyper-focus on Win. It was a stark reminder of how she'd spent her teens, living with a lovable but unpredictable older man who, despite giving her all he could, wasn't her father—a man she needed. With Alice home, the burden fell on Ben to step up. He became stressed and anxious, wanting to get Alice healthy, spoiling her with his undivided attention. Rowan wasn't surprised Ben was acting this way, it wasn't the first time.

Despite Rowan's rocky start with Grayson, she gave him props. He'd looked out for Win, messaged, and didn't let them go a week without knowing Win was okay. He'd sent her the location, a motel outside Rope's point, and the website and picture on google maps looked decent. Grayson gave her the freedom to come by at any time, but Rowan held back, even though she itched to see her sister.

Before Win left, they'd exchanged heated words, and Win accused her of trying to keep her in line. Rowan knew how it felt to be controlled, and she trusted her sister. Maybe she had been too overprotective? Win wasn't an idiot. She knew the risks she faced and would come home when she was ready. The pull to home must be bugging Win by now. Home on Hickory turf, Win would be stronger. Rowan marveled that she'd managed this long.

"Win does need to come home," Rowan finished his sentence. "No matter what happens, she has to face the music. If she doesn't, she'll get kicked out of school."

Ben visibly swallowed, raking his fingers through his dark, graying hair. "I've let this get out of hand."

Yes, you have. "You should have made her come home, Dad." Rowan blew out air. She'd said it aloud, and her father's face crumpled with guilt. "Why have you let her stay away this long?"

He turned and stared out of the window. On the bed, Alice gazed at his back, chewing her lip, remaining quiet. "I was trying..." he broke off, then turned to face her. "I wanted to show I trusted her. She went through hell this summer, and I wanted to give her time. Be a better dad than I was to you. But I screwed up...again!"

Rowan's lips pressed into a thin line, hiding the division she felt. Once again, Ben tried and failed to do the right thing; no matter what, Win would always be the baby. Rowan was the one who'd caused him pain by letting Alice go free all those years ago.

She felt a pang of guilt, recalling the day she'd opened Alice's cage and how he'd sobbed, broken on the floor. She cleared her throat. "You didn't screw up. But you give Win far too much trust. There's no way she'll come home of her own volition." Rowan shook her head. "Win belongs here. She can't stay away forever. It's a miracle we've gotten this far. Whatever Uncle Willard said or did must have worked, but it won't last. The woman who interviewed me was asking questions."

"I don't know what he said to them," he admitted. "God, this is such a mess."

"At least Rowan agrees with me," Alice said with a sharp sting in his direction. "I don't understand why you don't trust me."

"Of course, I trust you. She needs a bit of time...like when Evan brought you back. If you recall, home wasn't your priority!"

Alice snapped her mouth shut and looked away. Rowan rolled her eyes. "Mom... maybe Dad is right?" It still felt strange saying that in a sentence, Mom *and* Dad. "Maybe today was a coincidence? Grayson *would* call us if anything were wrong."

Distracted by a beeping in her jacket, Rowan stood and sagged next to Evan on the wall. She flipped out her phone, spying a message from Luke, and her heart pinched.

Hey. Can you call me? I blacked out this morning, and so did my dad. It was weird. Something feels wrong.

Rowan swallowed hard, and Evan read the message over her shoulder, and across the sound of her parent's bickering, she breathed a quiet, "Oh...crap."

On the bed, Ben's cell buzzed on the mattress, and all four edged closer. The screen lit up with the caller's ID. Ben grumbled, and Alice cried, "Ha! You see?" She slapped his shoulder for good measure.

Grayson *was* calling. Rowan's insides turned ice cold. Grayson didn't usually make day calls. Finally, it was Evan who snatched up the phone, as Ben visibly went gray with worry. After a very quick conversation, Evan hung up and nodded at them. "Yeah, you should go. Now."

Ben groaned and grabbed at his hair. "Okay...I'll get my coat."

Alice sniffed, vindicated. "You ought to know better by now."

"I'll stay here," Evan said when Rowan took her hand. Rowan nodded and followed her parents downstairs. "The four of us might be too much."

Rowan smiled weakly. "I think seeing my mother will be enough to freak her out."

Rowan dreaded what Win would say when she saw Alice. They'd all agreed it was best to keep it quiet until Win decided to come home. After Luke's Calling, whatever turmoil Win suffered was enough to make her flee, and Rowan could only imagine how awful watching him die must have been.

Losing him overnight, a guy she leaned on way too heavily, was enough to make her pack her bags. In the short time since Win had been in Cedarwood, she'd lost her grandfather, gone through her Calling, temporarily lost her boyfriend, compounded with losing Luke, and Ella. Win was still a kid and Rowan was amazed she hadn't cracked sooner.

In the hall, Ben stuffed a coat around Alice's shoulders, which she threw back at him in a temper. Ben locked gazes with his eldest, and they shared a weary smile, his hand at the small of her back as he ushered her out the door, with keys jangling in his pocket.

"Let's go get our girl," he said, "And bring her home where she belongs."

Of all the places on earth Rowan could guess Win might want to be, home, in this house, was probably the last place she'd choose.

SIX

The oak imprinted onto her closed lids like a burn. Blistering pain jerked Win awake, and she sat up, gasping. Grayson caught her shoulders and eased her to the pillow. "Steady."

"Where is he?"

"Who?"

Win sat, and her head thumped, her vision swimming as she fought swells of sickness in the pit of her belly. "The asshole who did this to me."

Ashen in the low, orange hue of the wall lamp, Grayson shook his head. "Win, I found you on the beach—alone." He scrubbed at his face, leaving red marks from the blunt ends of his fingers. "I shouldn't have let you go."

"This isn't your fault. I've been to the beach alone a hundred times since we've been here."

Sitting up, she leaned against his chest as he propped up the pillow behind her head. Bleary-eyed, she asked, "What time is it?"

He cast a glance at the bedside clock. "Nearly half past nine in the morning."

"Damn—I've been asleep all this time? He could be anywhere now!"

Grayson's lips parted. He went to say something, then changed his mind. Finally, he said, strained, "Who was he? Did you recognize him?"

Win recalled Wolfric's peculiar appearance, size, the untidy mane of black hair, and his clothing, still smoking from the fire she was sure she'd seen curled around him on the beach. But how could that be? Eyes widening, she unzipped her hoodie, and when her bare skin tasted cool air, she let out a gasp of pain. The burn stung, deep and down to the bone. Grayson's jaw dropped, and he went pale. "What the hell is that? A burn?"

"He did this to me," she revealed as Grayson's eyes traveled to the wound on her collarbone. "Wolfric—Wolfric Varga. Evan's brother."

"Why? Why would he hurt you?" Grayson went to touch it, but his fingers curled. Win could see guilt crease around his eyes, angry he hadn't been there. She folded her fingers around his and pulled his hand into her lap.

"He didn't do this to hurt me—not maliciously. He said it was a gift."

"A gift?"

"It was cryptic," Win agreed, shifting so her back didn't ache. "He said we had to fix the mess we made—the Spencer mess."

Grayson's thick brows knitted. He tossed his eyes around the room, then glared, muttering, "I knew that would come back and bite us in the ass."

Win's lip trembled, suddenly overwhelmed, with pain and emotion and one fact that was startling clear.

It was over. They locked eyes, and the way his lip dropped told her he knew it too. Spencer had come crashing through their sweet, blissful bubble with a deafening pop. Win's stomach coiled, and she drew up her knees. It was time to go home. "I don't want to go back."

Grayson bit his lip, giving her a look she recognized. His 'I've done something bad' face was too easy to read. She knew it well and cocked a brow. "What?"

"Don't yell at me."

"What have you done?"

"I called your father."

Win exploded. "*Grayson!* Why?"

He bounced off the bed, clawing his fingers through his thick blonde hair. "What was I supposed to do? You passed out cold. I'm supposed to be keeping you safe."

Win threw back the duvet, flinging herself across the room, grabbing clean jeans and a sweater, and throwing him her most venomous glare. "When are they coming?"

Grayson groaned, "I called about an hour ago."

"Grayson! Uh...I could...." Pounding around the bed, she threw open the door to the small shared bathroom. He chased her, but she slammed the door in his face, her eyes stinging with tears. Frustrated, she went to lock it, but it was broken. Wildly, her eyes swept the moldy room, finding broken tiles, the stained washbasin, everything that was awful and wrong in this space they'd hauled up in for the last four weeks. God, her father, could *not* come into the bedroom. She thought of the overflowing trash can, filled with food wrappers, cans, take-out cartons, and winced, shamefaced.

"Win...c'mon!" he called through the crack in the door.

"How do they even know where to find us?"

He exhaled loudly. "They've always known."

She ignored him, knowing how irritated he got when she gave him the silent treatment. She stripped off and threw on the shower. Steam gently filled the room. Condensation dripped down the mirror as the old fan battled to do its job.

He banged on the door with his fist. "You're being unfair, Win. What was I supposed to do? They trusted me to be look out for you."

She closed her eyes, got under the hot spray, and lathered up shampoo in her hair, washing out the salt from the ocean. Water hit the burn, but it didn't hurt. Gazing down, her neck at an awkward angle, she saw it was crusting over. Luckily, she healed fast.

Grayson wandered in, staring at her through the frosted cubicle door. After four weeks of close confinement, the two of them had quickly fallen into sync, neither one embarrassed or bashful, often having to share the shower because the hot water lasted ten minutes, and Win hogged it. To her horror, he stripped off and jumped in, and she was pressed against the slippery tiles as he reached for the shower gel.

"I'm mad at you—go away!"

"I gotta shower too, and you'll steal all the water—move over."

She cast him a look over her shoulder, wet, soapy, and handsome, and found it impossible not to let a smile pull at her lips. She couldn't be mad at him when he'd done so much for her. Squeezing around to face him, his eyes were drawn to the burn on her chest.

"We should get something to help with that."

She ran a hand up his chest. "It's healing already. Lucky me, huh?"

"Does it hurt?"

She shook her head. "I'm sorry," she said, feeling like a spoiled brat. "I don't want this to end."

Grayson chewed the inside of his mouth, staring at the tiled wall, his eyes glistening. "Neither do I."

He took her gently by the elbows, and Win let tears seep out of the corners of her eyes. She flung her arms around his neck. "I don't want to go back. I won't get to see you every day."

"We'll see each other, I promise!"

"No...you have to work, and I've got school...and this has been perfect."

Grayson's laugh rumbled against her chest as she clung on. "I'd hardly call it perfect."

She lifted her chin, face to face, and kissed him needily. "It is. You are perfect, and being here...I needed this. I needed you!"

Under the shower, he kissed her, lifting her onto her toes, and heat exploded down her back. He broke away. "I've loved every second of having you to myself. But this is right, Win. We need to go home. But we go together. I'll be there."

Sniffing, she wiped her nose as he kissed away tears rolling down her cheeks. A deep ache hollowed out her insides; she couldn't bear this to be over. She wouldn't get to wake up with him every morning. Grayson was endlessly fascinating, and he was hers. She tried to agree and speak, but it came out as croaky, "I know."

Win did need to go home. She couldn't pretend her absence from school worried her, that she was missing her old life. She missed Ella. But even thinking about home made Win gag. What was she going home to? Now armed with new worry, that Evan was in danger, made it unavoidable.

Grayson tapped her nose, bringing her out of her train of thought.

"That night in the woods, we did that...all of us. You, me. Rowan, Evan, *and* Luke. All of us share this with you. You aren't alone."

Wolfric was forced out of her mind as steam rose off the floor, coating the walls with slick condensation. Here and now was what she wanted, all she needed, and she never wanted to leave this room.

She leaned against his chest, resting her chin there, and smiled, bashfully. When he kissed her, she gasped for breath and arched into him as he lifted her off the slippery tiled floor.

Freezing cold water jetted through the faucet, and the pair broke apart, laughing. Grayson rinsed off his hair, as Win squealed, clambering out of the cubicle.

Win shimmied out into the bedroom, shivering and toweling off her hair. Her gaze roamed the walls, faded wallpaper, broken lights, and their trash cans overflowing. It was a dump, a wreck of a room inhabited by two teenagers for the last four weeks—eating crap, sleeping in, watching old movies, and not leaving the bed except for food. She threw open the windows, trying to aerate the cloying smell of damp.

A car crunching on the gravel outside made her straighten, and she flew to the window, pulling back the thin curtain.

"Crap!" she hissed, diving for her underwear and wriggling into a pair of jeans. Throwing on a shirt, she dived to the bathroom door. "They're here—get dressed!"

Wet hair soaking through her shirt, she shivered, stuffing her feet into shoes, and in the seconds she had, Win scouted the room, stuffing their strewn clothing out of the way. Grayson bounded naked across the room, scrambling for clothes.

Half dressed, his shirt hanging open, he took her hand and kissed her palm. He smiled, the one that drove her crazy. "I love you. We're together in this, okay?"

Her eyes misted. "I love you too."

Win stared out the small, dirty window as the truck stalled and the doors opened. She spotted Rowan's hair, and did a double-take, admiring how it was pinned up off her neck, making her look older, conservative. Her heart beat sped, as her father got out, his eyes raking over the dilapidated building. The website did make it look so much better. Warmth trickled from Grayson's fingers as he wound them through hers, and she swore nothing would ever make her let go of his hand.

But Win sucked in air, the room swaying, as her mother got out of the truck.

SEVEN

Ben Adler whistled as he shoved his hands inside his pockets and stared up at the ramshackle motel. From the window, Win could see his resolve wilting second by second as he spotted the dingy café and the strip joint nestled down the end of the lot. He looked greyer every moment he stood there as if the disbelief and disappointment were sinking in.

Win shrugged into a jacket, an icy jet of cold hitting her chest as she buttoned it up to her throat. Met with the sight she'd dreaded for the last month, she walked toward them, and they didn't see her approach from behind. Her breath hitched, eyes prickling with hot tears as the petite woman with a short mass of strawberry blonde hair, stiffened as if she sensed eyes on her back. Slowly, she turned, letting her pale eyes slide over Win, head to toe.

Win choked out, "Mom?"

Alice Adler stared at her for a long time before her lips twitched into a smile. Even though Win had grown up without her mother, the mouth, the eyes were so familiar. She was real and solid. Her hair hung loosely around her face, her cheeks rosy and full, bare of makeup. She looked better than Win could have imagined. Her pink lips split in a relieved grin. "Win...oh my God. *Win!*"

Heart hammering, Win burst and sprinted across the gravel, spiriting her mother in an embrace that lifted her off the ground. Alice gasped, tear-streaked, and smiled as she patted her daughter all over as if checking she was real. "Look at you—you're so tall and strong!" She grabbed Win's face and kissed her cheeks. "And, gorgeous!" She thrust a hand toward Rowan, who meekly joined the hug. "Both of you! My girls!"

Win choked back a sob as Rowan wound an arm around her waist and kissed her forehead. They locked eyes and giggled. "Hey," Rowan said, with a wobble in her voice. "I missed you."

"I missed *you*!"

They all laughed, hands linked, and Win was struck with how right this felt, how normal. Their mother was home, and she was human, real, and, most importantly, happy to be with them. Win dissolved into tears. "I'm sorry...I'm sorry I didn't come home. Why didn't you tell me?"

The question was aimed at Rowan, though there was no fire or anger behind it. It was Alice who answered. "We made the decision not to tell you. You'd been through so much...."

"You needed to get away," her sister answered simply. "After what happened that night, you needed a break. We just didn't think it'd be this long."

But Win sniffed, her eyes aching, barely able to form a sentence. "Are you angry with me?"

"No!" Alice squeezed her hand. "My God—no."

Rowan and Win's gazes caught, and she tried to read her sister's expression. Was there annoyance or resentment behind her stare? Win suddenly felt so selfish, running away when Rowan had been alone all those years, coping without anyone other than Grandpa. Rowan seemed to understand, and with a small nod, Win found nothing but love and understanding. "How can I ever be angry at you? I don't blame you for needing to take off."

"I need to tell you so much."

Alice squeezed her hand. "It's kind of why we're here."

Win's attention flicked to her father, who watched the reunion with fondness. His smile wavered as she broke from the trio and ran toward him.

"Dad!" Win flung her arms around him, but he jerked. His arms never quite met around her body. Instead, he smiled gruffly, drew back, and patted her shoulder with an awkwardness she was unused to.

"You look pale," he said.

Win's smile slipped, and her hand automatically went to her face, where her cheeks grew hot. "I'm fine."

He shook his head. "And thin," he said, looking her up and down. "What have you been eating?"

"We've been eating fine."

Win, painfully aware of Grayson listening in the door to their room, fidgeted with her hands. Ben threw his gaze toward him, his lips pressed thin. "When was the last time you two ate properly?"

Grayson narrowed his eyes, arms folded across his large chest as he leaned in the doorway. "We eat," he said, jerking his chin at the diner across the forecourt. Ben choked.

"In there?"

"It's not as bad as it looks."

The diner needed more than new windows and a lick of paint. It looked like it needed razing to the ground. On cue, a rat scurried out from under the black weatherboarding, hurrying across the forecourt. Rowan hissed in fright.

"And the bedroom...is that not as bad as it looks? Wait! I don't think I want an invite inside."

"Dad!" Rowan's tone was as chilly as the air. She stepped between her father and Grayson. "What exactly were you expecting? A quaint house by the sea? They're broke."

Ben scoffed, ignoring his eldest, his ire directed at Grayson. "How have you afforded this?"

"Grayson fixed things around the property for Mrs. Tate, the owner," Win explained, her chin wobbling. Her spine wilted like she was shrinking under the heat of her father's gaze, and she sensed something coming from him that she'd never experienced before. Barely concealed disappointment.

Ben shook his head, glancing at the dinner. "Let's get something to eat, shall we? Grayson, maybe you can pack Win's things while we catch up?"

"Don't talk to him like that," Win whispered, embarrassed tears threatening to form. The humiliation was enough to make her chest explode in a rash. Grayson, unphased, shrugged it off.

"The place looks like it needs burning down," Ben remarked, but it didn't go unheard by his wife.

"Ben, stop" she hissed, tugging at his shirt, and her blue eyes flashed. "He's a kid. And he did the best he could."

"Is this really the best you could do?"

Grayson didn't answer, only leaned on the door, unintimidated and steady. Win loved him all the more for it and couldn't understand why her father was acting like a jerk. "You knew where we were—the whole time," he reminded Ben.

"I didn't see you complaining while you were distracted with me. He took care of her, and that's what matters!" Alice said.

Win was flooded with warmth for her mother, recalling the small, frail bird she'd been only a few months ago. Little but strong. Alice smiled weakly and squeezed her daughter's hand. As they reached the diner door, Ben held it for his wife, and Rowan and Win huddled together as they slipped inside. Win felt Rowan's hand on her back, warm and strong.

You've rattled him, Win...don't take it personally...

Win glanced at her sister carefully as they chose a booth near the window. *It's a little hard not to.*

You're his baby...and he's let you shack up in a love den for four weeks with a guy he barely knows. He's having an internal breakdown. I can tell.

Hearing Rowan's thoughts in her head made her temples spike. A sharp influx of pain traveled her brow, and she focussed, staring at the chipped table. It had been a while since she'd heard anyone in her head, or spoken telepathically, and it showed. Win was a journey from Hickory land, and although she thought her body coped with the distance...maybe it *was* time to go home.

Ben waved over Mrs. Tate, the blonde, curly-haired owner, and she scribbled down an order of pancakes. Win's stomach grumbled at the thought of pancakes, she didn't want to admit that she and Grayson had been living off meager portions. Gazing out the window, they had a perfect ocean view, waves pelted the sand, the wash dragging out pebbles and rocks. Win's throat grew thick at the thought of saying goodbye to it.

Mrs. Tate hurried over with their pancakes. Ben sat staring at his food, chewing the inside of his mouth, looking uninterested. He studied her across his mug, and suddenly she didn't feel much like eating.

Win's belly swirled but she dug in anyway, chewing so hard that it slipped down and didn't stick. Rowan looked at her across the table. "I'm so glad to see you."

Win smiled around her food, and to her right, her mother pressed closer, slipping her hand over hers on her lap. "It's time to come home now, baby."

Win sucked in her ribs, forcing down the food. "Hmm."

"I know why you've stayed away," Alice said. "I'm *so* sorry. I'm sorry I didn't come home straight away. I know how much you needed me."

"It's okay," Win insisted, though it wasn't. Alice leaving was part of the reason she'd left.

"No, it's not. I've had time to get used to life—whatever this is. After what happened to you in the woods—what you saw—went through, I *should* have been there. I know why you ran. If I were your age and had a boyfriend who looked like that, I would run away with him too."

Rowan choked, and Win flushed to her chest. Alice giggled mischievously, but across the table, Ben blinked as though he'd been slapped in the face. "*Excuse* me?"

"Oh, Ben..." Alice rolled her eyes. "I'm teasing."

"When we've stopped gushing over Win's boyfriend, there's more to discuss...."

Alice nodded, and Win snapped her eyes in her father's direction. It was time to talk about this morning, and the burn under her hoodie throbbed as a reminder. She straightened in the leather seat, opening her mouth. "Something happened this morning on the beach...."

"You're going to be expelled," Ben interrupted, and Rowan gagged, spitting out a blueberry.

"Dad...jeez!"

Win froze. "What? *Expelled?*"

"I had a letter from the school office, and if you don't return to school soon, you'll be kicked out," Ben said, venom barely shielded in his gaze. "I'm sorry, sweetheart, but you don't have a choice. I'm taking you tomorrow, and we'll have a meeting with your principal. It's a miracle I've not been charged with something—your Uncle Willard is an asset!"

Win's throat constricted, fear threatening to suffocate her. She thought of Ella and Luke walking those halls alone, and her breathing quickened. Under the table, Alice grabbed her arm. "*Now* she looks pale. For God's sake, Ben...*this* soon?"

"They think she's out from sickness—her old illness before we moved here. Thank god Win has the records to back it up," Ben said with a shrug. "It'll be better all-around if Win can return to some form of normalcy."

You aren't going to be expelled.

Win glanced at her sister, whose green eyes were fixed on her over the coffee mug. *Really?*

Well...they want you back and they've made noise about doing a home visit, so he's not wrong.

"Dad is laying it on a little thick," Rowan said aloud, cocking a brow in her father's direction. "Win...you were about to say something?"

Breathing through her nose, she met their gazes one by one. She swiped at her eyes. "Something happened this morning on the beach. I met a man who said he knew me...and... he did this."

She unpeeled her shirt to reveal the mark on her chest; a faint welt etched on her skin. Ben recoiled with horror, and Alice peered closer, daring to touch the mark. "What is this?"

"He did this with his hands," Win explained. "He said it was a gift—whatever that means."

"Does it hurt?"

"Not anymore," Win said. "But Rowan—he was called Wolfric, and he said he was Evan's brother."

It was Rowan's turn to go ghostly white, her green eyes saucer wide. "Evan's brothers are dead."

"This one isn't." Win hated what was coming. Why did it feel like she was always hurting her sister? Giving her bad news? It had been Win who revealed to Rowan who Evan truly was. During her spirit walk with Mary, Win witnessed firsthand the power Evan hid from them. She was a witch, though Evan preferred the term *healer*, and she was old. Like, *fossil*, old.

Rowan shook her head, firm and assured, "Then she can't know he's alive."

Win swallowed. "I think she does, Rowan."

Rowan said nothing, only stared at her empty plate. "I'll talk to her." She lifted her chin. "What does that mean? This gift?"

Win sat back, happy to have her mother's thigh pressed nearer hers. "I don't know. But it means this thing with Spencer isn't over—we messed up Rowan. Wherever we sent him...we have to fix this!"

"I felt it," Alice admitted, earning a look of concern from her family. They listened intently. "Earlier today, I felt what this man did to you."

"Me too," Rowan said. "I had a dream, and later I threw up. And..." She drew in a deep breath. "I think whatever happened to me may have affected Luke as well...and Jake. Jake crashed his car, and Luke passed out. Something weird is going on!"

"What was your dream about?" Alice asked. Rowan paled, aware of everyone looking at her; she waved her hand.

"It was just a stupid dream...."

What? You're holding back... Win pressed.

Rowan stared hard at her blueberries. *I'll tell you later.*

"Luke passed out? Was he okay?" Win said, her voice drifting into the void as the bell chimed above the door, and Grayson shuffled in, kicking fresh snow off his boots. Squeezing into the gap next to Win, they all shifted to make room, and Alice offered him a smile. Win quickly told him what had gone on at home.

"I think he's fine. Fine enough to message me, anyway," Rowan said, circling back to Luke.

"So...whatever affected Win affected him too?" Grayson said, echoing the conversation around the table. "What does this mean?"

Ben threw him a look sharp enough to cut glass and rail-roaded the conversation. "Did you see him—Wolfric?"

Grayson paled under Ben's glare. "No." Win shifted uncomfortably, squirming and guessing where this line of questioning was headed.

"You mean you weren't there when she was attacked? Where *were* you?"

"Don't answer that!" Alice fired at Grayson, who linked fingers with Win under the table. His calloused thumb pads grazed her knuckles. "Ben, stop—you aren't being nice."

Win blinked, swayed, and shook her head as though bugs crawled across her scalp. It was an odd sensation, but when she looked at her mother, Alice's stare was fixed, her pupils dilated and lengthened, the black dots shaped like almonds. Rowan shook her shoulders. Ben smiled, evenly. "You aren't my alpha, Alice. You're my *wife*. That doesn't work on me."

"What was that?" Win asked, tingling. "Mom...was that..?"

Rowan chuckled, her shoulders rolling in a deep shudder. "Mom is flexing her alpha muscle."

Alice tutted. "It's involuntary—sorry!"

Astounded, Win stared at her mother, and even though she was small, whatever she just did, she packed a punch. She wanted to drop to her knees for those brief seconds and submit. It was a sensation of being boneless, helpless—it wasn't a good feeling and struck Win as powerful. Alice was a huge asset. What else was she capable of if she could do that with one glance?

"That was creepy," she said, looking at Rowan. "It never felt like that when you used to do it."

Rowan exhaled, muttering, "That's because I was never really an alpha."

"You will be one day!" Alice joked, despite the gloomy direction of the conversation. "But I do plan on living a long time." She gazed at Ben. "I can't understand why you're attacking him? We have more important things to worry about—whatever happened to Win affected all of us. Jake and Luke too. Something is terribly wrong."

Ben grumbled, crossing his arms. "Why don't we get Win home first? Let's try to get back to some kind of normal before we start involving the Frasers—god knows we need some kind of normal."

Ben stood and waved to Mrs. Tate, who was busy mopping the kitchen, trying to pretend she hadn't been listening in on her only customers in the run-down diner. Mrs. Tate hurried over with the check, placing it on the table, and Grayson and Ben reached for it simultaneously. Ben got there first, swiping it up. Grayson smiled at the elderly lady who'd housed them for the last month.

"Win and I are leaving today, Mrs. Tate. I need to settle everything."

"I'm going to miss you two," she said, grasping Grayson's shoulder, and Win smiled at her, hating the thought of watching this place disappear in the rearview mirror. "But the bills all settled."

Grayson blinked, confused, and Ben looked over his shoulder. "It wasn't me," he said.

Win and Grayson both shrugged. "Do you know who paid?"

"No, it was paid for over the phone about an hour ago. I didn't get their name."

Puzzled, Win stood and held out her hand for her mother. Alice held Win's arm as they wandered back outside. Ben sat impatiently in the truck's front seat while it chugged on the forecourt. With a fleeting glance, she spotted her bags loaded into the back. Grayson pulled the canopy over and clipped it shut, catching her eye. Win's stomach rolled, and the pancakes didn't want to settle. Leaving him here was gut-wrenching. She shook her shoulders, telling herself she was acting like a lovesick kid and needed to snap out of it.

Grayson pulled Win aside, tears already bubbling up in her throat. "You go with your family. I'll pack up here and bring your truck home."

She fisted his shirt, tears spilling over her bottom lashes. "When will you come?"

"I won't be far behind. I promise."

Win hurriedly wiped her face as tears leaked from her eyes. "My dad is being a jerk—though I don't know why."

Grayson let out a short laugh and took her cold face between his palms. "He hasn't seen you in weeks. I think he's freaked out—I get it."

"Don't stay away long." She stood on tiptoe and kissed him, wrapping her arms around his neck so hard that he groaned. She didn't want to let go, but she dropped back, rushing away before she burst into tears. Alice wrapped her arm around Win's waist, though she sensed she was there to support her mother. Alice leaned on her heavily as they walked to the truck. Grayson perched on the motel wall, arms folded, and Win didn't dare meet his gaze. He was going to wave goodbye.

Win wiped her eyes and wailed. "I can't even look at him."

"Oh, honey." Alice squeezed her, along with a gentle laugh. "He *is* cute."

"I *know!* Is he looking?"

Alice tilted her chin and gave him a wave. "Yeah."

"He kills me," Win snuffled a laugh through snot and tears as they piled in the truck. "You can distract me by telling me everything. I want to know how you are—human life."

Alice remained silent as she strapped in beside her daughters, and Win wondered if it hurt too much to talk about life as the falcon. Trapped for more than ten years, Alice lived with them, but apart, she was forced to watch her children grow up without her, unable to help when she was desperately needed.

Win strapped in as they pulled away, and the ocean chased after them on the right. She didn't dare peek out the window, she was already a quivering mess, and watching Grayson vanish, becoming smaller, and smaller was too hard. "You miss it? Flying?"

Alice swallowed and shook her head. It was too raw and too soon. "I can't, Win."

"I'm sorry!"

"No," Alice said, linking her fingers with hers. "I'm sorry. I was selfish—I ran from my family. From what I am. If I'd have come home...."

"I get it, Mom. You were scared."

Alice snorted and looked skyward, teary-eyed. "You can't even begin to know."

Win met Rowan's gaze across the top of their mother's head and was thrown a warning glance. *Pull back*, she said. *She isn't ready.*

Win wrapped her arm around her mother and was surprised at how well she fit, like they were pieces of a jigsaw made to slot together, so naturally right. "When you're ready, Mom—you know you can tell us—anything!"

Alice's gaze darkened, and she stiffened. "Some secrets are not mine to tell, Win. Some things are just too hard to speak of."

EIGHT

On the outskirts of a new town, on a dirt road peppered with small, colonial-style houses, sat a tavern. Horses whinnied in the stables out front, while inside the bar, the atmosphere was heady and thick with the smell of the old and unwashed. At a table near the back, lit by a lonely candle, a man sat alone. His long frock coat was pulled tightly up to his chin. Gloved hands curled around a tankard of ale, he wasn't sure what it was. It tasted nothing like the beer back home. It was earthy and dry, and he licked his teeth to scrape off the coating it left.

A man jeered, fell off a barstool, and everyone laughed as a fellow drinking companion hauled the man off the floor, dusted with hay and sawdust.

A barmaid hustled by, swiping the empty tankard from the stained table, and the man peered at her over his nose.

"Lonely in the corner?" she said with a smile, a hint of what she might be offering after dark. Spencer Fraser shot her a smile that would stop a heart in its tracks, not in a good way. The woman, drained of color, mouthed an apology and fled to the safety of the bar.

Nestled in his corner, Spencer narrowed a pair of cat-like yellow eyes; pupils split in an unearthly way—ungodly. Smirking, he thought that was apt, considering the time he'd been sucked into, beaten half to death by his little brother. Spencer was not a creature of God. He wasn't sure what he was anymore. It was far from human. Under his coat, which barely fit over his biceps, he was covered from head to toe in soft panther fur, delicately marled with faint rosettes. His feet were mutated into clawed paws, and he had no problem shifting back and forth from panther to half-human. It was a handy skill.

In the dark, he recalled the morning he'd been catapulted back in time to the year 1807, where he awoke on a bed of hay in the Hickory barn, with a sweet-faced child wiping his brow. She hadn't stood a chance. Drinking her up like a saucer of milk, her blood thickened with his own, mutating, fusing. The last-born child of the Hickory line was dead and somehow *alive* inside him, healing his wounds, powering up the wretched carcass on the brink of death. He'd been unceremoniously chucked through a time portal—by his brother and that Adler pain in the ass. Spencer chuckled darkly, tapping his long, tapered nails on the tabletop.

All his life, since he could remember, he saw things that weren't real, shapes, colors, and mists—images projected into his head as though he'd lived them. And the voice—constant, nagging, whispering to him at night. Jake, his father, never took him seriously when he spoke of the voice. But his grandfather believed. Robert Fraser, was the only one who ever really got him.

Spencer recalled a snowy night, one that changed his life. His mother had been killed in a collision on the Boxford Tunnel, her car hurtling into the icy river. Mercy, his home, loomed up at him from his seat in the back of the police vehicle, and his father ushered him inside. Later, alone with his grandfather, the old man stroked his arm with a cold, bony hand.

"This is a test, Spencer. One you'll pass again and again. You aren't meant for this life—a life of drudgery. You're a Prince, and you'll be granted a kingdom one day."

Robert Fraser was unhinged, and Spencer wasn't sure if it was his medication talking or the old man truly believed he was fit for a higher purpose. It didn't matter. Spencer was groomed, molded, and shaped into the role of a winner, the smart brother, the better brother. While Luke dallied in the wings. Did his grandfather realize the kind of monster he created? A monster who would get home to take back what was rightfully his, no matter the cost or the lives he took.

After killing Mary, and leaving her in a heap on the ground, he'd sniffed the air and followed the light. Like a violet thread, a trail lingered in the air—an essence of magic. Paws pounding the ground, he'd hurtled into the forest; deeply concealed within the pines sat a solitary cabin, smoke still pouring from the chimney.

After ransacking the place and ripping apart bedclothes, books, and furniture, he knew she'd vanished, her trail cold. Growling, he'd rolled in her sheets, soaking up every particle, every trace of DNA she might have left until her smell filled him up, and he was in some kind of pheromone-induced frenzy. He resisted the urge to pee all over the house. He wasn't quite at that stage yet, not fully panther. But the need to eradicate her presence, to mark her as his prey, was undeniable. The chase began, and now he was here.

Evan would pay for what she'd done to him. Though he didn't regret his mutated form, it came in handy. Right now, the witch was the only way he could get home.

Across the bar, there was a hushed murmur, and the crowd dissipated. Men hurried to find a seat, scraping stools across the straw dust. Spencer leaned closer, pricking back his ears, watching as a woman appeared from the bar's back room, and an immediate, appreciative whistle went around the room. Spencer sneered at them, their tongues hanging like pathetic dogs, and he glugged back a swig of the tangy ale, hops burning his throat.

The woman, beautiful, fine-boned, and with waves of ebony hair, climbed onto a makeshift stage, only a foot from the floor, and cast the room a slow, sly smile. Music started up, a band playing, and slowly, deliberately, the woman peeled off her cape, letting it drop in a velvety puddle on the floor.

A raucous moan went around the room as she tilted her chin, exposing her long neck. Dark hair rolled over her shoulders as she carefully, hole by hole, unlaced her corset, allowing the stays to trail through her fingers as she shyly bit her lip. Spencer eagerly shifted in his seat, peering over the heads to get a better look.

He hadn't been expecting a show with dinner! This was an absolute bonus. Grinning, he squinted through the haze of the bar just in time to see her peel off the corset and fling it to the ground. The men went insane, banging and clapping the tables, and Spencer almost felt sorry for her. A suggestive, coquettish smile played on her lips, allowing them to believe what she could do for them. Yet, her eyes betrayed her, dull hatred boiling under the surface of what she was being forced to do.

Spencer guessed the witch had to make money somehow. She couldn't work, couldn't use magic, without him spotting her trail.

The poor thing, he thought with a laugh, leaning his chin on his fist as he watched, licking his lips as she popped one foot up on a table and carefully rolled down a white stocking. Heat flushed through his blood, remembering Rowan. Rowan Adler, all sinew and muscle, lithe and tall, not a soft curve in sight—not like her. She had curves everywhere, and Spencer thought he was enjoying this a little too much.

Rowan, I wish you could see this...bet your girlfriend never told you she used to do this for a living! He would laugh aloud if it didn't draw attention to himself. Even his voice wasn't the same now, low, guttural, and terrifying.

The music faded, and the men jeered as the shivering naked woman threw her stockings into the crowd, and hurriedly gathered her clothing into her arms. Giving the crowds a wave as they tossed pennies, she smiled and ran to the backroom, her cloak billowing behind. Spencer was on his feet.

Pushing through a sea of sweaty, horribly turned-on men, Spencer gritted his teeth, the tang of sweat and arousal overwhelming. Shoving through the curtained-off area to a dark, candlelit back room, he spotted her by a mirror, struggling as she changed into a day gown. Her hands shook as she tried to lace her stays. Jerking, she spotted him in the mirror.

"Sir...I'm not accepting visitors this evening," she said over her shoulder. Spencer's brows flew up into his hairline.

Well, this just gets better and better. Digging around in his coat pocket, he pulled out a handful of gold in his palm. He'd stolen it from a traveler on the road, ripping out his guts with his claws and leaving the poor man to bleed out on an isolated dirt track. He'd taken his clothes and horse, leaving the man naked and mutilated. Spencer made sure she got a good look at it under the candlelight. "You sure?" he teased. "I leave a good tip."

And after what he'd just seen, he was seriously tempted.

Evan stared at the coins in his palms, then shook her head, turning away. "No. I'm sorry."

"Ah, that's a shame."

"Can you please leave?" She turned back to the mirror, fiddling with the ties at her back. In a fluid motion, he crossed the room, his hands at her hips, and she stared at him in the mirror. "What...Sir..?"

"Let me help you. You don't seem to be able to reach."

His clawed fingers deftly wound through her stays, threading each one through their anointed hole, and with each cross-over, he tugged hard enough to earn a yelp as the material pinched her flesh. In the mirror, her eyes frantically scanned him under the hood, his face hidden in shadow. "What do you want? I'm done for the night."

"What's this?" He ran his hand down her back, finding a fleshed-over scar where her bra line would have been. The skin was puckered, oddly formed in the shape of a crucifix. "Did you get branded, little witch?"

"Get the hell off me!" She wriggled, but he held her hips, his claws biting through the fabric of the gown.

Spencer traced the pad of his thumb over the scar, and she shuddered, letting her fear seep out of her pores. He drank it in, heady and thick. A total turn-on. Pulling and stitching her into the gown, he felt her ribs pinch and fear leak out of her, filling his nose, heating his blood. Draining of color, she gasped. "It's too tight."

"But just look at you," Spencer drawled, running the pads of his hands up and down her ribcage, imprisoned inside a herringbone corset, letting his nails rest on her ribs, right under her breasts. She panicked and spun. "Leave me alone!"

Balls of light appeared in her hands, her eyes blazing with humiliation and anger, but Spencer was quicker. His hands circled her thin throat and gripped hard, pushing his thumbs into her windpipe. Eyes wide, she flailed, wildly beating at his chest, as a tear escaped under her dark lashes.

"Don't try any of your tricks on me," he sneered in her face, revealing saliva-coated fangs. "You and I are going to work together. I've got a little job for you."

She gaped and choked, fingers clawing at his clothes, but he grinned and shook her till her eyes rolled. "If you can be a good girl and listen, I'll let go. Can you do that for me?"

Sensing her life was slipping, she nodded frantically, her hands resting on his chest. Evan gasped for fresh breath, oxygen running in her blood as he let her drop. "Wolfric said you would come. He said you were a monster."

Spencer tutted. "Well, that's rude. Did he tell you my name?"

Weakly, she shook her head.

"I'm Spencer, and Wolfric was right. I've come a long way to find you, Evan."

She looked confused. "That's not my name—I'm—"

"You've been going by Eunice for a couple of hundred years. I know what you're called in the future. What's your real name? I'd like to know, seeing as we will be working together so closely."

She shook, her lower lip trembling. "Euelea," she said. "I should have kept running."

"There was only so far you could go before I'd find you. I'll always catch you, even if you try to run."

Euelea leaned back against the dresser, her arms shaking. "What do you want from me?"

"Don't look so terrified. I only want you to do something you already know how to do. I want you to open the portal."

Euelea blinked at him. "The door?"

"Yes, that's right. In my time, you chucked me through it with a knife in my guts, and for that, I should bend you across that dresser and beat you senseless. But I'm in a hurry and want to go home."

Euelea edged away, arching her spine as far away as she could, but he crowded her, flashing that horrific grin, and sweat broke on her temples. He sucked up her fear like it was caramel. "And after...will you kill me?"

Spencer cocked his head. "Well—that's the thing. That was originally my plan. If I kill you here and now, then she won't get to see it. She'll never know what you were, what you meant to her, and it would be—fruitless. So I'm inclined to let you live unless you're a bad girl and don't behave."

"She?"

Spencer cackled. "Your beloved. Rowan. I kind of want to rip her guts out—metaphorically and physically. And if you die *here*, that won't happen."

Evan shook her head, confused and teary-eyed. "I don't know how to open it. I *truly* don't. Vecula...my sister could...but I...."

Spencer's yellow eyes narrowed. "But you can find it?"

Euelea swallowed. "I think so."

"Then let's start there." He wound an arm around her waist, pulling her close, too close, and she winced, her hands firmly on his chest, above his heart. "Maybe you can brainstorm it out while we travel?"

She didn't seem to be listening; her hand was still firmly planted on his breast bone, the dull throb of his heart beating under her fingers. With a sob, she looked up, eyes searching his. "You...you're one of two?"

Spencer stared at her, as her pulse beat in her throat. "Excuse me?"

"You're torn... split down the center." She closed her eyes, soft violet light pooling under her hands. She was reading his heart, drinking it in, looking where she shouldn't.

"What the hell are you doing?" Jagged teeth bared, he shook her, but it was too late. She'd seen...she knew.

"You aren't on your own." Her lips trembled as she lifted her finger and pointed to his head. "In there."

"Shut up!" His blow landed, knuckles against the bone of her jaw. Her head snapped back, and she crumpled and hit the dresser, her torso taking the brunt of the hit. The crack of her ribs filled his ears. She collapsed in an unconscious heap at his feet. Spencer flexed his hand and gathered her up in his arms.

He carried Euelea to the stables and flung her over the back of his horse, her feet dangling from the ground as he climbed to the saddle. Gathering her under his chin in a possessive embrace and tucking her into his body, he snapped the reins, hurtling into the misty night. Riding hard, the horse's hoofs flicked up mud and stones. He forced away the memory of what she'd seen in his heart.

Spencer didn't regret his decision. He wasn't going to kill her. But he'd sure have fun keeping her in line.

NINE

The truck rumbled into the lot, trailing through thick ice and gray snow. Ben edged it into a space and switched off the engine, throwing his daughter a look of despair. "Oh, come on, Win. You'll survive."

Win gripped the seat, her nails near white, and sucked in air. "I don't think I can do this." Her green eyes scanned Furlow's High, raking over the tall, imposing gray building with the long steps, circled by a low brick wall. Students milled around, hurrying to class. Inside the cab, it was warm and humid, while outside, the snow fell in fine flakes. "Dad...please...."

Ben frowned, his thick, grayish brows drawing close. "No, you are going."

Win swallowed and nodded. It was the same place, she told herself. The same building she'd gotten used to, actually quite liked, but how things had changed. "Okay," she breathed, remembering Grayson's words. She had this. "How long have we got?"

Ben chuckled and checked his watch. "Five minutes. It's not like you're going to the gallows, sweetheart." Win's neck tingled, remembering the vision, and she was unsure what prompted that memory to pop into her head. The tree, the spindly branches reaching skyward as if praying for forgiveness. She closed her eyes and shuddered. Flicking her eyes in his direction, she asked, "Dad...don't you think we ought to find Evan's brother?"

He pursed his lips. "Surely, that is the last person you'd want to see right now."

Win twisted toward him, unsure of how he'd react. He hadn't been a pillar of strength so far. He'd actively avoided her and hid when Grayson dropped off her truck. "In my vision...Wolfric planted something in my head...."

Ben held up his palm. "Sweetheart, I think you need to forget all that."

Win balked. "There's a giant burn mark on my chest that makes that pretty hard."

Ben took her hands and gently squeezed them, and Win relished the contact. He'd never denied her affection, except for yesterday; that look on his face troubled her. Like he was disappointed.

"Win, try and move past that. We have to all try. This right now is real. Getting you back in school and on track is what matters, and you and your mother...getting back to normal. It's all I want for us."

"But...Spencer is out there somewhere, Dad!"

"But he isn't *here*. Not now, and from what I saw, not ever."

Win opened her mouth to protest, confused, and her nerves ran raw. Was he really that naive? Did he truly believe that things could go on as normal? What was normal? Puzzled, she shook her head but gave a reluctant nod. This was the man who'd sent Rowan away at sixteen years old to live with her reclusive grandfather. A man who'd moved them to Boston, knowing that Alice might not handle it. Bound to the Hickory land by the curse, Alice eventually lost her connection to home, and the mutation took her, trapping her in her falcon form until Evan cast a spell this summer to set her free.

When she didn't speak, only stared miserably out of the steamy window, Ben jumped back in, but this time his voice was earnest. "Win—I was a jerk to Grayson yesterday. And I'm sorry."

Win half-smiled, glad she'd not been wrong. "Yes, you were. Why?"

"It's difficult. It's not easy—a dad seeing his little girl with a boy." His shoulders rolled. "Makes me feel *very* uncomfortable."

"You had no problem with Grayson protecting you with a crossbow? I recall you using him as a human shield. You can't have it both ways!"

"I know that, and I was wrong. He's a good guy—despite how things started. And when I see him, I'll apologize."

Win smiled, gently resting her head on the seat. "Thank you. You can tell him later. He's picking me up from school."

"Oh, *good*." Judging by his grudging snort, he didn't sound pleased. Win could read his expression. You can't go *one* night without him, it said. Win couldn't; she already felt bereft, waking up alone this morning and missing him. "I'll be sure to ask him when he plans on buying you a ring."

"Dad!"

"I'm kidding. Come on—let's get this over with." They got out of the truck, and Win sank into her heels, any strength she might have deflating. *Breathe. You can do this.* Ben's hand went to her shoulder. "Oh, I forgot to mention...I signed you up for driver's ed. It's time you passed that damn test."

Win stared at him, her feet like wood as they walked up the long steep steps to the school building. "Oh...*Dad!*"

"Don't whine. What with your mom home now? I can't keep dropping you all over the place. I'm not a cab service, and Grayson is too far away. Unless Luke or Ella take pity on you...."

"Fine—I'll do it!" She shut him down. Win was sure he knew about Ella, and it was a prod to make things right, but right now, her insides were churning so badly she thought she might vomit. Hugging her books to her chest, Win dipped her chin and followed him to the Principal's office.

Principal Geller, a tall, handsome man in his forties with ochre skin, slapped the file shut and threw Win a smile with gleaming white teeth. "So good to see you back, Miss Adler." He waved his hand in Ben's direction. "You made the right decision to return to school. We were worried."

The veil of a threat was there. The thought of expulsion was too much for Win. Having always loved school, the thought of not finishing was unthinkable. "I'm sure you're relieved, Ben?"

Her father squirmed in his seat. "Of course." He grabbed Win's hand and gave it a squeeze.

Principal Geller shot him a dark look over his coffee mug, taking a loud gulp. "Sure helps to have friends in high places. That old uncle of yours made things pretty difficult. I'm not sure the authorities will be so lenient if this happens again."

Ben cleared his throat, casting Win a fleeting glance. She met her Principal's gaze and with a firm shake of the head, she said, "It won't."

"Good to hear. We'll arrange a few sessions with the school counsellor. You've some catching up to do but it's nothing you can't handle—you were an honor student after all, and we are glad to have you back. We want to do everything we can to help you. *This* time. Next time...."

"There won't be a next time," Ben said, and squeezed her fingers.

She stared around his office, framed sports photos covering the walls, a few bookshelves stacked with old yearbooks. On his desk was a stale mug of coffee, and Win could taste it in her mouth. Though still bubbling on the surface, her nerves quietened a little, and she picked at her nails.

"Ben, why don't you leave Win with us? My secretary has a few forms for you to sign to enroll Win, but I think we got this? Don't we?" His smile, warm and honest, only half reached his eyes. Win returned it thinly.

"Sure," she breathed out. Ben's warm hand landed on her shoulder.

"Well, okay." He kissed Win's head. "You've got this, sweetheart."

"Don't worry, Ben. I've got a plan to slowly introduce Win back into life here at Furlow's—a little project she might be interested in. I know how she loves to write."

Win's cheeks burned at the thought of a special project, and at the extra attention. Couldn't she just walk the halls with her head down like she'd done so many times before? Ben smiled curiously. "Sounds interesting. I'm sure Win would love that."

He tapped her shoulder, and she looked up. *Don't leave me, Dad.* Her eyes sparkled with tears, and he deliberately avoided looking at her, knowing he would likely crack too. "I'll see you at home."

Principal Geller was rummaging in a drawer in his desk while Ben gave her shoulder a squeeze.

Win said a croaky goodbye as her father left, letting the door swing shut. Reluctantly she turned to her principal, who'd settled with some files on the desk, his gaze expectant. He cleared his throat. Win folded her hands in her lap, "So what's this project?"

"That's the spirit!" he said, pointing his finger. "Glad it's piqued your curiosity." Win resisted rolling her eyes as he picked up a pen and began clicking the end with his thumb. He buzzed his secretary. "Wendy, can we call Ella Torres from her class, please? I need to see her." Win went cold. "Oh—and Cole Ward, too?"

Oh...my god! The tiny settled butterflies in her stomach took flight and did a crazy dance. The relentless clicking of the pen made her temples throb, and she stared at it, wishing she could snatch it and throw it out the window.

Fraser Inc. Win blinked. Principal Geller was using Fraser Inc pens? Win straightened, peering at the untidy desk. All the desk stationery was marked with Fraser Inc, binders, notepads, stickers...Jake was everywhere. Like a cat marking his terrain.

Or a fox.

Then it hit Win smack in the face. *Jake.* Jake paid their motel bill. Win was confused by the odd gesture of kindness. It had to be him. There was no one else who would have stumped up that money. How had he even known where they were? Somehow, that man knew everything, and that irked her despite the fact he'd bailed them out. She remembered how Jake paid all Cole's hospital bills—guilt money.

A cold wash of fear pricked her spine as behind her, the door cracked open. She didn't need to look to know it was Ella. She could tell by her footfalls and the delicate floral smell that clung to her hair. Win gulped. *Shit...*

"You wanted to see us, Principal Geller?"

"Come in!" He stood, waving both Cole and Ella into the room. There was some awkward shuffling. Cole edged around the desk to pull up a chair. Ella shot Win a pale glance, her gaze indifferent as she found a seat as far away from Win as she could. Inside, Win's insides clenched. She stared hard at her friend, but Ella refused to cast her a glance.

"Good to see you, Win!" Cole exclaimed, slapping her shoulder as he sat down. Win gave him a weak smile.

"Hey, Cole." Her voice was sandpaper dry, and in her lap, she fiddled and picked at the loose skin around her nail beds, keeping her eyes low.

"Well, I'm guessing you two are wondering why I called you here, and I won't keep you long. I know, like me, you will both be keen to welcome Miss Adler back to school, and I thought a good way to slowly get Win back up to speed is for you three to take part in a small joint project for the school paper."

At the mention of the project, Ella's gaze snapped up, and beside her, Cole groaned aloud, flicking the zipper on his hoodie.

"Now, don't protest, Mr. Ward. You've done so well these last few weeks with Ella's help and mentoring—your grades have improved drastically, and I'm keen to keep the momentum going. Now, as you'll be aware, Fraser Corp is Furlow's school sponsor, and Mr. Fraser sits on the school governing body. He's a self-made man and owns the main house on one of the oldest founding estates in Cedar Wood. I want you three to interview him and write a piece on the house and its history for the school paper."

When no one spoke, Win's gaze flicked to Ella. She kept her eyes down, staring intently at her hands. Cole grunted, "Fine by me."

"It's all in school time. This isn't extra-curricular—god knows you have enough on your hands, Miss Torres, with Cole and all the tutoring you offer."

Cole leaned forward in his seat. "So, does this mean we go off campus?"

"Yes, that's right," Gellar agreed with a reluctant nod. "I'm sure that appeals to you, Mr. Ward?"

"Sure does. Sounds awesome!" He tapped Ella's knee. "We get to go poking around Luke's house."

Ella swallowed audibly, and Win had a feeling Ella had seen far more of Luke's place than she needed to. So had Win, for that matter, having spent quite an amount of time in Luke's attic coughing up dust bunnies.

Principal Geller seemed underwhelmed by their response. "The piece will be due in two weeks for the paper's next edition. I have no doubt you'll manage between the three of you."

Ella looked sick and sank into her seat. "Is there any way I can refuse, sir?"

Win's heart snapped, and Gellar looked aghast. "Miss Torres...I would have thought you'd love a project like this."

"I mean—usually I'd jump at it...." Her voice trailed off, and Win sensed that Ella couldn't bring herself to say the words out loud. "But I'm swamped already."

"But surely you want to help your friend settle back into school?" His eyes sparkled with confusion. "Is there some sort of problem here?"

"Not with me." Cole propped his feet on his chair, and Gellar shot him a glare so deadly, he quickly folded them under his seat. "I'm fine with anything that gets me out of the gate for a few hours a day."

After a long pause, Ella shook her head, avoiding Win's gaze. "No, sir. There isn't a problem. I'm sure we can make it work."

"Great news!" Gellar clapped his hands. "Mr. Fraser has granted you access to the house tomorrow afternoon, and you can use the school camera for photos. Which I'll know you'll use appropriately, Mr. Ward. No *accidentally* taking it home with you—I have the transcripts from your last three schools."

Cole grinned. "You can trust me, sir." That statement sounded sketchy at best, and Gellar frowned.

"Make it work, you three. Good to have you back, Winifred. I'm sure your friends echo that statement. Grab yourselves the permission slips on the way out!"

An unusual hush lingered in the air, thick and tense, so tight it made Win's shoulders draw up to her ears. Ella scrambled for her bag and dashed out of the Principal's office door, leaving it to bang behind her. Win shot out of her chair. She caught up with her by the lockers while Cole dragged behind, biting his nails. Making a big show of how he wasn't listening when he was. Dragging the toe of his sneaker on the floor, he nodded to Ella. When she squeezed past Win, she caught her hand.

Ella was quick to snatch it away.

"El—please wait!" Win begged, touching her shoulder with her fingertips. Her friend met her eyes with a cool stare.

Ella's shoulders stiffened. Hugging her books to her chest, she chewed her lip and said nothing. Win stepped closer, emotion and tears bubbling in her throat. "I missed you." Ella looked away.

"Can't we talk?" Win pressed. "Please?"

Ella shook her head, her eyes flicking to Cole, who was waiting by a vending machine. "I just can't right now."

Win held the locker for support, all the courage she'd had earlier drained out of her shoes. Ella refused to look at her, but her eyes were empty and cold when she did. This wasn't the Ella she knew.

"But we have to work together. You can't not talk to me. Ella—I tried to reach out."

Ella sniffed, ignoring the imploring look on Win's face. Then she shrugged. "I guess we'll have to make it work some-how...."

"What about the interview? You heard Principal Gellar, it's a joint project. You can't pretend I don't exist. Ella... *please!*"

Ella huffed and looked skyward. While across the hall, Cole coughed to make his presence known. "I have to get to class."

"I did nothing wrong!" The words flew out of Win's mouth, laced with anger and resentment.

Ella's mouth pursed, and with a slam of the locker door, she signaled the end of their conversation. "It's not about him—you don't even know what you did. And that's why I can't deal with you right now. I'm sorry, Win."

"Ella... please!" Win shot for her friend's hand. Ella gasped, staring wild-eyed at Win's fingers circling her wrist. Win immediately let go, hating how she'd left five finger marks pressed into Ella's flesh. Win, drenched in self-loathing, stepped away.

Ella flexed her hand, wiping at her eyes. "I need a little time."

Ella spun on her heels, stalking down the corridor, leaving Win to stare after her, mortified. Cole shot Win a weak smile, turning to follow Ella down the hall. Win stuffed her extra books inside her locker and blinked back tears.

Don't cry here....don't cry in school...

Her neck prickled, the hairs on her arms standing to attention. Win knew who was watching her across the hall before she looked.

Swallowing hard, she glanced over her shoulder. He was leaning against a pillar, his mouth pinched and hard, and his blue eyes fixed on her. Cold, unfeeling. Win's heart spiked as she took a step toward him, but he backed up, turned, and walked away.

Luke... she tried to reach out but found the space between them shut down, empty. Whatever connection they'd once shared, it was over. He'd closed the door.

TEN

Grayson and Win didn't speak on the drive home. Grayson's truck hurtled the icy roads back to her house, he was a fast driver, and she gripped the sides of the seat. Throwing her a look, he didn't press for conversation, even when she sniffed, and leaned her head against the foggy window. Bumping up the driveway, he parked and then twisted toward her.

"Out with it," he said.

Win pouted and promptly burst into tears. Every ounce of pent-up emotion rushed like a geyser, everything she'd forced back and held in. The breaking point came at lunch when she'd been forced outside after spotting Cole, Luke, and Ella at their usual table. Win saw them and smiled hopefully when Cole waved at her. He'd half risen out of his seat but was met with Luke's death stare and a firm head shake. The cold reproach stung deeply, and Win turned on her heels and fled the cafeteria.

Win collapsed into Grayson's arms. "It was so awful."

"I'm getting that."

"She won't speak to me," Win bawled. "I tried to talk to her—but she wasn't interested." Win quickly explained the forced joint project that she, Cole, and Ella had been assigned. Grayson listened, grinding his jaw, and she couldn't quite read his expression until he puffed out air. Win still had the permission slip in her bag, knowing her father would lose his shit when he read it. Rowan would have to sign it.

"Why do you have to interview *him?* Of all people?"

Win stared at him, his jaw tight and the muscles bunched. "You don't like him?"

Grayson scoffed. "Does anyone?"

"Not really."

Win was prepared to give most people a second shot. Jake Fraser sailed close to screwing up most shots he was given. Mysterious, infuriating, and annoying, he was reaching out in his misguided way. He'd paid their motel bill, of that she was positive, not that she was about to mention that to Grayson. His pride was already wounded that he'd been bailed out.

Win couldn't hate Jake for one more reason. He'd taken Luke back home. And even if Luke never spoke to her again, which was looking likely, she was grateful he wasn't alone. On the morning they'd trekked through the forest together, searching for Luke, she'd begged Jake to take him back. Under all the macho bravado, as much as he tried to deny it, Win was positive Jake had a heart, even if it was buried under expensive Armani suits.

Win jumped at Grayson, suddenly playful, throwing him out of his mood. "I've got this great idea! Why don't we run away?"

Grayson laughed, his scars running up his face. "That's such a good idea—why didn't I think of that?"

She leaned across and planted a kiss on his temple. "Think about it seriously...you and me in a rundown motel by the beach. Doesn't that sound perfect?"

He smiled and kissed her hand. "It was perfect."

Win sighed, and with a reluctant shuffle, they both got out of the truck. Inside, Evan had cooked, and Win endured an enforced 'normal' family meal. Ben eyed her boyfriend like an alien who'd infiltrated their base. Alice sat at the head of the table, head down, carefully chewing every mouthful as though it might stick in her gullet, and Win couldn't help a pang of sadness. She flinched as Rowan laughed, shrill and high, and Alice rolled her shoulders, bracing herself against the noise.

It was all very awkward. Evan chatted, and Win cast her a glance, wondering if Rowan had brought up Wolfric, her mysterious brother. For one split second, Win spotted something unusual, but it was gone so quickly, that she thought she imagined it. Evan listened intently to Rowan who was animatedly talking about the new busboy when her expression changed. Evan's eyes dulled, she winced in pain, and for one split second, a garish, purple mark appeared on her jaw, blooming across her cheekbone like a flower. Then as quickly as it came, it faded to nothing.

Win gaped. "Evan...?"

Evan's gaze flicked across the table at the sound of her name as she rubbed at the spot on her jaw, as though she were rubbing an errant ache. "Yeah?"

A little embarrassed, Win snapped her mouth closed. Had she imagined it? There was nothing there now, only Evan's smooth golden skin. But now, all eyes were fixed on her. She decided it best to confront the elephant in the room.

"So, Evan—your brother...Wolfric..." Win started, and a hush fell across the dinner table, knives and forks clattering on the china. "Can you burst into flames like he does?"

Evan swallowed her mouthful of food and placed her fork neatly back on her plate. Around the table, Ben grumbled, and Alice sat with her legs folded up to her chest, one toe on the floor as if she was prepared to bolt at any moment. Rowan spoke first.

"Maybe now isn't the time, Win?"

"When will it be the time?" Win countered. "When Spencer comes back?"

"Spencer isn't coming back," Evan said. "It's a one-way door."

"Your brother made it pretty clear that we messed up, Evan. I don't feel comfortable assuming all is well—and you failed to mention Wolfric was alive."

Evan exhaled hard, running her hands through her hair with the full weight of the table's gaze on her face. "I didn't say he was dead."

"You kind of did," Grayson backed her up, and a rush of gratitude flowed through her. "You said crowds killed him in Iceland."

Without looking at one another, she found his hand under the table and planted it on her thigh. He gave her a reassuring squeeze. Across the table, Ben squirmed, bringing back memories of the night Evan revealed who she truly was. "I remember that too," he said. Evan looked away, guilt creasing her features, and like a rabbit caught in a snare, she had little choice but to come clean.

"He *was* killed in Iceland," she admitted. "Vecula got him executed. She murdered a man in the village...." An icy hush went around the room, and she was fully aware of the weight of her confession, the impact that would have. Ben drained of color, and Alice inhaled through her nose. "We were about to be run out, and they would have taken us all—but Wolfric sacrificed himself so we could get away. Wolfric always looked a little...different. He knew it would be easy for people to assume the worst of him."

"The teeth," Win said in agreement and shuddered. "He does look frightening."

"He wasn't," Evan said, melancholic. "He was gentle. But it didn't matter in the end. Hatred has a way of seeping through the cracks, and they took him. It was awful."

"Jesus," Ben hissed. "Evan—I'm sorry."

The family was oddly silent, and Rowan grabbed for Evan's hand, their fingers linking over the table. Win was glad they weren't arguing. Rowan appeared settled, less edgy for the first time in Win's memory. Only a short while ago, her sister would have bolted, run from anything too emotional. "It was horrifying. And we had to watch from the shadows. But if you think that's bad—Isaac was worse."

"Maybe that's not an around the dinner table story?" Rowan quickly injected, which only piqued Win's curiosity.

"But he's alive?" Win circled back to the present. "Wolfric *is* alive. Explain that."

"He and I moved in different circles for years. I learned he was alive about fifty years ago. I don't know *how* he's immortal, and the rest of us aren't, only that Nassau gifted him, and that he can walk through time."

"He was on fire!" Win said.

"He likes to call himself a phoenix because he rises out of the flames. He has a strange sense of humor."

Win leaned across the table. "But I don't get this. Perhaps he went back, Evan? He went back and saw what we did? What if Spencer is disrupting our past?" She opened her shirt and revealed the scorch mark on her chest. "What is this gift?"

Evan blinked. "I truly don't know, Win. We never talked things through. After Iceland—Wolfric resented me for leaving and for Isaac's death. I followed my sister without a doubt. I'm ashamed. It's the worst part of me, Win. Living with what she did, what I allowed her to get away with. Wolfric hasn't forgiven me—maybe I don't deserve it."

Win was startled at her revelation; even someone as kind and good as Evan would think she didn't deserve to be happy, or forgiveness. Alice was proof that Evan was good, that she meant no harm. It made a lump swell at the base of her throat as she dimly recalled the time she'd asked her grandfather why— why he couldn't tell her what he'd done to Grayson's brother all those years ago, an accidental killing when he was the wolf. Shame. Shame and guilt for what he'd done, the loss of control, ate at him for years until it became too painful to say aloud.

"Do you know where he is now?" Grayson asked the obvious question, and Win berated herself for not asking that sooner. Evan shook her head.

"He's—around," she spoke carefully, choosing her words. "We haven't spoken in years. But I know he isn't far away—call it a sibling bond."

Alice made her presence felt, unfolding her legs and standing from the table. She rustled in the fridge, anything to end the grisly conversation. "Mom?" Win called over her shoulder. "Are you okay?"

"Fine," she said, her voice watery. Though by the way, her shoulders drew up to her ears, she didn't look fine. Her hand wobbled on the door of the refrigerator. Ben drew out of his seat and took her shoulders, and she melted into him for support. He whispered something in her ear, and tearfully she nodded. Cutlery clattered, and Evan rose to clear the table, followed by Grayson, who gathered up dishes and glasses. Win and Rowan exchanged a worried glance as Ben ushered Alice out of the room. Win half rose from her seat.

"Dad..."

"She's okay." Ben threw her a tight smile, waving her away. "She's fine."

Win stretched her arms above her head, feeling the familiar prickle under her skin. Being home on Hickory land was good, but she also needed to phase. Grayson cast her a glance over his shoulder as she joined him by the sink, hopping on her toes to kiss him. "I should go out for a while."

He wiped his hands dry. "Then I'll come with you."

Ben wandered back into the room, catching the tail end of their conversation. "Win can manage by herself, Grayson. She's home and safe now. Besides—I'd like to catch up with you."

Grayson's bottom lip fell, and Rowan snorted out a laugh at the table, her leg curled under her. Evan shook her head at Rowan, warning her off with a jerk of the chin.

"Me?"

Ben smiled wearily, scratching his jaw. "Yeah—you and me. That's not a problem, is it?"

"Uh—no."

Ben shoved his hands in his pockets and waved Grayson toward the family room. "You go, Win. And don't look so worried."

Inside, she was a quivering mess. The thought of her father cross-questioning Grayson and finding out his 'intentions' made her want to squirm. "I'm not worried," she lied.

Ben chuckled. "Then you better go. And don't stay out long. It's icy out there."

Grayson's fingers remained locked with hers, and she tugged him back for a kiss before he gave her a half smile. "It's fine," he said, squeezing her hand before heading after Ben. When they'd shut themselves in the family room, Win scowled and threw a dishcloth at Rowan, which she dodged. Rowan burst out laughing.

"Take it easy. He only wants to know when the wedding is."

Evan gave an exasperated cry, throwing Rowan a heated look. Win ignored her sister's wicked sense of humor, grabbing her bag and slapping down the permission slip on the table. Rowan peered over her shoulder as Win shoved a pen in her hand.

"Sign it, will you? I need a responsible adult, and you'll have to do."

"Thanks." Rowan scrawled her signature, and Win snatched up the slip before she'd even got a chance to read it. "What did I just sign?"

Win left Rowan bewildered and dashed to the boot room for her sneakers. "Trust me, you don't need to know."

Rowan laughed, uncurling her foot. "Be safe out there—Dad's right. Don't stay out too long."

Win poked her head around the door. "Aren't you coming?"

"I'm going to check in on Mom," Rowan sighed. "All the grisly talk probably got to her."

Win nodded, stuffing her arms into a jacket before flying out the door, hopping across icy puddles with ease. Above, fresh snow flaked from white, heavy clouds, and the trees rustled, opening their arms to greet her as though she'd never left.

The yard was dark and cold, with a fine mist spiriting across the ground. Win kicked up dead leaves in her wake, tracking through the familiar muddy terrain and unbuttoning her coat. The trees clawed in over her head, their branches stripped bare, adding an extra layer to her vulnerability. Usually, it was shady and secluded, and now going further into the under-growth, she could still easily spot the muddy pathways. Win felt winter's bite on her skin as she undressed, for the first time ever, feeling truly exposed.

Crawling to the ground, she bit back tears as she sneaked into her jaguar form, hot breath fogging the air as two canines erupted from her gums. Shaking off spikes of pain, like throbbing shots of venom under her skin, she bounced into a sprint, chugging as she trekked through the forest. It wasn't long before her paws hit Fraser land, the great estate of Mercy looming out of the darkness. Sadness pricked her heart as she circled its perimeter, her eyes keenly scanning the old building. Inside, lights flickered at windows, and smoke billowed from the chimney stacks, and Win wondered if somewhere in there, Luke was okay.

Luke's dismissal of her today cut like a knife. Everything she feared had come true, only now Ella was against her.

Feeling her throat thicken, she headed away, the pain of losing her friends enough to make her want to sink into the leaves and cry.

You left, a voice inside her head scolded her. *It was never going to be the same. Not after he confessed everything. And you've got bigger problems right now.*

Sickened, Win distracted herself by starting after a boar passed right under her nose. Instinct kicked in, and she was on it, batting it to the ground with a massive splayed paw before she bit out its throat. Blood bubbled and ran thick under her nose, and her glands salivated as she bit it hard, reducing it to dead prey within seconds. Shaking away the dizziness, Win wandered away from her kill, disgusted but strangely exhilarated at the same time. Predatory urges were harder to ignore thesedays, the compelling need to sink her teeth into something all consuming. She recalled how appalled she was at Rowan once for killing a mouse right infront of her.

The moon shone bright up ahead, and she wandered the woods aimlessly, wondering if Grayson was surviving her father's questioning. She set her mind on track, knowing that she must find Wolfric, and when she got home, she would start with the obvious places online. Wolfric was a man living in the modern world, and there was no way a guy who looked like that could go unnoticed or didn't have some kind of internet presence.

Branches rustled behind her, her ears pinned back, and instinctively, she sank low to her belly. Feet came closer, padding through the leaves, and she detected the scent before she spotted who it belonged to. She groaned, but it came out as a growly grumble. The feet stopped dead, listening.

Damn... She sunk to the dirt, hoping he'd just pass her by. She didn't need to see him right now.

Win...I hear you. You might as well come out.

Grunting, Win rolled out of the undergrowth, gaining height on him as she rose up, lifting her chin. A wolf stood toe to toe with her, his fur inky black and dense against the sky, he was only a pair of glittering blue eyes. Face to face they stared one another down. A low growl rumbled in the wolf's chest. Win drew back and bared her teeth, almost instinctually sensing hostility.

He sighed loudly. *I knew this would happen sooner or later...but I kind of hoped it would be much later.*

ELEVEN

Under the light of the moon, the black wolf's mane shone with a bluish tinge. Win took a moment to look at him, properly for the first time in many weeks. He was magnificent, proud, tall and lithe, and so handsome. She exhaled. It hurt how much she'd missed him.

Luke...can we please talk?

He pranced away, light and easy, like a dance step, and trotted into the tree line. It didn't take much for Win to catch up. She was twice his size and ten times more powerful. Not to mention fast. But she had a feeling he could give a good chase. She batted him with her tail, swiping out playfully, and he shot her a glare.

No Win, we can't talk.

This was going to happen eventually, she pressed on as her paws sunk into icy mud on the path they shared. *Our lands merge onto one another. We were always going to meet.*

Narrowing his cerulean blue eyes, he looked away. *You don't get it, do you?*

She followed him, undeterred, even though his dismissal hurt. He was jogging in a direction she wasn't as familiar with, through thorny brambles and crowded groups of birch. He wove deftly between them, shooting her side-eye. A stony path wound through the thicket ahead, and in the far distance, there was a dense patch of sky-high cedars, their branches drooping under the weight of snow.

Will you stop following me?

No...come on, Luke! Talk to me. We were best friends. There was nothing we couldn't say to one another.

His mane rose, heat rising under the fur. *Yes, that's part of the problem. My idiot confession.*

You're not an idiot...Luke...it was sweet. No one's ever said anything like that to me in my life.

He snorted. *Not even your white knight?*

Win stopped abruptly, and he paused, casting a glance at her. He was waiting for her response, and narrowed his gaze when it didn't come. Win recalled Luke's outpouring, how every intimate thing he'd felt for her came tumbling out, unfiltered and raw. It was heart-wrenching, soul-crushing, and she hated that she hurt him so badly. Knowing Luke, what it had taken for him to speak, to admit aloud, was courage she didn't think Grayson possessed. Grayson couldn't even bring himself to tell her the truth about his mother for all those weeks. But that was over now.

No, she answered truthfully. *Grayson isn't one to overshare. He isn't like me.*

But he loves you?

Win nodded.

Good, Luke said. *I'm happy for you.*

He darted off, vanishing into a tall, brambly bush, and when she went to follow, he poked out his head and growled. *Will you back off? I'm changing! And about to be very naked.*

Win scrambled away, shamefaced. *Sorry!*

Moments later, Luke, in his human form, crawled out of the bush, pulling a hoodie over his torso. It was expensive, as were the jeans he was wearing. Win admired him from afar, how different he was, taller, more muscular, and without the glasses, he looked so much like Jake, his jaw dark with the start of stubble. Win thought he looked amazing, so handsome it was startling. She was proud, and it swelled inside her. When he saw her waiting patiently, lying on her belly with her paws folded, his lips curled, nearly making it into a smile. But it dropped quickly.

"You know, I'm beginning to suspect that this *thing* you do...was the whole problem."

Win balked. *What thing?*

"This!" He waved his hand back and forth between them. "When we lived together, you were under my nose every *single* day. You drove me insane—borrowing my stuff, waiting in my room, sharing my space—I didn't know whether to strangle you or kiss you. The feelings I had...I couldn't fight it."

I know....

"Space from you was the best option."

Luke trekked off, taking long powerful strides that she easily matched. They'd wandered through a field with long, wet grass, tall enough to reach his thighs. Win admitted that she didn't recognize this neck of the woods, it was far from her terrain, and somehow in the open meadow, she felt exposed. Luke looked around, puzzled, as though he wasn't used to it. He'd wandered in any direction just to shake her off. "Think we are near the old church," he muttered.

Win shook her neck, her spine pulsing. She would need to change back soon. The clear air was full of stars shining bright enough to make the ice glitter.

When you went back to Jake...I had to get away. Ella didn't want to speak to me...I couldn't bear the thought of losing you both.

Luke exhaled through his nose and threw his hands skyward, his eyes flashing with sudden anger. "So you bailed on us?"

I didn't bail on you!

He choked out a laugh. "Ah, yes. You did Win. That's literally what you did."

Under her ribs, her heart pounded, angry and affronted, and a bitter taste coated her tongue. *How could I have stayed after what you said?*

He stopped waist-high in the grass. "Because you're her friend."

She didn't want to see me.

"Bullshit, Win! She *loves* you. She would have come around—forgiven you anything. But you didn't give her a chance to breathe or think. You just left."

I didn't think anyone wanted me around. I'd caused all of it.

Luke crouched, eyes meeting hers. "You didn't do anything wrong. It was me who screwed everything up. Me, and my messed up head." He gritted his teeth, staring into the distance. Muttering to himself, he started to jog, trying to get away from her, but she wasn't about to be pushed away.

Luke, please!

"No, Win!" he cried. "I'm so angry with you. We both are. And you don't even see why!"

Tears threatened to form in her ducts. She sniffed, and batted her head against his leg, forcing him to a stop. They'd crossed the meadow with the moon as their guide. She glanced up, eyeing the path ahead, and then froze as a wash of fear rolled through her.

Ahead stood a tree.

Planted in the middle of nowhere, on the edge of the wood, it stood alone, naked of any leaves, with its bare branches stretching to the stars. Its roots twisted and rolled at the base, burrowing into the earth. Win couldn't break her gaze. It couldn't be the same tree she'd seen in her vision. They were a couple of miles outside the town, in rolling farmland. Win had never traveled out this far. She would have remembered seeing this.

Luke strolled ahead, unaware that she'd stopped. She powered after him as he paused right under the tree.

"Win, you'd better go."

His tone, sharp and cold, brought her back to the present. *I get that you are pissed with me for leaving...I didn't feel like I had a choice.*

He tore at his hair in frustration, pacing back and forth, but no matter which way he went, she blocked him, toying with him like a mouse. She could pin him if she wanted to, and he wouldn't be able to stop her. "You did have a choice. We stood by you all summer. We were there for you when Grayson disappeared—when your mom went missing—all that crazy shit. And the first time Ella needed you—you left her!"

Ella didn't need me!

"You broke her heart, Win!"

The admission startled her to a halt, her claws digging at the damp soil underfoot. She let out a puff of air. *I...I'm sorry...I...*

"And you know what else sucks? You missed my birthday. You didn't even call or write, not a message. My eighteenth, Win. I had to spend it with my dad and Judy...that was lame."

Luke, on his knees, took her shoulders, his face clouded with agony and hurt at once. "You broke my heart too."

Luke...

"No!" He held up a finger and silenced her. "You followed me out here and wanted to talk— so listen. You left me. You were my best friend, and you *left* me. I had just gone through this insane, bat shit crazy experience, and you were gone. The one person I needed. Not for love, or sex, or anything like that. I needed *you*. My friend. God..." His eyes filled up, shining in the light. "Do you have any idea how much I missed you?"

Win hung her head, the spike of her breath hitching, making her dizzy, feeling every inch of the sorrow he projected. Shame and guilt ran through her, making her insides coil. *I missed you too...so much.*

"Ella needs time, and so do I." He stood, putting a sizable gap between them. "Don't follow me anymore, Win."

Win nodded, not moving as he rounded the oak. She choked back tears, wishing she could go after him, but the full weight of her wrongdoing settled on her shoulders, and she slumped in the grass, numb. Luke hadn't gone more than a few moments when he screamed.

Win hurtled through the dark, following where she'd seen his silhouette vanish. *Luke! Where are you?*

She sniffed around the wet grass, catching his smell, clean laundry, and soap scent in the air.

Where are you? Luke!

The woods were eerily silent, the bushes rustled, and her spine tickled as she peered through the dark. He was here seconds ago, and now he wasn't. Craning her neck, she stared at the oak, foreboding, looming over her, the moon's light glimmering through the naked branches.

Luke!

"Uh—down here!"

Oh, my god! What the hell are you doing down there?

"I fell in a hole." Groaning, he hauled himself out of the pit he'd fallen in, covered in mud and his shirt wet and torn. "Shit." He rolled out onto the grass and groaned as he looked skyward. "That hurt."

Win was at his side, staring into the black void below their feet, a narrow cavity in the ground that was surrounded by rotten, wooden slats. It was a door. Win gasped.

It's a tunnel, Luke. Like the one, we got stuck in on the night of the bonfire.

Luke wheezed through his teeth. "Yeah, no kidding. Think I cracked a rib."

Win smirked as she sniffed around the hole. It was old, the dirt solid and compact. *You'll be fine. This has been here for years.*

The grass formed knots around the door. There had been so much snow in town it must have rotted away. *What's down there?*

"There was a ladder. That's how I climbed out." He sat up, clutching his ribs, and threw her a wry smile. "Nothing changes, does it? I always get bruised and beaten when I'm with you."

She nudged his shoulder with her snout. *It'll heal. I'm more worried about someone killing themselves falling in this thing. We should cover it up.*

"Win, no one comes here except us. But..." He winced, getting to his feet. "Okay."

Bundling twigs and forest debris in his arms, he covered the door, packing as much dirt around it as he could, while Win gathered some fallen, thin branches to conceal the door. *I don't think I've walked out this far before.*

"The church is through those cedars." Luke fell back on his bottom, panting lightly, still in pain. He pointed through the cluster of trees, a stony, worn path winding into the distance. "It must be one of the old tunnels they built in the 18th century. Creepy, huh?"

Very creepy....that tree...don't you think it looks...weird?

Luke shifted and looked in the direction she was gazing, the great knotted oak swaying in the breeze. "Hmm...I don't know what's weird anymore."

Win decided to push aside her unsettling vision, Wolfric, the whole thing. Luke didn't need to hear it right now, and she had no right pulling him into her drama, not after what he'd just said.

Win settled beside him, staring up at it together. It was strange out here, and she shook off the odd, crawling sensation of being watched. It was as quiet as a graveyard, the air dense and thick, like eyes watching them from the darkness.

"Let's walk back," Luke suggested, rattled, as though he'd sensed it too. He rested his hand between her ears, giving her a scratch as they walked. She purred loudly, then quickly pulled away when she realized what he was doing.

It's probably not a good idea to pet me.

Luke chuckled. "Sorry—habit."

Are we good? Even... a little bit good?

"Not really," he exhaled out in pain, favoring his injured rib.

Win gathered the courage to ask what she'd been dreading all evening. But it was now or never, and part of her had to know. She wouldn't settle if she didn't know.

Do you still...have those feelings for me?

Luke looked skyward and scratched at his hair, his ears reddening with embarrassment. "Honestly?"

Honestly. She braced herself, unprepared even though she'd asked the question.

"Then...no. If you're asking me if I love you...of course I do. But this is different. It's not...romantic. I don't want to have sex with you if that's what you're asking?"

Eww...that's good, though.

"I'd honestly rather bang Mrs. Ward."

Win burst out laughing, but out came a snorting chug. *Cole's mom? That's so wrong, Luke!*

"It's the southern accent and high-waisted jeans—I'm obsessed."

Luke cackled, and Win laughed so hard she snorted saliva out of her mouth. *I can't say I'm not relieved, and don't ever let Cole know...although you can do better than Mrs.Ward*

Luke frowned, his eyes downcast. "I *had* better. But I screwed that one up."

Ella would take you back in a heartbeat. You know she would.

"Yeah...I'm not so sure." He paused, staring into the dark, his mouth pinched. "My 'I'm in love with your best friend' confession may have obliterated my chances." His fingers found her head again, and he rubbed her casually between the ears. They had reached the borders of the Mercy estate, the old place dark and gloomy under the moon.

Suddenly, Luke ducked to the ground, eye to eye. "Win, I need to explain." He looked pained, struggling for words, and held up his finger when she went to speak. "When I told you how I felt that night, a lot of it was true. If I had stayed, it wouldn't have gotten any better. But I was dying...I was confused and broken...and scared. And you were there, and you were...you. I clung to you as much as you did to me. As soon as I left, I saw it, clear as day."

Win nodded, relief and love washing through her. *I get it.*

"I won't ever make things difficult—with Grayson. You have nothing to worry about from me. I swear—it's over."

Luke...thank you.

"Things just got very confusing for a while. And I—" He looked away, searching for his words, awkward, stuttering. "I always want you in my life. We're linked now. I drank your blood. You run under my skin...but I can learn to deal with that if it means we stay close."

Win's mind conjured the images of that night in the woods, the way he'd clung to her, and she'd wept, allowing him to take her blood, drinking it so it would heal him, to push him through his Calling.

I want you in my life more than anything.

"I want things to go back to the way they were. But Ella just needs some time, and she needs *me*. I have to stand by her for now. I know she'll come around. But till she does—I'm with her."

Win sniffed. *I understand.* He smiled, boyish and handsome, and patted her head. They were linked, bound by blood, and it gave her comfort to know they could exist together as friends. Win was relieved he felt the same, their friendship too important to waste over messed-up feelings caused by an ancient curse and too close proximity.

Something itched under her skin, on her breast bone, distracting her from her train of thought. She rolled her shoulders to ease it away, but it came back as a fiery explosion.

"So..." Luke drawled, and she knew he was about to embark on awkward terrain. "How's Captain America?"

Win made a face, despite her sudden discomfort. Luke was bound to ask about Grayson at some point. *He's...wonderful.*

Luke smiled sadly. "Good."

How's your dad? Her skin burned, making the corners of her eyes water. But she and Luke were talking, and she didn't want it to stop, so she gritted her teeth.

"You mean the world's worst father? That's official, by the way. I bought him a mug," he answered with a chuckle. "He's okay. He tries. How's your mother?"

Win made a movement that looked like a shrug. *She's trying, too...it's weird. And I haven't been home long, we've still got a lot of catching up to do.*

Win explained the joint project she, Cole, and Ella had been assigned, interviewing his father. Luke, puzzled, whistled through his teeth.

"That won't be awkward at all," he joked. "But my dad will love that—having a chance to brag and show off the house—and of course, talk all about himself. Good luck with that."

I'm more worried Ella won't speak to me.

He sighed loudly. "I can't help you there."

Yeah...thanks.

Luke shoved his hands in his pockets and nodded to his house. "Well, that's that then."

They both laughed, and he ducked forward to pat her between the eyes. "Goodnight."

Night...

When he had gone, Win released a long exhale of pain through her clenched teeth. Pounding through the woods, she didn't stop till she found the spot where she'd hidden her clothes and didn't waste a second morphing back to her human form. Dressing at lightning speed she ran to the house, her eyes watering at the blistering sensation under her skin.

The house was quiet, and everyone was in the family room, the lamps glowing as she dashed through the hall. Rowan caught her on the stairs as she hurled past, flinging herself into the bathroom, and ripping off her hoodie.

"Win!" Rowan knocked on the door. "What's wrong?"

Win gasped and stared at her reflection in the mirror, her breathing ragged as her eyes traveled down her chest.

"Win..."

The pain had started when she had been walking Luke back to Mercy, not long after he'd fallen into that cavern. Eyes on her in the dark, the tree looming over them...watching. It began as a faint itch, melding into a deep throb under her skin.

It became unbearable, like a lighted match held against her pale flesh, her skin bubbled and blistered, and what faded a day ago was now back with a vengeance. The burn Wolfric inflicted upon her on the beach had morphed into an outline, her flesh raised in an angry, red welt....it looked like...Win didn't want to admit aloud what it resembled.

"Win!" Rowan said more urgently. Win could sense her sister's fear through the wood. "Let me in now!"

Reluctantly, Win unlocked the door and let it swing open. Rowan pushed inside, gaping at her half-naked sister. "What the hell is that?" She gaped, open-mouthed at the burn on Win's clavicle.

Win blinked back tears, the sting needling and raw. She scooped cold water from the faucet and splashed the wound, and to her horror, her skin fizzed. "I don't know," she said through gritted teeth. "But I have to find Wolfric. He did this to me...and I have to find out why."

Rowan fled the room. "I'll get ice," she said, creeping quickly down the stairs, careful not to alert their parents. Miserably, Win stared at the burn, the mark so clear, she couldn't deny it.

It was a bird.

TWELVE

Win didn't find it hard to avoid her parents. When she rose for the day the next morning, sunshine shone through the window, piercing the heavy snow clouds, and Rowan greeted her with a coffee and a nudge to get out of bed. "I'm taking you to school," she said, kicking her sister with her bare toe. "Mom and Dad aren't up yet."

Win made a face. "Laying in?"

Rowan shrugged. "Mom is restless and doesn't sleep well, and for some reason, last night was a bad one...something unsettled her."

They shared a look, unspoken worry lingering between them. Rowan urged her to hurry up, and Win recalled the sound of footsteps pacing last night, but she was too distracted with her skin blistering to go find out who it was. Perhaps Alice sensed something was wrong? Win was becoming increasingly aggravated that her father was keeping her at arm's length, protecting Alice like a bodyguard.

Win hurried into her clothes, running a comb through her tangled locks. "Maybe it's me being home?"

"Maybe," Rowan said with a sigh, though she seemed edgy. "Every day has been a rollercoaster since she's been home. Dad is massively preoccupied."

Win nodded, at the exact same time, a tile slipped from the roof and crashed to the ground outside. Hickory desperately needed a makeover and more than a lick of paint. Ben promised it would be on his list of priorities, but that was before Alice. They both smiled in unison as another tile hit the ground outside. "Maybe we should ask your boyfriend to fix up the house?"

Win snorted as they both trotted downstairs side by side. Grayson had left by the time Win arrived home last night. It sounded as if Ben had made his feelings pretty clear by how Rowan described his face when he left. Win messaged him goodnight, but he hadn't replied. That wasn't unusual for Grayson, he was useless with his phone, but she missed him and his shape in bed. Two nights without him were hellish.

Under her sweater, her skin tingled, the burn was crusting into a healed-up mess. Icing the burn last night helped, but it stung like hell, pulling her focus from the real problem, finding Wolfric.

Rowan wove the truck through the sludgy streets, and Win was surprised when she got out of the vehicle in the school lot, falling into step beside her. "I'm heading to the library before class," Win told her. "I was going to look up Wolfric online. The Wi-Fi at home is patchy."

"Another thing for the list," her sister replied. "I'll come with you. It's a good idea, and I want to see him for myself."

Rowan smiled as she followed her inside the building, and Win tossed her a puzzled look. "You mean you want to get a look at Evan's mysterious brother?"

Rowan paused, her face creasing, and Win froze on the step. "What?"

"On the night you got that burn...I dreamed about an oak tree."

Win gasped, then punched her sister in the arm. "You could have said something! Backed me up in front of Dad so I didn't look like a moron!"

"I know!" Rowan wailed. "But...can you blame me? A spooky tree? *I* would sound like a moron."

"I saw it last night," Win said. "When I was out hunting—it's out by the old church, and I'm certain I've not traveled that far. It was the same one I saw in Wolfric's vision. I can't leave this, Rowan—even if Dad wants us to move on."

"I believe you, Win. I don't feel like we should be brushing this under the carpet. Evan isn't terribly talkative about her family."

"Evan isn't talkative about anything that draws focus to her."

Rowan paused on the Library steps, throwing her younger sister a glare that could ice to the bones. "Don't start on her, Win. Do you know how long it's taken me to trust her again? I know she has secrets. I know she wouldn't hurt me, or you."

Win planted a warm hand on Rowan's shoulder. "I'm not starting. Let's find this guy and figure out why he barbequed my skin."

Inside the old building, it was quiet, and the computer stations were busily whirring to life. Win headed to a station and pulled out a seat as the screen blinked into action. Rowan dropped into a chair beside her, hands in her pockets and chewing her lip as she looked about the room. Win smiled. "Is it weird that you might be working here?"

"If I get Becky's seal of approval," Rowan reminded her. "Yes, it is. I used to hang out here."

"With Spencer."

Rowan nodded, thoughtful, as she sat back in the chair. Win launched the search engine and Google sprung up on the screen. "Everything I ever did is linked with him...in this place."

Win swung to the screen and typed in the name Wolfric Varga. Within seconds the search loaded, and the top line was for Professor Wolfric Varga, listed on a team page at Boston College in Newton. Win's mouth dropped open as she clicked through, and his page appeared, along with his profile photo.

"Shit. That's him!"

Rowan sprung forward in her seat, it creaked under her weight. "That was fast!"

Win rolled her eyes. "It's the web, Rowan. No one is off the grid...apart from maybe Grayson."

"This is so weird." Rowan narrowed her eyes, her hands still in her jeans, and edged her seat closer. It was a thumbnail, but it was clearly him. Win recognized the wiry black beard, the sharp brows, and dark, deep eyes that stared out from the screen, with deeply tanned skin. "He looks like Evan."

"He's a professor of History...at Boston College. He's been right here all this time!"

Rowan whistled. "It's so strange. What the hell did this guy do to you?"

Win fanned the burn under her sweater, it prickled when the fabric got too close. "I need to go and find him."

Rowan slapped the table, and Win jumped in surprise, but her sister was grinning. "This is perfect. Boston College has an open day this weekend! I saw the flier in the school office when I had my interview. You should go. Dad wouldn't suspect...we'd be just looking at colleges for you anyway."

Humming nervously, Win shut down the search. "He did say to look him up."

A boy-shaped shadow fell across their station, and Win's head snapped up to spot Cole lingering nearby. He stood awkwardly by the desk and lifted his injured hand in a wave. Win gritted her teeth and smiled, reminded of their scheduled interview with Jake. "Hey Cole," she said, lifting out of her seat.

"Hey." He ran his good hand over his shaven head. "I saw you come in. Thought I'd let you know that I've got the permission slip for the camera—though I'm not sure why Gellar trusts me with it."

Win frowned. "Why shouldn't he?"

"Stealing is *one* of the reasons I got kicked out of my last school." He grinned, his dark eyes flashing with mischief. "Guess he believes in second chances."

Rowan chose that moment to rise out of her seat behind Win, shaking out her hair. She stood shoulder to shoulder with her sister. Cole's jaw sagged.

Rowan beamed at him. "Hey—you're Cole? We met before...but last time, you were unconscious!"

The reminder seemed lost on him. Rowan was there when Cole was mauled by Spencer in the woods. Cole was too busy eyeballing her.

Rendered into an appalling silence, Cole's pupils dilated, and under his sweater, his heartbeat went into a freefall, every pore in his body emitting boy pheromones. Win shook her head, dismayed, a little disgusted, and compelled to fill the gaping silence stretching like a chasm between them. "Cole—this is my sister, Rowan."

Cole didn't speak, only stared, and Win sensed the cogs frantically turning in his brain, desperate for something witty or clever to say. Instead, at last, he managed a weak grin. Rowan sensed the strange awkwardness and patted Win's shoulder. "I'll see you at home."

When she'd gone, Cole released a breath. "Shit!" He clutched his chest.

"Cole—*what* was that?"

"*That* was your sister?"

"Yes."

"Luke lived with *her,* and it was *you* he had a crush on?"

Win pretended to look hurt but then snickered. "Thanks!" Hurrying for a subject change, she glanced down at the stack of papers he was holding, spotting the Boston College flier at the top. "Are you going to this?"

"Um, yeah," Cole replied, still reeling from his embarrassment of being stuck without a voice in Rowan's presence. "We were going this weekend. Luke isn't working and Ella wants to see the place....I mean, you can come along, I guess?"

It was sweet that he was trying, and Win smiled. "It's okay. Thank you, though."

"I'll see you out front at two," Cole said. Win nodded and watched him leave. She hit the button to return to the Boston College profile page. Wolfric's dark face stared from behind the screen.

I'm going to find out what you did to me...

The image of Mary circling the oak repeated in her mind. Win gritted her teeth and tried to clear her head. The voice she'd heard...Stacey...Casey...The name was there on the tip of her tongue. But it was muffled and unclear. Why was this image important?

Win went to her first class, trying to forget the image she'd seen. That tree...under the moon, its branches splayed like fingers clawing the sky. *Casey...*

Why did she need to see this? Her burn stung under her sweater, the garment's fibers made it tingle, and finally, during Math, Win asked to be exuded. She went to the bathroom, hoping she could douse it with cool water to take the sting out, and when she revealed her skin in the mirror, she gasped in horror.

It was more than a pair of wings, more defined than the fragmented outline she'd seen last night. It was a bird, its wings splayed, lifting from fiery waves beneath.

A phoenix rising from the ashes.

THIRTEEN

Ella threw her car on the driveway of Mercy, and behind, the large iron gates swung shut with a clang. In the backseat, Win shifted on her bottom, her gaze drawn up to the old, gray Victorian building with its lead windows and long wrap-around porch.

Snow settled on the windshield as Ella switched off the engine, bundling tight inside her coat. She glanced at Win in the mirror, then quickly looked away, while Cole bit his nails next to her. "Quit with the biting," she scolded him, and he flushed red.

"I'm so nervous," he admitted, clutching at the camera bag, and Ella waved her hand.

"It's Luke's dad. He won't bite."

Oh, wouldn't he? Win exhaled, her lips curling into a smile, but she felt like a spare part sitting in the back of Ella's car. She fidgeted and sat on her hands, awkward with no one acknowledging her. So far, Ella had avoided eye contact and changed the subject if Win spoke. Cole talked around her, sensing the tension, unsure what side he should be on.

"Besides, you know him."

Cole smoothed out the small amount of sandy fuzz on his head. "He's so cool, though."

Win laughed, and Ella shot her a glare that instantly made her shut her mouth. Ella huffed and threw open the car door. "Let's just get this over with."

"Did you prepare questions?" Win asked over her shoulder. Ella snorted indignantly and pulled out a neat, pink file filled with papers.

Win smiled and willed away an eye roll. "Of course you did." It would kill Ella to be unprepared, even if she hated being forced into this.

"I wrote about ten questions on the house's history and then a few more personal ones—that's if he doesn't mind."

"He won't mind. Jake is a talker, especially if he's the subject," Win quipped, and Ella ignored her. Instead, she looked to Cole.

"What did you write?"

Cole looked aghast and held up the camera. "I'm shooting the pictures, remember? I can't think of everything."

They walked to the house, gravel crunching underfoot, and instantly Win spied the stained glass panel of the Virgin Mary, head bowed in prayer. How many times had she been to this place now? Mary's prayers didn't do anything to help once you stepped inside Mercy. "What about you, Win? Did you prepare anything?" Cole asked.

"No," Win drawled, and upon seeing Ella's annoyed expression, she added, "I'm sure I can come up with some on the fly."

Ella's knuckles wrapped lightly on wood, and when they got no reply, she firmly rang the bell, which echoed down the hall. Win rubbed her arms briskly, her burn throbbed, and right now, she wished she could strip off and dump herself in some fresh snow.

The outline of a large, busty female appeared behind the glass panel, and the door cracked open, revealing Judy— Win's nemesis. Judy's smile cracked when she spotted Win standing at the back of the three, lurking in the shadows. "Winifred...you again."

"*Hey*, Judy."

Hands in pockets, Win gave Judy a meek grin as she squeezed past in the doorway, following Cole and Ella into the hall. A clock ticked on the mantle, and the room smelled of dry, dead lilies, that clawing scent still lingering in the air. But strangely, for once, the house seemed warm and lived in. Win recalled the walls being papered with a faded, old green print, but now they were crisp cream and gold floor to ceiling. The hallway fire was lit, spilling out heat from the grate, and a pristine cream rug ran the length of the polished wood hall. Cole stamped his feet and rubbed his arms. Judy smiled at them each in turn.

"If you three will follow me into the kitchen—Mr. Fraser is in the gym, but he'll be with you shortly."

Cole threw Win a wicked grin as they followed Judy down the steps towards the back kitchen, a room she remembered. It had once been the house kitchen, filled with servants and large enough to feed a fleet, and now it was wall-to-ceiling chrome, sterilized perfection. They all sat at the chrome bar, pulling up stools.

Judy's bleached bob bounced as she hurried about the room and brought over a tray. "Help yourselves while you wait," she said, nodding at a plate full of chocolate and caramel donuts.

Ella's fingers inched across the table, but Cole swooped on the caramel-splattered one before she could reach. She giggled and nudged his shoulder, but when she gazed up and spotted Win smiling, she looked away. Win sagged, deflated, and stuffed a donut in her mouth.

It stuck in her throat, and she washed it down with the juice Judy left them. When no one spoke and the silence between the three of them lingered, Cole slapped his good hand down on the table. "Come on, you two—enough of this crap!"

"What?" Ella was affronted, while Win stared at the loose skin around her nails.

"I see this afternoon as an absolute win," Cole pressed on. "I'm not in Biology, *and* I get to spend the afternoon taking photos of this old house. Can't you two lighten up?"

Ella chewed the inside of her mouth, refusing to look at Win. Cole puffed in annoyance, drumming his fingers on the tabletop. Win's nerves ramped up the longer Jake kept them waiting, and she half wondered if this was his game plan. Jake did enjoy playing with her, like a fox with a chicken. She folded her arms, but the door banged open, and they all jumped.

He wafted in, hair damp from the shower, wearing slacks and a t-shirt, and if it was possible, he looked like he was getting younger. Jake was the same age as her father, but he was fitter, toned and darker-haired. Across the table, Ella cleared her throat and wiped sugar off her lips, bolting straight.

Jake smiled, white and charming, and Win sensed Ella's heartbeat rocket up a notch.

"Hey, sorry to have kept you waiting. I see Judy looked after you." He rounded the table and planted a large, warm hand on Win's shoulder. "Good to have you home safe and sound, Win. How was the little vacation?"

Win bit back her frustration, knowing full well he was goading her. Instead, she smiled. "So good I didn't want to come back."

The moment the words slipped out, she regretted them. Ella's lip dropped. Win huffed, knowing she shouldn't have bitten. That remark would have hurt her. She distracted herself by placing her notebook and pen on the table. Next to her Cole clicked his pen repeatedly.

Click, click, *click*. Win nudged him under the table.

"Lovely to see you both, too." Jake smiled at Ella, and Cole, his white smile sincere and charming. Under his gaze, it was impossible not to blush. Poor Ella was blotching up. "Now, what am I in for?"

Ella coughed nervously. "Well, we just wanted to ask some questions about the house's history. Mostly about the family, the history, for the school paper."

"You like history, right?"

Ella nodded, her cheeks reddening. "Yes, I love it."

"Luke told me."

She suppressed a giggle and grabbed for her notepad, flipping it open. "Can you give us a brief history of the house?"

"Sure." Jake shrugged. "Well...it was built in 1786, I believe. Don't quote me yet! By my ancestor, Jacob Fraser. He was a reverend, who came over from England and became the minister for the town, by order of King George....the fifth, I think?" Jake tilted his head, a patient and interested expression on his face while Ella scribbled notes.

Cole and Win exchanged looks, wondering if they should be doing the same.

"What part of England?" Ella's eyes twinkled. Ella was a history buff and despite her earlier protests, Win could tell she was loving this. She adored anything antique, old houses, anything with a backstory, and her mother was a curator for the Lincoln museum. Seeing Ella focused, with her tongue poking out, made a smile break on Win's face. She missed her friend so much.

" London—Whitechapel. But his wife was from Doohoma, in Ireland."

"And that's who this place is named after, right?"

"That's correct. Olivia Mercy Brown." Jake leaned back against the chair behind. "I could give you a tour?"

Ella jumped. "Yes, please!" Beside her, Cole sniggered.

Jake slipped from the stool and motioned for them to follow. "Come on then."

Ella followed him, while Win and Cole lagged behind. He fiddled with the camera around his neck, clicking the buttons on and off. It irritated her so much that she slapped his shoulder. Cole glared at her, annoyed. "What?"

They followed Jake into the marbled hall, where only a month ago, Win stood dripping wet after she was caught wandering onto the estate. Jake had been concealing Spencer, trapped in panther form.

"So this is your wing?" Cole marveled. Jake chuckled, throwing them a casual glance over his shoulder.

"Well, I used to be a bit precious about my privacy. I had the boys living up the other end only because it was what I was used to. But now Luke shares this side of the house with me."

An unexpected glow of relief washed through her. When she glanced up, he was looking directly at her. "It's good having him around," he said.

"You two look more like brothers!" Cole said. "You look so young...younger than my dad!"

Jake shrugged at the compliment, keys rattling in his pocket as he went to unlock the door to the old end of the house. "Good genes, I guess!"

"Or perhaps you sleep in a cryogenic chamber?" Cole joked.

Jake cackled, ushering Ella through first, his hand on the base of her spine. Shooting them a dark look, he lowered his voice, a devious smile playing on his mouth. "Or perhaps I drink the blood of virgins?"

He winked at Win over his shoulder, and she fought back a snort, hating he could get a laugh out of her. She squared up next to him.

You are so gross.

Sorry, that was too easy to pass up. Win jerked, having forgotten Jake also had a talent for talking telepathically. Damn curse. He grinned, wickedly, knowing he'd startled her.

Win tutted, shaking her head as they went into the drawing room. Win remembered this room. She'd caught Luke and Ella down here once, hidden in a back room, in a compromising position. Win sagged inwardly. That felt like a lifetime ago.

"So, this is the drawing-room." Jake waved his hand around the expansive room. It was a shrine to the past, with wingback chairs, gilded paintings, and heavy, brocaded drapes hung from every window. The room swept into a beautiful glass orangery with a marbled floor. "It would have been used for balls, dinner parties—you name it. It's quite ornate, and all the portraits are original, and family members."

Cole admired the ones hanging on the wall. One was Callum Fraser. Win noticed it instantly, having seen it a few times before. The young man in the painting had a forlorn, lost look in his eyes, black hair swept off his forehead, and a frock coat and cravat tightly around his neck. Win regarded him with a tilted head, wondering if he'd any inkling of what would become of him. Callum Fraser, dead at eighteen and doomed to be a ghost story for tourists.

"Whoa! You weren't wrong about family genes—that's uncanny," Cole said.

Win and Ella stood beside him as he snapped away with the school camera. Jake folded his arms and watched them with interest. "Five generations of Frasers have owned this place."

"I mean...the jaw line...the hair...blue eyes...."Cole babbled in admiration while lining up his shot.

"Would you like to be alone with the portrait?" Win joked, and behind his back, her eyes met Ella's. She was laughing, though trying her best not to. Cole scowled, his cheeks blistering pink.

"Maybe you should take some notes, Win? Make yourself useful?" he snapped.

Cole clicked the camera while Ella wandered the room. She passed a whiskey decanter, fingering the delicate glass. Win's attention was drawn to a rack of bagged-up clothing stuffed in a lonely corner. It was surrounded by shoe boxes, and all the clothes were encased in suit bags. Her eyes widened with interest.

"What's that?" She pointed.

Jake chuckled, his brows rising. "Eagle-eyed aren't you?" he joked. "That's all for an exhibit at Lincoln Museum. It's vintage clothing. They asked if I had anything worth loaning, and I had a room full."

"Vintage?" This was Win's favorite word. She recalled many happy hours with Ella, rummaging through the thrift stores in town. Without thinking, she fingered the bags. "What kind?"

Ella noticed Win's tone and was drawn to the rack, like a bee to nectar. "My mom was talking about the exhibit. Isn't it fashion? From the sixties?"

Jake shrugged off their interest, pretending he wasn't enjoying their reaction. "Fifties, sixties, and seventies... it's mostly my mother's things. There are some really old pieces in there—designer. Some things my father had made for her in Paris." He looked at them, both girls homing in like sniffer dogs. He grinned. "Want to have a look?"

"Uh..." Win began.

"*Yes!*" Ella cried.

Jake slipped past them, yanking the rack into the middle of the room. Cole groaned, throwing his hands in the air. "What am I supposed to do?"

"You can continue the tour?" Jake peered over the wrack, pulling all the bags off and laying them across a sofa. "I don't mind you poking around. Except, stay clear of the East wing. That's where I keep the bodies."

Jake laughed at his own joke while Win gaped, and Cole stuttered a nervous chuckle.

"I'm kidding." Jake sobered, and Win shook her head.

Not funny. I've seen your attic.

Cole shrugged and headed out the door, ignoring both Ella and Win diving into the pile. Win carefully pulled a silk gown from a bag. Deep grape in color, with an open back and puddle neckline, she turned it over in her hands and read the label. It was a Givenchy dress. "This is beautiful!"

Jake smiled, with a twinkle in his eye. "Don't you have prom coming up?"

"Next year," she answered, glancing at Ella, who was looking through the clothing bags on her hands and knees. "I've not been dress shopping yet."

Ella glanced up and then looked away, guilt creasing her features. "I have mine."

Something like hot lava flooded her chest. This was the final straw. Ella had been dress shopping for prom—*without* her. Jake sensed the tension and cleared his throat. Ella piped up, "My mom wanted to take me. After...to cheer me up. My dress is gold."

A lump formed in Win's throat, and she looked away, utterly miserable. They had promised faithfully they would go together. Loneliness crept in, and she sank her teeth into her lip, desperate not to cry. Ella's mother wanted to spoil her heartbroken daughter and buy her a pretty dress. The weight of misery made Win want to sink into the plush carpet.

"Gold, huh?" Jake asked, clapping his hands. "I have something you might like!"

Win watched as Jake dropped to the shoe box pile. Rifling through the boxes, tossing the lids aside, he bit his lip before he cried a triumphant 'ah ha!' He pulled out a pair of slingback, spaghetti high heels, the straps coated in tiny, gleaming diamantes sparkling under the light. On his knees, he presented them to Ella as if he were proposing marriage. Ella's dark eyes went wide. "Oh, my God!"

"They're a size six."

"I'm a size six!"

Win couldn't help but let out a short laugh as Ella whipped them out of Jake's hands. "Can I? I mean...you don't mind?"

"Try them on!"

Ella squealed, parked her bottom on the sofa, and ripped off her shoes and socks before Jake had even handed them to her. She stuffed her feet in the shoes, sticking out her tongue as she struggled with a tight, unwieldy buckle. Jake planted her foot in his lap and fastened the strap. Ella beamed, rotating her ankles and admiring how her foot appeared, the dark red paint on her toes shining. "They are gorgeous! Win—what do you think?"

Win snorted. "So you're talking to me *now?*"

Ella's eyes filled up, shining, swallowing back whatever anger she'd been storing. It took her a few moments before she looked Win in the eyes. "What do you think? I want to know."

Win smiled, unable to resist. "They're pretty, Ella."

"They're Christian Dior," Jake told her. "You're welcome to borrow them."

Ella jumped to her feet, squealing in delight, her skin flushing pink. "Thank you! Mr. Fraser, thank you so much! Really, you don't mind?"

Win stared, mouth agape as Ella unashamedly threw her arms around Jake's neck.

Is this how you get women to marry you? Dazzle them with pretty shoes? Win said to him, unable to hide her cynicism, even if her friend was beaming like the sun.

Unprepared for the blast of affection, Jake shoved one hand in his pocket, raking the other hand through his hair. Win watched him carefully. He glowed, and she realized he was enjoying every moment of this. He caught her staring and poked out his tongue.

Works though, huh?

Ella tried them out, walking up and down the plush carpet runway style, when Jake turned his attention to her. "See anything you like, Win?"

Win presented her much larger foot in his direction. "I have clown feet. If they're all size six, I'm out of luck."

Jake made a face, looking thoughtfully around the pile. "W ell....what about this?" He grabbed at a small box and pushed it into her hands. "I mean—" He waved his hands around the pile. "All of this belonged to your great aunt. It's as much yours as it is mine. That was hers. There are some things even Rowan might like."

"Open the box, Win!" Ella appeared, poking her head around Win's arm, so excited Win had no choice but to prise the box open. Inside was a pendant, a delicate silver Hare on the end of a fine chain. Emotion bubbled in her throat. Iris, her great aunt, was a Hare, and she'd been living apart from her family for years. She met Jake's eyes. "It's so pretty."

"It's yours," he said, ushering Ella aside as he crossed around back of her. "I'll put it on."

"Oh...no..."

"Put it *on* Win!" Ella chimed in, her eyes flashing with tears. "It's so delicate. You should have it."

Huffing and deciding that Jake had some charming mystic power, she allowed him to lead her to the gilded mirror on the wall, where he fastened it around her neck, brushing her hair aside so she could see. "There, perfect." He smiled at her in the mirror, and she unfastened her zip to see how the pendant sat on her collarbone when suddenly his smile vanished.

"What the *hell* is that?"

Win jerked at his tone, at the worry flashing across his eyes, and knew he'd seen the burn. She zipped the hoodie up to her throat, placing her hand at the base of her neck.

"It's nothing!"

"What the hell is it? Show me—now!"

Across the room, Ella was drawn by Jake's voice. She hurried to Win's side, prising her hands out of the way as she eased down the zip. Groaning, Win allowed her friend to look, hearing the sharp intake of breath as she revealed Win's garish burn.

"Oh gosh...Win that looks painful!"

"Have you had that looked at?" Jake shot at her. "Been to a hospital?"

"No, it's fine!" Win lied. "It's nothing—I had an accident."

Jake met her eyes, blue steel boring into her wide green doe eyes. "With what? A hot poker? You're lying."

"I'm not!"

"I can see straight through you, Winifred. Who did this to you?"

Ella drew away, sensing Win's annoyance, and went back to rummaging while Win zipped up her sweater. "It's none of your business, Jake."

"Win if someone hurt you...if you need help...."

"I'm fine!" she spat, annoyed at his insistence. He drew back, his expression confused, a little hurt she was refusing his help.

Win skipped away but glanced over her shoulder, feeling awful that she'd snapped at him. "The necklace is lovely, Jake. Thank you so much."

Jake ignored her, clearly irked by her refusal to tell him the truth. Flipping out his phone, he waltzed into his office, tossing her a glare before he went. Cole returned, fiddling with the camera dials, and looked at the two of them still on the floor with the clothing pile. "Can we get out of here? This just got very boring."

Ella and Win exchanged a small smile, gazing at the disarray they'd caused in less than ten minutes. "We should tidy this up."

The three of them hauled the zipper bags back onto the rack. In the corner, Cole made a pile of shoe boxes. Jake wandered in and chatted to Cole, as Win and Ella shuffled about on the floor, gathering up all the garments and folding them back into their bags.

Win ducked to retrieve another unzipped bag, and as she hauled it off the floor, a pink, ruffled garment slid out onto the carpet.

Win cooed, lifting it up and examining it. "Ah, this is so cute!" she said, holding it between her fingers. It was a little girl's dress, made for a very small baby girl, covered in pink ribbons and white polka dots. On the hem of the dress in fine embroidery was a name, stitched in pink thread. Win's color drained as the dress slipped out of her trembling fingers.

Katie....

Ella looked up. "Aww," she said, then her smile dropped. "Win?"

Katie...not Casey...Katie...

Win choked out a breath, looking up and meeting Jake's eye. He'd gone white.

"Who's Katie?" she whispered.

"What...is that doing in there?" Jake snatched the garment out of Win's hands. He mouthed something wordlessly, his eyes black, fathomless as he stalked out of the room. "*Judy!*"

The woman poked her head around the door, and Jake flew at her, waving the garment under her nose. "What the hell is *this* doing in the collection for the museum?"

Judy paled, clutching her throat. "I'm so sorry...I don't know...."

"Put it back upstairs, now. It doesn't belong in there!" He caught himself, turning away from the girls, and Win could sense him breathing through his nose, willing himself to calm down. When he turned, his smile was fixed and neutral. "Girls...I'm sorry, but I'll have to get back to work now. Judy will see you out. If you could email me the rest of the questions, I'll do my best to get that to you."

"Jake..." Win called after him as he fled the room, but he ignored her. Win stared at Ella, both dumbfounded.

"Okay, you've seen enough." Judy ushered them out into the hall. For what felt like the hundredth time in her life, Win was shoved onto the front porch. The wind whipped around them as the older woman slammed the door, and the Virgin rattled in her windowpane.

"Well...that was weird," Cole quipped, rolling his eyes as he strolled back to the car.

Ella and Win stared at one another, alone on the front porch. Win exhaled, and met the eyes of her friend, assessing her carefully, edgy and awkward. For a while, Win had Ella back, even if for a few minutes. Ella surprised her by reaching for Win's hand. Win squeezed her fingers as they walked back to the car. Then they both burst into tears.

"I'm so sorry!" Win wailed.

"No—I'm sorry!" Ella threw her arms around her, standing on tiptoe. "I missed you."

"I missed you!" Win hugged her friend so hard that she felt Ella's ribs cave. "Luke is such a dick! I hate him for what he did."

"A giant, stupid *dick*!" Ella agreed with a snort, wiping at her eyes.

"He should have never broke up with you. He's such an idiot!"

"I know...but he's my idiot!"

Win sniffed, wiping her nose and laughing. The rush of relief was heady, intoxicating, and if Ella was her friend, suddenly everything in the world was okay. "Can we never not talk again? This has been rough."

Ella wiped her eyes and nodded. "Deal. I love you!"

"I love *you!*"

Hugging again, they ignored Cole's disgusted groans from the back of the car. Ella ignored him, her fingers trailing to the collar of Win's sweater, flattening it with her fingertips. "We have to talk about that burn, Win."

Win was elated, flooded with adrenaline, love, and relief. Her smile was real and cracked her face. "I have *so* much to tell you."

"And I want to hear it—but there is one thing I'm worried about...."

Win cocked a brow. "What is it?"

Ella drew in a breath, her grin mischievous and full of love. Just herself again, at last. "After what just happened in there—do you think there's any chance he'll still give me those shoes?"

FOURTEEN

The windows in Hardy's fogged with condensation. Droplets of water trickled down the window panes as they dashed out of the snow. Shaking flakes off her coat, Ella flung it into the booth and grabbed Win in yet another long hug. Win giggled. Ella only reached her chest.

Across the bar, Luke, who was working his shift, had gone a very stark shade of white as the three of them bundled inside out of the cold. Cole waved and joined Luke at the bar.

Ella slid into the booth, and Win sat opposite. They grabbed hands, and both laughed. A rush of warmth spread through Win, head to toe, relieved and elated at the same time. It filled her up, and right now, her chest was full and ready to burst.

"Win..." Ella began, lowering her eyes.

"No, let me say this first!" Win gripped Ella's hands tightly. "I shouldn't have left. I was wrong to walk away—especially when you needed me. Can you possibly understand how—scared and alone I felt? It was like starting over again. And I couldn't stand the thought that I'd hurt you."

Ella's dark eyes shone with tears. "But you didn't hurt me. You didn't do anything. *He* did." She tossed her gaze at Luke, who was making a huge show of wiping down the bar when really he was listening, turning increasingly pale and sweaty by the second. Ella sniggered. "I understand how you must have felt."

Win shook her head. "I've screwed everything up. I ran away—from you, Luke, school. I'm behind on my college applications—"

"I can help you!"

Win smiled. "I've got some serious catching up to do. I want you to know—there was never, *ever* a chance. You get that, right?"

Ella nodded. "I know. And I understand why he had those feelings—he was mixed up, and you are both...so similar in lots of ways. He loves you."

"But not like that."

Ella smiled weakly. "I just want it to go back to the way it was."

Win stared at her. "And you wouldn't...you know...?"

"Take him back?"

"You didn't stop seeing him...after?"

The words were too awkward to say aloud. Win knew her friend had a big heart, but Luke had stamped on it with his even bigger feet. Ella smiled wistfully. "He's my friend, Win. He was my friend years before we ever dated, and I didn't want to ditch him after what he went through. After you left...."

"Okay." Win didn't think she could take the guilt. "I think I get it."

Ella smiled. "I mean, look at him! He's a hot mess. He thinks it's me who needs him, but...."

Jittery and on edge, Luke accidentally knocked a glass flying but caught it reflexively. He hovered around the bar, his eyes darting over occasionally while Cole kept him talking. Win threw him a smile and waved her fingers. *Relax, we're catching up.*

He nodded, reluctant to leave as someone called him from the bar. The place was near empty, and the air was thick with frying oil from the lunch rush. Luke buzzed around the tables, cleaning and collecting glasses, and Win grinned inwardly, knowing this was driving him insane.

Eventually, Ella steered the conversation to the burn on Win's chest, and once the waitress planted steaming hot chocolates in front of them, Win laced her fingers around the mug and unleashed. It felt good to pour everything out, including what happened on the beach; Wolfric's strange appearance, and the vision inflicted upon her. Ella listened, enthralled, her mouth hanging open.

"So, this vision...you saw Mary?" she pressed, and Win nodded in agreement. "And what was she doing?"

Win lifted her hands in a wave. "Doing weird Mary stuff—she was singing, a name, over and over. Like in a creepy movie. Seeing Mary feels important—like its connected to Spencer. I'm kind of going on my gut here."

Ella shuddered and lowered her voice, leaning closer. "Your gut isn't usually wrong. And you think she was saying...Katie?"

Win checked Luke wasn't listening. The whole incident with Jake left her rattled. The look of shock on his face was hard to forget. The tiny, pink outfit was not something he'd wanted in that collection, and it left a hollow feeling in the pit of her stomach. "Up until an hour ago, I would have sworn she was calling for Casey or something that sounded like it. But when I saw the little dress and the name stitched on it ... I'm convinced now it was Katie. "

Ella seemed unsure. "Should we ask him?" She nodded in Luke's direction. Win shook her head fiercely. That haunted expression on Jake's face was enough to dissuade her.

"I'm not sure we should mention it. I mean, you saw Jake's reaction? Luke is already weird about his mother, and I've got a feeling there is much more going on than Jake would admit to. I kind of want to do my own digging before I say anything."

Ella nodded in agreement. "I understand—I mean, he's been through enough lately. Okay, when we know more, we'll tell him."

"Right." Win smiled, then her eyes lit up with mischief. "Should we call him over? He's clearly dying to know what we're talking about."

Ella grinned. "Do it!"

Win put her fingers in her mouth and whistled, then both girls burst out laughing. Luke's jaw dropped at being so openly mocked. At the pool table, Cole was oblivious. Luke sauntered over, wiping his hands on a dishcloth. Win whistled again, and Ella howled. *"Win!"*

Hands-on hips, he loomed over their table, his hair falling around his ears. "I'm sorry—did you just *whistle* me over? Like a *dog*?"

Win covered her mouth, trying to control herself, while Ella patted the seat next to her. "Come on, boy. *Sit!*"

Luke's face screwed up, and it took a full minute for both girls to compose themselves. Luke slid into the booth next to Ella, folding his arms. "That's not funny."

"It's not funny," Win said around laughter. "We're sorry. Would you like a treat? Or a belly rub?"

Luke slunk in the seat. "Hilarious. So—I see you two are talking again?"

"You should thank your father," Win said. "He got us to bond over vintage shoes."

Win half wondered if that had been Jake's plan all along.

Luke's smirk softened his eyes, and he said, "That does sound like something he'd do." He looked at both of them, his smile sliding up his face, blue eyes relieved. "I'm happy, though. Can we go back to some kind of normal?"

Ella's expression darkened. "I'm not sure what kind of normal we can go back to. Win has something to tell you."

After a few minutes of relaying the story again, Luke listened and then let out a long breath when she was done. "Alright—show me the mark."

Win protested, which only made his nostrils flare. "Not here."

"Yes, here. Show me."

Reluctantly, Win unzipped her hoodie, avoiding Ella's pained expression as she revealed her ruined patch of skin. Luke hissed and leaned over the table, squinting. When he went to touch it, she slapped his hand away. "It hurts, Luke."

He bumped down in his seat, his expression grave with concern, and she guessed what he was thinking. "It looks sore. Shouldn't that be healing faster?"

"It was," Win admitted. "Up until I saw you last night—we were by that Oak, and it started up again. But it might be a coincidence? It's better than last night."

"Hmm, I don't know. That place felt off—that burn—it looks like...."

"A bird," Ella finished the sentence. "We need to find this guy."

"I found him already!" Win said and watched as both their jaws dropped. "He wasn't hard to find—Wolfric Varga is a History professor at Boston College. I was going to find him at the open day they are having over the weekend."

"*We* will find him at the open day," Ella corrected her. "We were all going anyway. It's perfect—only, we can't say anything to Cole."

"I'm sure I can distract him," Luke said, folding his hands on the table. Al, the owner, appeared at the bar and waved at him to get to work. Luke groaned. "I wonder what other secret siblings Evan neglected to mention?"

Win rolled her eyes in unison with him. "I want to trust her. Rowan adores her. But this keeps happening, over and over. She knows something is coming—something bad."

"Something Spencer shaped," Luke finished, gritting his teeth. "I knew that this wasn't the end."

"Wolfric said we messed up. *I* messed up."

"We were all there that night, Win. We can fix this."

"Except my father is in some kind of denial," Win groaned and rubbed her eyes. "He just wants this to go away."

Luke scoffed and threw the dishcloth over his shoulder before sliding out of the booth. Ella's eyes trailed up his long torso, a pink explosion in her cheeks giving away her feelings. Win hid her smile. "We all want him to go away—but this is Spencer. He won't go quietly. And I imagine he's extra pissed with me."

He sauntered away, giving them both a wink and a smile. Win and Ella exchanged a look, finishing the last of their hot chocolates.

Win wasn't prepared to see Jake's black Mercedes parked in the driveway when Ella dropped her home. The hood was dented and scratched, a stark reminder that he'd crashed it only a day or so ago. Overhead, the clouds were spitting light rain, and it dripped onto the windshield; and Ella threw a concerned look as she parked the car. She smiled hopefully.

"Maybe he isn't here to yell at you?"

Win chewed her lip. "I don't like that he's here at all."

"Do you want me to come in with you?"

Win thought about it, but it was late, and Ella was already swamped with extra work helping Cole, so she shook her head. "Thanks, but I'll message you."

Ella leaned and gave her a long hug. "I'll get you in the morning."

After Ella drove away, Win lingered on the porch step, her scalp prickling at the sound of raised voices from inside. She threw her bag across her shoulder and decided to be brave and not listen in. Jogging up the steps, she threw open the door and was met by the tension of the atmosphere inside. Stepping into the kitchen, Jake stood behind a chair, leaning on it almost as if he owned it. Wearing his long wool coat and gloves, his eyes flashed as she entered the room.

At the table, Alice sat curled in a chair, with Rowan sitting in a seat close by. Ben was leaning by the sink. Jake gave her a tight smile. "Speak of the devil, and she appears," he gritted out, and her cheeks flushed. The necklace, still hidden under her sweater, suddenly felt very heavy and present.

Ben caught sight of her lurking, waving her inside. "Win—Jake seems to think you're in some kind of trouble."

Cagily, Win edged into the room, feeling the hostility wafting around her like a fine mist. In her chair, Alice hugged her knees, rocking gently, her lower lip chewed so hard it was swollen. Her pale eyes darted back and forth between her husband and Jake, and Win sensed every instinct Alice had, told her to leave that room. Rowan steadied her mother with her hand.

"Have you seen the mark on her chest, Ben?" Jake asked with a sneer. "It's a third-degree burn. It should have been treated."

Ben waved his hand. "Win is fine. She hasn't complained about any pain. If it were troubling her, she would have said something."

Jake cocked a brow. "Would she?"

Rowan met Win's terrified gaze, and she shoved her sweaty palms in her back pockets. "It's fine," she croaked. Jake crossed the room, took her arm, and dragged Win in front of her bemused parents. Win squirmed out of his grip, but not before he'd ripped down her zip and revealed her skin. Ben's complexion drained, and Alice gasped. But she was staring at the necklace around Win's neck. Alice's eyes filled up.

"Win..." Ben started.

"Does that look fine?" Jake fired.

"It's none of your business, Jake!"

"Why did you let her leave?" He wasn't listening. Instead, he directed his ire at Ben. "Why did you let your child go off alone with a man you hardly know anything about?"

Win's temper flared. "It's nothing to do with Grayson. This happened...."

Jake held up both hands. "You're right—I don't need to know. It's none of my business, and I came to do what I intended. I knew you were hiding this." He pointed at the burn. "And now, your father knows perhaps he'll at least take you to the damn hospital."

Ben sneered. "Well, now your conscience is clear, you can get out!"

Alice squirmed in her seat, Jake's eyes blazed in her direction, the muscles bunched tight in his jaw.

"My conscience is perfectly clear, Ben. How about yours? I can see you have been a little preoccupied lately. If Win was my daughter, she wouldn't have been gone for four weeks. If she was my daughter, I would have dragged her home by her hair!"

Ben's face fell, his eyes darker and deadlier than Win had ever seen them. "You don't have a daughter, though, do you, Jake?"

Alice hissed audibly, covering her eyes. "Oh...Ben."

Win and Rowan exchanged horrified looks, and across the room, Jake looked like he'd been hit by a truck. His face crumpled, something like agony crossing his eyes. Win sensed his heartbeat drop like all the air had been sucked out of his lungs. But whatever that was, it was fleeting. He lifted his chin, his eyes blazed, and through gritted teeth, he said, "You goddamn asshole, Ben Adler."

He hurt him... she thought, her lip dropping.

Her hair wafted as Jake shot past, his coat flapping behind him, and she flinched as the front door crashed. The Mercedes fired up and sped out of the driveway, stones flying in its wake. Win blinked back tears, though she had no idea why she was so emotional.

Alice flew out of her seat. "How could you, Ben? How could you *say* that?"

Ben clenched his jaw and gripped the sink, turning away from his wife. Alice fled the room, despite Rowan calling after her. As Win passed, Ben grabbed her arm. "We should see to that burn—he's right about that."

"It's honestly fine, dad." It hadn't pained Win all afternoon, and although the deep red welt had blackened, the sting had faded, and Win hoped her Therian healing was taking care of it. She prised his fingers off her arm and hurtled up the stairs after her mother.

Win wasn't about to let this moment fade. She banged into the shared bedroom and found Alice sitting on the edge of the bed in the dark. When she spotted Win, she drew up her knees, using the hem of her skirt to wipe her eyes.

"Mom..." Win crossed the room and planted herself right next to her mother. Thin-boned, and frail, Win knew that Alice was a hell of a lot stronger than she looked. "I know you've been through hell, but now is not the time to keep quiet. Something is wrong here—we all felt it. And as much as I hate it, Jake is connected to this."

Alice chewed on her nails, staring listlessly out of the window. When she didn't answer, Win gave an exaggerated huff.

"Rowan says not to push you. And Dad is pretending it's all happy families. I get it. He's worried. You aren't ready—well, I don't buy it. Evan brought you back to us for a reason, and I think that reason is about to make itself clear. We can't run from this. He is *going* to come back. I don't know when or how, but Spencer...is coming."

Alice sniffed and rested her chin on her knees, giving Win a watery smile. "When did you get so grown up?"

Win didn't back down. "Spencer has hurt me. He's hurt Rowan enough, and if he does anything to Evan then that'll destroy her. He'll keep coming for me. In his twisted mind, I'm the way this ends for him. My death equals the end of this curse, and the guy is obsessed with seeing it through. Well, I'm not going to sit and wait for him to find a way back to us. I have to face him...but I can't do it with my hands tied behind my back. Wolfric did this to me because he knows we need to man up and get ready. I can't stand by knowing he's coming and do nothing. I have to protect my family."

Alice wiped at the corner of her eyes, the truth bubbling below the surface. Finally, Win asked the question she'd been dreading. Part of her was terrified she'd hate the answer.

"Mom...who is Katie?"

Alice lifted her chin and exhaled, long and hard. "Oh, Win. I don't...I can't...."

"Mom!" Win cried, temper fraying inch by inch. The Hickory family were expert liars, shielding everyone from the truth. Win supposed that was how Alice was raised by John, another master deflector. Keep the family safe, hidden. Win wanted nothing more than to keep everyone she loved safe. "Start talking. I'm done with lies."

Alice swallowed, gripping her skirt with her white hands. "Jake was my best friend growing up. What you see, who he pretends to be, isn't him. He was kind, not cruel."

Win had suspected for a long time that there was more to Jake and Alice's relationship. He alluded to that much on the night Spencer went through that door and Luke went through his Calling. In true Jake fashion, he'd flaunted his knowledge, delighted that he knew something Win didn't. But friends...that confused her. She hadn't suspected a friendship. Jake was hard to like.

Win inched her hand across her mother's knees to clasp her hand. "I don't think he's cruel. But your *best* friend?"

"I know what you must think. And I know he's insufferable. But when I knew him, he was kind, sweet...and fun."

Win made a face. "It wasn't...." Her cheeks flamed. "God...you never...?"

"No," Alice said through a sniff. "I may have had a small crush *once*. He did grow up handsome."

"Hmm." Win knew the Jake effect well. When she first met him, it was impossible not to blush while looking directly at him. But she knew him better now.

"We were friends...and believe it or not, he was your father's too. That's what made it all so hard."

Win's brow furrowed, listening intently. "So...the cool, arrogant act—it's just an act?"

"Some of it is. There was a time we were everything to one another. Best friends, inseparable all through school and college. He left for New York and married Olivia. And I married your father—and there was a time when we existed, and this horrible, toxic thing between us was never a thing."

"What happened?"

"The worst thing that can happen to a parent. But, we didn't imagine that the person we thought we *knew* could become so bitter, jealous, and twisted that you weren't safe anymore. Jake wasn't the same man, torn up and broken. So we left because we thought that was the better choice."

Win sagged under the weight of her mother's words. "When you left Cedar Wood, you knew there was a huge risk that you would become stuck as the falcon. You knew the risks, Grandpa warned you...and you still left? Because of Jake?"

"I didn't have a choice left. You and Rowan weren't safe. And that was my choice. A sacrifice I would make again and again."

Win's eyes filled up, her throat clogging, prepared to ask the question again, even though she thought she might already know the answer.

"Mom...who was Katie?"

Hot tears spilled over Alice's pale lashes. "Katie...died. She was Spencer's sister."

FIFTEEN

Alice's tearful confession rendered Win speechless. Alice had dropped a bomb from a great height, and Win was dizzy, clutching for the truth. Spencer once had a sister. Did Rowan ever know this? Did Luke?

Before Win could question her mother, Ben appeared like a warding sentinel, shooing his youngest daughter out of the room, insisting his wife needed rest and not an interrogation.

Win retreated, at a loss for words. It hurt her heart, remembering the small, unworn dress wrapped with care in a bag. It was frustrating to have a tiny sliver of truth presented to her and then run into a dead end. Win decided to form her own plan. Her father, master of all lies and keeper of secrets, was determined to get her to focus on home, life, and school, but Win knew this was a fool's errand.

Spencer would come back. There was a reason they were all connected, the very day Wolfric chose to fry Win's skin and give her this mysterious gift, they all experienced something. It wasn't a coincidence, and Win itched to know the truth.

Wolfric was the key, and Saturday couldn't arrive fast enough. On the morning of the road trip, Win woke to a steady stream of sun edging around the curtain. She washed and dressed her burn. It felt cooler, and the welt faded from vivid red, to darker beige. It stung if she touched it, but she dressed carefully and pulled up her hair, the silver chain with the Hare glinting around her neck.

Poor Jake, the thought sprung into her mind. The look on his face when he saw the dress...Win couldn't forget it. Pain. The dark, haunted look of a man torn apart.

Distracted by something heavy clanging against her window, she jerked in surprise as a shadow fell across the pane of glass. There was a noise of feet squeaking on a ladder, and curious, she threw open her window and poked out her head, unprepared for what she saw.

Her grin split her face. "What are you doing here? Wait—are you stalking me again?"

With the breeze ruffling his hair, Grayson climbed easily from the ladder and hoisted himself on the ledge. Win snaked her arms around his neck, and he smiled, pressing a kiss to her mouth. "A ladder sure beats climbing up with my bare hands."

Win cocked a brow. "Why are you creeping around my window?" Then her smile dropped, remembering Rowan's joke about Grayson helping fix things around the house. "Oh god—my dad—he hasn't...."

Grayson waved away her concern, planting himself on the ledge. "It's fine. I don't mind."

"I mind! You aren't a handyman."

"He needs some help around here, and I offered to do it—look at it this way." He grabbed her hand and kissed the back of it when she went to butt in. "I get to see you and get to know him better. We didn't exactly start out on the right foot."

Win fumed, her nose wrinkled as she leaned on the ledge, her skin going goose-pimply in the morning air. "He better let you stay over for this!" She found his mouth when he offered it up to her, below her like Romeo on the balcony. Win sparkled with an idea, and she nodded for him to crawl inside, her brows raising suggestively. "I can lock the door— no one will know you're in here."

Someone coughed and cleared their throat noisily at the bottom of the ladder. Grayson's mortification was complete; he ground his teeth and nodded emphatically to whoever was outside.

"I can hear you, Win," Ben said. "I'm *holding* the ladder."

Win giggled, utterly mortified, laughing into her folded arms. "Sorry, Dad—but I don't think this is fair. You let Evan practically live here."

"I'm not having this conversation, Winifred. Have a good time in Boston!"

Grayson's glassy clear eyes met hers, and he gave her a long kiss. "Be safe," he whispered. "I'll be here when you get home. I want to know who this asshole is as much as you."

Win nodded and put a finger to her lips, knowing full well if Ben guessed what she was really going to Boston College for, he'd lock her in her room. Gripping the back of his head, she left him with a hard, urgent kiss, a promise of what she would have let him get up to if they'd had five minutes alone. Throwing on a coat, she hurtled downstairs, where Ella had already pulled into the drive. Luke leaned on the hood, talking to Rowan.

Her sister gazed up expectantly when she spotted Win trotting across the drive. "Be careful on the road—it's still icy," she warned. "I hope you find what you're looking for."

"Not a word to Dad," Win said. "And please be nice to Grayson. At least make him lunch."

Rowan chuckled and let out a long sigh, stretching her arms overhead. "I'll look after him, don't you worry."

"I don't like the way you said that," Win said with a short laugh before hopping in the back of Ella's fiat. She stretched out her long, jean-clad legs, nudging the back of Luke's seat. Annoyed he'd automatically claimed the front, she gave him a shove with her knee. He turned and scowled at her as Ella reversed out of the snowy drive.

"It's two hours to Boston—you better not be kicking me with your huge boat feet all the way."

"Then swap over?" Win stuck out her tongue.

Luke wasn't biting. "Ella needs help with directions."

"No, I don't," she snapped. "Besides, you only yell at me. You two better not bicker all the way there. Cole can have the front when we pick him up."

True to her word, when Ella pulled up at Cole's, Luke was swiftly evicted, forced into the narrow backseat with Win. It wasn't easy, the two of them being tall. Luke, having filled out considerably in size, was wedged into the corner. Building up a sweat and his hair curling at his nape, Luke dragged off his coat and accidentally elbowed Win in the gut.

She swore and kicked him in the shin. "Watch where you put your hands!"

A low vibration, like a growl, rumbled under his ribs, and Win smirked as he tossed his coat away, fanning his neck. He'd broken out into a hot rash. "Open a window!"

"It's freezing!" Cole protested from the front. Then to add insult to injury, Cole cranked his seat to accommodate his two long legs, forcing Luke to sit with his knees up to his chest. After ten minutes, the heat grew unbearable, and Win shrugged out of her coat. Cole grinned at them both and wafted a box of cookies under their nose.

Win shook her head, but Ella dove in. "My hero," she said with a wink.

"Is this new?" Win asked, referring to Luke's jacket, an expensive, wool-lined denim design, folded between them.

"Ha! Don't you even!" He flung her a wolfish grin. "You know what I don't miss about living with you? Cold water and my clothes never being where I left them."

Luke's eyes narrowed with interest as Win fanned her neck, eyeing the necklace lying on her collarbone. He reached and touched it with his fingertips. "I saw this yesterday. Where'd you get it?"

Win flushed, willing away the guilt on her face. "Jake gave it to me—it was your grandmother's."

Luke's boyish features split in a teasing grin, and he laughed, shaking his head. "You mean he put a *chain* around your neck? Wow, I can't believe you fell for that."

Liquid heat pooled in her belly, her nerves taking flight. "What do you mean *fell* for it?"

Luke laughed, though Win had no idea why. It was a kind gesture. "This is what he does. It's textbook Jake Fraser."

Win colored pinker by the second. "What are you talking about?"

"Making women fall for him. It starts with little things, like paying for stuff, kind gestures, *jewelry*, dinners, and then before you know—boom—he's convinced you to marry him."

"Luke!" Win spluttered. "It wasn't like that. Besides—it wasn't just me. He literally put shoes on Ella's feet. He even buckled the straps."

"Thanks, Win." Ella whined from the front seat, glaring at her in the rear-view mirror.

Luke sighed heavily, with a sleepy smile on his face. Folding his arms behind his head, he narrowly missed elbowing her cheekbone. He closed his eyes. "Then Ella is lost too."

"He was being *nice.*" Win punched his arm.

"I'm kidding," Luke said. "Kind of. This is him all over. You should have been around during the Carla years."

Luke referred to his most recent stepmother, now safely divorced from Jake and living in Hawaii. Win had never met her in person, but had seen pictures, and like Spencer's mother, she was a cool blonde, predictably ten years younger. Jake's type. Win could only imagine the clothes, the bags, and the shoes Carla would have accumulated in their short marriage. Now *that* was a closet she'd dive in headfirst.

"Isn't that what fathers are supposed to do? Spoil their kids from time to time," Win asked, though it had been a long time since she and Ben had spent any real-time together. Something gnawed at her conscience, and she was aware of Ella's dark eyes flicking to her in the mirror. She was circling dangerously close to the dark truth she'd learned. "I mean—I guess he would have loved a daughter?"

Luke laughed aloud but didn't open his eyes, folding his arms across his broad chest as he napped. "Are you kidding? It would be his dream."

"Didn't he and Carla ever want kids? Try for a girl, maybe?"

Win edged around her words, and Ella stared at her warily in the mirror. She felt her cheeks burn. Luke glanced out the window, bored and uninterested in the turn the conversation had taken. "I mean—he wanted to."

Win was surprised. "He did? He doesn't strike me as a...." She couldn't find the words, and Luke's lip lifted in a half-smile.

"Someone who wants lots of kids? No, not really. But he did want more. She was a career woman, not interested. She was too young for him anyway." Luke snapped his head in her direction. "Why are *you* so interested?"

"I'm not!" Though she was pretty certain, he could tell how hard her heart fired. He narrowed his eyes. Desperate to steer attention off of her, she shrugged in a bid to look nonchalant. "I think you give him a hard time, that's all."

Luke cackled and wagged a finger in her face. "There! Right there! I told you—it's what he does. Makes you like him—feel sorry for him. Win, don't feel sorry for him—not ever. He doesn't deserve it."

Luke's expression darkened. He grumbled, and stared out of the window, kicking Cole in the back of his seat for good measure. Win snapped her lips closed around her retort, but swiftly recalled how Luke felt about his mother, a woman who walked out of his life. Win had her theories, not that she'd voiced any aloud. But on the night of Luke's Calling, she'd questioned Jake, and was almost certain she hadn't left willingly.

Jake sent her away...maybe for her own safety. Spencer and his mutated form floated into her mind, and she shuddered. Jake allowed Luke to go through the process of emancipation, letting his youngest son sweat, and work like a dog, desperate to break the ties binding them as a family. Jake hadn't fought it. And Win was certain she knew why.

With Spencer around, Luke's life was in danger, perhaps since he'd been a small child. The image of the pink dress returned, and her stomach swam. It was a stark reminder of what danger they were all in. Win wasn't sure she truly wanted to find out what happened to Katie.

Careful to shield her thoughts, Win bit her lip and looked away, content to watch out of the window. Katie, a daughter he'd lost. The image of it made tears spring to her eyes. Win settled in the seat as Ella drove, speeding along the highway, content to watch the scenery pass in a blur. Snowy tracked fields, and sprawling farm buildings dotted the landscape. The weight of the pendant hung around her neck like a noose. She fingered it gently, now sure of one thing.

Whoever Katie was, Luke had no idea she'd ever existed.

SIXTEEN

Win pressed her nose against the glass as Boston college came into view. Drawing in breath, her eyes wandered over the array of stone buildings, with small lead windows arranged around an immaculate, lush green lawn, packed with stalls for the fair. A guy on the gate pointed them toward the bustling car park, and Luke whistled over his shoulder as they crawled into the lot. "Impressive," he said.

"It's beautiful," Ella said from the front, cranking on the brake. "I want to live here already."

Win's stomach plummeted. She could love it here all she wanted, but a future in a place like this wasn't on the cards. Overwhelmed with sudden disappointment, she felt it settle on her shoulders before she'd even climbed out of the back. Luke got out and stretched his long arms overhead, looking around.

"Can't you see us here?"

"No." She looked at him sharply and shook her head. "I can't."

He made a face. "What? We could do this."

She avoided his gaze, wondering what part of their curse he hadn't gotten. Both of them were bound to Cedar Wood. Guilt coursed through her. Swinging her pack over her shoulder, and falling into step with him as they walked through to the crowded main square, the narrow pathways weaved through impressive stone buildings. Her mouth was dry, and she didn't want to remind him of their predicament. Didn't he realize he'd face a four hour daily commute to go to school here?

Curse aside, Win was fairly certain Boston wasn't in the Adler budget.

Cole scratched his head, craning his neck as he looked up at a gray, stone-washed building named Gasson Hall, a gothic-style structure with a steepled clock tower. He groaned, his thoughts clear. "Well—I can say now, for sure, I won't be coming here. There's no way my mom could afford this."

Beside him, Ella nodded. "I'm not sure we could either. Still, it's nice to dream."

Nice to torture ourselves... Win thought, rolling her eyes at Luke, who'd remained silent, chewing the inside of his mouth. Money wasn't going to be an issue for the Frasers.

"There is always football," Ella said, nudging Cole's shoulder. He shrugged, resigned to the fate awaiting him. He winked at her with a smile.

"We may need to double my tutoring hours."

The four of them wandered through the maze of tented stalls on the Quad. Within five minutes, they were loaded with armfuls of fliers for various clubs, associations, and activities going on within the campus. It was friendly, buzzing with activity, and part of Win felt utterly selfish for bringing Luke here. Cole grabbed a map as a guy waved them in the direction of the Stephenson Theater.

"There's a talk for freshmen going on in about ten minutes if you hurry," he told them with a smile, so earnest she found herself returning it. Win cleared her throat as Ella thanked him, and they locked eyes. Cole was busy chatting to a blonde girl at a refreshment stall. Win grabbed Ella, and Luke ushering them away, and lowered her voice so Cole wouldn't hear.

"I feel awful."

"Why?" Ella gasped.

"I'm not here for any of this," she said, waving her hand around the magnificence. "Why don't you guys look around—go for the talk in the theater. I can find Wolfric."

"No, we're coming with you," Ella said, casting her eyes in Cole's direction. "We just need to ditch Cole somehow."

"No. You guys were coming here without me two days ago. And now I've hijacked your day. Please, I'll be fine!"

Ella's nose wrinkled with annoyance. "I'm coming with you. Don't fight me on this."

Ella's expression was too defiant and Win knew not to fight her. "Fine."

"I can distract, Cole." Luke glanced carefully over his shoulder. "I'll take him to the football stadium. Then I'll lose him and come and find you guys."

Win linked arms with Ella, grateful for her friend's warmth. They made an excuse to Cole and darted away into the sea of colorful stalls, avoiding older alumni who were there to entice them in, thrusting fliers into their hands. Ella sighed wistfully. "Isn't this wonderful?"

"Yeah," Win admitted, dejected.

Win trekked across the green, stuffing fliers into her pack, and then noticed a stall for the 'History Appreciation Society'. Behind the table sat a small, blonde-haired girl with red streaks through her bangs. Win pressed on a grin and marched up to the stall. "Hey," she said shakily. "You wouldn't know if Professor Varga is somewhere here on campus?"

Clearly bored, the girl's brown eyes brightened. "Sure. He's always here. Are you interested in History as a major?"

"I am," Ella piped up beside Win. The girl grinned, happy to meet a fellow History fan.

"I take History with Professor Varga. He's great—grumpy—but he knows his stuff."

Yeah, I'm sure he does! Win beamed. "He's a family friend." This wasn't entirely a lie. "Do you know where his office is?"

"If you walk around Higgins Hall and cross the Labyrinth, you'll see the Bapst Library—his office is at the back."

Win dragged Ella along, her pace quick and light, and determined not to get caught by Cole. "Once we find him, you go and enjoy your day. I don't want to drag you down with me," she insisted as they approached a vast, stone-speckled building. Ella nudged her in the ribs, pointing to a grassy area with interweaving stone paths, and colorful flower beds. Some students were on laptops on the benches, and most were prospective families with their kids. It echoed as they walked through, serene and peaceful. "You belong here, Ella."

"We have a job to do, Win," she said, avoiding the tone of Win's statement.

Crossing a green lawn, a beautiful building with bleached red and grey stone loomed up before them, its steeped roof jutting skyward toward a thick cloud. It was the Bapst Library and, by the looks of it, one of the oldest places on campus. Surrounded by a low iron gate, they went inside and hopped up the stone steps. Ella's eyes shone with tears as they went inside, the place eerily silent. Win scowled at her. "Do *not* cry!"

"It's so beautiful." Ella wiped a tear from her eyes. "I won't get to come here."

Win squeezed her hand as they walked inside, their shoes slapping on the stone floor. "You don't know that." The walls, lined with stacks of bookshelves, created a maze of literature and knowledge all around them. The air smelled like books, old and worn. Long oak tables and chairs were lined back to back. Not pausing to drink in the ambiance, and knowing her friend was growing fretful of having an impossible future presented before her, like a carrot on a stick, Win pulled her toward the back of the library.

Vanishing into the maze of book stacks, Win spotted a glass door, leading to a walkway. "There."

They bustled through the door, finding themselves in a long, silent glass hallway with small offices sprawling off the sides. It didn't take long to find his door. Taking a long breath, Win wrapped her knuckles against the oak wood, pausing before gently nudging it open with her fingertips. It wasn't locked and swung open, revealing an empty, and untidy office.

"Maybe he's at the fair?" Ella said, pushing in behind Win, her eyes roaming the array of stacked, messy shelves, and leftover coffee mugs on his desk. "We missed him."

Win's neck tingled, her hairs rising off her skin in a warning. The shape of a man crowded the empty doorway. Win had about a second to shove her hand over Ella's mouth as she turned, and spotted the man smiling at them curiously. Win was a fraction too late, as Ella shrieked, "It's a vampire!"

Win died inside, suppressing a giggle despite the situation. Wolfric glared at them, aghast.

"I am *not!* That's an insult."

"Sorry," Ella mumbled against Win's palm.

Wolfric Varga gave them a savage grin, slamming the door shut with finality that shuddered through Win's bones. "You didn't miss me. I'm right here—and it's about time you showed up."

Wolfric eased past the girls, and Ella sagged against Win's body, drained from fright.

"Why didn't you warn me?" Ella hissed as, out of earshot, Wolfric pulled out the chair of his desk. He dusted off his jacket. He wore a surprisingly neat, tweed ensemble, and with his wild hair pulled back in a short ponytail, he didn't look as unkempt as he'd looked the night on the beach. She supposed there must be some kind of dress code here, even an ancient witch with a love for heavy metal must adhere to.

Win frowned. "Warn you about what?"

Ella gestured to the huge man. She pointed to her eye teeth, and Win snorted back a chuckle. "About the teeth!" Ella hissed.

Wolfric, overhearing the last part, rumbled out a short laugh. "It's alright, Miss Torres. I don't bite—unless absolutely necessary. Please sit down."

They slipped into the empty chairs. Across the room, Wolfric folded his arms, studying the two of them with his chocolate, brown gaze. Even during the day he was intimidating. Broad from shoulder to shoulder, he looked like he could carry a globe on his back, his face worn, sun-kissed, and framed with a scruffy dark beard. "It took you long enough." He aimed the quip at Win, and she scoffed.

"It's not like you gave me much to go on—except this." She yanked down the neck of her sweater, revealing her ruined patch of skin. Wolfric grimaced, as he leaned over the desk, and reached for a pair of glasses, perching them on the end of his nose. Ella chuckled, but Wolfric shot her a glare that made her mouth shut.

"What? I'm short-sighted. I'm immortal, not perfect." He nodded to her burn. "Sorry about that. Hazzard of the job, I'm afraid."

Win narrowed her eyes, folding her legs as she leaned closer. "What the hell did you do to me?"

He grinned without opening his mouth, his eyes darting to Ella, who seized the arms of the chair with white fingers. "You mean you haven't figured it out yet?"

"Uh—*no!*" Win drawled. "That's why I'm here."

Wolfric stroked his beard. "I'm sorry. I couldn't stay and tell you more. The jumps—they're draining. The older you get, the worse it becomes. And when you passed out, I took my cue to leave."

"Jumps?" Ella repeated.

"I saw you on the beach—on fire." Win gritted her teeth. "What did you do to me?"

He spread his palms in an open gesture. "It's time. You have time—you can go back. Fix the past, the mistakes you made, and set the course straight."

"Wait!" Win's fingers flew to her temples. "I can time travel? Go back to the past?"

"Correct. Only back—never forward. *That* would be so much easier."

Ella sucked in her breath, while beside her Win seethed. "How could you do this to me?"

Wolfric's expression darkened. "You and your friends sent that monster back in time, right to a place he had no business being in. Now it's up to you to fix it. You have to figure out a way to bring him home before he hurts someone."

"But how do you know where he is?" Ella rose off her chair. "Why can't you help?"

"I went back, but it was too late. Spencer was already gone. He murdered Mary Hickory, your ancestor—something which wasn't supposed to happen, not by his hand. He's going to find her and make her raise the door. If we get to him first, we might have a way to control it."

Win was confused, which only seemed to irritate him further. "You mean Evan."

"Yes—my sister," he barked, which made Ella jump. "And if he decides to kill her in the past...."

Win's skin washed with ice. The bruise she thought she'd seen explode on Evan's jaw, there one moment and gone the next. "She'll be dead in this time....Rowan..."

"It'll wipe Evan off the earth. Do you want that to happen?"

"No!" Win's eyes filled with tears.

"Neither do I. She's my little sister, and despite all her flaws, I love her. I'm sorry for what I had to do to you. And I can promise you it won't be easy."

"What exactly did you do to me?"

"I gave you some of my gift—an act which nearly killed me—and yes, we *can* die. Only I have a little habit of rising from the ashes."

Ella's eyes widened, and Win guessed they might be thinking the same. The mark on her chest, the burn, the splay of wings. A phoenix. Ella uttered the words, "Is Win immortal now?"

Wolfric chuckled. "She's Therian, she's already going to live a *long* time. But no. She has the power to go back. I call them jumps. You get a jump for every year you've been alive."

Win reeled, her head spinning with this information. Clutching her chest, she leaned over her knees while Ella rubbed her back. "Seventeen," she confirmed. "Win gets seventeen jumps."

Wolfric nodded, his gaze darkening, leaning his elbows on his desk. "Right."

"And how many do *you* have left?"

Wolfric cleared his throat, a little awkward. "Two."

Ella gasped, and Win lifted her chin, her lips pursing with anger. Wolfric at least had the decency to look abashed.

"Two? So that's why you did this to me? Because you're running low?"

"I had to!" He growled, and both girls flattened against the chairs. "I used a jump to go back and warn my sister to move her ass. Once I make that last jump..."

"What? What happens to you?"

Wolfric stood abruptly, so hard the chair flung back against the wall. He paced, raking his hands through his hair. "I don't know exactly. But I have a theory I'll grow old and die—or worse. I'll fade away, erased like I was never even here. Like footprints on a beach, I'll be swept away, back where I belong. So I thought it was about time to pass on the mantle—to someone who could fix this chaos."

Win sniffed, stilling her breath, and straightening like she could brace what lay ahead of her. Her fingers traced the burn, the imprint of wings on her flesh. "I saw you appear in a ball of flame."

Wolfric gritted his teeth. "Yeah—it ain't a picnic."

"Is that how it happens? I catch on fire?"

"Um, yeah." Wolfric's chest puffed. "I call it the Phoenix flame."

Win cocked a brow. "Did you make that up yourself?"

"Maybe." Wolfric looked embarrassed. "I admit I don't know how all this stuff works—why I was given this gift out of all my siblings. Nassau didn't love many things, but he did love the Phoenix, a creature with a soul—kind of like you. He said it was a gift from the Sun and a witness and judgment of time. Fire purifies the earth so new things can grow. Like being burned and rising from the flames reborn."

"Well, catching on fire sucks," Win said, throwing herself back in her chair. Hadn't she taken enough pain and suffering this year?

Ella made a noise, a gentle clearing of the throat, that caused them both to look at her expectantly. When they did, she was perched on the edge of her seat, her lower lip wobbling. "How did you do this to Win? What are you? Because I'm fairly sure Evan doesn't have that kind of power. Unless she's majorly holding out on us."

"Well, would that be a surprise? Evan lying? But no, you're right. She doesn't, not that she isn't powerful. She is but in a gentle way. We all had different talents, but the god Nassau thought he'd gift me with the flame...which I didn't know I had until I woke up in my own grave."

"Nassau?" Win said. "We've heard that before." She looked at Ella, and she nodded.

"The night we brought back Iris," Ella nodded to the chain around Win's neck. "His name was in the chant we used."

"Ah, yes. The first time the stone door appeared for you in the woods. Quite a foursome you made, raising it from the mist."

"How'd you know *we* did that?"

Wolfric grinned. "I know lots of things. I know it rose for you again on the night of Luke's Calling, and you sent Spencer through it. He'll try to use Evan to raise it."

"She can," Win confirmed. "I saw her do it when she brought back my mother."

"Right," Wolfric said. "But in the past—Evan hasn't done it before, only alongside Vecula. And he'll try to get her to bring it from the ground, and if she falters, if she gets scared—he'll kill her."

Win rubbed at an ache forming in her temples. It was too much. She felt nauseous with the weight of the past slung on her back. Ella inched forward in her seat.

"You didn't answer my question—not really."

He cocked a brow at her, at the puzzled expression on her face. "What one do you want me to answer?"

Ella drew closer, chewing her lip, her brow furrowed with worry. "Who was Nassau? He gave you the flame—who was he to you?"

Wolfric ground his teeth, but after a moment, a smile, tired and resigned, crossed his lips. "I wondered when you'd ask."

After a pause, in which silence lingered between them, Win prodded, "Well?"

"Nassau was a god," he said slowly, his expression unsure, cagy. "He was also our father."

SEVENTEEN

Silence fell like a blanket. Ella sagged in her seat, while Win only blinked rapidly. Sunshine gleamed through a crack in the window, lightening up dust motes dancing in the air. When Wolfric didn't jump to fill in the giant, god-like gap, she said, "I'm sorry—what?"

He grumbled under his beard, idly flicking an empty Styrofoam cup into the trash. Flicks of coffee splattered inside the can. "He was our father. We were the mortal children of a god."

"But...you're immortal now?"

"Yes—Vecula saw to that."

Win opened her mouth to speak, but her ears pricked back, recognizing the stamp of familiar footsteps thudding down the hall outside. The door slammed open before she could rise to her feet, and Luke stormed in, nostrils flaring. "Found you!"

"Luke..." Win went to stop him, but he shoved her aside, greeting Wolfric around his side of the oak desk. Wolfric stood, towering over him by a foot. Luke squared up to him, his chin defiant, as he narrowed his eyes.

"Is this him? Is this the guy?"

"Uh...Luke, we were talking..."

Luke didn't wait for a response; he shoved the larger man in the chest. Wolfric rocked on the balls of his feet. Red-faced,

Luke looked confused as the hit hadn't landed as he'd intended. He went to strike again, but Wolfric caught both his wrists with fluid grace. "Please. Do sit down."

Win groaned and rubbed her temples. "Luke, for god sake..."

"It's fine. Let him get the show of male testosterone out of his system," Wolfric said with a casual wave of his hand, patting Luke's shoulder so hard he collapsed into a chair. "You did good, kid. You moved me a whole inch."

Luke spluttered. "What did you do to Win?"

"We covered it five minutes ago. I'm sure she'll fill you in."

Luke narrowed his eyes, growling low in his chest. "How about you fill me in?"

"How about you show me some respect? If you are so desperate to mark your territory—I'll let you piss in the corner. Hell, I'll even put some newspapers down. *Don't* touch me again."

Luke withdrew, his shoulders slumping, and Ella snorted into her palm beside him. "Okay."

Wolfric smiled. "You aren't the only guy around here with a sharp set of teeth."

Luke went a stark shade of white. "I can see that."

Win kicked his foot, throwing him a glare sharp enough to crack ice. She evened her smile and glanced at Wolfric. "Sorry about him."

"How did you find us?" Ella asked, and Win suddenly worried about Cole.

"Cole got distracted by the Eagles cheerleading squad—so I ran."

Wolfric nodded. "Good plan. They are very distracting."

"You found us fast," Ella marveled, and Luke scoffed with a roll of the shoulders.

"I could find you in a stadium of sweaty football players, El." He meant it as a compliment, and Ella blushed pink, darting her gaze to her hands in her lap.

Wolfric watched them with interest and huffed dramatically. "How cute. Well—*as* I was saying. We were born to Nassau, his mortal children. We weren't his only children. He had hundreds. Together we were known as Primus, the *first* children of a new, dangerous time. Primus was the first language, ancient and now, pretty much eradicated."

Ella said, "Primus...so you were the beginning...of everything?"

Wolfric nodded. "We were the new generation of a race predating the history books. A time of gods, magic, and monsters...and evil. Our language still exists, interlaced with Mayan...Latin...Egyptian, even European tongue. No one stayed with Nassau long if they wanted to live—he was rather unpredictable. The Primus disbanded across the globe, and you'll find traces of us everywhere...if you look closely enough."

Luke cocked a brow. "So you guys really are as old as dirt."

Wolfric snorted. "Older." He took a long inhale, preparing to continue. "You'll find evidence of us in Nordic folk tales, Arthurian legends, even ancient Egyptian paintings. We aren't the root of the tree, we are the seed."

"If you tell me you were at the Last Supper, I'm leaving," Win quipped, though she wasn't joking.

Wolfric looked grave and disappointed. "No, I wasn't there...but my cousin was!" He burst out laughing, and all three of them stiffened. He wiped his lips as his laughter sobered. "I'm kidding." Rolling his eyes at them, he continued.

"Our mother was a high priestess, a powerful witch. One of his favorites—which made his betrayal of her all the more cutting."

Luke swallowed. "What happened?"

Wolfric sat back, arms crossed at the chest. "Moved onto a younger model. A princess. You know how it goes. Men can still have a midlife crisis no matter the century."

"He sounds like my dad."

Wolfric chuckled sadly, and Win sensed talking about the past weighed heavy on him. "My sister—Vecula, was enraged with his betrayal. She murdered the Princess in cold blood, and used blood magic to bind us to her—immortality for her family forever. I think in her warped way, she wanted to prove she was more powerful. Nassau took his rage out on our mother. He executed her, and broke Vecula's heart. We had no choice but to flee the continent or we'd suffer the same fate."

Win sucked in her ribs, trying to ignore the dull ache forming at the base of her skull. Heavied by the revelation, she sank in the chair. "That's awful."

"Wherever my sister fled, she left a blood trail in her wake. She got my brother Itzma killed."

Win frowned. "You mean Issac?"

"Yes, yes," Wolfric corrected himself. "That was his given name, but over the centuries, we took names to blend in. Vecula, Wolvan, Euelea, and Itzma—they were our given names. Funny, Vecula never dropped hers. She loved her home, and for as long as I can remember, all she wanted was to go home. To make peace with our father."

"But she got herself hung in the eighteenth century?" Win concluded with a deep shudder.

"She never stopped trying to get home. The night she cast the Hickory curse, she wanted to use the power to open the door, but what she didn't know was she had crafted the very thing needed to open it. Cursed blood—your blood. Sometimes she wasn't that smart—hence the hanging."

"So—you were witches?" Ella said with piqued interest. "What else can you do—apart from burst into flames?"

"Well," Wolfric cleared his throat gruffly. "I didn't know I could, not until I died a grisly, horrible death. My gift was the power of persuasion."

Luke scoffed. "You mean mind control?"

"Not really, more like a suggestion, planting a seed. If I could control minds life would be so much easier." Wolfric shrugged. "I can pop thoughts into your head—help a student pass a tough exam, get seated in restaurants a bit faster—all very rock and roll stuff." He looked darkly at Win. "Wake you up out of a dream."

Win shivered, something about his tone making her back stiffen. What did that mean? She tried to shake it off, listening as he spoke. His voice was like a motor, deep and rumbling. You could drift off easily if you listened too long. Maybe that was his gift?

"Isaac was a warrior, though he took no love of that."

Ella blushed. "Tougher than you?"

"Oh, stronger, faster. Evan was a healer, and Vecula was the sorceress, a blood drinker—an evil bitch. You should have seen *her* fangs."

Fragments of thought floated in Win's mind, his statement about dreams bothering her deeply. Something was pushing at her conscience, wanting her to remember, then it hit her between the eyes, and she bolted upright, slapping the table. "Oh—my god! *You?*"

Wolfric looked affronted but grinned "Me?" he asked innocently.

"You—my dream. The night I walked through the door, back to when I saw Joseph Hickory butchered—the night the curse was cast. I *couldn't* have opened the door myself. I wouldn't have known blood opens the door...."

He clapped his paw-like hands together. "I may have given you a little nudge."

A little nudge? It was a darn sight more than a nudge. "But..." Win spluttered. "What did you do?"

"I put the idea in your head—filled in the blanks."

Win cocked a brow. "We'd never met before that night on the beach."

Wolfric smacked his lips, awkward. "I'm not proud, okay? You were playing pool in the bar you three practically live in, and I waited till I got my chance. A whisper in the ear is all it takes."

Win went white. "Oh my god...and then...?"

"And then nothing. You did the rest. You slept walked right where I told you to. I managed to raise the door, and boom, you went back in time."

"I was covered in blood when I got back!" Win yelled, her face pink. "That's creepy! Massively, *horribly* creepy!"

"So you can raise the door, like Evan?" Ella asked.

Wolfric grumbled, unused to the relentless line of questioning. "Yes. Like Evan and Vecula, I have that capability." He suddenly looked tired, frustrated as if he were dealing with students. "Honestly, I don't have the time, patience, or the crayons needed to explain this to you. The door presents itself when magic is used, like the night you called Iris. But I can call it out of hiding."

"Because you have god blood?" Ella affirmed, and Wolfric snorted.

"I guess."

The whole side conversation was lost on Win. She was still seething about being led through the forest, starting an entire chain of events leading to her witnessing the brutal mutilation of her ancestor. "Why? Why did I need to see that?"

"Look!" He stood, and she snapped her mouth shut. "You needed to see what really happened that night. I *needed* you to see it, to believe what you are—what you can do."

Luke snorted, indignant, infuriated he was side-lined. "And what is that exactly? What is it Win is capable of that I'm not? Or Rowan, or Alice?"

"Spencer *can't* open the door!" Wolfric blurted. "The guy isn't too bright!"

"Win can," Ella confirmed. "Win's blood opens the door."

Wolfric's smile was thin, grave, and didn't meet his eyes. "She needs to believe she's capable of doing the very thing she was put here to do—what she was born to do. A curse born Hickory—one who doesn't believe she has power."

Ella, Luke, and Win exchanged horrified glances, and Win's throat went dry. The words charged inside her, right on her tongue, so real she could taste it, and tears pricked her eyes.

Willard told her many times, but she hadn't believed. Not then. Now with this bear of a man watching her with a twinkle in his eye, she felt it, deep and raw. Tears spilled from her eyes, and she thought of her grandfather, a gray, shaggy wolf. She thought of Iris, the pendant sitting heavy on her clavicle. The White wolf, locked behind glass, lonely, trapped, but deadly if she was unleashed. All they risked, sacrificed, so she could be standing here, alive and breathing.

Win could be deadly too. She'd spent too long denying it, hiding, and now she knew what she was put here to do.

Her family—She had to save her family. Wolfric leaned across the desk, and Win, caught in his dark gaze, was powerless to look away.

"Winifred Adler, you come from a long line of powerful, formidable women—and men. People who fought for their families. Your grandfather threw himself in front of an arrow—for you. No second thoughts, no regrets. His mother, died to keep her children safe. And I lost...." His eyes shone, wet in the corners as he broke off, quickly recovering himself before continuing. "I knew a woman who took a bullet for her family to protect them. She didn't even blink in death's face. Your family isn't *cursed.* Not really. It's a gift. It's time you believed you are one of them."

Win gripped the edge of her seat, terrified of what he might say next.

"That's right," Wolfric said as if he'd read her thoughts. Maybe he had? "You were put here to save them—to save the whole lot of us."

EIGHTEEN

Euelea woke, her neck stiff as she tried to look in the direction the relentless dripping sound was coming from. Drip, drip, drip. A shudder rocked her body, and cold air circled her bare feet.

Wincing, she lifted her neck, something sticky and dry pulling in her hair. Carefully she touched the tender spot on her head and winced, her fingers brushing matted, dried blood.

The rolling sickness of an empty stomach made her dizzy, her elbows shaking as she leaned on them. She took in her surroundings, having spent a few uncomfortable hours on a bed of hay. She was in a stable or some kind of animal house. Light flooded through the barn door, along with cold, frigid air. Euelea's skin was sensitive, and she wondered if she could be burning up. How far had they traveled in the night?

Shaky, and weak-kneed, she crawled to her feet, grabbing one of the barn doors for support. Then her back split open, and she screamed. Tears welled in her eyes as she dropped to her knees, burning pain slicing up her spine.

She remembered. He'd used his claws. The prickling sting dulled as she fell forward, sobbing, the memory surfacing. After stealing her from the inn, Spencer rode the horse till it had nothing left, till she begged him to let it rest, sensing the poor creature was starving and dehydrated, strings of saliva dangling from its lips. But instead, he'd morphed before her eyes, transforming by some ancient method of transfiguration into a terrifying animal—a cat, long, sleek, and deadly. He killed the horse, letting its blood run across the stony path, taking his fill while Euelea sobbed for him to stop. Her fingers grappled with stones and rocks, seeking one that might act as a weapon. When he transformed back, she'd ran at him with a rock, pelting him as hard as she could. Lashing out, all five nails traced a bloody line through her dress, and the tender flesh of her back.

He threatened to kill her a lot, she noticed. Rough-handed, throwing her across his shoulder, tossing her around like she was nothing but a toy. Yet, he hadn't, and she knew why. He needed her to open the door, when and if she eventually raised it for him. A spark of hope kept her going, it was her bargaining chip. Spencer didn't know she couldn't open it. It was the only reason she still breathed.

How long had she been asleep?

Euelea's head throbbed as she stood again, her throat dry as she paced the barn, her bare feet cold against the straw-covered ground. Suppressing a cry, she stumbled to the door, bloodied fingers reaching for the lock when it burst open. Euelea staggered, afraid, as a man stepped across the threshold. He stopped, open-mouthed when he saw her. "Who are you?"

Euelea fell against the slatted wood, the smell of animals floating through the door behind the man. He was strong, bearded, and wore a wool tunic over a faded shirt and breeches. He was a farmer, and this was probably his barn. His gaze raked her head to foot. "My god—who did this to you?"

Euelea's eyes darted around the barn. Where was Spencer? Shakily she choked out, "You need to leave—forget you saw me."

"This is my home. I can't pretend I haven't seen you." Carefully he took a step closer, holding up his hands to show he was unarmed. "Let me take you inside—my wife can help you."

"No." She moved as he stepped closer. "Please."

"Come with me—I won't hurt you."

He was kind, he was just being kind. And the stupid fool would get himself killed if he stayed. Euelea darted past him in an attempt to run, to make a dash toward the sunshine streaming through the barn door. If she could just run, get out, feel the grass on her feet, she knew she could put distance between her and Spencer.

But the farmer caught her wrist, she yanked out of his grip, stumbling. "Don't. You need to leave me alone. He'll hurt you."

The farmer's large brows knitted. "You mean the monster who did this to you?"

A low rumble echoed out of the far corner, and she spotted two yellow eyes peering from the dark. Any hope dwindling in her chest faded, and died on the breeze. Of course, he'd been here the whole time, waiting for her to escape. So he could have the fun of running her down, humiliating her over and over. Her pulse spiked as the massive creature crossed the room with lethal speed and agility. A yell escaped its throat as it barged her aside and flattened the stupefied farmer with both paws.

"No! Don't please!" Euelea yelled as, with a snarl, the thing cocked its head, and looked at her over its shoulder, weighing her reaction, making sure she had the perfect view. The man gaped, sprawled on the ground, his fists beating dirt as Spencer lunged. There was a crunch so sickening she screamed and covered her ears, followed by the gentle sound of lapping and chewing.

Hot tears streaked down her face. "Why did you kill him? He didn't hurt you."

Without warning, Spencer shifted, morphing back into his human form, rearing up over her, filthy, naked, and mutated. She cowered as he slipped past. The smell of urine filled her nose, and with a hot, embarrassed flush, she realized she was standing in it, pooling down her legs and onto the stone. His brows rose. "You mean to tell me all these years on earth, and you piss yourself at the sight of a little blood?"

The farmer's blood leaked over the cobbles, and she inched backward.

Spencer flashed her a toothy, blood-stained smile. "You look pale." He thrust her to the ground by her shoulders. "Rest—we've got a couple of days' journey before we reach Cedar Wood." He wiped her sweat on his thigh as he hauled her up and checked her over, turning so he could look at her back. "You heal fast, don't you?"

Her sliced skin was gradually knitting. Born a healer, Euelea was an asset on the battlefield, she could help with most injuries and ease pain. She'd tried to focus on herself the last couple of days, healing whatever he inflicted on her. The slice on her back was taking longer, and the weaker she got, the less she could help herself.

Shaking, she drew up her knees, sinking into a corner, and watched as he threw on his long coat. It wasn't large enough to cover the thick muscle underneath. The fur running the length of his body shone; if she didn't hate him, he'd be fascinating. The longer he remained mutated, the more cat-like he became. His upper teeth touched his lower lip, barely concealed in his mouth. Animalistic snarls floated out with his speech, and she admitted to finding him horrific, lurching if he stalked close. In all her years alive, she'd never seen anything like him, a creature created by blood magic—by Vecula on the fateful night they cursed the Hickory family. This was all her fault. Tears leaked out of her eyes. "Why did you have to kill him?"

Spencer threw her a sharp glare. "He was going to take you away from me—and I don't share well."

Something clawed at her chest, a gripping, hollow sensation, and no matter how she fought it, exhaustion pulled at her eyes. She let her head sag, and it was dark outside when she opened her eyes. Hunger knotted in her belly, and Spencer prodded her arm till she woke fully. Euelea shrank away.

"Come on, Evan. You smell awful, and we have to get on the road. There's a river at the end of the meadow. You can clean up."

He stood, towering over her, and held out his hand. When she recoiled, he grabbed her elbow, forcing her to her feet. Staggering alongside him, he didn't pause to let her adjust as he dragged her outside, all her nerve endings protesting as the cold air hit her lungs.

True to his word, he led her to a river, a sharp stretch of water twisting through a dense cluster of trees. Above the sky was inky dark. Over the last few days, they'd traveled at night to avoid being spotted. It wasn't unusual for a man and a woman to travel together, only Spencer didn't resemble any man these people would have seen before.

"There." Spencer pointed a yellow, clawed finger at the dark water. "Go wash—and make it quick."

Flushing, she looked for a place to change in private, which only served to amuse him. He grinned, revealing his hideous teeth. "Are you serious? After the little display in the bar, you suddenly feel shy?"

Euelea firmed her chin, her resolve dropping. Humiliation stained her cheeks red as she stripped off her gown in defiance, knowing full well he watched her every move. His eyes were glued to every inch of her body as she waded into the water. She let out a shaky gasp as cold water iced her skin, her teeth chattering as she sank deeper.

Her back stung, but she swallowed a cry, submerging, wondering if it would be easier to sink and close her eyes. Let the water take her, let the mud grip her feet till she couldn't stand. Wolfric made her promise to live. He'd planted something inside her, a seed of hope entwining with her soul, and making her see what might be possible. When Vecula died, Euelea drifted, lost without her sister's guidance. Without her sister's mission, where would she go? She only knew she wanted to do good, right the terrible wrongs caused by Vecula. When Wolfric found her in the woods, not only had he ignited hope, he'd told her one day she'd be loved.

Rowan. Someone worth fighting for. Someone to live for, even if it was hundreds of years from now. Once they got back to Cedar Wood, he'd force her to raise the door, and when he realized she couldn't open it, only cursed blood would, then she'd be dead. Rowan would be a distant dream, a nice fantasy to keep her warm for a short time. Euelea stiffened her shoulders, casting him a quick glance, where he stood, watching.

God, she was going to make him work for this. She wasn't about to back down, not without fighting him every step of the way.

An idea formed, so urgent she couldn't ignore it. Warily, she cast him a glance at the bank, watching her bathe. There was a glint of interest in his eyes, something male shimmered below the surface, and whatever warped creature he might be now, she wondered if she could appeal to the man underneath. Closing her eyes, she sucked in her breath.

You can do this....if it gives you a moment to get away....even the smallest chance.

"I know you're watching me," she said, a haughty tone to her voice as she lifted her chin, turning so she watched him from the corner of her eye.

He didn't even bother to pretend. "It's a great view from here."

Brazen, she rose from the water, letting it stream down her naked body as she strolled to the bank, keeping her steps slow, deliberate, unrushed. Taking up her clothes, she stuffed her dress over her damp head, yanking the gown down over her hips, making sure he got a full view as she dressed. Spencer's eyes heated, and he crossed the gap between them, roughly turning her around so he could lace her into the bodice. Euelea cast a glance over her shoulder, letting a laugh escape her lips, even though inside, she was repulsed, shaking. Her voice nearly cracked as she said, "Most men usually like undoing these—not the other way around."

He yanked her stays, and she gasped as her ribcage tightened. His breath tickled her neck as he leaned into her ear. "I'm not most men."

Swallowing dryly, she lifted her eyes to the stars, and prayed silently. He was too close to her neck, her pulse beat frantically. All it would take was one strike. She pressed back into him and visibly shivered. "I'm so cold."

Without missing a beat, he rubbed her arms. Euelea closed her eyes, willing strength in her soul to remain steady, even when he said nothing. She knew he was staring at her neck, knew what he was daydreaming about. It was so visceral her skin crawled. Cagily, she turned to lift her chin as her eyes played with his, biting her lip. Then she stood on tiptoe and kissed him. Spencer tensed, rigid with shock, but Euelea clung on, grabbing his hair and holding him, even though her stomach rolled as her tongue touched his teeth.

He went slack, made a growl against her mouth, and closed his eyes. She kissed him, and kissed him till every thought of killing her was vanquished, and he was a squirming, confused mess. The moment he gave in, the second he kissed her back, she hit him with it.

Violet light pooled out of her mouth, bleeding into his, possessing him till he made a startled, surprised noise in the back of his throat. She pulled away, breathing hard, and terrified. Not at what she'd done, but at what she'd seen. Lost in the kiss, he couldn't shield what he'd hidden. Something dangerous lurked in his soul, like a clawed-fingered parasite, with its nails embedded so deeply she didn't know where Spencer began, and this thing ended, fused and melded as one. She let him go, and without an anchor, he staggered, his eyes heavy-lidded and sleepy.

Please, dear god, work...

"What the hell did you just do to me?"

Panting, she clutched her chest as he swayed, a blank gaze settling over his features. The look on his face before he fell was enough to play on her mind as she ran. Confused, beaten, and a little crushed that she'd played him at his own game. Spencer slumped and fell face down in the dirt, fast asleep. Wolfric had warned her not to use magic, it would leave a trail. But god, she planned to put some distance between them before he woke up.

Live for Rowan...

Euelea picked up her skirts and ran. Spencer wasn't wrong. He wasn't just any man.

He wasn't alone.

NINETEEN

The tall red brick buildings of Boston were replaced by the sprawling fields and farmlands of home. Funny how Win thought of Cedar Wood as home, even after spending the day in the place she'd grown up.

She glanced at Luke with his knees pressed to his chest beside her in the car. He caught her looking and gave her a thin smile. Curling his hand around her wrist, he gave it a squeeze, and affection swelled inside her. His eyes went a strange shade for the briefest moment, like faded sea glass with golden flecks.

Win hid her gasp. And before she could say anything, they were blue, bright, and piercing. She felt a snap in her chest, annoyed with herself for being needy, and he could feel it. It was pretty impossible to hide anything from him.

You better not try any of that time jumping without me. Luke said it without lifting his head.

In front, Ella and Cole were unaware of the private conversation going on in the back. Win sniffed.

I won't. Though she wasn't sure, she meant it. He rolled his eyes, and she could tell some part of him didn't believe a thing she said. Closing his eyes, he napped against the doorframe while Win chewed at her nails. She opened the window to let in fresh air. The wind rustled her hair and her clouded thoughts drew to Wolfric. And the tail end of their strange conversation in his office.

"So, how does this thing work?" she'd asked once the whole 'you are the savior of Cedar Wood' conversation dwindled to an awkward close. "How do I—jump? Use the flame?"

Win harbored a strong, sickening suspicion she knew *exactly* how she was supposed to jump, though she needed him to say it aloud.

"Well, now we're talking," he said with a savage, slightly unnerving grin. Rays of sun from the window glinted off those sharp teeth, his brow bar shone. "It's not that complicated."

Win nodded in encouragement, aware of Ella, and Luke hanging on his every word.

"You need to focus—something I know you're good at. Think about the time period you want to visit, picture it hard, until you can almost see it—smell it. Then you say the magic word."

Luke snorted. "Are you kidding me? How does she come back? Click her heels together three times and say there's no place like home?"

Win elbowed him, annoyed by his sarcasm. "It does sound pretty simple. Too simple."

Wolfric sniffed, indignant. "Would you call bursting into a ball of fiery death simple? I've done it many times. And it hurts like a bastard."

Win shuddered, not liking the idea at all. "Point taken—what's the *magic* word?" She felt like a loser saying it out loud, especially when Luke choked back a snigger.

"Ah, not here. I'll write it down. No sense in saying it aloud in here and burning down the oldest building on campus." He threw her a serious glance, while he scribbled something on a scrap of paper. "Don't even think about it until you're ready."

He tossed it across the desk, and Win folded it into her jean pocket. "Anything else I ought to know?"

"Practice," he said. "But leave several days between jumps. It'll drain the life right out of you—and you being Therian, it might mean you can't shift. Visit places—safe places that you know you won't run into trouble. And no matter what, even if you're tempted—no interfering with yourself!"

Win's lips curled into a smirk, and next to her, Ella howled into her hands. She cocked a brow. "*Interfering* with myself?"

Wolfric spluttered, realizing his blunder, turning a stark red under his beard. "You know what I meant. Don't talk to anyone or interfere with the *line*. Even if it means you want to help—you do not get involved. All is as it's meant to be."

"You mean she shouldn't start betting on sporting events?" Luke joked, and Wolfric growled in reply.

"So damn cute, aren't you? Exactly—no interfering—with yourself or anyone else for that matter!"

"Kind of like you did?" Win poked his arm. "It's alright for you to go back and warn Evan but I can't?"

"Oh, come on!" Wolfric folded his arms. "I think that's what's known as exceptional circumstances."

"But why can't I go now? Rowan will only ask me the same thing when she finds out about this. Why can't I go back to the past and end this now?"

Wolfric took her shoulders, that trembled under the weight of his fingers. "Slow down. There's more at play here. It has to happen at the right time when we can deal with this for good. Evan knows this."

Ella gasped. "You mean—she knows this is happening? Why hasn't she said anything?"

"Its complicated, but the moment Spencer went back through the door and found her, her memories would have started to change. He's altering her past so now, in this present, she knows exactly what is happening to her. She knows how this will play out."

Win's eyes widened. "Then why can't she just *tell* us what's going to happen?"

Wolfric screwed up his fists in frustration. "Because if she *tells* you then there's a risk it might not happen at all! You might make a different choice, take a different path than the one you're meant to be on. Jeez—don't you kids watch time travel movies?"

"Those are mostly bullshit," Luke deadpanned. Beside her, Luke's phone buzzed, and he gritted his teeth. "Damn! We need to rescue Cole. He accidentally walked into a physics seminar."

Wolfric rose along with them, his expression pensive as he landed a huge paw-like hand on Win's shoulder. "Make sure you do practice runs in big open spaces. Don't set your house on fire—believe me, I've done it. I can't stress enough that you need to leave time between jumps to heal—don't be tempted to go after Spencer yet."

Win balked. "But if Evan is in trouble...."

"Evan has always been in trouble—she's been a pain in my ass since she was old enough to speak. But she's not stupid, if I know her, she'll stay well hidden, and if he catches her, she'll find a way to stall him. Let time run its course. When you go through it needs to be controlled. We need to bring him back to the time and place where we can actually deal with him—properly this time. You'll know when the time draws closer, trust me."

Win looked up at him almost fondly. It wasn't hard to like him, gruff and crotchety as he was, he was big and safe, and for some reason, she trusted him. "You keep saying *we*. Does this mean you'll be there?"

He grinned and gave her chin a sharp pinch. "Would I miss you kicking that monster's ass? Never. I can't wait."

The car bumped over uneven ground, the Massachusetts terrain opening into wide-open meadows, and snow-speckled countryside. From the driver's seat, Ella glanced in the mirror at Win. The hardest part of today was not talking about it in front of Cole, who sat in the front playing an irritating game on his phone. It pinged and buzzed relentlessly. Beside her, Luke dozed, and Win clenched her jaw, itching to get home and tell Rowan and Grayson what she knew.

The weight of responsibility settled on her neck, and she physically forced all her pent-up anxiety to take a hike. Drawing on what strength she had, she had to face this—no time to choke. Spencer was coming. Evan was in danger, and if anything happened to her...Win could barely think of it. It would destroy Rowan. And Spencer had hurt her enough to fill a lifetime.

Flicking her eyes out to the window, she remembered the vision of Mary walking in aimless circles around the Oak tree. Mary was unhinged, of that she was sure, but usually her ramblings meant something. Something deep and buried. *Katie...Katie...*

What the hell happened to you, Katie? How does this lead to Spencer? Why did you show this to me?

It had to mean something. There had to be a connection. Win chewed her lip till she tasted blood.

Wolfric said she should do a practice run. Win knew exactly what time she needed to visit.

TWENTY

A narrow branch yielded under the eagle's weight. She sank down, and droplets of ice water fell onto the head of the man standing below. He shivered, and rubbed his scalp, narrowing his pale eyes as he peered between the trees. Grayson huffed, and pretended he hadn't seen her when Rowan knew he had. She jiggled the branch, and a great chunk of ice fell from the branch and landed on his neck.

If an eagle could laugh, that was the sound Rowan made, an odd clucking noise. Especially as he leaped sideways and tore at his shirt. "I know you're up there," he gritted out.

Rowan dropped from the trees and landed on his shoulder. She did enjoy riling him, and spent most of the afternoon tossing casual insults at him as he straddled a ladder in an attempt to fix one of her shutters.

Rowan felt a little mean. He'd done an excellent job, primed to ignore her and throw her a cold glare every time she made a quip. And he can't have felt at ease, knowing he'd spirited away the youngest member of the family to live in sin in a motel for four weeks.

Perched on his shoulder, she peered at him closely, too close, studying the grey flecks in his glass pale eyes with a hunter's precision. Grayson tilted his head, staring, his eyes drawn to the curve of her golden feathers, the flecks of hazel and chocolate woven into the detail of the markings like brushstrokes of a painting. He lifted his gloved hand to touch her.

Rowan squawked and pecked his finger, hard. "Ow! What was that for?"

No touching! She knew he couldn't understand, so she rose both wings, the span larger than a six-foot man, flapping till it rustled his hair off his forehead. She hopped to a log while Grayson yanked off his glove with his teeth. He sucked his finger as Win appeared out of the bush.

What did you do to him?

Rowan ruffled her feathers. *He tried to pet me.*

Not nice, Rowan. Win prowled around Grayson, winding under his thigh so it almost lifted his foot off the ground. Throwing her green eyes at him, he grinned, seemingly able to understand what she was thinking. He scratched her ears, and like butter melting, she purred and pushed her nose into his hand. "Don't be jealous," he said. "I've never been close to a bird that size."

Rowan's stomach bubbled at the show of affection. Something about it made her tingle, their closeness, ease in each other's company. He understood her without having to speak. Shoving away the odd sensation, she darted to a patchy area of bush and rolled back into her human form, stretching out her neck as she stood. Pulling her sweater over her head, she met them back in the clearing. Win threw her a snarl.

Rowan laughed. "I'm for looking, not touching," she said, nodding to the bush. "C'mon you next. Before it gets dark. We should get this over with."

Grayson scratched at his chin, nodding in agreement as Win sauntered into the bush. He laughed as she gave him a swipe with her thick tail. Rowan tucked her thumbs into her jean pockets, awkward while they stood there and waited.

Grayson sucked at the blood on his finger again. She clicked her tongue. "Sorry."

"Are you sorry for nipping me? Or for calling me a stalker ten times today?"

"You *were* looking in my window." She smirked, but hid it, dipping her chin.

Grayson huffed. "I was fixing your shutters."

"You did good," she said, giving him a thumbs up. She relented, hurrying out a reluctant, "Sorry about the finger."

He looked up, surprised. "I've come to expect no less."

"I'm worried," she admitted, ignoring Win's cries of pain from the bush. "I'm worried about what this means."

His lips moved into a slow smile, and she looked away, swallowing. Rowan didn't do feelings, not out loud. Not even to Evan, who was inside the house cooking, oblivious of what they were about to do.

"I'm worried too," he said. "At least we have that in common."

Rowan swayed on her feet, the realization of what Win was attempting making her dizzy. Win arrived home from Boston college and dragged them both outside, out of earshot of their parents, and Evan. After making quick work of what she'd learned from Wolfric, they both reluctantly agreed to let her test this crazy theory. But Rowan insisted she phase first so she'd have nothing to pull her focus away from the task.

"I'm scared something will happen to Evan," she said, and then snapped her mouth shut, hardly able to believe she'd let it out, and who she'd let it out to. "I'm scared she won't survive this."

"She *has* survived this," Grayson reminded her. "Already."

"I know, but why can't we just go now...?"

"I don't pretend to understand this either." Grayson tilted his chin in her direction. "But Win was fairly insistent that we can't know how this plays out, it could risk the outcome. So, we're just along for the ride."

Rowan kicked a stone over with her toe. "I don't like not knowing what direction I'm headed." She rubbed her arms while next to her, he released a deep chuckle.

"Me either." Their eyes met briefly before she ducked her chin.

Rowan wasn't an idiot, she'd spotted the decline in Evan over the last couple of days. She seemed off, tired, and was hiding in large, winter clothes. Rowan knew she was covering up, and it ate at her, she couldn't swallow the thought that something terrible was happening to her girlfriend.

Grayson nodded softly, his shoulders rising in a shrug. He didn't budge when she sat beside him on the log. Rowan hadn't been particularly nice to him. The first time they'd met properly, she'd punched him in the mouth. He was solid, and for a moment, she saw the attraction, why Win loved him so much. Grayson didn't say much, but his presence was reassurance enough.

Grayson cleared his throat. "If Win doesn't see this through—then something bad could happen to any of us. I saw him that night, what he's capable of. He won't stop, Rowan."

She stiffened as Win fell out of the bush, her jeans snagging on a branch. Rowan sighed, despite the comical tug of war Win was having with the brambles. "But why does it all have to fall on her?"

Grayson held in a laugh as Win frantically attempted to untangle herself from the bush, catching her hair in the process. "I believe in her. She's got this."

"I would give anything to switch places," she said, letting her words slide away as Win, free of the branches, jogged toward them. Win cocked a brow at the two of them, sat shoulder to shoulder.

"Are you two bonding?" she teased. Grayson blushed, and Rowan crossed her arms around her waist protectively. "Don't bond too closely while I'm gone. I will come back!"

"You have twigs in your hair," Rowan said sweetly, ignoring Win's jealous remark.

Win fingered her tangled mane and plucked out the debris. "Oh."

"Shall we?" Rowan stood tall, and folded her arms behind her back. "I can't say I'm thrilled about this, Win. Where exactly do you plan on jumping to?"

"I have a plan—kind of."

Rowan followed behind, lagging like a gooseberry as they trekked further into the wood. The paths were worn and soggy, piles of fresh snow melting into a grey sludge. She folded her arms across her chest, her lungs tight. Win had only needed to say the words, Evan's in danger, for Rowan to spin into a freefall. Suddenly the world went grey, her feet like lead as she tried to imagine a place where Evan didn't exist.

It was simple. She couldn't. Evan arrived in Cedar Wood, almost as if she'd answered a silent prayer Rowan made. Her savior, the other half of her heart. Rowan was built to fight, to protect, but how could she protect against a man who was senselessly bent on destroying her?

Hadn't Spencer had his fill of torturing her? Over and over. But Rowan knew it had never been about her. Rowan was just his ticket in, and it made a knot clog in her throat. All the years together, the shared experiences, Spencer had been her first for so many things. And none of it had been real.

Rowan watched the way Win casually wound her arm around Grayson's waist, the way he looked at her, brushed her hair out of her eyes. Win was precious to him.

Evan came to save Rowan. She'd mended her heart. And now Rowan had to protect what she loved. And, unfortunately, it meant trusting her kid sister.

Win paused, sniffing the air and glancing around. They were in a snowy clearing, with tall, drooping cedars acting like a shield. "I think here should do."

Rowan sidled up to Grayson. He'd been carrying a blanket under his arm this whole time, and Rowan wondered if they would need it. Her stomach lurched at the thought.

"What do we do now?" Rowan didn't like being vulnerable, she looked to Grayson, who only shook his head. Win stood on tiptoe, planting a kiss on his jaw, and then scurried away to stand well clear of them.

Win pointed a finger at both of them. "No matter what happens—for god sake—don't tell Mom and Dad."

"What do we do? Just hang out and wait?" Grayson asked.

"I guess. I mean, I have no idea how this works. Wolfric said the jumps only last about an hour, and then you are sucked back. So with any luck—I should end up right here."

"And what if you don't?" Rowan panicked. "Where are you even going?"

Win sucked in her breath. "If this works...then it could be huge. There's something I need to see."

Rowan let out an exasperated sigh, and paced the clearing. Tangling her hands in her red hair, she looked skyward. "Okay...I trust you. Maybe pick up the lottery numbers while you're there?"

"I can't talk to anyone," Win said. "Wolfric was pretty clear. I can't interfere with...myself. Oh god, this has to work."

Win balled her fists, and closed her eyes, and without realizing it, Rowan edged closer to Grayson. The quiet of the woods closed in, the air heavy and tense, and with her shoulders drawing up to her ears, Rowan watched, utterly helpless.

Win took a scrap of paper out of her pocket, scanned it, and reread whatever was written there several times over. She settled on the balls of her feet.

Please don't die...

Rowan...I can hear you.

Rowan pressed her fingers to her lips, breathing through her nose as Win became as still as water on a pond. The muscles of her face relaxed, and she looked as if she were deepening into a meditative state, her chest rising, and falling slowly. Her fingers loosened, and the piece of paper floated to the mud.

Win let out a long exhale, her lids fluttering, lips down-turned and relaxed. Then she opened her eyes and whispered, "K'a'ajale."

Heart knocking against her chest wall, Rowan frowned and dared a peek at Grayson. The breeze stirred around them, and without warning, she swallowed back a nervous giggle. Nothing was happening. She opened her mouth, about to whisper to Grayson behind her hands, when smoke wafted under her nose.

With a flick of her green eyes, Rowan glanced at her sister, who looked as confused as they did. Win wiggled her fingers, her mouth open in horror.

Smoke, black and dense, curled from Win's outstretched fingers. She gasped as though her brain had only just caught up with what her eyes were seeing. Win's pain receptors kicked in, as she screeched, sending a shockwave of ice down Rowan's spine. Rowan fell to her knees, gasping as right in front of her, her sister went up like a candle. Flames licked and tore at Win's pale flesh, the claggy smell of burning skin unable to shake off. Grayson stood still, his mouth hanging open, his fist clenched as Win's shrill cries of agony filled the clearing.

"Oh god, Win!" Rowan sobbed. "This can't be right. We have to help her!"

Rowan, on her feet, blinded by hot tears as she dove for the blanket, determined to end her sister's anguish. But Grayson grabbed her waist and threw her to the ground. Eye to eye he pinned her. "She said this would happen, Rowan. We have to let her do this!"

Win rolled on the leaves, the once lovely planes of her face contorted in agony, her flesh bubbled and charred, until she was only fire. A thud echoed through the small space, a burst of shooting flame licked the trees. Rowan's skin tightened, the searing hot flames too much from even this distance.

Smoke billowed from the area where only seconds ago, Win stood. Now the soil was burnt, crispy, and Win vanished in a plume of smoke.

TWENTY-ONE

Smoke, as thick as tar, clogged the lining of her lungs. Like a fish out of water, Win gasped for air, bug-eyed as her back hit dirt. Above rose steady plumes of smoke, her flesh seared, tingling as the flames evaporated.

She sucked in clean air, rolling her body on the ground, the relief of the sting bringing fresh tears to her eyes. "Oh, shit," she cried, rocking on her back, and hugging her knees. Watery-eyed, she moved to all fours, her sweater smoking. She smacked at her arms, putting out the flames. "Oh my fucking god." Collapsing, she breathed deep, her fingers clawing dirt.

The clearing was empty. Grayson and Rowan were gone. Where the hell in time was she?

Moaning, she rocked to her feet. Wolfric hadn't lied. It hurt like a bastard. Above, the sun streamed through the canopy, and the air was humid and moist. If she had to guess, this was a Cedar Wood summer, she recognized the clingy way her clothes hugged her skin, her hair at her nape already sweating. Striping off her sweater, she tied it around her waist, down to her t-shirt underneath. Fanning herself, knowing she didn't have a great deal of time, she jogged through the woods, her feet aching in a way she hadn't felt for a long time.

Out of breath from a short distance of running, she halted, clutching her chest as a stitch exploded under her ribs. Bent double, she heaved, wondering if this was the effect of the jump, if it had knocked the energy right out of her. Slower than usual, eventually, she crossed the meadow that opened up into the main town. She rushed to leap the fence of the Laundromat, but she could barely lift her knees.

Grumbling, she took the longer route, annoyed Wolfric hadn't mentioned that she'd be totally useless after a jump. She longed to get her speed back. Her feet hit the cobbles of Main Street, and using her arm as a shield from the sun, she gazed down the familiar street, with its bustling cars and quaint shop fronts. The paintwork on Hardy's looked fresh, the neon sign hung above the door was brand new and didn't have a broken bulb in the letter A, unlike in the present. Win passed the convenience store, swiping up a paper, scanning for the date.

July 14th 2007

Win frowned. In this time, she was about one month old. She'd tried to focus back in the forest before she went up in smoke. She squeezed her eyes tight and attempted to follow through on what Wolfric told her to do. But instead, one burning question kept forcing its way into her mind.

What happened to Katie? Win had no idea why she'd brought herself here. And with an hour on the clock, before she was sucked back, she didn't have time to waste.

Tapping her hips, she glanced up and down the street, half tempted to duck into Hardy's and see if her grandpa was in there. The thought made her gut twinge....what she wouldn't give to see him right now.

Standing under the awning of the convenience store, she wiped the sweat off her brow, when a familiar scent wafted under her nose. Lifting her chin, she poked her head into the street and spotted a woman headed in her direction. Armed with a red-haired toddler, and pushing a stroller, the woman was trying to pacify the younger one as she bustled past Win. Win drank in her smell, knowing her scent.

It was Alice. Her mother—only younger, with fresh, pink skin and a gleaming mane of long, strawberry blonde hair. Win's mouth fell open.

Mom...

"Don't complain, sweetheart. I'll get you ice cream when we get to the park, okay?" The lady paused, taking a moment to tie up the young toddler's mane of hair which had gathered in a sweaty tangle down her back. Win's heart leaped. It was Rowan, and she could have only been three years old. Which meant the baby in the stroller....

This is crazy...was I meant to be here? To see this?

Win ducked out from under the canopy, hands in pockets as she carefully trailed behind, keeping a good distance. In this time, her mother was fully Therian, and would eventually pick up on being followed by a stranger unless she was so preoccupied with her daughters to notice. Rowan was miserable and whiny, tugging on her mother's skirt with the anguish of a hot, hungry, and bored child. Alice stroked her head, smiling and waving at another woman she'd spotted across the street.

She was happy here...she's so young.

Win trailed her mother through the town, quickly recognizing the path she was taking as she veered off down a side road that led to the modest town park. A green acre of land filled with colored swings and slides, monkey bars, and a climbing wall. Win spotted the ice cream truck parked on a verge at the same time as Rowan. The little redhead hopped on one foot in excitement.

Alice laughed and parked the stroller by the truck, quick to get Rowan what she wanted, thrusting a vanilla cone into her chubby hands. "Come on, sweetie. I think I see Tyler over there!"

Win ducked behind a fern, a good safe distance away, sinking to her heels right as her mother's head turned sharply in her direction. Alice narrowed her eyes and looked away, dismissing what she'd thought she'd seen. Preoccupied, she grabbed a cloth from her diaper bag and wiped Rowan's sticky face. Sinking onto a park bench, Alice checked the baby, hidden under a sun canopy, smiling fondly as she tickled the little one's bare toes. Win's chin wobbled. It was perfect here.

Wolfric had given her a gift, allowing her to witness this moment. Sweat cooled on Win's neck, as she sank to her bottom and watched Rowan dart to the sandbox to play with another boy.

Rowan played tug of war over a stick with the little boy, both of them in fits of giggles as they played in the sand. Tyler's mother was nearby, chatting with another group of mothers. Alice smiled, content, and turned her face to the sun. After a few moments, her attention wavered, the baby made a noise in the stroller, and she was instantly alert, fussing over her. There was a loud buzzing in her bag, and Alice scrambled for a phone she had to flip open to answer.

Win made a face, concealing a smirk. What kind of archaic invention was *that?* Alice smiled into the phone, lowering her voice as she had a conversation Win couldn't quite pick up on.

Over in the sandbox, Rowan and Tyler appeared to be fighting over a bucket. In a quick motion, the little boy got to his feet and chucked a handful of sand in Rowan's face. Swallowing dust, Rowan shook out her red curls, her chin wobbling as she instantly burst into tears. Tyler's mother swooped in, red-faced as she scooped him up. Rowan sat miserably in the sand and bawled.

Alice clicked the phone shut and dashed across the playground, holding out her arms. Win crawled out of her hiding spot, her skin tingling. Something was wrong, and her eyes drew to a shape looming from behind a tall, thick trunked oak. The woman had been there for a while, and at first Win hadn't taken any notice of her, assuming she was another park mom watching her kid. The woman peeled away from the trunk, stalking purposefully for the stroller.

Win's mouth went dry. She couldn't move. She wasn't supposed to get involved. She couldn't call out or scream...and something told her this moment was why she was here. *This* was the moment she had to see.

As the woman neared the stroller, Win glanced back and forth between her and Alice, who was oblivious while she struggled with Rowan. The toddler was in the midst of a tantrum, throwing her hands in the air and kicking her legs, beet red in the face.

Mom...look up...please!

The stranger was a blonde woman, her face ghostly pale in the sunshine, her gaze fixed on Alice as she grabbed the handlebars of the stroller. Win's stomach went into freefall, liquid heat exploding across her palms. Maybe she was only admiring the baby in the stroller?

Mom... please....look up.

Words bubbled to her lips, desperate to rip forth, to warn her mother. The woman looked about, then, with brazen authority, unparked the stroller and walked away with it. Win broke out into a sweat under her arms, panic exploding in her chest.

You're here to see this...you have to see this. But every maternal instinct in Win's body told her she had to move, her throat tight as she stood, creeping out from her shady spot. She watched in horror as the stranger reached the park gate, and rather than being weighed with an unwieldy stroller, she ditched it on a grassy verge and scooped up the baby inside.

Win's body froze, rooted to the spot. *Mom...please...look!*

Alice wasn't looking. Win's words stuck, but she closed her eyes and projected as much authority into her inner voice as she could. *Alice! Alice!*

Rowan sniffed, crying in fits of temper as Alice forcibly dragged her to the park bench. But Alice froze, her face seizing in terror as she saw the stroller was no longer there. Her mouth dropped open, and like a lead weight, she dropped Rowan's hand.

"Win...oh my god...Win?"

Hair flying around her, she whirled, confused, terrified, and Win couldn't do a damn thing to help. Alice spotted the discarded stroller, and the noise she made, the cry of terror from her throat, was enough to alert everyone else in the park. Other mothers joined her at the abandoned stroller, all frantic, offering help. All the while, Alice stood there, confused, white-faced, and helpless.

"Help, please..." she cried, trembling, tears streaking her face as the man from the ice truck ran across to let her know he'd called the cops. "My baby...someone took my baby."

Win shivered, recalling the conversation she'd had with her mother. Words failed Alice, the pure fear she'd experienced as a parent traumatic enough to keep her silent.

Can you imagine the worst possible thing that can happen to a parent?

In that moment, Alice wasn't Therian, not a hunter, not a fighter. She may have strong senses, but fear and shock reduced her to rigidity. She was a mother with a stolen baby, rendering her helpless and immobile.

Win, however, was none of these things. Feeling power kick into her muscles, Win dove out of the park gates, determined to find the woman who'd taken her.

It didn't take long. Win lifted her chin and sniffed the air, catching the blonde woman on the corner of Main Street, scrambling for keys in her pocket. The woman's pretty features were taught, anxiety making her fingers tremble as she fought to unlock her car door with a bundle in her arms. Win stood, breathless on the sidewalk as the woman got in the front seat, not even bothering to strap the child in a proper carrier before she roared the engine to life.

Clutching at the stitch ripping under her ribs, Win cursed. This is not the time to be weak! The car hurtled past, the woman's haunted face at the wheel. She was out of her mind. Win half wondered if this had been her plan. If she'd watched Alice, concocted this, and waited for her to become distracted. It made her skin crawl.

Win ran after the car, her muscles struggling to keep up with the strain she was putting them under. Keeping to the buildings, she hurtled at full jaguar speed, her lungs squeezing as the car reared off the main road and headed out of town. Win bent double. "Shit!" she cried. "Shit!"

Win blazed after the car, her red mane flying behind her, sweat pooling at the base of her spine. Her feet slapped the asphalt hard, as above the sun blistered her scalp, and somewhere along the way she lost the sweater tied around her waist. The car wove erratically along the road, flew sideways into a concealed driveway. It paused as a set of iron gates swung open. She drove into Mercy.

"No," Win panted, not believing what she saw. This woman...this was Olivia Fraser. Jake's first wife, it *had* to be. Win, out of breath and aching, broke into a jog, veering off the road and into the woods. It wasn't like she didn't know the back way into Mercy. Ahead she spotted the rusty gate leading into the courtyard. The woman was already out of the car. Win pressed her body against the wall of the stone building. She peered around the corner as the woman mounted the steps with the baby in her arms.

She hollered, and banged on the door. "Let me in! Jake, please let me in!"

A crank of a lock was followed by muffled, harried voices as Olivia vanished inside the vast building. Win bit her lip, her sneakers slipping on the stones as she edged around the building, pulling herself up at window ledges, peering through the dark glass. Dropping to her feet, she ran back to Jake's end of the house. She'd done this before, breaking and entering, spying. Pricking back her ears, she strained for any sound, hoping she'd find them somewhere on the ground floor.

"Olivia...what the hell have you done?" It was Jake, frantic, terrified. Inside the room, a baby wailed. "Who's child is this?"

"Where's Rose?" came Olivia's sharp, cold reply, calm for a woman who'd kidnapped a baby girl.

Win crawled under the ledge, the window was open, and a drape fluttered in the breeze. She settled on her heels. Rose...that was Luke's mother? Jake had already remarried, and in this time, Luke would only be a few months older than Win. Win scowled. Jake's love life was a complete mess.

"She's taken Luke for a walk in his stroller...you can't be here, Olivia!"

"She's perfect, Jake...will you just look at her?"

"Olivia...this is insane!"

"Look at her, Jake, she's so pretty...so perfect...will you hold her?"

Jake made a noise in his throat, a strangled cry that sounded like a growl. Then he sobbed. "Why are you doing this to me, Olivia?"

"Jake, please look at her. We could give her such a good life—together."

"I have a life—my wife is heading home with my son right now. It's over, Olivia. It was over long before Katie died, and you know it. God—don't you think we've suffered enough."

"I know you want this...."

"Olivia....who is this child?"

There was a long pause, and Win could hear feet pacing and Olivia's ragged breath. Part of Win's heart tore, sensing the pain she must be in. Olivia was grieving, possessed by loss and loneliness. It can't have been easy, seeing the man you loved remarry, cast aside. Win's heart hurt for her.

"Is this...is this Alice's baby?"

Olivia sniffed.

"Olivia...my god...what have you done? How could you do this?"

"I remember how upset you were when you found out she'd had another daughter...I know how jealous you are of Ben. I feel what you feel, Jake. I wanted her too."

"Not like this...*fuck*...we have to fix this!"

Jake paced, and from beneath the ledge, Win could sense his mounting terror. How would he fix this? How could he return a baby? How could he make this go away like he did everything else? Win flushed with anger toward him, angry he'd pushed Olivia aside, leaving her destroyed by grief. While he moved on, married a new wife, started over, and replaced what he'd lost. Olivia *couldn't* move on. She was stuck. He should have stayed and helped her, not cast her aside like a problem.

"Olivia, you must stop this fixation with Alice Hickory."

Win frowned. What the hell did that mean? Inside the room, the baby murmured, and someone comforted her. Dying to look, Win stretched her neck, craning her chin over the ledge. Jake scooped the baby into his arms, rocking her against his chest. He smiled down at her. "She's lovely."

"She could be ours. I knew you'd love her."

Jake snapped a cold, blue stare in her direction, the muscles in his jaw bunched. "She's not ours. We have to take her home."

Olivia snarled. "I won't."

"You will—or I'll call the cops myself. Olivia—don't you realize what you've done?"

Olivia grappled for his arm; her mascara-streaked face taught as she clung to him. "You don't love Rose...not really. We could be so happy."

"And what about our son?"

Olivia fell to her knees, wailing into her hands. "There's something wrong with Spencer."

Jake swayed with the baby in his arms, swinging towards the window. Win hissed and dropped to her knees. "What the hell are you talking about? He's a sweet little boy—there isn't anything wrong with him."

Olivia cried, "You are a goddamn idiot. Spencer is wrong....I feel it."

Jake forced a laugh, but Win's blood ran like ice. Under her skin, an itch burned, and she panicked. How long had she been here? *I'm so close...I have to stay...*

"Now I know you're really insane."

"Jake... I don't know how...I know it. I feel it."

Sickened and weary, Win needed to leave. Any moment she may be sucked back, and it couldn't happen here, right under this mossy ledge. Grinding her teeth against the dull, burning itch under her skin, she accepted defeat. Edging out from under the ledge, she ran through the woods, wiping her eyes. Her flesh tingled, and she picked up speed, terrified she wouldn't make it. Dashing through the undergrowth, she spotted charred ground and hoped to god this worked. She hoped Rowan and Grayson waited for her.

Closing her eyes and trying to shut out the memory of Olivia's sobbing, she wriggled her fingers and waited. Something rustled in the bushes, and Win's eyes sprang open following the sound of a low, almost inaudible growl.

Oh...crap!

Win stood face to face with a large shaggy grey wolf. He sniffed the ground, confused, narrowing two yellow eyes at her.

Win bit her lip. "Hey, Grandpa."

The wolf nuzzled her sneaker, clearly confused. John Hickory was out searching for his grandchild in the only way he knew how to help. And he'd found her. Only she didn't look like the baby he was hunting.

Win ducked to her knees, letting her fingers tickle his mane of hair. He drew back, sniffed her fingertips, and then gave her a lick. The rough pad of his tongue traced over her skin. "It's me—I know this is crazy."

The wolf narrowed his eyes. *This can't be real...you smell like her...*

It's me...Grandpa...

Winifred?

Win burst into tears, letting out everything she'd stored up for the last few months since he'd been gone. Sobbing into his mane, she wound her arms around his neck, her heart throbbing as she drank in his smell, pine needles, and leaves. "Oh, Grandpa...I've really screwed this up."

Where is the baby? Where's my granddaughter? Are you the reason she's missing?

"No, no!" Win shook her head, wiping her eyes with the heels of her hands. "And I know this is crazy, but I can't stay. The baby is fine, she's safe—and she'll come back."

Why can't you stay?

"I can't explain...you have to forget you ever saw me here."

I'm not sure I can.

God, what had she done? Stroking his fur, she remembered how warm he was. She choked back tears as, under her skin, a fire raged. It was about to happen.

She willed away images of the night he'd died. The arrow wedged under his ribs and his last hot breath on the night air. Tears streaked her face as she buried her face in his neck. Words wouldn't form, and an awful hollowed-out sensation dwelled in the pit of her belly. She'd never see him again.

If she warned him now of his fate when she went back, would he be waiting for her at home? With his feet up on the couch watching CSI Miami like he'd never been gone, they'd never burned him, or said goodbye. The arrow that killed him was meant for her. Pressure behind her heart made her ache, and the warning died on her lips, knowing he'd sacrificed his life for her.

Be brave...it's all you can do in the end... He'd said that once. It was like a dream, ones she frequently had, where they were together, talking and laughing. And then she'd wake with a damp pillow and wet cheeks, remembering he wasn't across the hall.

"I love you, Grandpa...I love you so much." Win glanced up, terrified she'd keep crying if she looked at him, but to her surprise, he was looking at her neck. Or, rather, the silver Hare pendant. Nuzzling it with his nose, she stroked his head. It hurt she couldn't even tell him where Iris had died.

"You'll see Iris again...I promise you."

How do you know?

I know, she promised. *You'll be together again.*

Where did you get that?

"I'm not sure you'd believe me if I told you."

I gave her that when she turned eighteen.

Startled by the pricking fire gathering under her skin, Win jerked to her feet, warning him back with her hand. She closed her eyes, not wanting to see him vanish as she burned like it was him who dissolved into smoke.

You could save him...you could tell him...now before it's too late...

The wolf blinked, confused. *Tell me what?*

Her heart spiked, and she battled with the words on her tongue. You'll die...you'll try to save me and die for me. Instead, she whispered, "I love you, Grandpa."

Win backed away, closing her eyes as flames caught her body, and within seconds, she was gone. In the last moment, before she left that plane, as the fire blazed in the wolf's eyes, she thought Wolfric hadn't given her a gift. He'd given her a curse.

TWENTY-TWO

Euelea ran, her lungs full of icy air. A low vine caught her ankle, and with a slap, she landed face down in the mud. Breathing hard, she got up. There was no other choice.

She ran and ran, through densely packed trees, her bare feet tore open, the sting almost unbearable. Sweat dripped down her back.

Don't stop, don't stop. A voice echoed in her head, her inner strength slowly waning. Adrenaline pushed her forward, she had to keep running.

Spencer was behind her. She didn't know how far back he was, but in his panther form he wouldn't take long to close the distance. Unless this was another little game he was playing. Cat and mouse. Hunter and hunted. An endless game of hide and seek. Euelea knew he'd be enjoying this. He would catch her, but she was going to make him work.

Pausing, she caught a tree, bent double as a stitch exploded under her ribs. Where was he now? She'd lost him in the market at Lincoln, when daylight hours were her savior. After breaking away at the river, she'd headed for people, homes, light, and noise. Anywhere he couldn't easily hide in the darkness. But as she'd wandered the busy market town of Lincoln, a shawl pulled around her shoulders, he'd found her in the crowd, and she'd fled.

Her stomach growled, knotted and acidic, having eaten nothing for two days. Fuelled with the fleeting gasp of hope, she kept running, even when she thought her knees might buckle.

Noises up ahead distracted her, and she slowed her pace. Attracted to the bubbling and crashing of water over rocks, she walked through a clearing, finding a narrow running brook. She walked alongside, climbing down the bank to drink from the stream. Coldwater flooded her system, and she gasped, her sudden thirst overwhelming. She walked the brook till it wound and twisted into a dense, dark wood.

Then she saw a cabin. A small wood-cladded cabin, nestled in a group of trees, right on the bend of the river. There was even a little bridge to cross to the other side. It was isolated and dark, and hope sparked in her chest.

Food. Euelea, propelled forward by hunger pangs, crept closer to the dusty, leaf-covered porch, and peered in through the filthy window. It was dark inside, but that didn't mean it was empty. The remnants of smoke lingered in the air, and around back, she heard the clucking of chickens in a pen. Someone lived here.

Keeping low, she tiptoed to the door, giving it a push with her fingertips. And to her surprise and elation, it swung inward. Darting her eyes behind, she scanned the woods. Nothing moved except trees in the wind. Maybe he had lost her trail? The silence was interrupted by the growl of her stomach, and she ducked inside, gently pulling the door after her. Why would they lock their doors? It was isolated.

Inside it was dark, and it smelled like the forest, like a group of men lived there. Muddy boots were thrown against the wall. Guns in racks lined the walls, and with a startled breath, she saw rows upon rows of hunting knives displayed like trophies. Swallowing, she wandered to a small kitchen, a stove tucked in the corner, its embers still glowing. Hot milk sat in a pan, steam drifting from its lid. Euelea didn't waste time processing where the owners were.

She grabbed the pan and tipped its contents down her neck, not caring if it scolded her lips. There was bread on the table, and it tasted stale and dry, but she chewed frantically and swallowed down a pang of nausea as it hit her empty stomach. Her eyes raked the room as she ate, she spotted a pretty floral apron hung behind the door and instantly felt sorry for the woman who had to live in a house full of unwashed men.

Spoiled fruit sat in a bowl on the table, and she forced it down her throat, gasping as a bitter tang exploded on her tongue. She choked, coughing seeds into her palm, but she was grateful to the woman who bought the delicate fruit bowl and kept it stocked.

"Who the hell are you?"

A voice boomed behind her, and with a loud clatter, she dropped the pan of milk. It dripped down the table leg and over her bare toes. Tremors shook her body as she spun, coming face to face with a hunter and a shotgun pointed directly at her head. Trembling, she held up her hands. "Please, don't shoot—I'm leaving, I swear."

"The hell you are!" Hidden in shadow, he peered at her over the top of the gun, and she caught a glint of white-blonde hair and glassy eyes. He pointed the gun at the chair. "Sit."

"I needed to eat," she begged, panic surging up her chest. She couldn't stay here. Spencer would trace her here in no time. She needed to keep moving. "If you let me go...."

"I said—sit." Despite the calm, deadly tone of his voice, the end of the barrel shook. Euelea edged into the empty chair, palms up in an open gesture of surrender. Within seconds he'd shakily lit several candles around the dim room, and her eyes flickered against the intrusion of light. Tearing off his hood, he dumped himself in the chair across from her and thrust a candle in her face.

"What's your name?"

"I...Euelea...Euelea Varga..."

"Where'd you come from?"

Words caught in her mouth, blinking rapidly as the light touched her irises, and she struggled to adjust. Peering across the flame, she could see him clearly. He was young, probably no more than eighteen or nineteen, with a thick crop of white-blonde hair and unwavering pale eyes. Were they green or blue? She couldn't tell, and it hardly mattered. A shadow of stubble crossed his jaw. "Are you on your own here?"

His gloved palm slapped the table so hard, she jerked. Then he sneered. "I'll ask the questions...." He waved the candle over her, and something in his expression faltered. Euelea wondered if he saw the blood matted in her hair, or the claw indentations on her neck. "What happened to you?"

"N-nothing."

He cocked a brow. "Don't look like nothing. Looks like someone beat the Jesus out of ya."

Euelea noticed the intensity of his gaze soften, his earlier bravado slipping the longer he looked at her. She wondered just how appalling and pathetic she must look. Like a poor mouse tortured by a cat.

"I need to leave—now." His gaze flickered at the urgency in her tone. "Someone is coming for me, and if you get in his way...."

"Did he do this to you?" The boy waved his hand over her form. "Who is he?"

"Please forget you saw me," she begged, her eyes wet and shining. "All I wanted was food."

She went to move, to try and slip out of the chair, but his hand on her shoulder forced her back. "I can't let you go. Not if I know someone is going to hurt you."

"You won't stop him."

The boy tapped the gun, now straddled on his lap. His grin was confident, almost arrogant. "I don't know many men that can stand up to this."

"He isn't like other men," she insisted. That was true, wasn't it? It was what kept her moving these last few hours. What she'd seen in his soul...the whispers in his head....

"Please!" She took his arm. "I need to go."

"I'm Jack." He ignored her pleas. "Jack Riley. My brothers aren't home. They won't be back till morning and my sister-in-law is with them. You can rest in her room."

"No!" She took his gloved hand and pressed hers to it. "That's so kind of you, Jack. But I'm putting you in terrible danger—he'll kill you. He won't even blink before he kills you."

Jack leaned back in his chair, a cocky smile playing on his lips. His front teeth were chipped, and his nose, which she guessed must once have been straight, looked as though it had been broken. Despite that, he was wholesome, handsome in a soft, kind way. He wasn't listening, which was infuriating. "Well, ma'am, you walked into my kitchen beaten sick. We're Rileys, and if you don't know our name, then you should. We're hunters. Do you think I'd let you leave looking like that?"

She'd guessed they were a hunting family, judging by the gun display and the distinct smell of unwashed men in the air. "It doesn't matter who you are."

He leaned on his knees. "This is what we do. Trust me."

"You aren't listening—a gun won't stop him. He's too fast."

Jack scratched at his scalp, shooting her with a dead-eyed glare. "What is he?"

Euelea let a caged breath escape her lips. "A monster."

He chuckled, revealing his chipped teeth. "Is that all? You should see some of the things we've caught over the years. I don't think we have a problem here."

Outside, the chickens whipped into a frenzy, squawking and making enough racket to make both jump to their feet. Whooping and screeching tore through the air, loud enough to wipe the smug expression off Jack's face. What came next sparked dread in Euelea's gut, making her slither to her feet and grip the table. The animals went silent, like a candle had been snuffed out.

She broke into a sweat. "Jack—he's here! Let me go now, or he'll kill you."

Euelea didn't want another dead man on her conscience. After what Spencer did to the farmer in the barn, she couldn't stand to have Jack's death on her conscience too. Elbowing him out of the way, she hurried into the dark corridor, but the boy was hot behind her. He pressed her against the wall in the dark and put his finger to his lips. "Don't move."

"I've got to leave, now!" she whispered. "He'll follow me, and you'll be safe."

"Too late for that. I closed the door after me when I came in."

Staring down the hall, her breath lodged as she spotted the front door wide open and swinging in the breeze. Jack's hand clutched hers in the dark, drawing the gun against his chest. "He's already inside."

TWENTY-THREE

Win opened her eyes, and every muscle complained, groaned, and twanged as she sat up. Grayson pulled her upright into his arms, and Win sagged against him. "Am I back? Did I screw anything up?"

His lips twitched into a smile, relief creasing the corners of his eyes. "You're back."

Rowan knelt beside him, pulling Win into a tight embrace, her face buried in Win's thick hair. Win hugged her, not sure she could tell her sister she'd seen their grandfather without dissolving into tears. Instead, she held her tighter.

"We've been here over an hour—we didn't think you'd come back," Grayson said.

"I'm okay," Win said in reply, noting the worry lines around Grayson's mouth. He looked awful, wrung out, and worried. It was a lie. No part of this was okay. "We need to get to the house."

"Win. You cannot do that again!" Rowan shifted to her bottom, ignoring the urgency in Win's voice. Grayson hauled Win to her feet. "I've never seen anything so awful. Please—there has to be another way."

Win leaned heavily on Grayson's arm as they trekked back through the forest. It was cold and dark; their breath fogged on the air, reminding her of the ghosts she didn't want to face.

The terrible, grim memory of what she'd seen flashed in her mind. "There isn't another way."

Rowan took her other arm. "Was it worth it?"

Had all the pain she'd endured been worth what she found out? Win saw her mother, young, happy, if only for a while. Watching Rowan play in the sand, sweet, innocent, unburdened with the heavy responsibility of caring for her family in the future. Holding her grandfather again. Win's eyes welled up.

"It was worth it," she said, as they reached the house, mentally preparing to face two people inside who knew how to keep more than one secret. "But our parents have a shit ton of explaining to do."

Rowan held her tight as they mounted the steps. Win looked at Grayson, and squeezed his hand.

"Maybe I should leave?" he suggested as they stepped into the back room, kicking off their muddy shoes. "This is family business."

"You are my family," Win said, ignoring his worry. "And this affects everyone." She glanced at Rowan. "You should call Evan—she needs to hear this too."

Rowan bit her lip anxiously as she dashed through the house. Drawn to the family room, the warmth of the fire beckoned. Win's chest tightened, and for a split second, she hoped. She imagined John Hickory. His feet slung over the arm of the couch, coffee in hand. Her throat swelled when she spotted her mother and father curled up on the couch instead.

Could I have warned him? Could I have changed anything? She swallowed her answers. This was the terrible truth of what Wolfric inflicted upon her, something he'd endured for centuries, and it was guilt that would forever gnaw at her conscience. The what-ifs. Ben glanced from the television, the glow of the screen lighting up his face, his smile soft when he spotted Win at the door. Alice dozed on him, she looked like a kid, knees up to her chest, snuggled under his arm.

"Win?" he said, then his smile dropped. Rowan, Grayson, and Evan crowded into the room behind her.

"What's this about, Win?" Evan asked, slipping into a chair, her lovely face creased with concern.

"I know—about the kidnapping when I was a baby." She waited for her father's response. Slowly Alice sat up, her features contorting in panic, and Ben held her shoulders. Win felt awful—she didn't want to inflict this on her mother.

"I know who took me and what happened that day. Why didn't you ever tell us?"

"How do you know any of this?" Ben fired. Win looked away, her fists balling, and caught Rowan's eye with a warning glance.

"It doesn't matter how I know. I do, and I need the truth."

Behind her, Rowan fell into a chair, her jaw slack. "Is this true? Someone took you?"

Win opened her mouth to answer, but Ben swooped in, standing in front of Alice like a protective shield. Alice sobbed into her hands. "That's enough, Win. We don't need to relive this again."

"But—this is important! It's why you left home." She peered around her father's body, locking eyes with her mother. "You sacrificed your own life...you must have known the risk you were taking leaving here. You ran away!"

"Of course we did!" Ben snapped. "We were happy here—we had a life. But he *hated* that. After what happened to Katie—Jake lost his mind. What he did to us...."

Win shrank, feeling Grayson's warmth behind her, but she tossed her head in confusion. "Jake...?"

"Stole you—he broke your mother's heart. Someone who he claimed to love. He betrayed us and made life so difficult for us both—we had no choice but to leave."

"What do you mean?" Rowan interjected.

Ben seized his hair in tufts as though he could pull it free. His voice choked with emotion, and Win could only guess how awful those moments must have been.

"Jake wrote letters...got me blacklisted from every bank in town. I couldn't afford to rent an apartment, so we were forced to move back in here with your grandparents with two kids. My name was mud everywhere. Alice lost her job at a nursery. He made us miserable...he got John arrested every chance he got—if he crossed Fraser borders. Not to mention the threats...."

"Threats?" Win balked.

"Gloria, your grandmother was constantly harassed. Horrible phone calls, the line going dead—classic nuisance stuff. There was only one family it could have been. He was vile, vindictive...he nearly destroyed us."

Alice stood, finding her voice as she moved around her husband. "I didn't see any other way forward. Ben couldn't find work. We left to get as far away as possible. Staying here, we'd be forever linked with that family. And you would never be safe. How could I stay knowing you'd end up running into them at school? After what he did—how could I trust it wouldn't happen again?"

Rowan choked. "Well—clearly, *that* didn't work out."

Win felt Rowan's ire boiling below the surface. In the end, it hadn't helped. Rowan returned to Cedar Wood when she was sixteen, but at that point, Ben was a single father and had no idea where to turn with his troubled teenager. John was the only option.

Ben was aghast. "We didn't know, Rowan. We had no idea what would happen once we moved to Boston—that your mother wouldn't make it. We were stuck living here...constantly watching our backs. We wanted to live and be happy."

The entire time her father had spoken, the blood had slowly drained from Win's face. Something was off here. Something didn't fit. Had Jake done those things? When she'd listened under the ledge, he was remorseful— ashamed. He wanted to move on, not torture his neighbors across the woods. Right now, judging by her father's expression, Win didn't dare push. Alice took his hand. "Ben..."

"Do you have any idea what he put us through?" He was worn, wrung out, reliving those moments in his head. "I died...a *thousand* times in the two hours you were gone. We were helpless, powerless to do anything. Our baby was gone, stolen right under our nose, and anything could have happened to you. Do you have any idea what a complete failure I felt? I wanted to die."

"Dad!" Rowan was on her feet and flung her arms around his neck.

Win couldn't speak, her mouth like cotton wool. Alice left Cedar Wood, knowing the risk she faced. No mother would undertake that lightly. The look in her mother's glassy eyes revealed the truth they believed, even if Win wasn't buying it. Saying nothing, she clasped Grayson's hand and backed out of the room, suffocated and needing space.

Upstairs, Grayson settled on the bed and pulled her into his arms. "You should sleep."

Win smiled at him weakly. "Not without you."

"I don't think I'll be allowed a sleepover after that. Do you?"

Knuckles wrapped lightly on wood, and Evan poked her head around the frame. "Can I come in?"

Win sat up, wedged between Grayson's legs, her back pressed against his chest. Evan crept in and sat on the edge of the bed with a gentle smile. She carefully pressed a hand on Win's thigh, and sparkles of violet light traveled out of her fingertips. The aches plaguing Win's muscles released, and she went heavy-lidded. "What was that?"

"You've been through hell—literally." Evan sat back, her expression somber and remorseful. "I remember Wolfric going through the same thing. It takes a lot out of you—the jumps."

"You could have said you were a daughter of a god, Evan. Or your family were the founders of a lost civilization." Win eyed her as she spoke, recalling the term Wolfric had used. Primus. The first to walk the earth.

Evan clicked her tongue. "He mentioned that, huh?"

"I mean, it's not like we wouldn't get it," Win said, and Evan hid a wry smile. "There was never a need to lie."

"Not many people would understand about my family—the things we were capable of. I only ever wanted to help, Win. To try and put right the things Vecula did." Evan let out a shaky sigh. "And now you've met my brother, you know how odd we really are."

Win chuckled, leaning on Grayson's shoulder, momentarily distracted as he shifted position behind her. "He isn't so bad. Grouchy—cryptic, which I'm used to. He was pretty cagey about what happens to him after he makes that last jump."

Evan sat back, folding her arms around her knee, her expression thoughtful and somber. "We don't know. It's been years since we spoke. We've actively avoided one another.."

This confused Win. There were plenty of times when she and Rowan didn't see eye to eye, and only recently they'd shared some pretty epic spats. But not ever seeing her again, or avoiding her was unthinkable. "Why? You're all each other has in the world."

Evan allowed a beat of silence to pass. "And that was true for centuries. I turned my eyes away, and forgave Vecula for the wrongs she caused. Wolfric was the only one who stood up to her, and he died for it. He sacrificed himself so we could run. And I was...scared. Scared she would leave me too, and I'd be cast out, alone. But in the end...I was."

"And you survived," Grayson finished.

"So our relationship is...fractured," Evan added. "We love one another, but we can cope without the other. Not all siblings are like this family, Win."

"I get that," Grayson said gruffly from behind. "I may be able to compete with Luke for the world's worst big brother. I had one too."

He tossed her a cynical grin, avoiding her gaze when she shifted to face him. Grayson didn't often speak of Henry, his older brother who'd died years ago. It struck Win how interwoven their fates were, four very different families, Hickorys, Frasers, Vargas, and Riley's, all with interconnecting puzzle pieces. All victims of what the elder generations inflicted upon the other. This generation had to be better, didn't it? They couldn't keep making the same mistakes over and over.

"Win, don't try anything for a few days," Evan warned. "Jumping drains the soul—don't be surprised if you have trouble phasing. You were burned, and over time it chips away at you."

Win nodded, making her smile as even and sincere as she could. There was no way she was going to be held back, not with so much at stake. Evan tilted her head, her expression doubtful as she lifted off the mattress. She toppled, falling sideways and went stark white. Grayson rose, catching her by the elbows. Evan let out a nervous laugh, trying to shake it off, but Win sat up in alarm.

"Evan?"

"It's nothing—I'm fine."

It wasn't nothing, her golden skin drained as she leaned heavily on Grayson's arm.

"You don't need to lie," Win admitted, taking Evan's cold hands. "I know—Spencer is hurting you. You remember."

Ghostly white, Evan attempted to steady herself without the use of Grayson as an anchor. "Then you know I can't tell you anything. All is as it has to be—for now."

When Win went to protest, Grayson warned her off, shaking his head. Evan left the room, assuring Win she was fine. After Grayson left, Win sank to her mattress, alone with her turbulent thoughts and lost with everything she'd learned today. She rubbed an ache at her temples.

One thing she was certain of, whatever truth her parents believed, was a lie. Jake hadn't stolen her. Olivia had. Win decided there was no way she would confront her parents again tonight, not after seeing her mother visibly wilt before her eyes.

Jake allowed them to believe this, even if it meant Alice leaving Cedar Wood. As much as Luke complained about his father, Win was convinced it was an act. Jake wasn't a bad man. He'd made some rotten choices, some appalling life decisions, and he should have cared for his first wife when she needed him. But bad...*evil*...it didn't add up.

It grated at her she still didn't know what happened to Katie Fraser. A part of Win knew she was desperately clutching at straws; that this could be nothing. But Mary showed her this. And it didn't feel like nothing. All the while, Evan was suffering and it weighed heavy.

Win groaned, pulling herself out of bed and heading for the bathroom. She poked her head over the banister. Downstairs her parents and Rowan were talking in hushed tones. The glow of the fire spilled into the hallway, and Win shuddered. The thought of going through that again...her hairs rose on her arms as if imagining the searing pain ahead. After washing, she scurried back down the corridor, passing Evan and Rowan's room, the door slightly ajar.

Win froze, her mouth dropping at what she saw. Inside the room, Evan was undressing for bed, pulling off her dress, revealing the smooth skin of her naked back. Win's chest seized, eyes unable to focus. Toward the base of Evan's spine were five long deep scars, perfectly healed as though time eroded them to skin-colored welts.

They were more than scratches. Whoever hurt Evan had claws.

TWENTY-FOUR

In the blink of an eye, Monday rolled around. Win trudged back into school, armed with new information, and burdened with memories of a time where she'd only been an infant, causing heaviness in her step.

Upon waking on Sunday morning, Ben abruptly whisked Alice off for a day out to clear their heads after the ordeal the day before. Win knew it was snippy and selfish if she complained. She couldn't stand to see her mother in any kind of turmoil. She'd only just gotten her back, and now they were avoiding her.

"Dad, please let me see Mom," Win pleaded the morning before they left. Ben avoided her gaze, packing up snacks, and bundling Alice into the car before wagging a finger in his daughter's face.

"She's had enough, Win. I don't know what you think you'll achieve by pushing her."

Win boiled inside, and willed down her temper, saying shortly, "How about the truth?"

Ben glared at her, exasperated. "Why do you keep on pushing? Don't you understand? I just got her home. We were making progress before...."

Win's eyes flew wide as he snapped his mouth shut. "Before I came back?"

Ben groaned, flung a coat over his arm, and headed for the car, where her mother waited, strapped into the front seat. "I didn't mean that. Win...some truths just need to stay buried."

In History class, Ella grabbed a seat next to her, and through a series of whispered communication behind hands and raised books, Win managed to recount most of her experience.

Ella listened, then after a long pause, she whispered, "Have you told, Luke?"

"No," Win hissed. "Are you crazy? How can I drop *that* into the conversation?"

Ella agreed. "He's been through a lot. This would hurt him...finding out he had a half-sister. It's so sad."

Ella's musing was the very thing that made Win's blood run cold, something she didn't like to imagine. It was linked to Spencer, and she couldn't shake off Olivia's hopeless cry. *There's something wrong with him...*

Had he been bad, even then? Win shuddered, remembering the pale scars down Evan's back. Someone had hurt Evan in the past, and it made Win gag to imagine what she could be going through. When Win questioned Rowan the next day, her sister avoided the subject. Win suspected Rowan was desperate to deal with this herself. Evan was quiet, tired, bordering on exhaustion. Rowan knew something was wrong, but in true Rowan fashion, she was shutting down.

"I have to try again," Win said as their teacher closed the door, signaling the start of the class. Ella nudged her, shaking her head.

"Use the flame? No way, Win. Evan said not to. You need to rest between jumps."

"You didn't see the marks on her back. I *have* to try again. I feel like this is all linked to Katie..."

"You don't *know* it's linked to Katie," Ella said behind her hands. "Though...your visions do tend to mean something."

"Exactly! I can't wait for this to come to me. Though...bursting into flames *really* isn't appealing."

Mr. Rainer paused at Win's desk, placing a note by her open textbook. "It's from the office," he said before strolling away to start the class. Win picked up the note, read it, and lifted her eyes skyward.

"Drivers Ed! Are you *kidding* me?"

Win leaned her forearms on the desk and rested her head. After the last week's events, she completely forgot her father signed her up. Her new instructor was due to arrive in her free period. Ella patted her arm in mock sympathy.

"You do suck at driving."

"But now?"

"Oh, and by the way, I finished the project for the school paper. Jake emailed me over some more information, and I cobbled together a report."

Since she'd returned to school, all of her teachers were keen to load Win with missed assignments, new books, and notes for her to catch up on. School was the furthest thing from her mind, despite the niggling worry she'd fail the next pop quiz.

Win whined into her hands. "Ella...I'm sorry!" She glanced at her friend hopefully. "Perhaps I can help submit it...lay it out for the paper?"

Ella clicked her tongue. "I did that already."

Win banged her forehead against the desktop. "I'm such a loser. You know I love you, right?"

"I know," she sighed. "It's a good thing Cole took some decent pictures too. We did kind of slack off. Oh, *oh!*" She grabbed Win's arm in excitement. "When I got home Saturday after the college tour—Jake sent over the shoes. So it was totally worth it."

"Isn't he just Mr. Wonderful?" Win had meant it with a generous dollop of sarcasm, but it seemed lost on her friend.

Ella smiled, far away and dreamy. "He is."

"You'd be better off with the younger one."

Ella scowled at the suggestion. "I don't think so. Luke is officially friend-zoned."

Win swallowed back a snort of disbelief. Ella might have friend-zoned Luke Fraser, but she could sense Luke pining. And she hadn't missed the forlorn gazes he threw Ella now and again. Win half wondered if this was her friend's plan, to torture him to death.

Mr. Rainier threw a stinging glance at them, and both girls shut up. Win tried to listen, but she was tired, her eyes scratchy and raw, and her trail of thought railroaded no matter how she focussed. She was also anxious about getting in a car with a stranger. Lunchtime came and went, and her new instructor arrived during free period in the parking lot.

Luke and Ella walked her to the lot, and they paused on the steps as the car rolled in. It was a small, light blue Volkswagen, and the door bumped open, followed by a large, pot-bellied man with thinning hair and sweat patches under his arms. Win's stomach flip-flopped as Luke slapped her shoulder, chuckling. "He looks ready for a heart attack—try not to push him over the edge."

"You are such a jerk."

Luke sniggered, even when Ella elbowed him in the ribs. "Have fun."

Win whimpered, climbed in the car and tried not to breathe as her instructor puffed coffee fumes in her face. A stressful, turbulent hour later, Win crawled the car into the lot, keenly aware it was jerking and juddering, and several students watched with interest. The instructor bellowed in fright as she pulled up at the curb, the smell of tires crunching on stone filling her nose. Shaking, she pulled on the handbrake and gave him a hopeful smile.

He was fuming. "We have a lot of work to do."

"I'm just nervous," Win tried to explain, but he scribbled something on his clipboard as she climbed miserably out of the car. Shoulders slumped, she grabbed her bag, humiliated as she crossed the lot. Sniffing the air, she lifted her chin, recognizing the spicy aftershave, and spotted Jake, perched on a brick wall, drinking coffee from a metal mug. He grinned wickedly as she approached, a key witness to her atrocious entrance.

"Well, *that* was embarrassing."

"I'm out of practice," she said. Jake cackled, tossing his eyes to the instructor in the distance, who was checking the hood of the car, running his palm over the paint. Win gritted her teeth, her hands were sweating.

"Did you damage the hood?" Jake asked.

"There may or may not have been a *slight* bump with a parked truck."

"Oh, Win!"

Win huffed, ignoring the mischievous twinkle in his eyes. He clearly loved taking every opportunity to tease her. "Bye, Jake."

He wiggled his gloved fingers as she waltzed away, chin lifted, avoiding the gazes of several classmates, laughing at her abysmal failure. She paused on the stone steps when she got a foot away.

A wicked idea sprung into her head. Eyes down, Jake scrolled through his phone, oblivious as she watched him. Why did she have to use the flame to learn the truth? Jake wasn't evil. Couldn't she appeal to the better nature she hoped lurked under all the sarcasm? She'd done it before.

Taking a breath, she went back, halting at his highly polished shoes. Surprised, he glanced up and smiled. "Yes?"

"Why are *you* here?"

"I had a meeting with the principal about some funding...." Jake narrowed his eyes at her. "Is that a problem?"

"No." She clapped her hands nervously, and his lips melted into a line, his curiosity piqued. He knew darn well Win wouldn't strike up a conversation with him for no reason.

"Don't you have class?"

"I have a free period," she lied. "I was getting lunch...but...I was hoping to go into town."

"So...you want me to give you a lift?"

Win nodded. "Do you mind?"

Perplexed and side-eyeing her warily, Jake waved her toward his Mercedes. "Sure." He unlocked the car with his keys. Without pausing to consider if this was a smart idea, she darted ahead, threw open the driver's door, and jumped in. It smelled leathery and expensive. Brazenly, she strapped in, sneaking a coy glance at him through the glass. His jaw hung in confusion, but he quickly caught onto her plan when she tossed him a pretty smile. Shaking his head, he knocked on the glass.

"Oh, no. *Forget* it."

"Please!" she begged, and waited for him to cross to the passenger's side. He slid in and threw her a death glare.

"Out—now!"

Jumping at him, she grabbed his wrist, shooting him with the most adorable, doe-eyed, dad-manipulating smile she could manage. "Teach me to drive—I suck. You saw it."

"Yes, I did!" He yanked his arm away, her charm clearly not working. "I want to live to a ripe old age, thank you very much."

Win pouted. "You said if I needed anything I could ask you."

Jake waved his hands in exasperation. "I meant money—or *literally* anything else. Can't you ask your boyfriend?"

Win shook her head. "He's too distracting."

Jake shook his head, appalled. "I didn't need to know that. What about your father?"

"He yells at me."

"Luke?"

"He makes fun of me." Win clicked her tongue.

Jake puffed, a red streak crossing his nose, like Luke when he was flustered. "Well...I guess...maybe...."

"Yes!" Win grabbed his arm again. "Can we try now?"

Jake laughed. "No, you're not driving this—I have something at home. Carla's old car is in the garage. You could drive it off a cliff for all I care."

Twenty minutes later, Jake rolled his third wife's Peugeot out into the courtyard, and with a clicker, the garage door closed behind it. With a weary sigh, Jake fired up the engine and waved her into the driver's side. Taking off his coat, he flung it in the back and then rolled up his sleeves. Win smirked.

"You must mean business if you're rolling up your sleeves."

Jake's expression soured, mouth downturned. "Why did you say that?"

Win was confused, more by the look on his face, as though he remembered something that bothered him. "I just...never mind...."

Careful, Win told herself. Only a night ago, her father said some awful things about him. Jake was the reason her family left town. *Vile, vindictive...* but looking at him, Win couldn't see any of those things.

He makes you like him. Luke's words echoed in her head. Shaking her shoulders, she threw him a bright smile, unsure how she was going to get any information out of him.

"Ready?" he said, more to himself. "Please don't kill me."

Carefully she rolled out of the Mercy gates and onto the main road, the steering wheel light under her hands. She swerved carelessly, distracted as he switched on the fan. Jake swore through gritted teeth and grabbed the wheel.

"Eyes on the road!"

After a few minutes of aimlessly trundling along, Jake clicked his tongue at the amount of traffic overtaking the small car, zooming past at speed. The roads were wet, sludgy, and gray. Win's fingers gripped the wheel, and she kept accidentally stamping on the brake too hard. Her cheeks went red hot. Jake let out a short laugh.

"Win...you drive like a ninety-year-old woman."

"I do *not*!"

Jake waved his hand at her driving position, knees curled around the seat, her chin jutted over the wheel. He burst out laughing, a surprisingly nice sound. "If you sit much closer, you'll be kissing the glass—pull over."

She did as she was told, compliant as he folded back her seat, adjusted the distance, and melded her into a better place for her spine. She nodded in appreciation. This was starting off better than she expected.

"That was your first problem—what are you bad at? Tell me."

"Everything... signaling, reversing into a space, driving into a space...parking."

Jake pinched the bridge of his nose.

"Parallel parking...emergency stops..."

Jake snorted and rubbed his temples. "Okay! How about just going forward?" Win nodded, and he waved his hand. "Then do that."

"Just drive?"

"Just drive—get used to it. You make me nervous. And that's bad because I rarely get nervous."

Win sucked in her ribs, passively agreeing and keeping her eyes fixed on the bleak road ahead. Silence lingered between them, and she knew she had to make this count. This couldn't be for nothing. She tapped her fingers on the wheel, nervous and shaky.

He'll see right through you...be careful...

"When was the last time you did get nervous?"

Jake balked at the question, giving her a long, hard look. For a moment, she didn't think he'd answer. Rolling off his gloves, he bit at his nail. "My wedding day."

Win grinned. "Oh really? Which one?"

"Ha!" He didn't seem to mind the joke. "All of them."

He rested his chin on his fist, staring out of the window. Win bit her lip, intent on keeping the conversation flowing, hopefully to her advantage.

"So, I have to thank you for something."

"What for?" He looked at her in surprise.

"Our motel bill," she said. "It was you who paid. I figured it out."

Staring out the window, his lip curled. "Well, aren't you a smarty pants."

"You didn't have to do that for Grayson."

He looked at her soberly. "What makes you think I did it for him? Or I did it at all?"

Win rolled her eyes. "No one else would have laid out that kind of money. And it doesn't matter why you did it, but I know you did. So...thank you."

Rain drops settled on the wipers. To her surprise, he didn't say anything, only tapped his fingers on the window frame. Win's words dried up, and she wished he wasn't so closed off. They drove in silence and the silence felt awkward. The way he stared at her profile every so often made her skin prick with sweat. This was futile, and she realized she had *no* idea how to talk to him. Jake was so completely opposite to her father, a coolness in his eyes, unreachable and aloof.

Win's attempt at conversation was going nowhere. Grinding her teeth, she realized she sucked at driving *and* interrogation. Her chest was damp, and she fanned herself, aware of the odd glances he was tossing her way. He made her turn around in a side street and bit his tongue as she bumped the curb. Jerking the car back and forth, they were soon on their way back toward Cedar Wood. He hadn't yelled at her yet, which was a bonus.

Win wasn't about to suffer this humiliation only to come away no better off. Tongue sandpaper dry, she frantically searched for *anything* to say, any conversation starter. But to her surprise, it was him who spoke first, leaving Win to wonder if he felt as awkward as her. "How was your trip to Boston College?"

Win exhaled in relief. "It was good—enlightening. You went there, didn't you?" She vaguely recalled Luke mentioning it.

Jake smiled wistfully, folding his arms. "I played football."

Win remembered finding his Polaroid photo in the attic over the summer. "Yeah—I bet you couldn't wait to leave this place behind."

Jake smirked. "Not really—do *you* want to leave this place behind?"

"I mean—" her voice faltered. "A college like Boston isn't on the cards for me. Even if things were different." She didn't want to admit her family could never afford it. "Luke might make it work."

Jake scoffed. "Win, you don't know that. You're smart, and I'm sure there would be a way you could manage the...." He struggled with his words as though he still didn't believe the family ties he'd inherited. "...the *challenges*. Luke might be able to afford to commute, but there's no guarantee he'd get in. Especially if he doesn't pull up his grades."

"He does okay!" Win argued. She was steering the flow of conversation, determined to box him in somehow. "With Ella's help."

"Luke's got a hell of a lot of distractions—and he never was the brightest. What with everything that's happened...."

Win's brow furrowed, her fingers tightening on the wheel. "You mean *my* family?"

Jake laughed. "I mean you."

"That's over," she protested, red-faced and dismayed once again he'd won the top hand, rerouting her train of thought and pushing her down an avenue she didn't want to broach, especially with him. "We talked things through."

"Win, you didn't see him after you left—he didn't leave his bedroom. He cried and listened to sad country music, over and over. Trust me, I was there!"

Win clenched at the implication, gut-wrenching guilt eating at her conscience. But she lifted her chin, suddenly aware of how she was going to manipulate this conversation.

"Maybe that was true—I missed him too. But we've talked, and I know he feels the same as me. And we're bonded now. We *have* to make it work. Our friendship is too important and he knows that."

"Does he?"

"Yes!" She was exasperated. "You don't believe in platonic friendship?"

Jake's smile slipped, his eyes glazing over. "It's a bit different if it's one-sided."

"But it's not!" Win spluttered. She found him so irritating, as though he was determined to dig around with her guilt and make her as uncomfortable as possible. "We chose to make things work. He's more grown-up than you give him credit for—we're blood buddies now!"

Jake laughed, scratching at his jaw. "Yes, you certainly are."

"Didn't you ever have a best friend?" She cocked a brow in his direction. "Like my mother, for example?"

Jake snapped his eyes, staring at her for a long time. "Is that what she told you?"

Taking a juddering breath, Win tried to keep her eyes on the road. "I know you were kids together...I know you hurt her."

Jake stared at her profile, grinding his teeth, and she panicked. She'd been too obvious, too fast, but if she attempted to side approach the subject, he'd find a way to divert her. Maybe it was best to get to the point.

He glared at her. "Where are you going with this?"

Win started to bake under her sweater. God, where *was* she going? She had to make this work. Rain drizzled from the sky, and he leaned across and turned on the wipers.

"I'm not going anywhere," she lied.

He folded his arms. "You're baiting me, Win. I can tell. Why?"

Her fingers trembled. "I'm not."

Without warning, he grabbed the wheel and threw the car over to an embankment. A car honked as it sped past, and Win broke hard, her knee jarring. Jake twisted toward her, yanking on the handbrake. "What is this about?"

Win pressed hard against the door, face to face with a man she'd grossly underestimated. Leaning close, blue eyes flashing with anger, he looked as dangerous as he was handsome. Win choked out her words, "Nothing—I swear!"

"You're a liar!" He wagged a finger in her face. "And I might be many things—but a liar isn't one of them. What do you want to know?"

"I don't want to know anything...."

Jake sneered. "So what is this? Tell me the truth!"

He wasn't a liar? Finding her voice, she straightened. "That's hilarious coming from you. You've never told the truth about Luke's mother."

Jake smiled nastily. "There's lying, and there's avoiding."

"You lied about Spencer—you knew he was responsible for those killings, and yet you let us take the fall!"

"Again—*avoiding*. No one outright asked me—no one comes to me unless they *need* me, Win."

"You've lied about knowing my mother—about being her friend. You've *omitted* to tell the truth about anything. Why would anyone come to you? You aren't exactly approachable."

"You don't know what you're talking about."

Win's cheeks fired up, aware the windows were steaming up. The car rocked as cars rushed past. He was angry; she'd plucked a nerve, but undeterred, she finally had her in and wasn't about to back down. "When you caught me trespassing—you *knew* Spencer was out there hiding—killing innocent people. You could have warned us."

He laughed, raking his hands through his thick black hair, growing impatient. "Could I? Would you have welcomed me? You've seen how your father reacts to me."

Win fought back. "Only because you've destroyed the friendship you once had!"

"What the hell are you talking about?"

"Spencer hurt Cole—*that* was on you. You knew and could've stopped him. You must feel guilty because you paid for all his bills. I *know* you feel guilt."

"Win..."

"You let Luke put himself through that ridiculous emancipation. Do you know what he had to give up to make that work? How he worked and struggled alone. He did it because he actually thought he'd be better off—you didn't give a crap about him or his welfare!"

Jake bared his teeth. "Win, enough!" But she wasn't backing down now, like a cat and a mouse. It was she who cornered him, fighting back with as much venom as she could summon up. Her eyes welled with frustrated tears.

"My mother suffered because of you...."

His eyes went black. Like a shark about to hit its prey, he reared back. "Win...."

"She did..." Win spat. "They left town because you forced her. We lost ten years of life with her—because of your jealousy. You destroyed their lives!"

Jake deflated, aghast at the accusations thrown in his direction. It was him who underestimated her. On a roll, and with a fire in her gut, Win couldn't back down. She was wild-eyed and near hysteria.

"Jake, don't you get it? I can't let Spencer hurt anyone else. I can't let him come back and destroy what's left of my family. You knew Spencer was bad. You chose him over Luke—over Oliva and Rose. Again and again, you've protected him. Olivia knew—she warned you!"

The tan from his skin went gray, and Win made a killing blow.

"I *know!* I know Olivia took me."

"Win stop..."

"I know about Katie!"

The air went oddly still, they locked eyes, and all the fight seemed to drain out of him, the twinkle in his eye, the smirk on his lips, all died on the mention of her name. It floated in the air between them like a ghost.

He deadened his expression, all warmth, and humility gone. "Get *out* of my car."

A part of her knew she'd wounded him, hurt him deeply, more than just his ego. She'd struck at his heart. But she shook her head resigned, knowing she'd do it again. "Please tell me what happened so I can understand. I don't know how to fight him—and a fight is coming."

"*Fight* him? He's gone, Win!"

When a beat of silence passed, she grabbed his arm, and he tried to snatch it away. "You're wrong. Spencer will find a way back. He's coming to kill me, Jake. He'll kill me and then everyone I love. Don't let my death be on your conscience too."

Tears escaped from her lashes, and her heart hollowed out, unable to believe she could hurt him anymore. The words lingered there, like a kick to the soul, and she hated herself for stooping so abysmally low. Jake leaned closer, his face inches from hers. She made no attempt to draw away. "Get *out*."

Hand fumbling for the handle, she fell out of the car and hit the asphalt. Rain splattered from above, and she fell in the path of a truck. It honked the horn, and Win ran, her feet slipping on the wet ground as she dashed into the forest. She heard him calling after her, his voice in the breeze, but she was too enraged to care. Why had she even bothered? Why had she tried to appeal to his better nature?

Seconds later, he was chasing her, soaked in seconds, his shirt sticking to his skin. He ran. "Win—don't run!" he yelled. "I'm sorry!"

Panic exploded in her chest, her muscles firing up as she sped away, leaving him to stand in the rain, gaping.

Jake had *no* better nature. Stony, cold and bitter, that was all he was, with a wall constructed so high you'd need an army to tear it down. Aimlessly she ran, angry, boiling with rage. So close...she kept edging so close only to fall flat on her face.

Evan's scars...What was happening to those she loved? What was the point of this stupid curse—of being *chosen*, better, powerful if she couldn't do a damn thing when it mattered?

Rain fell in sheets, ice cold against her skin, and darting into a clearing, she stopped, breathless and fatigued. This wasn't over. She couldn't allow this to be over.

Into the wind, she screamed, "K'a'ajale."

TWENTY-FIVE

Waking in a ball of searing flames, Win screamed and rolled in damp grass, smacking at her arms and legs until the flames died. Gasping, choking, she wailed as a wash of hot lava enfolded her limbs and she waited for the tingling sting to subside.

Could this ever be something she would get used to? Clutching her throat and sucking in clean air, she shuddered, her skin sensitive like she'd stepped in a boiling bath. Opening her eyes, she was greeted by dazzling sunshine and threw her arm across her face.

Sitting up, she found she was in the forest, but it was shadowy here, unfamiliar—except she recognized that tree.

The oak twisted and bent loomed above her. Win stood shakily and, with trembling fingers, touched the trunk.

Okay...so I'm here again...but I don't know when. The pads of her fingers stroked the great tree. Win scratched at her head, circling the base of the massive tree, here for centuries, and tracking the same path she'd seen Mary walk in her vision. A tree like this didn't grow in one hundred years—even five hundred. It was older than the town—maybe as old as Evan and Wolfric.

Win froze, putting her hand on the bark. Vibrations of an invisible current tickled the palm of her hand.

She swallowed and jerked her hand away, staring up at the tangled mass of limb-like branches clawing their way skyward. Panting, she placed her hand back—there—a current. It was only faint, but she could feel its power, like the stone, gentle pulsations tingling up her arm. Dropping to her knees, she ran both hands down the tree, near the base where its roots burrowed deep underground.

Why am I here? What do you want me to see?

Win closed her eyes, the vibrations growing stronger the nearer to the ground she got.

How can this help me stop Spencer?

Opening her eyes, she touched the entangled roots. *The earth...underground...the tunnel.*

On her feet, Win scouted for the door that, in the future, Luke fell through on the night they met in the woods. She crawled on her hands and knees, raking her fingers through the long grass. It had to be hidden here somewhere. Kneeling, she sniffed the dirt, running her fingers through leaves, when she caught her thumb on something sharp. Wincing, she sucked up blood from a tiny graze on her thumb and brushed aside dirt and debris, spotting a wooden trap door.

"Yes!" she cried, tossing aside branches and soil. It was well hidden, untouched for years, and grass and moss made the door home. Using her nails, she dug, like a raccoon burrowing through trash, until she could slide her fingers under the door. Her skin split on rough wood. She snarled and used her biceps to prise the door open. With a crunch, she yanked it free.

Wiping sweat off her neck, Win stared into the hollow, open mouth of the door, and her nerves kicked in.

Now you have to go down there.

Taking a breath, she launched herself down the steps. Clutching the ladder, she headed feet first into pitch black. Shivering, she rubbed her arms, standing at the base and looking up into the dazzling sunlight. It was chest achingly narrow in the cavern. A breeze rustled her hair she eased her way blindly through the dark. Seconds later, her night vision exploded, irises focussing on every vine coating the tunnel wall. Reminded of the night of the bonfire, Win fought back nerves.

Stumbling, Win cried out as she lost her footing, the walls on either side opening up, as she stepped into a narrow room. On the back of the wall, she spotted the exposed roots of the oak, which she had no doubt was right above her head. The air was damp and claggy, the taste of soil settled on her tongue. Using the roots as a guide she followed them as the vines curled into the earth. This was the soul of the tree, its heart, still alive and thriving centuries later.

Win froze as Wolfric's voice popped into her head.

We aren't the roots of the tree...we're the seed it was born from.

Win tripped on a root, blinking in the dark. Her eyes found a shape hidden in the shadows. Slowly her vision adjusted. Her mouth dropped, but her brain refused to process what she saw.

A skeleton lay at the matted base of the oak, entwined in the roots of the tree as though it were bound by nature, the roots curling around the bone, capturing it in a macabre embrace. Its jaw hung open, and even in death, it looked as though it were screaming.

Win hit the air, gasping as she crawled out of the hole. Bile rushed up her gullet, and without warning, she vomited into the grass. Dizzy and blinded by the sunlight, she spat out saliva. "Shit!" She squeezed her eyes shut.

Win didn't wait for her hands to stop trembling, a wash of terror rushed through her as she covered up the hole, fitting the trap door snuggly in place. She tossed it over with dirt, rocks, and branches. Sagging, she fell to her knees and sobbed, unable to shake the image of what she'd seen. *It's been here all the time, bound in the oak...*

Panting, she shuffled to her feet, wiping her mouth on her sleeve. She didn't have time to think or ponder on who the skeleton once belonged to.

Feet were headed toward her. Darting her head left and right, she paused to listen...not one but two sets of feet were coming right at her from two different directions. Maybe this was what she was really here for? She fled into the undergrowth, scrambling under a thorn bush, settling on her haunches. She waited, and after a while, she sniffed the air, smelling spicy cologne, pepper, and cinnamon. It was Jake.

Win ducked closer to the ground, praying he wouldn't spot her. Win peered through the brambles as he appeared in the sunlight. This must be at least ten years ago, perhaps more. He looked younger, his hair slightly long, and unkempt, but he was wearing a shirt with the sleeves rolled up and jeans. He leaned against the oak, biting his nails impatiently.

Jake was waiting for someone. Suddenly he shifted, and stood straight as the person he was meeting wandered through into the clearing from the opposite direction. Win hoped she'd covered the hole well enough. As Alice walked closer, Jake looked nervous and edgy, arms crossed over his chest. She was wearing her hair long, and a floral dress flapped about her feet.

"Thank you...thank you for coming to see me." His voice was strange. She'd not heard him sound like that before. Vulnerable.

Alice stopped about a foot in front of him, arms folded. "Say what you have to say, Jake," she said. Although her back was turned, and she couldn't see her mother's face, her voice was muffled and thick. Like she'd been crying. "Ben is packing the car. We leave tomorrow."

"I'm so sorry," he said, and she let out a short laugh as though she'd braced herself for a confession or more from him.

"Is that it? *Sorry?*"

"I can't change what happened."

"You could have stopped—anytime."

She let a beat pass, and Win wished she could see her mother's face. She could imagine the tension in her expression, her voice was strained enough. Tired and defeated.

"Alice...."

"The phone calls—they frightened my mother. How could you do that to her, Jake? How twisted *are* you?"

Remorse was etched into the lines around his eyes, and Win strained her ears, impatient and frustrated. Wasn't this the moment he confessed he didn't do any of those things? She waited. But Jake kicked away from the oak with his shoe. "I know."

Win frowned. The prickling sensation on her arms told her this was a lie. Why was he lying? Why was he protecting Olivia?

"I can't forgive you...not after Win. How could you do that to *me*?"

Alice covered her face, and Win's eyes welled up, her mother's anguish twisting a knife in her heart. He scratched the back of his neck, awkward and shy, not sure what to do. Win guessed her mother would smack him in the mouth if he dared touch her. Jake drew closer. "Alice, please...listen to me...I need you to listen to me."

"I'm listening," she said, not pushing him away. Win's throat tightened. This was so raw, adult, and private. He was vulnerable, open, and Win thought he'd be mortified if he ever found out she'd seen this. She felt like a voyeur being here, watching. But like a car crash, she couldn't look away.

This was why she was here. Jake stared at her imploringly. "I don't think it's safe here—for Rose."

What?

"What?" Alice pushed at his shoulders, and he sagged back on his heels. *"Why?"*

"I think something is wrong with Spencer."

Yes! Win nearly whooped aloud. Finally, the truth was rising to the surface.

Alice stalked, and paced the grass back and forth. "What on earth are you talking about?" Suddenly she stopped, throwing her head right in Win's direction, as if sensing her there, like the day at the park. Narrowing her eyes, she peered into the bush. Win stifled a cry and flattened to the ground. Alice looked away.

"Alice...."

"You accused my father of trespassing—had him locked in Lincoln jail. You got Ben fired from his last job....I've lost everything because of you."

It wasn't his fault. It was blindingly clear. Win wanted to catapult from the bushes and sing it out loud, and she couldn't suppress the relief she felt. Jake didn't do those things. She felt it. So why was he lying? Who was he shielding? *Say it*, Win begged silently. *Tell her it was Olivia. You never wanted to hurt her.* But the words never came.

"Alice...something is wrong with Spencer—no, listen to me!" He caught her by the shoulders when she went to stalk away. Roughly she pulled out of his grip. "Olivia knows...we both do...he isn't like other boys."

"What do you mean?"

"I don't know...I...have this awful feeling...he's wrong. And I know this sounds insane...but Rose....It's like he *hates* her."

Rose? What happened to Rose?

"Don't!" Alice yelled, holding up a finger to silence him. Passively he stared at her, pleading with his eyes, broken. Not like the Jake she knew. "Don't you dare say another word! What the hell is wrong with you? He's a sweet little boy. How dare you even come to me with this after you took my baby? You're sick, Jake, sick to the soul. And to think I loved you once—you were everything to me, my best friend."

His face contorted with thick tears. "Alice....please. I need to know if this is because of the curse?"

Alice froze on the spot, and Win strained her head out of the bush. "Oh my god...you blame me?"

"I don't! But you can hardly blame me for thinking it. What with our history...."

Alice laughed, the crazy laugh that came from months of stress and anguish. "You do. You blame us."

Jake stopped her relentless motion by grabbing her shoulders. "I need to know if it's because of the curse...my mother was Therian, Alice. And Spencer is...I don't know what to do."

"I'm not listening to another word you have to say. I'm going, Jake. Ben and I are leaving and taking our children so we can live in peace and be free of your obsession."

Jake dropped to his knees, grabbing the hem of her dress. "Alice. If he turns...I don't know what to do. He's so different. I can't describe it. He scares Rose...he scares me."

Alice stared down at him, lifting her chin. "Do I scare you? You've known me since we were eleven years old. Have I ever scared you? What I am...has that ever scared you?"

He shook his head brokenly. "No."

"Then why would you think this has anything to do with the curse?"

He spat, "Because...the curse, it's rooted in darkness. That's where it comes from—death, blood, evil."

"Maybe you should look inward." With a hard jerk, she yanked her dress out of his hands. "Whatever darkness that boy has...it has nothing to do with my family."

Win's watched as her mother paused by the oak, fingering the bark like it held memories within. While he was still on his knees, Alice touched his shoulder with a trembling hand.

"I'm sorry for Katie...what you and Olivia went through breaks my heart. I can only imagine what it's done to you...but what *you've* done to my family and me...is unforgivable. Goodbye, Jake."

Alice stalked away, the sun on her back. Jake lifted his head and moaned, a sound Win had never heard erupt from a fully grown man. It was pain, deep and unearthly. She cried, pressing her hand over her mouth.

Alice was wrong. She hadn't listened—she didn't even want to listen. How could she not see the truth? Had he broken her that much?

An itch spread across Win's neck, deep, hot, and she rolled her shoulders. But when she looked down, she saw her palms alight. "Oh...crap!"

The fire spread all over, engulfing her before she had time to shriek. Rolling around in the bush, she spotted Jake getting to his feet, wiping his eyes as he peered into the dense wood. "Is someone there?"

Win let out a shrill scream, loud enough to send birds rocketing out of the trees. Spotting the blaze, Jake ran towards her hiding place. "Who's there?"

Win rolled, half running, half stumbling, a blazing, human ball of fire. She closed her eyes and let it pull her back through time, vanishing into smoke at Jake's feet.

TWENTY-SIX

Jack pressed Euelea into the wall with his forearm. Only the soft rise and fall of their breathing could be heard in the dark. "Stay behind me."

She grabbed a fistful of his shirt and tugged him through an open door behind her. Roughly he caught his breath, flattened to the wall with the palm of her hand. Euelea's hand shone with bright violet light. Shuddering, his eyes met hers. "What are you?"

"You don't want to know."

"I can help you."

Groaning, she shook her head. "You'll get yourself killed, Jack. And...you're good. You don't deserve this mess I've landed you in. *Please* stay hidden. I'm going to draw him away."

Ahead, the door swung in the wind, and somewhere in the dark, Spencer waited. With a final stay-put motion with her hand, she pressed her finger to her lips and pleaded with her eyes for him to stay fixed. Drawing in her ribs, she forced away terror, stepping on silent feet into the long, dark corridor.

Her breath juddered as she took a step, sweat beaded on her brow one at a time. She had to get through the door and lead him away from the cabin, away from the boy who would get himself killed. Euelea didn't want another death on her conscience. Wasn't it bad enough what she and Vecula did to Joseph Hickory? Wasn't it enough his daughter, Vivienne, died in a jail cell, alone and frightened, frozen to death with the threat of a public hanging bearing down on her?

And all those souls who came before—murdered in Vecula's name, while she stood by and enabled her sister's reign of horror, doing nothing, not helpless or unable. She chose not to help. She decided to look away, thinking if Vecula got what she wanted, maybe she'd stop or toe the line. It stopped with Jack. It had to. Even if it meant Spencer caught her.

One foot in front of the other, she neared the door. Her foot touched the frame of the door, so close to freedom. Breath tickled her neck, and her shoulders stiffened.

Spencer peeled out of the dark, knocking the air from her lungs as he hit her from the left. She staggered and crashed into the wall, her skull thudding on wood, and for a second, her vision whited. Claws scraped the flesh of her neck as he hauled her up by her throat.

"You aren't going to kiss and run this time," Spencer snarled in her face. She gasped, his teeth inches from her temple while his clawed fingers dug into her ribs. She whimpered but closed her eyes, summoning her strength. Balls of violet light shot from her palms, hitting him squarely in the chest. Spencer flew back against the wall opposite, sending picture frames crashing to the ground. It bought her seconds, and she was through the door.

But he was faster. His screech filled her ears as she ducked left and right in a frantic bid to outrun him. Hidden in the shadows Jack Riley waited and she needed to draw Spencer away .

A gunshot broke the silence and sent birds rocketing from the trees. Euelea glanced up, heaving, when she spotted Jack on the porch. "Euelea run!" he yelled, cocking the barrel and pointing it directly at Spencer.

"Jack...no!" she cried. Stupid boy, why hadn't he listened? Spencer halted in the dirt, his long coat flying behind as he whirled in Jack's direction with a new, infused interest.

"What is about you, Evan? You've really nailed the damsel in distress act," he muttered, wiping spit off his chin as he doubled back with frightening velocity in Jack's direction.

"No! Leave him alone!" Euelea threw another fireball of light, hitting Spencer's broad, muscular back. It knocked him off course, but he pounded the dirt. Jack's expression went from grim determination to horror in seconds once he spotted what he'd shot at. Once he saw the monster straight out of a nightmare hurtling in his direction.

Spencer barrelled into him, knocking Jack off his feet, and he landed with a crack. There was a shrill scream, and wrenching of muscle as Spencer dislodged Jack's shoulder from his socket, wrestling the gun away with ease. Claws splayed, Spencer angled to lunge, to deal Jack's death blow, but she threw herself between them.

"Spencer, please stop!" she begged, her face a mess of snot and tears. "I'll come with you now. I'll do anything you want. Don't hurt him. Don't hurt anyone else for me."

Breath heaving, Spencer staggered back, grinning cockily. Under her, Jack writhed in pain, his skin waxy pale and his lips gray. "Run...please..."

Spencer watched with interest as she hovered over Jack, quickly assessing his injury. "Let me help him," she said, appealing to whatever humanity dwindled under the fur. "And I'll come with you. I won't try to run."

Digging his hands in his pockets, Spencer tossed Jack a cruel smile. "Be my guest."

Sweat trickled down Jack's brow as she eased him up, shifting to her knees beside him. The bone in his shoulder protruded at a grotesque angle, and Euelea straightened his forearm as he wheezed in agony. With a sickening crunch, she angled his arm across his chest, pushed hard, and the bone slipped into the joint. Jack went white with pain, he collapsed, panting in shock. Euelea stroked his brow and placed a hand on his shoulder, closing her eyes as warm, violet light seeped from her palms. Jack stared up at her, awe and admiration creasing his features. "What will happen to you if you go with him?"

"Sleep." She stroked her fingers over the ridge of his nose. "I'm so sorry you got dragged into this."

Jack resisted the pull but wavered as sleep slackened his jaw, his head sagging on the ground.

Straightening her shoulders, she stood and faced Spencer. "Let's go."

Euelea glanced over her shoulder, hating to leave the poor boy sprawled on the porch steps for his brothers to find. She followed Spencer into the woods, and they silently walked for minutes. He watched her cagily from the corner of his eye, assessing her step, waiting for her to bolt. Part of her knew he wanted her to run, so he could play.

"Aren't we going to talk about the kiss we shared?" He was teasing, but something shimmered below the surface, hatred boiled, and she sensed the humiliation in his chest. She'd made a fool of him. For one brief moment, she'd beaten him, played at his own game, and he was stung.

She stopped against a tree, and in the dark, he was backed by moonlight and looked even more like something from a child's fairy tale. "There is nothing to talk about."

He stepped closer. "Maybe I've changed my mind?"

Prickles of anxiety washed her palms. "About what?"

He shrugged. "About everything—maybe I should keep you around a little longer? Have a taste of what Rowan loves about you."

She swallowed hard. "You're sick."

Her back pressed against the tree, he closed the gap, grasping a fist full of her hair and yanking it, so she had no choice but to look up at him, the pale column of her neck exposed. "I might be sick—maybe we belong together? After everything you've done, you're no better than me. No more high and mighty. Maybe I'm a little hurt you left me knocked out cold?"

Seething, she brought her knee between his legs hard, and it connected with the right spot to make his eyes fling wide. It bought her seconds to move. Two hands caught her legs, and she was face down in the leaves. Sobbing, she brought up her hands to protect her face, but his fist landed in her ribs, and with a crack, she felt one spring and break. A shrill cry escaped her mouth as he turned her over, straddling her hips with his legs.

"You promised me, Evan. No more running!"

Euelea threw him a crazed grin, anything to wipe the look of victory off his face. "You won't get what you really want."

He snarled. "And why is that?"

"You...can't open the door...*idiot.*"

It took a few seconds of blinking for the truth to settle and the cold realization all he'd done was for nothing, before he spat, "What?"

Euelea laughed, the kind of strained, crazy cackle born of fatigue and fear. She'd revealed the truth, the very reason she was still breathing, but she didn't care. "Neither you nor I can open the door. We need blood. *Cursed* blood. Your plan won't work."

He slapped her hard, but she laughed through blood-stained teeth. "If we can't open it this side...then we'll have to make sure Win comes to us, won't we, Evan?"

Her blood froze, and the laugh died on her lips.

It wasn't her real name, and he was confused, and she wondered fleetingly if he was as exhausted as she. Wildly they battled, arms and legs flailing till he pinned her with his hands and gaze. "Stop fighting me! You won't win this."

"Why?" she spat, tears rolling down her temples. "Why are you doing this? Who is it you need to hurt so badly?"

"I have to end the line." She gripped his shoulders, his face inches from hers. His lips pulled into a grimace, revealing bloodied teeth, and a copper tang sailed under her nose.

"End the line?"

"It has to end—then this nightmare will be over."

Clenching his collar, she reached out, touching his temples with her hands. Shaking, blood drained from her fingers. His thoughts were chaotic, jumbled. The whispers...he didn't believe his words. It was something he'd been told, brainwashed for years until he didn't even know what to think.

"Why?" she asked again. "Why do you need to end the line?"

Saliva gathered on the tips of his fangs. "It'll make *this* all go away."

"What? What will go away?"

"It'll make her go away—she'll leave."

Startled by his admission, Spencer drew away, weight lifting from her hips as he slid to the grass. Trembling, he drew up his knees, his face sweaty and shining under the moon's light. Euelea lifted to her elbows, carefully easing into a sitting position.

With increasing bravery, she crawled on her knees toward him, stopping at his feet, and let her hand trail to his head. She closed her eyes and saw only black. Something or someone shared this space, his head used as a guest house. She could sense black swirls of malice and hatred encircling the beating organ in his chest. "Who is this? Who are you hiding in there?"

His eyes flew open and reflexively caught her wrist. "Too far, witch."

"You're protecting someone...your heart doesn't belong to you...your soul...is black...empty."

A cry left her mouth. Pain tore through her arm as he yanked her to the ground, shaking her so hard her vision whited, and her teeth clashed. When he dropped her, she fell limp, stars clouding her eyes. Euelea opened her eyes at the precise moment he struck her ribs with his boot, the blunt force sending a scream of anguish through her clenched teeth.

She rolled to her side, drawing up her knees, pain slicing through her torso. Something snapped in her ribcage. Spencer drew breath and hit her again. "Now, let her come. Think we've given her a pretty good incentive."

On her belly, she crawled, nails scraping the dirt. She quivered and shook, uselessly dodging his blows as he struck her repeatedly. A spark of hope died. Rowan's name left her mouth and she went quiet.

TWENTY-SEVEN

Rain fell in sheets, dousing the flames as she arrived right back where she left, in the forest near the roadside.

Numb, her hair flattened to her scalp, Win didn't know where to turn first. As she jogged into town, cars raced alongside. She hoped Jake would've gone straight home after their argument.

Win bent double, panting, her mind in free fall as she tried to process all she'd learned in that short hour. The body under the oak, alone, was enough.

She picked up speed, running straight past the turn for Hickory house. She ran for Mercy, cutting through the woods, arriving at the imposing iron gates. Instead of ringing the buzzer, she ran around back. Why change the habit of a lifetime?

This was it. She was here. It was the final push, and Jake wasn't going to wriggle out of her grip this time.

Ducking under overgrown vines, she snuck around to the old, disused servants entrance. The door was unlocked and creaked open. Icy water dripped from her clothes as she wandered the stone hallway, leaving a wet muddy trail in her wake. She pushed open a door, warmth greeting her from Jake's end of the house. He was here. Following his scent, she tracked into the family room, kicking off her ruined shoes and leaving footprints behind her as she trudged over the immaculate cream carpet.

Jake was sitting at the fireside, a full whiskey tumbler in his fingers, staring into the flames. As she hovered in the door, he spotted her and his face cracked in relief. Win thought she must look like a bedraggled mess.

"Oh, thank god," he cried, instantly off the couch and stalking toward her. "I didn't know what happened—you ran so fast."

Before he could push her away, Win threw her arms around him. Emotion bubbled up in her chest.

"I believe you," she said, holding him tight. "I believe you, Jake."

Win wondered when someone last hugged and squeezed him hard because they loved and needed him. Utterly lost at what to do with his hands, he settled for awkwardly patting her shoulder.

She pulled away. "I know—everything."

His brow furrowed. "Know what?"

"I know why you sent Rose away...and in the end, you believed Olivia. I know you took the fall for everything she did...everything she did to my Mom and Dad."

Shakily, he pulled out of her arms and slid back to the couch, grabbing the whiskey tumbler. "How can you know that?"

She dropped beside him, wondering if she should hold his hand, but he looked too wired, already rattled by the unexpected hug. "Let's just say...I have a little gift."

Jake snorted. "Don't you have enough *gifts*?"

She didn't have time for his quips. "I've seen the past, Jake. Olivia was the one who took me as a baby."

Jake blinked back tears in his eyes and settled his glass on the glass tabletop. "After we lost Katie, Olivia went out of her mind. We both did. Alice had just given birth to this perfect baby girl—you." He smiled, but it didn't reach his eyes. "And she...couldn't handle it. Jealously tore her apart, my friend-ship with your mother made it worse. We knew one another when...God, we were so young."

"But you let Alice go? You let her leave town thinking all those things she did...were because of you?"

Jake took both of her hands. "Win, listen to me. I didn't know what would happen when she left. If I had any idea of what would become of Alice...."

"I know!" she insisted, willing him to believe. The room was hot, the crackling fire was comforting, and Win was wet and dripping. The heat licking from the hearth warmed her skin.

"Why have you pushed everyone away?" she asked and got her answer in the depths of his stormy eyes.

"It was easier to let her go. Olivia was intent on destroying your parents—she was wracked with jealousy. When Olivia died in the crash, the one that killed your Grandma, Spencer came home to live with Luke and me. And that's when I truly knew what he was capable of. Sometimes I convinced myself I imagined things—that I was crazy—but..."

"I believe you," Win said. "Can you talk about Katie?"

Grey tinged his complexion, memory settling in the creases around his eyes. Thinking about Katie aged him. "I never got to hold her. It was over before it began. But for nine months—I had a daughter."

Win trembled, listening. "What happened to her?"

"Olivia and I were already divorced when she got pregnant with Katie...but we started things up again. It was an accident, but a happy one." He dared a peek at her and Win choked in distaste. "I *know*. I'm a walking cliché. We decided to try living apart while she was pregnant, and then she'd move back in—but I went to every appointment, every scan. I bought clothes—we named her. She had a nursery here. I *wanted* her to grow up in Mercy. It was the plan."

Win remembered the tiny pink dress stitched with her name, a dress she never wore.

"Olivia was close to giving birth, and I stayed at her town apartment. One night...she woke up and said Spencer had a nightmare."

Win's skin erupted in goosebumps, and she rubbed at her arms. Jake stared into the fire, which she thought must be easier than looking directly at her. "She put him back to bed—said he'd been upset. But in the morning...." He scrubbed at his face, his voice breaking. "I can't Win...."

"Okay..." She took his shoulder and squeezed it.

"It was over by the time we got to the hospital—Katie was gone. They put a medical term on the death certificate—placenta abruption. Olivia was devastated. We both were."

Words stuck in her throat. It wasn't enough to say she was sorry. Sorry, wouldn't be good enough.

"Nobody knew we were trying to patch things up—not even my father. But Alice and Ben knew. I told Alice everything. And after Katie died...Olivia and I stopped trying to fix what was always broken. A few months later, I met Rose, married her, and then Luke was on the way."

"Jake..." Win couldn't hide her dismay, amazed that she could empathize with a woman who stole her in broad daylight. "How could you do that to her?"

"I know, Win." His head hung between his broad shoulders. "Olivia—well, you know what she did. I abandoned her, and she took out her rage, her jealousy on Alice—resented her because we were close. But I didn't imagine that she'd steal you, not for a second. I was so ashamed I could have pushed her so far. So I let your parents think I did it."

Shame...her grandfather's words echoed on the crackle of the flames. *I've got so many things to be ashamed of...*

"Luke was six when she was killed, Spencer nearly thirteen. She didn't exactly give Rose an easy time of it as the ex-wife. Let's say she made her presence known any chance she got. Poor Rose only made one mistake her whole life—marrying me. Look what I exposed her to."

"After Olivia died in the accident and Spencer moved back home, I started to see the truth—there *was* something wrong with him. Once they'd grown into young men, I began to think I was crazy and imagined everything. I married Carla, and we moved away. After the disaster at the bonfire and Spencer's arrest, I bailed him out and flew him to Hawaii, far away from Luke. When I got filed for Luke's emancipation—I thought perhaps it was a blessing. He'd be gone, and I wouldn't have to worry myself to death that Spencer could hurt him."

Win hadn't moved an inch the whole time he'd been speaking. She half wondered if he'd forgotten she was there. Despite the warmth of the fire, she shivered, and without thinking, he automatically cradled her into his side. Unfortunately, it wasn't the end of the story, and a detail she'd learned by the oak nudged at her.

"Jake," she said. "Why did you send Rose away?"

At the mention of his second wife's name, his eyes glossed up, and his chin dimpled, holding back whatever emotion choked him. Win thought just how like Luke he was.

Win tried to fill in the gap when he appeared lost for words. "Luke said once that Spencer locked her in the attic. He did nasty things to her. Pushed her down the stairs...."

Jake's head snapped up, and Win caught his expression. *Oh...no...* Now she was emotional.

"Was she pregnant?"

Jake's answer was to scrub his face with his hands, wrung out before he managed a nod. "Only a few weeks, but it was too late. She broke her leg, and when she was healed, I made her leave. I couldn't risk having her here."

"But..." Win spluttered, still confused. "She left Luke behind?"

"It was my caveat. I paid her to go, Win. She was young and wanted to go back to school, so she left and returned to her family home in Washington State. Luke...she wanted to take him. But I didn't want to lose him too. Besides, Spencer...tolerated him. He didn't seem interested in Luke, only hurting Rose."

"Why didn't you do something about him? If you knew he was..." Win didn't outright say the word. *Evil.* She didn't think anyone could be truly evil, though Spencer was making it increasingly hard to believe. Jake's shoulders slumped.

"Spencer could be kind, he could be fun and charming. There were times I believed I'd dreamed the whole thing up. With Rose gone, he was settled. Can you possibly understand? I didn't want to lose another child. He was my first, I saw the best in him."

Win swallowed. "You protected him."

"I failed him."

Win didn't reply, the words hung between them. Jake hadn't only failed Spencer.

"This is such a mess, Jake. You have to tell Luke the truth about his mother." Appalled, Win recalled the afternoon they'd sat on the porch and Luke's emotionally fuelled slip up. "He thinks she's dead."

Jake stared hard at the fire as though the right thing to say would spring out of the flames, but eventually, he bobbed his head in agreement. Win guessed he must feel as wrung out like her, tired, drained. Sometimes revealing the truth only made the weight heavier. Now the real work needed to begin, and Jake was a master of avoidance.

Win inched nearer, unsure if he could take another hug, another display of affection he was so bad at. No wonder Luke was so cool and aloof when they'd first met. Jake seemed distant, tapping his fingers on the glass tumbler.

"I failed Spencer's mother. I cast her off when I should have helped her. I didn't want to fail our son too. I didn't want to lose him. I knew what he was—what he is."

"Thank you for telling me the truth." Win tilted her head, watching for his reaction. "Do you hate us, Jake? Do you hate my family? My Mom and Dad?"

Pain made his eyes glossy and wet. He lifted his gaze, rolling the tumbler between his palms. "I'm a jealous man. I always was. The three of us, Ben and Alice were inseparable as kids—funny you, Ella, and Luke remind me of how we used to be. I never envied their relationship, *ever*. But when I lost Katie...and they had Rowan, *then* you. I was bitter and jealous, I admit it. I couldn't be happy for them, not after Katie. I tried to move past it, but jealousy is a parasite. It eats at you, worms its way into your heart. They had two perfect little girls, and I'd lost mine."

"But you don't hate them? You don't hate me?"

He looked as though her question alarmed him. "I couldn't ever hate you—or them."

Win sighed with relief, not sure why her chest tightened, holding onto his words. She liked him a lot. Despite all his flaws and how annoying he was at times, it was impossible not to warm to him. She couldn't stand the thought of anyone hating her.

"Win. I'm sorry for what I said about you and Luke in the car. I was trying to push your buttons. I know he's a sore spot."

His apology startled her out of her train of thought, and she smiled, embarrassed. "For what it's worth, I think you two are handling everything very well. You made a good choice to remain friends. I would hate to think of you two growing up hating one another. Neither of you deserves that."

"What do you deserve?" she asked, and he snorted.

"Not much."

"You deserve a family—and have one. We're waiting for you when you're ready."

A blush crossed his nose. "You think your parents would ever forgive me? Would they even listen?"

"I think they would," she said with a firm nod. "The truth is all they've ever wanted. You *must* tell Luke. He deserves to know about Katie."

Cheeks warm, she threw her arms around his neck and hugged him hard. He chuckled. "Are you sure you aren't being nice because you think I might buy you a car?"

A laugh escaped her throat. "I have a perfectly good, beaten-up truck, thank you."

He cocked a brow. "A prom dress then?"

Win rolled her eyes. "No—but I saw a dress in the collection you have in the parlor that I wouldn't mind getting my hands on."

He laughed and clapped his hands. "Okay, it's yours. If you promise to tell me how on earth you suddenly know all my dark secrets? And can see the past?"

"Ah, you might want more whiskey for that story."

"Did this help you?" Jake asked. "Now you know the truth. Did it give you the answers you were looking for?"

She deflated, hardly able to tell him after he'd just revealed his past, something which he'd struggled with, that, it didn't help at all. Katie died a natural, tragic death and she still didn't know how to win this fight against Spencer. All she had was the ancient skeleton under the Oak, another jagged puzzle piece. Buzzing from her jean pocket made her jump from the couch. It was her phone beeping. Smiling bashfully, she grabbed it and slid it open, Rowan's name flashing on the screen.

Turning away from Jake, she smiled at the receiver. "Hey...I've got..."

"Win—where are you?" came Rowan's frantic reply, and Win's blood chilled, her smile slipping from her lips.

"I'm...it doesn't matter...what's wrong?"

Rowan sobbed at the other end of the line. "Win—I'm in Meadowford General. Evan collapsed at home...she fell and wouldn't wake up."

"I'm coming! I'll be there."

She whirled and found Jake already on his feet, rolling up his sleeves. She didn't need to explain. He'd already heard Rowan's voice, the frantic tone unmistakable.

"I'll drive," he said.

TWENTY-EIGHT

Footsteps hurrying across the gleaming, polished floor made Rowan fidget in her seat. Her spine was stiff from sitting too long. She stood, her nails digging into her palms as she relentlessly paced. Covering her eyes, she stifled a sob. This wasn't the time to lose it, even though she'd bawled down the phone to her sister. The corridors of Meadowford General were busy, uniformed nurses and doctors hurrying from door to door, and Rowan was one of many waiting for news on a loved one. That didn't make her feel less alone. The lingering smell of disinfectant in the air made her feel queasy.

Rowan's temples throbbed, tension spilling into her neck muscles, her jaw tight from grinding her teeth for the last hour.

In her pocket, her phone beeped. Pulling it out, she stared down at the message from her father.

Hold tight. We are coming straight to the hospital.

Rowan's head snapped up as the doctor she'd spoken with earlier dashed past. He was young, receding but with a calm face, and she'd detected his unwashed scent. The guy was probably tired, and on the tail end of his shift. Rowan caught his shirt sleeve as he passed. "I'm sorry... is there any news on my girlfriend?"

He blinked at her, shaking his head as though trying to recall their conversation, staring at a clipboard and clicking his fingers. "Yes...Evan Varga, right? She's just had her MRI. We'll be wheeling her up soon."

"But she's awake?"

He smiled, but it didn't reach his eyes. "She's awake."

Rowan let the fabric of his shirt drop from his fingers, disliking how he'd said that. Sickness swelled inside her, and she grappled for the chair and sat back down, her legs draining of strength.

At first, when Evan fell in the kitchen, Rowan thought she'd been joking. They'd been cooking, talking, and drinking, even though it was still early afternoon. With a teenger-free house, and keen to forget the drama, Rowan opened a bottle of wine, and Evan didn't need much convincing to join her. Mid conversation, while the pasta boiled in a pan, Evan's face dropped. Her smile slipped like the dinner plate in her hand.

Rowan watched the plate fall, hit the wood, and crack with a smash, fragments scattering across the kitchen floor. Laughing, Rowan lifted her gaze but quickly stopped. Evan groped for her blindly, her eyes deadening, rolling, and then she was gone like snuffing out a candle. Rowan barely had time to catch her before her dark hair spilled over the floor. Sitting cross-legged on the kitchen floor, with Evan sprawled across her lap, Rowan shook her lifeless body, willing her awake.

Pleading with her to wake up, Rowan grappled in her jeans for her phone, too scared to let her go. Evan's skin was clammy and cold, her fingertips freezing. Rowan called an ambulance, alone in the house with her parents out and Win gone, cold dread clawed at her. She didn't know what else to do. Holding Evan's lifeless body, she waited, the seconds turning to long, yawning minutes until blue flashing lights flooded the kitchen.

As Evan was strapped to the gurney, her shirt rode up, revealing the toned curve of her abdomen. Rowan flinched, what she saw making chills erupt up her back.

Claw marks. They were new since the ones on her back appeared a day ago. Marks Evan tried to hide. Five identical, long scars across her belly, faded to the color of flesh as though they'd been there for years. Or a century or two. Unfortunately, it didn't go unnoticed by a paramedic, who cleared his throat, and rolled Evan's shirt back down.

"Did she have a run-in with a dog?"

Rowan's voice dried up, and he peered at her, puzzled. "Those been there long?"

Rowan didn't answer, her voice trapped in her windpipe. Rowan knew Evan's body, and with a flush, she admitted, probably more intimately than she knew her own. She'd never seen those marks.

Collapsing in a chair, Rowan wrung her hands, her anxiety building until movement from the elevator caught her eye. The doors sprung open, and two porters wheeled out a large, unwieldy hospital bed. Evan sat bright-eyed and upright, with her dark glossy hair spilled over the white pillow. Rowan sprang out of her seat as if someone had set her ass aflame.

Emotion knotted in her throat as she grabbed Evan's hand. "I've been so worried."

Evan gave her a watery smile, her eyes wet, and she weakly squeezed Rowan's hand. "Don't start crying. I'm fine."

The porters wheeled her into a side room, fitted with two armchairs, cupboards, and a television. It was cold, sterile and Rowan fought the urge to gather her up and whisk her away in the truck. "The doctor will be around shortly," a porter said, wheeling Evan's bed into place.

Rowan pressed her lips to her temple when he'd gone, her skin cold to the touch. "Are you warm enough?" She pulled the thin sheets up over her stomach, and Evan laughed, waving her away.

"I'm fine."

"What happened?"

Evan didn't answer. Rowan narrowed her eyes. Did she look smaller, frailer? A year older than she'd looked this morning? Fine lines creased her mouth. "I don't remember a thing. I blacked out."

The way Evan directed her gaze away, her mouth pursed, made Rowan's stomach turn. That was her avoidance face. "I know you aren't telling me everything. What did he do?"

Evan swallowed, brushing back her hair. "You know I can't tell you."

The door slammed open, and two shapes filled the door. One was Win, her hair wet and frizzy from the rain. Behind her, Jake Fraser stood in the doorway, the look on his face uncertain and oddly shy, like he was an intruder. Rowan couldn't keep the venom out of her voice, staring at him over Win's shoulder. "Why is he here?"

"He drove me here." Win rushed and wrapped her arms around Rowan's neck.

"Why are you together? Why are you wet?"

"I'll wait outside," Jake said, awkwardly shoving his hands in his pockets, and Rowan didn't miss the grateful smile Win gave him. When he'd closed the door, Win dragged her eyes to her sister.

"I can explain—boy do I have a lot to explain. But now isn't the time." She rushed to Evan and grabbed her in a hug. "What happened?"

Evan shook her head. "All I know is I blacked out—like someone turned off the lights—and the next thing I remember is waking up in the MRI machine."

"That isn't all." Rowan uncovered Evan's abdomen, gently pulling aside her hospital gown. All three hissed in unison. Evan's belly caved as cool air hit her exposed skin. The claw marks were there, faded to nothing more than light scars. Evan choked back a cry, as horrified as Win.

Win lifted her eyes to Evan's face. "I hate this. I want this to end. Can't I just go back now...?"

Evan covered up, hugging herself for comfort. "Win, no! You know how this has to play out."

"No, I don't! I'm going on trust here, Evan. I'm trusting you and your brother when you've told us some serious lies in the past."

"Win," Rowan snapped, her eyes darkening but Win waved her hand.

"I'm sorry. I know you wouldn't hurt us. I'm just waiting, and I'm fighting with my hands tied. I'm not fighting at all! And here you are suffering because of a mistake I made. What can I do?"

"Wait," Evan said. "You have to wait."

"You have to give us something."

Evan burst into tears, and Rowan wrapped her arms around her, feeling like her thin bones could crack if she pressed too hard. "My memories of that time are...it's hard to describe. They're like flickering shadows, I can see his face. I can feel his hatred. And I know somewhere in his warped mind, he thinks he's right and he won't stop. But if I tell you *anything*—I run a risk that it won't play out as it should. Sometimes knowledge isn't always power."

"He won't kill you," Win said, and Rowan was amazed at the assurance in Win's voice. How could she be so confident? Then Win said, "He needs her to raise the door. And he won't kill you without getting what he wants first. We have time."

"Time for what?" Rowan asked.

"To fix this," Win gritted out. "I have to fix this."

The door opened again, and Rowan caught a brief flash of Jake sitting in the chair in the hall, head down, eyes on his phone. The sweaty-faced doctor bustled in armed with a clipboard, then grabbed the charts at the foot of Evan's bed. He flipped her a brief, unconcerned smile.

"How are you doing?"

Evan's hands twisted in the covers of the bed. "I'm fine. *Really*. Can't I just go home?"

He nodded, and Rowan puffed in relief. "Actually, yes. We've no reason to keep you in. All your vitals checked out fine, and the MRI was clear...." His voice trailed off, eyeing her carefully over the board, and puzzlement twinkled in his eyes. "So, there isn't any reason to keep you in any longer than you need to be. I would put this down to a bad case of dehydration...or perhaps hunger? If this continues, you'd need to come back in for tests. But I'd be happy to let you leave in a few hours once you've eaten and your bloods come back."

Rowan exhaled a long breath she'd been holding. "Thank god."

"Although." The doctor clicked his tongue, his hazel eyes looking curiously at the pretty woman in the bed. "I have one question... something that cropped up during the MRI. This might sound odd...but have you ever been in a serious car crash... fallen down a cliff or anything?"

The last part was intended as a joke, but Rowan's jaw bunched, gazing purposely at Evan, watching for her reaction. Evan chuckled and shook her head. "No...why?"

The doctor produced a copy of the x-ray film. He rested it on Evan's knees, running his bitten nail over the image of the skeletal projection of Evan's torso. "You have extensive damage to your ribs. I can count at least six fractures there, but the funny thing is we can't age them. We can usually assess how long the fractures have been there...but we can't get a fix on that." Again, he ticked his tongue expectantly. "Anything you want to tell me?"

A horrible silence filled the room, Win edged closer, while under the sheets, Evan shot him a confused smile. Finally, she said, "No—nothing I can think of."

The doctor raised his brows and blew out air. "Well, okay. I guess I can always try and gain access to old hospital records...."

Rowan gulped fear down, her hand slackening like a weight in Evan's grip. The young doctor worried his upper lip with his teeth, tutting and lost in thought. Evan sprang forward in the bed.

"I'm such an idiot—it was so long ago. I was nine and got in a car accident. We worked on our family farm, and my older cousin took one of the trucks into the field, and he rolled it. He was sixteen and didn't have his license, so I recovered at home, and my family didn't report it. I completely forgot."

Staring hard at Evan's profile, Rowan kept her expression neutral, astounded that her girlfriend could whip up bullshit out of thin air. Across the bed, Rowan and Win's gazes locked briefly.

Whoa, she sure lies fast, Win said, and Rowan ignored her. The doctor pursed his lips, staring at the x-rays, and finally shrugged his shoulders.

"Okay, guess that explains some of this damage. In fact it could explain these compressed vertebrae." He pointed to the film again, tracing his finger to the base of her skull. "You could have extensive nerve damage from an old injury, one that could cause temporary black outs, which might be an ongoing issue. I'll leave you to rest, and we'll get some paperwork to release you...providing your bloodwork doesn't reveal anything else interesting."

The doctor, distracted and keen to get on, hurried out of the room and let the door click shut behind him. Win whistled, and Rowan fought for control by the side of the bed. Her tattered nerves frayed to raw ends, and she sobbed into her hands. Somewhere in the past, Spencer violently inflicted those injuries upon Evan. Injuries which were now permanent—ongoing issues Evan would need to deal with for the rest of her life.

Powerless, helpless, Rowan bunched her fist. She hated that he could control her, bend her to his will, and reduce her to nothing.

I won't be nothing. Fight rose inside her, fired by the need to protect what she loved. "Win—we need to end this."

Chin firm, Win nodded, and Rowan wondered when her kid sister had risen in the ranks, as powerful as any alpha. "I have news—big news. You need to see something."

"I'm not leaving Evan."

"Go!" Evan urged. "I'll be fine here."

Rowan opened her mouth to protest, but outside in the hall, there was an array of voices rising in pitch. With a sinking feeling, she realized it was her father, who had probably just run straight into Jake. Win gritted her teeth, "Damn it," she said, waltzing out into the hall.

Rowan was hot behind, folded arms and mentally bracing herself for the argument. Ben stood over his wife, who'd flopped in a plastic chair. Holding her hand and shielding her, Ben blasted Jake, who'd risen to his feet.

"You've no right to be here."

"I was dropping Win to the hospital, Ben, nothing sinister about that."

Alice's chin dropped, breathing hard as she clutched Ben's hand. It was almost too painful for her to look at him. Rowan furrowed her brow. "Evan's fine," she quipped, annoyed as both sets of parents were too engrossed in their spat to notice or ask.

Ben sighed and threw up his hands. "I'm sorry, honey. What happened?"

"Now isn't the time to discuss it," Rowan said. "She can come home later."

Alice sagged. "Thank god!"

Ben's smile quickly shifted into a sneer as he threw a sardonic glare in Jake's direction. "There....she's fine. You can leave."

"He can't," Win piped up, standing by his side. Jake jerked in surprise, then patted her hand. Ben's jaw fell open.

"This is family business," he said.

"He is family," Win argued. "And right now—this thing going on between you—shelve it! I don't have time for this bullshit—Evan *doesn't* have time!"

Rowan burst with pride, her chest swelling as Win stepped between her parents and Jake, like a small warrior. "Jake has something to tell you," she said, and kicked his toe when he protested. "So I suggest, *parents*, go grab a drink together...you'll need it. Don't come back until you've cleared the air. And dad—*please* listen to him."

Ben spluttered. "There is nothing he can say...."

"Dad—we need everyone on the same side. Mom...." Win knelt in front of her mother and took both of her trembling hands. It looked as if Win was about to be gentle, her expression soft, but instead, she cocked her head and said, "It's time to man the hell up. Be the alpha we need—because right now, we need you. The person who gave you a second shot at life is being attacked and laying in a hospital bed with bone fractures and scars they can't explain...and I can't allow that. Not anymore. Do you understand?"

Alice's expression blossomed from confusion to pride. Finally, she lifted her eyes and nodded her agreement. "I understand."

Win took out her phone, darting out of earshot as she held it to her ear.

"Who were you calling?" Rowan watched, her mouth growing dry as Win returned with a disappointed expression on her face.

"Wolfric," she answered. "I've left him so many messages. It's coming...he said I'd know when it was time, and I think it's here. But I can't get through to him."

Rowan sucked in a breath, folding her hand around Win's shoulder. "We'll get hold of him."

Win tried to smile, shooting Rowan a grateful glance. "You coming?"

Rowan gave her a mock salute, and Win's grim expression broke into a laugh.

"I'd follow you anywhere," she said.

TWENTY-NINE

Darkness had fallen across the wood, and on the brow of a hill, Win spotted the shadow of the black wolf, his bright eyes gleaming. When he saw the group appear from the woods, he pelted down the hill and bumped his head against Win's in the act of hello. Win stalked around him, allowing him to adjust and sniff her. If she wasn't so tense, she'd tease him about the weird sniffing. Luke had no clue he was even doing it. Rowan and Grayson stalked out of the forest and caught up.

By the time they'd arrived back from the hospital, it was cold, dark, and the yard was frozen, all the old machinery glistening with frost in the moonlight. Stars twinkled above. Win thumbed Grayson a message to meet them at the house and was filled with gratitude the second Rowan pulled up and spotted his truck.

He climbed out of the cab, dressed in ripped jeans and his battered hoodie. He'd come from the lumber yard, but had his crossbow strapped to his back in readiness. Win sprinted across the yard and flung herself into his arms. He chuckled into her hair. "You missed me?"

She drew back and kissed him about ten times till he laughed. How could they have been together in that motel only a week ago, untouchable and blissfully unaware of life outside those walls? "Thank you for being here. I'm going to need you."

He let her slip down his body, his smile melting. "I'm not sure I like the sound of that."

The pull to shift was pulsing through her, itching under her skin. They'd trekked to Mercy in the dark, discovering Luke was gone, out for a hunt. Win scurried into the long grass behind the old house, while Rowan and Grayson patiently waited for her to shift. It didn't take long to find the young wolf, Win sniffed him out quickly.

I see Captain America decided to show. Luke ran around Rowan's legs, and she laughed, bending to scratch his ears. The wolf lifted his chin, his back legs quivering as she got him good and rough under the neck. "Be nice, Luke," she said.

We don't have time for your sarcasm. Win jogged ahead, her growl rumbling in her chest. *You need to see this.*

She led them to the oak, and she shuddered on approach, the gnarled tree a bent and distorted silhouette against the inky sky. *It's there...Luke the door...*

Nose in the grass, he was already sniffing around. He yelped and scratched frantically at the old door they'd covered up with debris a week ago.

Win joined him, using her teeth to prise the wood away. Grayson leaned and tore a chunk of the rotted door away, his back muscles flexing as he tossed it away. Gritting his teeth, he glanced around, pointing to the oak. "I've never seen this...what is this place?"

It's what's under it that's the problem. The cat nudged Rowan's shin, and her sister pulled back her hair as she launched herself backward down the hole. She cocked her head and threw Grayson a spiky smile. "Are you coming?"

Grayson rolled his eyes, shrugging off his crossbow and laying it in the grass. "Ladies first."

Tutting, she dropped to the cavern floor, clicking on the flashlight she'd stashed in her jacket. The beam of light pointed out of the hole. "Well, aren't you a gentleman."

Grayson dropped through the hole, and Win inched her head over the edge, her gut tightening as they vanished into the depths of the pit. Above the hole, Win and Luke were nose to nose. He crawled past and dropped through the hole with a whimper, his claws scraping the earth as he toppled forward.

Aren't you coming?

Win's insides swirled at the memory. *I don't need to see it again.*

As she paced, her breath chugged on the air, waiting for anything to let them know they'd found it. Part of her was afraid she'd imagined the whole thing. Maybe someone could have moved it? What if she'd been dreaming everything? She soon got her answer as, within minutes, Luke's head popped through the hole. Scurrying to safety, he shook his fur, then, without warning, he puked up the woodland creature he'd feasted on before they showed up.

Win made a face. *Oh man... you saw it.*

I saw it. Luke's eyes bugged as he vomited again.

Next, Rowan hauled herself out of the hole, arms trembling as she crawled away, and then heaved, clutching her torso. "Holy....hell," she cried. "I can't see straight."

Did you feel it? Win meant the strange tingling sensation in her limbs, pulsating through her muscles when she'd gotten close to the body. It'd left her dizzy, and nauseous and her first instinct was to get into the fresh air and heave.

"Feel it? I can taste it." Rowan held her hips, trying to straighten. Behind them, Luke recovered, spitting bile out into the grass.

Well, that was disturbing.

Grayson was the last to appear, his biceps straining as he pulled out of the hole and rolled. Staggering to his feet, his strapped the crossbow to his back, but Win frowned. He looked at her as if reading her expression. "I'm fine. I have a strong stomach."

"It's not that." Rowan sat, her elbows propped on her knees. "I felt something down there...it was strong...old. Maybe it wouldn't affect you?"

Power. Luke said. *I felt it.*

"We should call Wolfric," Rowan suggested. "Surely he would have answers?"

Win worried, grinding her teeth as she recalled the string of unanswered messages she'd sent him. She was worried maybe he'd jumped, done something rash. The messages were unread, left waiting for him. Where the hell was he? Win couldn't help but feel a little pissed he'd vanished right when they needed him. The past was racing to catch up and Win was filled with a heaviness that she was still fighting blindfolded. She's hoped by uncovering the truth about Katie, she'd be better off, only she was more confused. Mary had lead her to Katie, to this tree and the body underneath, and it couldn't be for nothing.

Grayson hauled the old, rotten wood back into place. Scratching his chin, he stared at the hole, kicking rocks and stones over it. Win couldn't describe what had made her head swim when she last went into the cave, only it sent her reeling, dizzy. The scent and taste of power had coated her tongue, and she'd experienced a deep sense of sorrow...hatred, and anguish.

Win closed her eyes, fighting back images she'd seen. Here in the woods, something happened to Mary. There was a piece of the puzzle refusing to fit. No matter how you turned or forced it to slide into place, it wouldn't budge. She sensed fear in that cavern. The body was left alone, buried deep below the earth, never to be discovered.

"Who would warrant being buried so deeply underground?" Rowan asked as if following Win's train of thought.

"Someone unpleasant," Grayson said, shifting the weight of his bow to his back. "Someone they were afraid of."

Rowan visibly shuddered, stretching to her feet. "I need to get back to the hospital. I can't leave Evan alone for long—I'm sorry." She directed her words at Win. "But I can't stay here knowing she's alone on that ward. You'll have to lead this one."

But no jumping Win! Rowan fired at her silently, though a deadly seriousness flashed in her gaze. *Don't try it again...it's too dangerous. You weren't supposed to jump so soon after the first one.*

Win made a noise that signified she understood. Luke nudged her with his wet nose. *Please listen...for once in your life.*

In silence, they trekked back to Mercy. Trotting side by side, Win eyeballed Luke, wondering if Jake would choose to tell him about Katie. The truth, it seemed, was hurtling for them, pieces of a jigsaw slotting together, and she didn't want to be the one to tell him about his lost half-sister. She hoped Jake would make time, try to make things right, and maybe reunite him with the mother he'd hidden away. Heavy with knowledge, they pelted ahead, running through the rusty back gate.

Luke pranced away to shift in private, and Win wandered to where she'd stashed her clothes. She lifted her nose, the air alive with the smell of cigarettes. Her brows flew skyward as she grabbed her jeans and sweater with her teeth and chased Luke into the bush.

He was naked and yelled, darting behind a tree. "Win! What the hell?"

Cole! It's Cole! He's here...

Luke's jaw dropped. He lifted his chin, his eyes narrowing before he hissed. "Ella's with him. Get out of here. I need to get dressed!"

I need to change. Why are they here?

Luke went still, raiding his memory bank, and then slapped his forehead. "We said we'd meet tonight...damn...get out of here before he sees you. This could give him a heart attack."

Win ignored Luke's cries of mortification. She darted around frantically, desperate to find a place to shift without exposing her naked self to Cole, Luke—everyone. Panic exploded inside her as she bounced back into Luke's hiding spot. Mortified and red-faced, he shoved her out, no mean feat. She was heavy and rolled on the grass.

"Win! I've got no clothes—get out of here!"

She scrambled in circles. At the last second she dashed across the yard but ran straight into Cole and Ella's path. Ella shrieked and grabbed Cole's arm.

Cole stood stark still, lit by the glow of the butt of his cigarette. Ella's mouth dropped, her eyes bobbing back and forth, and she gripped his hand, prepared for his reaction.

A long waft of smoke trailed from his lips, his eyes wide as saucers. The butt dangled and dropped to the gravel, where Ella stamped on it. After a while, he took a whole step back, dragging Ella with him. "Oh...crap!"

"Cole, it's okay!" Ella shook his arm, trying to snap his attention back to her. "It's not what you think!"

It was *precisely* what he thought. Cole had been attacked by Spencer only weeks ago, left maimed and bleeding in the woods, struck by an oversized panther. Win didn't move, and in the act of submission, to prove she was tame, she fell to her belly. She bowed her head and purred for all she was worth. Cole's eyes widened in terror. Luke jumped out of the bush, half-dressed, and Cole staggered in surprise. "What...what the hell is this?"

Rowan and Grayson wandered through the yard by this time, both cagily approaching Cole and Ella. Rowan eased toward him slowly and put an arm around his shoulder. "It's alright—it's just Win."

"Win? *That's Win?*"

The jaguar flattened her ears, then crawled across the ground, nudging Cole's shin with her head. Cole let out a shaky breath, then, after a long pause, placed his hand on her head. Encouraged by his bravery, Win's tongue poked out and lapped at his hand. Cole's skin tasted of salt and tobacco. Win's show of affection didn't have the desired effect. Cole cried out in horror at seeing a pink cat's tongue poke through his fingers.

"Too much, Win." Grayson warned. "Give the poor guy a second to adjust before you start licking him."

Cole looked sharply at Ella. "You know about this? Why aren't you freaking out?"

Luke hopped on one foot, trying to shove the other into a sneaker. He shot Cole a bashful smile. "We can explain!"

"Dude—why were you naked?"

Ella burst into giggles, and Cole flapped his hands, bemused and horrified. "Why are you laughing?"

"I'm not laughing at you," she said. Cole, aghast, stared around the strange group, his eyes finding Rowan in the dark. Then he spotted Grayson, his scars and his crossbow, and with a downturned mouth, he whispered to Ella.

"What the hell is going on?" He cast a wary glance at Grayson. "Why does that guy have a crossbow? Are we going to shoot something?" He gasped. "Is he going to shoot *Win?*"

Luke exhaled, throwing his hands in the air. The game was up. "Maybe we should get a drink?"

The windows fogged with steam as they sat in a back booth at Hardy's. Rowan and Grayson had declined to stay, the two of them leaving the friends to hash out the disaster that unfolded in Luke's yard.

The dinner rush was over, and the bar was empty, apart from a few stragglers playing pool. The popping of the ball irritated Win's nerves as she gazed across the table at Cole. Next to him, Ella clutched his forearm to keep him from bolting. Luke's heat seeped through her jeans, and Win edged away from him, a sweat building on her brow. They met eyes for a second, worried and trying to gauge Cole's reaction.

"So..." Cole drawled after a lifetime of empty silence. "Luke is a wolf...Win is a jaguar...." He stumbled over the words, his gaze quickly flicking to Win's face. "And your sister...is a bird?" She blushed and sank into the seat.

"An eagle," Win corrected him, then shut her lips. Cole was draining of color by the second.

"Is this some kind of joke?" He battled inwardly, his thoughts trying to fit together. Ella squeezed his shoulder. "I know the Hickory stories, but...."

"I know it's crazy," Ella said.

"You knew all this time?"

Ella nodded. "Since the party at Luke's last summer. Win revealed herself to us—two cat eyes in the dark are hard to miss."

Cole fumbled with his drink and scratched at his chin. "Oh, the *bonfire*. Guess my invite got lost in the mail?"

Luke made a face. "C'mon. None of us were friends then." He looked pointedly at Ella.

"I'm kidding...but this is...a lot."

"I'm sorry, Cole." Win shot out her hand and grasped his clenched fist on top of the table. "We like you. We really do. After what you just saw, we can't keep lying to you."

Cole's eyes widened, and he flexed his injured hand on the table. Cole was deep in denial. His mouth worked, eyes like saucers as his complexion went from rosy to porcelain. He wriggled his ruined hand, the one Spencer mauled. "The animal who attacked me? Who was that?"

Luke squirmed next to Win. "My brother, Spencer."

"The guy you sent through the door to another time?"

Luke tapped his fingers on the tabletop, his teeth grinding. "Uh-huh. I realize this looks bad."

"Is that...why you've been nice to me?" Cole asked in weary disbelief, as though his worst thoughts had come true. The idea their friendship was out of sympathy had only just occurred to him. "Is that why we're friends? Because you feel *sorry* for me?"

"No!" Ella spluttered.

"No way, Cole!" Luke chimed in. "That isn't true."

Ella threw her arms around his neck. "We *love* you. I know how bad this looks, but we couldn't not tell you, especially now with all this crazy stuff happening."

"Cole..." Luke blushed, shamefaced, and avoided Win's curious eyes. "We're *friends*. You're better to me than my own brother ever was."

Cole exhaled hard and clenched his fist. He shook his head. "Okay. I'm sorry I even said that."

The four of them remained silent for a long time, and Win met Ella's worried glance across the table. She wished she could read what her friend was thinking. Every one of Ella's fingers dug purposely into Cole's arm to keep him from fleeing. Win's heart lurched as finally, Cole shifted his gaze, staring at them each in turn.

"So...Luke is a wolf, and Win is a cat..." he confirmed again, glancing at Ella. "What are you...a friendly little otter?"

Luke snorted, and Win breathed a sigh of relief. Ella chuckled. "I'm not...I'm *nothing*."

Win balked. "That's not true."

"She's the smart one." Luke threw her an adorable smile, and Ella went pink around the ears.

"*Everyone* is smarter than you," Cole said, though he wasn't laughing.

Ella bristled, circling back to his earlier comment. "Otters are jerks. They look cute but kill for no reason."

"Complete assholes," Luke agreed with a snigger.

Win laughed. "Only *you* would know that, Ella."

Luke looked at Ella across the table, and Win sensed something catch fire in his blood. His pulse pounded harder. "I always imagined Ella as a cute little bunny," he said, resting his chin on his fist. Ella's lips pursed, her eyes heavy-lidded, and Win detected the flush of hormones racing through her friend's body.

Wrinkling her nose, Win snorted in disgust. *Please...don't start anything up with her if you're not serious about it. Otherwise, I will have to kill you this time.*

Hearing her loud and clear, Luke side-eyed her. *You're kidding, aren't you? She doesn't trust me, not anymore. She really is the smart one.*

Win didn't reply, only nudged his toe with hers. The resignation in his voice was tough to hear, he was lonely, and he'd broken Ella's heart and didn't know a way back. It occurred to her she was more deeply in tune with him than ever. She felt his sorrow and guilt. He hid it well, but sometimes she saw it in his eyes, and it weighed heavy on her that she'd caused it.

Luke sipped at his coke, his eyes fixed on Cole, as if he might spring from his seat in fright. Win wove her hands around her drink, and Cole looked deep in thought as though they'd casually been discussing a sports game, not a curse cast over a hundred years ago.

"You seem to be taking this rather well." Ella chewed her lip. Cole's eyes flicked between the three of them.

"It kind of makes sense," Cole said to Luke. "You do give off some intense doggy vibes."

Luke's jaw dropped. "Doggy vibes?"

Cole waved his hands around, gesturing to Luke's face. "You act so weird around my mom—your nose looks way bigger without glasses...and there's the smell..."

"Smell?" Luke sniffed his shirt, then tapped the bridge of his nose. "What's wrong with my nose?"

"He's kidding!" Win flung Cole a glare, but he was already cackling into his drink. "Aren't you?"

"There's nothing wrong with your nose," Ella protested.

"If I left you alone with my mother...would you try to hump her leg?" Cole dissolved, laughing, and Win choked on her drink. Meanwhile, Luke glowered.

"No, but I might take off your *other* hand," he threatened. Cole shut up, pressing his lips in a fine line before bursting again. When he recovered, rolled up his sleeves.

"Okay...so how does this work?"

Win folded her arms, not sure what he was doing as he upturned his pale wrist, thrusting it in her direction. "Huh?"

"I want in. How does it work?"

"What the hell are you talking about?" Luke cried.

"I want superpowers too!" He flexed his wrist and wiggled his eyebrows suggestively. "I don't mind you biting me, Win. It would be super awkward if Luke did it."

"I wouldn't bite you if my life depended on it!" Luke cried.

Win grinned, took his hand and folded it across the table. "Not how it works, Cole. Its blood. We're all cursed."

"How do I get myself cursed?"

Win let a genuine laugh escape her lips, the sound odd in her ears, hardly able to remember the last time she'd laughed. "Maybe you are cursed, but it's not a Hickory one."

"Cursed to be moron," Luke deadpanned. "Somewhere in the world there's a tree working hard to replace the oxygen you're wasting."

Cole threw a fork at him, which he dodged, and it clattered to the floor. Ella placed her hand back on his arm, her lips curling into a smirk.

"Cole, we have bigger problems, and you turning into a wolf...or a zebra isn't what we need right now. If Luke bit you—you'd die."

"You nearly died!" Win reminded him. "The panther...the monster that did that to you...*that's* what we are. He's what we have to fight! Only he's chosen a different path, a violent one."

"This is so cool," Cole said, his grin almost splitting his face. Win hung her head, not the reaction she'd been expecting. In exasperation, she threw up her hands.

"No one is biting you, Cole. You get to stay human, with no whiskers in sight. But...I'm glad you're cool with it."

Cole's face darkened, the muscles in his jaw bunching. "I want to help," he said after a long beat. Laying his ruined hand flat on the table, he turned it over, revealing the scarred flesh on his palm. Teeth marks forever imprinted on his body. Spencer had left his mark on everyone she loved, Rowan,

Cole, and now Evan. The giant panther bite lay under her clothes, a scar running along her hip, an injury that plagued her even now.

"I'm not the smartest...." Cole said. "I'm not much use, I know. But I was good at something once, and it might have gotten me through college. I know I'm not healed, but that bastard fucked up my hand, and now I can't play basketball—like I used to. And now you tell me he's hurting *you* and your sister's girlfriend, and ultimately it's *you* he wants...no, just no. So I'm in. Whatever you need."

Win's chest swelled with emotion. "Thanks."

"Well, you did save my life in the woods that day. Without you two, I'd have been Spencer meat."

"So...what do we do next, Win?" Ella piped up, she'd wound her arm through Cole's, giving him a side hug, but her eyes fixed on Win with expectation. Win felt the heat of their gazes, and her cheeks fired. She forced all her bottled-up anxiety back into the soles of her shoes.

"I don't have a plan," she admitted. She couldn't admit aloud to Luke that even after doggedly pursuing Jake in search for the truth, she was still in the dark. Luke still didnt know he had a half-sister.

Luke eyed her suspiciously as if he could already tell she was itching to jump again. "You heard Wolfric—and Evan. No jumping, Win. You've been through enough."

Win didn't say a word, not prepared to promise anything right now. As she followed Cole and Ella out of the bar, Luke tugged her shirt, bringing her close and lowering his voice to a whisper. "Please...don't do it. We'll figure this out together."

The earnest look in his eyes was enough to make her nod, although she crossed her fingers behind her back. He rolled his eyes as though he knew she wasn't listening, tension and anxiety of her recklessness building under his chest. When he shuffled away, she caught his hand. "Talk to your dad—it's important."

Luke cocked a brow. "Why?"

"Promise me you'll talk to him tonight—he has something he needs to tell you."

He shirked out of her grip, giving himself a shake. "Okay."

It was odd leaving the bar, walking slightly ahead of them, and she wondered when she'd shifted into this role or accepted it. But one thing gave her strength. Her friends had her back.

THIRTY

With her head spinning from the turn of events at the bar, Win arrived home to a dark house. One lamp flickered in the hall and she figured her parents must be out, thrashing out their issues with Jake. Grayson peeled out of the dark, and she jumped in fright. "You scared the crap out of me!"

"Sorry." He had the decency to look abashed. His hands were firmly shoved in his pockets. "Rowan went to the hospital, and your parents aren't home."

"With Jake, I guess," she confirmed, tugging him closer by the bottom of his jacket. He was at her back as she unlocked the door, heat grazing her cheeks as she shot him a coy smile over her shoulder. "Which means the house is empty...."

"Don't get any ideas!" he warned. "I like all my limbs intact."

Teasing, she turned, back to the closed door as she tugged him in for a kiss. She missed him and wound her arms around her neck. "You're killing me, Grayson."

He grinned against her mouth. "You are greedy, Win. We had a month to ourselves, and right now, I don't want to piss off your dad. I think he might start to like me."

Win scowled and pushed open the door, walking into the empty hall. "That's because you're handy with a nail gun...and a crossbow. The *perfect* boyfriend!"

"How did it go with the kid?" he asked later, as they sat on Win's mattress eating leftover pizza from the previous night. Win sat cross-legged against a pillow, stuffing a slice of Ham and pineapple into her mouth. It reminded her of how they ate in the motel, sitting on the bed opposite one another, eating out of whatever takeout carton they'd managed to afford.

"He took it well—too well. He thinks it's cool and wants to be—I don't know—a bear or something. He doesn't realize it's a lifelong curse."

"Maybe he's looking at it the right way?" Grayson suggested, swiping the last slice before she got her paws on it. "I always thought it was a gift, not a curse."

Win mulled it over, something sparking in her memory. "Wolfric said something similar."

Grayson chuckled. "Well—he and Evan are the children of an ancient god—he's bound to be right about some things."

Tossing the pizza box on the floor, Win crawled into his lap, linking her fingers through his, gazing at the bitten ends of his nails. Her ears pricked up, hearing tires in the drive. "They're home."

Grayson flung her off him, standing and brushing crumbs off his jeans, and Win laughed. "Calm down!"

Footsteps thundered up the stairs, and Win straightened, recognizing her father's uneven tread as he neared the door. She was keen to know the news and waited as he paused outside the door. To her surprise, he knocked. After a moment, he pushed it open. "Everyone decent in here?"

Win blushed, and Grayson groaned and stared hard at the ceiling. "Come in, Dad."

Ben poked his head around the door. His expression relieved when he saw them sitting on the bed. "You ate—good."

Win jumped up, pulling up a chair for him as he crossed the room, but with his hands behind his back, he gazed at Grayson awkwardly. "How did it go?" Win asked when he didn't sit down.

Ben exhaled. "It was intense. And I'm not sure what I think. But...I believe him. And I believe he's sorry."

Win sagged in relief. "I'm so relieved. How was Mom?"

"She's turned in—it's late after all. I think she wants to spend some time alone with him, thrash things out."

Win balked. "And you don't mind?"

"I trust her, Win. *Him*...I'm not so sure. But, we have to make this work, don't we?"

Win jumped, and threw her arms around her father's neck, and for the first time in what felt like an age, he squeezed her and kissed her cheek. "Dad..." She fell back on her heels and shot him with her best pout. It worked on Jake, so why not? "Can Grayson stay?"

A beat of silence passed before Ben said, "On the floor? Sure."

"Dad!"

"Floor or nothing!" Ben glowered, shooting an imploring look at Grayson. "He gets it."

Win grumbled as Ben ruffled her hair, a gesture full of warmth, something she'd missed these past weeks. Already on his feet, Grayson grabbed up the bedroll, still propped against the wall from the last time he'd stayed. Not that he'd lasted on the floor. Ben said goodnight and shut the door behind him. Win jumped into Grayson's arms, but he gently pushed her away. She scowled. "Are you really telling me you're planning to sleep down there?"

He crossed the room chuckling, yanking off his shirt. "I think you've forgotten how well I resisted you before—you think I don't know about the times you *accidentally* bumped into me in the woods." He smirked at the indignant noise she made. "All those cute excuses you cooked up. You never wanted to learn to shoot a bow."

Win gasped. "I'm so transparent!" she mocked. "My seduction techniques must suck. I tried *so* hard!"

"I'm stronger than I look."

Suddenly, he let out a yelp and fell on the bed. Win tried not to laugh as he clutched his toe. "You have a loose board under the rug—shit that hurt!"

"You poor thing!" She ran her fingers through his hair in mock sympathy. "Not so strong, huh?"

He laughed. "Don't make fun of me, Win." He tugged off his sock, revealing his swollen toe. "Guess I'll be fixing that tomorrow."

Win frowned, dangling her leg over the bed and pushing on the squeaky board. Grayson unrolled his bed and threw himself on it, moody and cross. Win giggled, grabbing her wash bag from the vanity. "Don't be too worried about my dad," she said. "He likes to believe I'm saving myself for my wedding night. I think he's in some kind of fatherly denial."

Grayson snorted, folding his arms behind his head. He threw her a wicked smile. "Too bad you're ruined for any decent man. I'll have to stick around."

She smiled shyly. "You are a decent man."

A wanton expression crossed her face; grinning devilishly, she waved her hand over his body. "*But* you'll have to start packing in those calories—build up that strength you claim to have. If you stick around when I go into my heat—you'll be really useful."

Sniggering, she ignored his confused expression, his brows drawing as he said, "Your heat? What's that?"

Laughing, Win called over her shoulder as she opened the door and stepped into the hall. "Ask my sister. I'm sure she'd love to tell you all about it."

A real, contented smile crossed her lips for the first time in a while. She chuckled, closing the bathroom door behind her as he called down the hall. "Win...can't you tell me? What's the heat? *Win!*"

In the pitch black of the room, the loose board squeaked. Win was instantly awake, and cold. She shot up in the dark, shaking away temporary dizziness from her deep sleep. A deep chill crossed her arms, and every hair stood on end.

A shape of a girl floated past the end of the bed.

Win's blood iced, and the shape lingered, drifted, and with a flash of dark hair, and black eyes in a pale face, Mary vanished. Win swallowed a scream, flicking on her lamp with such force, it scooted off the bedside cabinet.

Orange light flooded the room, and Win stood on numb legs. "Shit!" Despite waking up freezing, she was sweating.

Win's skin broke into goosebumps. Collapsing on the bed, she willed away the tremors in her hands, unable to shake the vision of Mary's ghost crossing the room. How long had she been there watching her sleep? Grayson jerked awake, used to her odd sleeping habits. "What's wrong?"

"N-nothing..." Her voice shook. She didn't want to admit she'd seen a ghost. It wasn't like the first time she and Ella contacted Mary. This...Win shuddered. It was different. Mary wasn't invited, yet she seemed to have an open-door policy.

"I heard a board squeak—must be the one you...." Win didn't finish her sentence. She fell to the floor, yanking back the old, patterned rug that had been there for years. Her grandmother's furnishings, her drapes, things she'd chosen. Win never wanted to alter this room. But that board...

There *wasn't* a loose board. Not in all the time she'd lived here. But under the glow of the lamp, there it was. A wood panel, lighter in color than the others, recently replaced and only held by two nails. She stuck out her tongue and carefully slid her finger under the board. Grayson sat up, his interest piqued. "What are you doing?"

"This is new! It wasn't here..." she trailed off as she tugged it free, the nail wielding as she pulled. Peering under the board, she spotted an envelope, and recognized the messy, scrawled handwriting on the front. It said, *To my grown-up Win.* Trembling, she grabbed it. Grayson crawled onto the bed. "What is that? A letter?"

Shaking, Win peeled it open, careful not to rip it. She wiped a stray tear sliding down her cheek. How could she not realize this might happen? Wolfric warned her implicitly not to meddle in the past, not to speak to anyone—but in her grief, she'd forgotten she'd seen her grandfather.

Mary. She woke you up... you have to see this...

Win unfolded the letter in her lap, letting it rest there for a beat before holding it under the lamplight.

To my grown-up girl,

If you're reading this....well, shit. I'm probably gone. If I'm not, and you find this, then we will have an interesting conversation.

I never forgot what I saw in the woods. I know you told me to forget you, pretend I never saw my grandbaby all grown up. But that kind of thing is hard to shake. You look like my sister, by the way. Iris. It took me a moment to realize it wasn't her standing before me.

You were right. You were returned, found by a woman inside the convenience store. Someone left you in aisle six, in a basket. We tried to go back to normal, but I never forgot what I saw, and it got me thinking. You are changing so quickly, it scares me, and as I write this, right now, you're helping that boy move in downstairs. You practically flattened him in the yard, nearly ripped his head off, and now he's moving in. Jake's boy. I never thought I'd see the day.

We haven't seen eye to eye lately. I said some things, you said some things. We fought about the boy you like, the one from the woods. You see those scars on his face? I did that.

I think he's good. He's a Riley, and we don't have a good long-standing relationship with that family. They tend to murder us...Mary, Louisa, Annie...my mother. But I liked him. You can keep him in line. He doesn't strike me as the murderous type.

You are changing, Win. And I'm dying, growing older by the second. I didn't want to go so soon. I feel as though I just got you back. And I've not prepared you enough for the things you'll face. I've not told you things you need to know. But somehow, I feel like you'll make it. You are strong, Win. And I love you so much. I'm so proud of who you've become.

By the way...if you read this in time...the Calling is pretty gnarly. It's not a pleasant experience—just saying.

Win dabbed at her eyes, and chuckled through salty tears. "Yeah, thanks for the warning, Grandpa."

Ps. The chain is for you. When I saw you wearing Iris's pendant, it gave me hope she was still alive somewhere. This was mine. I had them made together. She was the other half of my heart. You make us whole, Win. I love you, my firecracker.

Win dropped the letter in her lap, and Grayson took it carefully. She fastened her lips as he read, waiting for his reaction. He laughed at the same spot she did. "Gnarly? *That's* putting it lightly!"

"Mary woke me up," she said, ignoring the look on his face when she said it aloud. "She wanted me to read this letter."

Win tried to envision John writing this months ago, shortly before Luke moved here, in a present she'd altered. She imagined him waiting till she was out and hiding this letter under the floor. One fleeting moment in the woods, and she'd changed his whole life, but in a good way. She'd made him happy.

Win emptied the envelope's contents into her hand. And out rolled a delicate silver chain with a wolf as its pendant. Without wasting a second, she fastened it around her neck, feeling its weight on her collarbone. She fingered it gently. "He never got to know Iris was here the whole time. He waited all his life...only to find out she was gone."

Grayson plumped a pillow under his head, pulling back the duvet. "Let's sleep on this."

"What if she's still...here?" Win's eyes darted around the room, scanning the nooks and corners, her hairs standing on end. "I saw her, Grayson."

Grayson pulled her under his arm, forgetting he was banned from the bed, but Win shook her head when he leaned to turn off the light. Within seconds he snored, and Win tutted, annoyed at how easily he'd drifted off. Wriggling, she twisted, folding his forearm under her head, using him as a pillow. She tried to close her eyes, but every squeak or groan of the window pane kept her awake.

Mary woke you up...it wasn't for nothing...

Easing out from under him, Win threw her legs over the bed. Mary's diary was under the bed, coated with a thick layer of dust. Win dragged it out, hopping on the bed and unfolding it in her lap. The room was dark, but she squinted, staring at Mary's faded handwritten scrawl, her ancient ancestor's garbled ramblings.

Mary was an infant at the time the curse was cast. She was a curse born Hickory, doomed to suffer the fate of her sisters and her ancestors to come. Except she hadn't. Spencer had murdered Mary. Wolfric said she wasn't supposed to die like that, not by his hand. His words came back to her as she flicked the pages. The last thing she wanted was to tangle with Mary again.

Win thumbed through the worn pages. They crinkled as she folded them back. She poked out her tongue in concentration, wishing she could have slept, content, like Grayson. She couldn't rest.

Win narrowed her eyes, and read a passage near the end of the diary, and she noticed how Mary's writing became loose-handed, frantic...careless.

Tonight I walk, and I will join with him at last. I will become what my sisters fear and embrace the animal inside me. What will I be? A bird-like poor Vivienne. A fox-like Louisa...or maybe the wolf...like Eliza. I will be free and join with my maker...

Win shivered. Join with her maker? She rolled her shoulders, reliving the night Mary had been in this very room. She remembered the blood on her neck as she was about to depart the spirit plane.

"It always has to be this way...I go to him, and I die...." Mary had said it. But what did it mean?

Her grandpa's letter sat folded by her bed. His words echoed back to her. Mary, Louisa—killed by a Riley. Mary was supposed to die, but not by Spencer. Preparing herself, Win read on.

The stone fills me with power...I know I can cross and join him. He will give me his light and make me what I should be...not this wretched carcass I must endure...blood will open the door.

Win flicked the pages and then found the entry stopped. Mary's writing trailed into nothing, as though she'd been erased from history. Did she want to cross...cross where? To become like her sister, forcing her Calling. But Win knew that never happened. Mary died that night, shot dead by Grayson's ancestor.

Startling her, Grayson woke up. Shifting to his elbow, he watched her with sleepy interest, the chain around his neck glinting in the light. "What are you doing?"

Win hummed. "Light reading."

"Doesn't look light—judging by your face."

"It's here, Grayson," she said, tapping the closed book, the smell of dust wafting under her nose as she shoved it back under the bed. "How is Mary linked with this? With Spencer? With the body in the oak?"

"Don't you think you should sleep?"

Frustrated tears pricked her eyes. "I can't."

"Win, please." He looked worried, letting his knuckles trace over her bare arm. "There's nothing we can do, not tonight."

She snuck under his arm, tracing the bones of his hand with the pads of her fingers. She closed her eyes and prayed Mary wouldn't make another appearance. Her hand found the chain around her neck, the two pendants hanging together, and she wished John would return. His ghost would be one she'd love to see.

"Win?" Grayson's voice rumbled against her shoulder blade.

"Hmm?"

He held her tighter, keeping her from leaving the bed one more time. "Promise me you wont do anything stupid."

When she didn't answer immediately, he poked her arm. "Win?"

"Okay, I promise." She bit down on her lip, thinking of Luke and how she'd lied right to his face. Was it her imagination, or did Grayson's grip increase slightly?

It wouldn't matter in the end. If she decided to leave, he wouldn't be able to stop her.

THIRTY-ONE

Light spilled under the crack in the door, and the heavy tread of labored footsteps trudged up the stairs. Disrupted from sleep, Win leaped from the bed and threw open the door. Rowan mounted the stairs, carrying Evan, asleep in her arms. Rowan kicked her bedroom door open with her toe, and Win followed her sister on quiet feet. Rowan folded Evan into bed, and right before she covered her with a duvet, Win spotted the marks on Evan's thigh.

Rowan and Win locked gazes, horrified as the long, jagged scar ran right from Evan's hip down to her calf, like she'd been sliced with a knife. The skin healed, knitted and neat, as though the wound had been inflicted years ago—in another century. Win held her arms out to her sister, and Rowan broke and ran into them. Her shoulders trembled as she sobbed.

"I can't stop him, Win," she said, her wet cheek pressing against hers. "He's hurting her, and I can't stop him."

Tearfully, Rowan lay down beside her, and Win edged out of the room, allowing their privacy. Win stood alone in the empty, dark corridor. The house was silent, and breathed as if lulled into a deep sleep. She could hear her father snoring down the hall. Light crept through the windows, and it was nearly morning.

Win padded to her room as a cold draft snaked around her feet. Hairs on her neck stood on end. She froze, feeling eyes on her back. Willing herself to turn, the glimpse she caught of Mary was so fleeting, she swore she nearly imagined it.

But she'd been there for a split second, hovering at the end of the corridor. Shivering, Win shut the door, drawn to the window, where the drapes were half-open. Swallowing, Win knelt on the window seat, her blood-chilling.

Mary waited in the yard, with her back turned, facing out to the dark, snowy woods. She thought of Evan, laying beside Rowan, bruised and beaten, and going through hell in the past. With her mouth dry, Win yanked the curtains shut and fingered the chain at her neck.

Win had sent him there. This was her mistake.

This ends now... If she used the flame and jumped now, she could end this. If she found him, faced him head on, this could be over.

Still dressed in her pajamas, she leaned over Grayson and kissed his temple. "I'm sorry, don't be mad at me," she whispered in his ear, heaving a relieved sigh when his only response was to roll onto his stomach. She opened the door with a cat's precision, leaving it ajar in case it creaked as she closed it.

Tiptoeing down the stairs, her heart raced, she threw on boots and coat and dashed out the backdoor. Slapping across the yard, she hurtled over the frozen ground, cold air stinging the back of her throat.

Wolfric hadn't warned her what would happen if she pushed her jumps. He'd been vague about most aspects of his little gift. But her body pulled into focus. The burn on her chest pulsated under her skin.

I can do this...for Evan...

Finding a small clearing, she rooted to the spot, fire tickling her palms like her body already knew what to expect. She whispered the word repeatedly in her head, her feet going numb as ice seeped in through her shoes. Her eyes opened, her focus waning as she heard feet rushing through the undergrowth straight at her.

Whipping her head, the black wolf exploded out of the bushes in the distance. Luke careered toward her, gaining speed, and her heart burst into a panic. Win spluttered, annoyed somehow he'd known. Like she could ever hide this from him. How could you hide from the person who knew everything about you?

Back off, Luke!...I have to do this!

Don't you dare, Winifred Adler...don't you dare jump!

She closed her eyes, but before she could spit out the words, Grayson ran through the bush, half-dressed and screaming her name. Pursued from two different directions, she squeezed her eyes tight and tried to block them out.

"Win! Don't do it!" he yelled, jumping a log in his path. "Please wait!"

"I have to," she cried in reply, her voice rippling in the wind. "I can't watch her suffer another second!"

The ancient word bubbled in her throat, panic seized her, and she spat it out carelessly, shouting it in the morning mist. Luke gained distance as she somehow managed to say the word, but in her own tongue, as if some hidden part of her *knew* the ancient language, claimed a connection to it. She screamed, *"Fire!"*

"Win, *no!*"

Grayson and Luke nearly collided, both hurtling to a stop as Win dispersed into a ball of flames, and the girl they loved was nothing but ash.

THIRTY-TWO

Ablaze with shimmering heat, Win couldn't open her eyes. Gritting her teeth, stark white light burned behind her lids, but something felt wrong. Her skin puckered, blistered, and peeled away from bone, the searing temperature of the flame enfolding her like a blanket.

This wasn't ending. The jump hadn't brought her to Evan, she was trapped inside the fire.

Where was the cool relief? The drop-off as she reached the other side? The Hare and Wolf pendant melted, the silver bubbling hot against her flesh, so hot it stuck to her chest. The burn on her collar bone sizzled as smoke and fumes clogged her throat, suffocating her till her eyes rolled and bugged.

Roaring, deafening, thunderous noise filled her skull. The sound of fire, like rockets taking off from a launch pad. Panting hard, she opened her eyes, and nothing was left of her human body. To her horror, she realized this wasn't ending. She was trapped. Wolfric warned her about jumping too soon. Light pooled out of her nail beds, an orange blaze searing from her fingers as she slowly dissolved into ash.

Suspended in flame, she stared through the smoke. Her body was gone, dissolved in flame, and she was just floating consciousness. Tears leaked from the corners of her eyes, telling herself she had to hold on. Win was trapped in the jump, reforming and burning, over and over in an endless cycle.

Ahead of her on the brow of the hill, stood the oak. Its naked limbs scratched for the sky like fingers desperate to claw their way out of the earth.

Mary Hickory juddered in her vision. The black-haired girl circled the oak repeatedly, her fingers tickling the bark. Mary's dress fell in tatters at her feet. She was smiling as she walked, aimless, heady. She paused and stared out at Win, as if she could see her through the smoke, her empty, black eyes locked on hers.

Angrily Win spat, "What do you want me to see? I know Katie is dead. I know that's why my parents left."

"Katie was just a moment in time—a sad, unfortunate event. Like Callum, like Olivia. Like your grandfather. Ghosts who never really left us."

"Like you?"

Mary smiled, revealing her little jagged teeth. "Like me." She turned her back and circled the oak. "It's buried here, Win. You have to see. She was...magnificent."

Terrified, Win gritted her teeth as the scene shifted, and through the rolling haze of heat, she saw a woman standing on a scaffold beneath the oak. She was bound, hands behind her back, wearing a filthy torn gown, barefoot with her long, black hair hanging loose around her face. Dark, hollow eyes stared blankly out of her gaunt face, defeated but strangely unafraid.

A small group of men rounded the tree, watching with mounting horror as the minister read words from a bible, his stormy glare flicking from the ancient book to the bound woman standing below the tree.

Jacob Fraser stood behind her and faced a jeering, feverish crowd as he read from a prayer book. "Vecula Varga, you have been found guilty of the murder of eight men, the unholy practice of witchcraft, and altercations with the devil. You are ungodly, a demon, and sentenced to hang by the neck until you die. May God have mercy upon your wretched soul."

Suspended in horror, Win had no choice but to watch. In her last moments, Vecula looked out upon the baying crowd and began to chant, sweat beading on her forehead.

"Kuxtal...Katan...Otoch...Manik...Vikli..."

The minister reared, afraid of this unholy woman and what spilled from her lips. With a nod to the executioner, he kicked the platform from under her feet. Win cried out, her head filled with the sickly, squirming sound of a woman strangled to death. Her feet kicked, and she swung in a horrible pendulous momentum until she went still. Vecula hung perfectly still, eyes wide and chanting those words.

"Kuxtal...Katan...Otoch...Manik...Vikli..."

The crowd sensed the peculiarity. Something had gone very wrong, and someone screamed. People fled as Vecula hung dead-eyed and spinning from the oak branch till the last word died on her lips.

Win cringed as a fresh wave of heat engulfed her body. Torn away from the scene, she bared down and screamed as her hair fizzled, frying to nothing on her scalp. She saw the oak...young, with fresh green leaves, and the hole dug at its base when she dared to look.

Vecula's body was thrown into the hole, buried, forgotten, deep, alone. The townspeople threw stones in the hole, and spat at the dead woman, braver now she was dead.

They covered the hole, and time passed, the leaves crisped and fell, and the world moved on. The oak shimmered with light, its roots twisted and bent, and below Vecula dissolved, her hair shrank to strands, skin pulled back from her lips, eye sockets empty and worm-eaten, while the roots of the oak bound her, trapping her in death.

Win screeched an unholy sound as waves of heat rippled through her, the scene dissolved, and she saw Mary Hickory alone in the woods, kneeling at the base of the stone. Mary held up her arms, enraptured as blue light tore through her body, her ebony hair billowing in the breeze. Win guessed she was here to complete her Calling...to join...with her maker as described in the diary entry. Mary blazed with blue light. It seared from her mouth, and her eyes as she slowly began to take animal form, her body shrinking, molding into its new shape.

The Calling was near completion.

A hunter peeled out of the woods. Hidden in the shadow, he fired an arrow, piercing Mary's jugular with accurate precision. Mary convulsed as blood spilled from her gullet, soaking through her nightgown as she fell face-first into the grass.

This was Mary's true death, not the one inflicted by Spencer.

The blue light wasn't enough to save her, and the electric pulsations that pushed her toward her Calling pulsed, waned and exploded into the clearing. A stream of black energy left Mary's body, like tiny particles of black dust. It formed a crude bodily shape and vanished into the woods like a specter. The stone went cold, dark, and disappeared into the mist.

Win saw the oak through the passage of time. The oak's leaves blossomed and blackened, the roots deep into the earth, where Vecula lay buried and forgotten.

"I can't take this anymore," Win screamed. She was barely holding on, suspended in light, ablaze. The heat tore through her muscles, shredding the ligament underneath. "I have to stop."

It's close...the last piece...this can't be all there is.

The oak sat in the sunshine, and Win followed behind a pretty blonde-haired lady—Olivia Fraser, tightly holding her child's hand. Spencer. Olivia waddled, her baby bump weighing her down as they trudged through the grass. They walked in the woods, armed with picnic blankets and toys, nothing strange or sinister. Finding a spot near the old oak, Spencer played, then darted to the old tree.

"Spencer, come back," she called, tossing off her shoes as she dashed through the woods to catch him.

The oak stood on the brow of the hill. Spencer gained speed, ignoring his mother as she gave chase. Spencer's arms opened, and he fell, grappling the oak's trunk. Black light shimmered around the tree. The same particles of dust that left Mary's dead body fell around the boy, soaking into his skin. "Spencer, come here," Olivia laughed with relief as she caught up with him, scooping him up in her arms.

Win's gaze widened...the oak shimmered and pulsated. Olivia took his hand and led them back to the blanket, where she packed up and took them home. The peaceful scene shifted to a dark bedroom, where under a thin sheet, Olivia writhed, sweat-slick on her skin as her young son stood over her while she slept fitfully.

"Mommy, there's a monster in the house...."

Spencer's words should have coated Win's skin with ice, but it sizzled, and she was engulfed with terror. Win tried not to look. This was the night Katie died. It seemed like a horrible, tragic coincidence Olivia fell ill right on the day something dark and evil entered their home. Win already had many reasons to hate him, but this wasn't one of them. *Something* was inside Mercy. As much as she wanted to toss blame for Katie's death at Spencer's feet, she sensed he was innocent. The rest, not so much.

Win felt cold, but it wasn't a relief from the heat. Struck with crippling fear, she willed herself back to the present and prayed for this firey torture to be over. Was it over? Could this finally come to an end?

Win had experienced several jumps in one hit, her body regenerating and healing, only to be burned up again like a spacecraft on re-entry.

The image juddered and blurred Win's vision, and as her skin peeled and blew like ash on the breeze, she screamed. Sucked back through a blazing vortex of orange light, she woke screaming and rolling in Grayson's arms.

"Shush...Win you're home... it's okay!"

Luke moved closer, and the wolf pushed his wet nose into her face. She wrapped one arm around him. He whimpered and lay beside her. "I'm okay...I think...."

She wasn't okay. There wasn't one part of her that was okay. Smoke rose from her clothing, and under her healed flesh, her muscles ached, raw, bitten, and chewed up by flame. Underneath her bones begged for respite.

Grayson's eyes were stormy, angrier than she'd ever seen him. "You lied to me—you promised."

Breathing hard, she rolled, her body across his lap, her skin tingled. "I'm not sorry, Grayson. I had to."

"I hope it was worth it," he snapped, mirroring what Rowan said only a few days ago. Lungs tight, like she'd been squeezed in a juicer, she lay her hand on his shoulder and then looked to Luke.

"Call Ella..." she panted. Black dots formed across her eyes, her vision spinning out of focus so hard vomit surged up her gullet. Retching, she swallowed it down.

"It was worth it...Vecula never left Cedar Wood...she's still here. She's *always* been here."

THIRTY-THREE

It was his last chance. After this jump, Wolfric didn't know the fate that would await him.

But he had to try. All day he'd been in a foul mood, grumping at students, blasting his temper at unsuspecting drivers behind the wheel of his car. His fist clenched so tight he thought he might end up stuck that way. Impatience irked him, and he headed to Travers, his local bar on Boston common, to drink away his stress. Something needled him. It was anxiety, worry.

He was worried about the kid. She didn't deserve a grain of what he was putting her through. He was worried about Evan, suffering god knows what in another time, a place he couldn't easily visit.

So he drank, and it burned his throat, so he drank some more. Numb and inebriated, he stumbled through the snowy streets when he slumped to his ass.

Blinding pain shot through his temples, and he couldn't breathe for a second like a fist had tightened around his gullet. A knot formed in his stomach, the cord binding him to Evan sang, vibrating, across the years.

Evan was dying.

Clutching his chest, he heaved and wobbled in his boots. God, why had he drunk so much?

Wolfric stumbled into an alley, his boots sloshing through puddles. Catching his breath, he felt for the wall, cold and wet, closed his eyes, and imagined Euelea. Yet again, he was breaking his one rule. Evan was his exception, and had been since she was an infant. Even though she'd lived through this, her thread was unraveling and it scared him.

Come on babe, show me where you are...

He grunted, imagining her, seeing her with his mind's eye till she was so vivid and real he could smell her. Her pain, and anguish screamed at him across the decades. Wolfric choked. He needed to be with his sister.

The words left his lips. "Ka'ja'le." An unimaginable sting encased his old, weary body, and within seconds he burned, crisping and frying like meat in a hot pan. Gritting his teeth, he balled his fists , yelling through the pain as he arrived smoking at the other side.

Okay, where the hell are you?

Where he'd arrived, night had fallen, and it was bitter, the air so cold it threatened snow. He sensed she was out here, and panic built in his chest. Was she hurt? Wounded? How could he have left her to this fate? Stalking through thickets of trees, wet leaves and mud stuck to his boots, and guilt clawed at his gut. He was the worst big brother—the absolute worst.

Campfire smoke lingered on the breeze. He melted into the tree line, spotting the glow of embers through the trees ahead. His breath halted as he crept closer, his boots squelching in the mud.

Please...be alive babe.

Spying a fallen log lying discarded nearby, he ducked and grabbed at it with one hand, prepared to fight if the bastard attacked. The smell of blood floated in the air, soaked into the ground. You didn't live as long as him without recognizing the smell of fear.

"Shit—Evan!" he choked on his words, spotting her laying on her side by the fire. Shaking, he knelt, carefully turning her over. Anger lodged in his throat, as he brushed strands of matted, bloodied hair from her face. She was breathing, alive but barely.

"Evan...wake up, please. *Euelea*!" He cradled her head in his lap, the sight of ugly welts covering her arms and legs making vomit surge up his chest. She'd been beaten sick. Spencer had tossed her about like a ragdoll. Breathing, shallow and uneven, her eyes fluttered open. "Wolfric?"

He tried not to bawl as he held her, cradling her body to his chest. But both her dark eyes were bloodshot red, and a stray tear leaked out of the corner. "I'm so sorry, babe. Evan, forgive me for leaving you."

"Wolfric?" Her eyes shifted, suddenly lucid, awake, and panicking. "You can't be here."

"He's not here, don't worry."

She gripped his forearm with a ferocity he'd not expected. "No, you're wrong. He is here somewhere. He'll have seen you coming—"

"Evan, listen to me!" He shushed her, mortified as pain crossed her features, and she fell back over his lap. "Listen to me...you have to hold on. For as long as you can."

Shaking, she sniffed back tears. "I can't hold on much longer, Wolfric. I'm so tired. I just want it over."

"Evan, listen to me. Remember who we are. We are *Primus*—the first family. We haven't survived all these years to be wiped out by an overgrown frat boy with a grudge. We are stronger—you are stronger. Hold on!" His fingers gripped her shoulders, and he wiped an escaped tear as it tracked down her cheek. She shook her head weakly.

"No, Wolfric. You underestimate him, it's more than a grudge. I can't explain it. There's something bad in his heart...."

"Evan—"

"Go...please!"

"I'm not going to leave you to this fate. I can't stay long, but you have to hold on. I will come back for you."

"Wolfric go—now!"

"If I can't make it back here, I'll send someone—a girl. Don't be afraid of her. She'll help you."

"*Wolfric!*" Her scream filled the clearing. Too late he felt breath on his neck. The creature tore into him, arms and legs around his waist, claws embedding into flesh.

Wolfric hollered, a guttural sound loud enough to terrify small children, and he tossed Spencer free of his back with strength the monster hadn't bargained for. Opening his palms, Spencer rolled, licking his canine teeth. It wouldn't be long before Wolfric was pulled back through the flame, and in that second he made his decision. If he killed him now, so be it.

"Touch my sister once more and I'll rip you in half," he growled. Air fogged between them, both panting as they circled one another. Staring him down, Wolfric admitted he didn't like his odds. He hadn't expected Spencer to be so large, the seams of his frock coat practically shredded by the muscle present underneath.

Glancing quickly at Evan laying helpless in the dirt, he gnashed his teeth, seething with loathing and anger. Spencer rendered her useless, bleeding and limp, and even with what little magic she possessed, she'd have been no match. "You're a piece of shit," he cried. He wished he could take her with him, but there was no time.

Rearing, Spencer lunged, grappling the taller man to the ground. Fists flew, and under his weight, Wolfric's knuckles pounded ribs relentlessly till he heard a snap. Wolfric decided to show Spencer what his fangs were really for. Grabbing the man's forearm, Wolfric sank his fangs into skin and Spencer roared, black-eyed with pain.

Spencer rolled sideways but Wolfric grabbed a fistful of hair, crushing Spencer's mutated face into the ground till he heard his nose break and blood pooled around his head. Panting from exertion, Wolfric rolled, but not fast enough. Spencer flew, pinning him with his thighs, and sank his teeth into the forearm Wolfric brought up to protect his throat. It was a dull, piercing sting, and with a yell, he shook him free.

They both crawled to their feet, dirty, bloodied, and sweating. Wolfric sensed the familiar prickles of fire in his palm, and with a savage grin, he licked his lips. The two men, equal in size and build, circled one another like sharks, Spencer dead-eyed and focused, Wolfric boiling with rage.

"You aren't going to win," Spencer said, wiping blood off his chin. "I'm going to get what I want in the end—I always do."

Wolfric's eyes shone with emotion. "You didn't have to hurt her," he yelled. "You didn't need to beat her. I'll kill you myself."

Evan groaned on the ground, barely able to lift her head. "Wolfric...please leave..."

"Even she agrees," Spencer said with a nasty grin, jerking his head to the beaten woman on the ground. "Even she knows you aren't a match."

Wolfric's palms blistered. It was coming. Spencer lunged and pinned him to the ground, wrapping his clawed fingers around his throat and squeezed. Wolfric's eyes bugged, air shut off in his windpipe. Flailing, he grabbed Spencer's jaw, digging in his fingers in a savage twist. Spencer was too strong, and Wolfric sweated, as his vision swam.

"I may not be a match for you...but I know someone who is. You *are dust*, Spencer Fraser."

It wasn't much, but his smile dropped for a second, a second of doubt. Spencer released him and rolled off. He tore a hand through his mane of tangled, sandy hair, leaving blood and gore in its wake. "If you mean Win, then you're out of luck. She's never been able to live up to the task...the lofty pedestal she's been placed on. When it comes down to it—she never comes through. She'll always fail."

Wolfric chuckled as, step by step, they neared one another. "I think you might be surprised."

Spencer leaped. In a frenzy of teeth and claws, he wrestled Wolfric to the ground, but this time he went willingly. Flames curled out of his fingertips and grabbed Spencer's coat, holding him close in a tight embrace. "Burn you fucker!"

All too late, Spencer realized he was alight. The flames caught his coat, licked through to his soft fur underneath, and with a howl he rolled free, leaping around the clearing, frantically patting away the flames engulfing his body.

Wolfric went up in a blaze of light, but he cast one last look at his sister laying on the ground. "Hold on for me, babe. We are coming for you."

The last thing Wolfric had the pleasure of seeing before he was sucked back, was Spencer howling and dancing in agony, entirely on fire.

THIRTY-FOUR

Every muscle under her skin was taught, and stung. Juddering, she woke in a pool of sweat, hair stuck to her forehead. Saliva coated the inside of her mouth, and her innards rolled. Win rolled sideways, where by a miracle, Luke held a bucket. She vomited into it, sobbing and spitting.

Luke peeled a strand of hair off her face before it fell into the contents of the bucket. "Ew—gross, Win."

Dimly, she recalled nursing Luke in his hour of need, and she'd been far less squeamish. Teeth chattering, she fell back on a soft pillow. She was in a room, a nice room, reminding her of the inside of a fancy hotel. The pillow under her head was squashy, and the sheets soft. "Where are we?"

"One of the guest rooms," Luke filled her in, cocking his eyes at someone in the corner. Win detected Grayson, painfully rolling her neck in time to spot him rising from a wingback chair by the window. "We didn't think it was a good idea to take you home."

Shivering, she nodded weakly. "Good plan." Home was out of bounds. Her parents didn't need to see her like this. Right now, her skin was sensitive, like she'd been flayed alive, and despite the wracking shudders taking over her body, she was burning up. Grayson pressed a hand to her forehead and it came away slick.

"This isn't good." He looked angry, his nostrils flared. "Why don't you *ever* listen?"

"I'm not sorry," she whimpered, rolling and yanking the bucket out of Luke's grip, in time to puke again. He pulled a face, visibly swallowing.

"You're going to empty," Luke attempted a weary joke.

"I need to get up."

"You need to rest." Luke fixed his icy stare on Grayson. "This wouldn't have happened if *you* had been watching her."

"Watching her? She's not a kid," Grayson grumbled a reply. "She made me a promise and I believed her."

"Ha! Well, that'd be your first mistake. First of many."

Acid burning her throat, she ignored the both of them as they bickered across her body. Her head sank into the pillow, every fiber she possessed willing her to sleep. But how could she after what she saw? The pieces were finally slotting together. The oak...Vecula...and Spencer. Had Vecula cursed Spencer? An ache split her temples and she shut her eyes as light flooded the room from the hallway. A door banged open and a shape filled the space.

"What the hell is going on?" Jake barked. Luke slipped from the bed holding up his hands.

"Dad...*indoor* voice!"

"What's the matter with her?" Jake, still in a robe and slippers and carrying a coffee, paced across the room. He disregarded the mug, planting it on the bedside cabinet, then pressed his hand to her head.

"Uh..." He winced as he wiped her sweat on his robe. "Is she sick? You could have said before I touched her!"

"She jumped," Grayson filled in the blanks.

Jake slipped onto the bed next to her, rolling her carefully onto her back. His features went taught, fixed in a hard grimace, as he gingerly pulled a thin sheet across her. She was still wearing her pajamas. "She's burning up. Have you called Alice?"

Luke and Grayson exchanged a worried look across the bed. Jake grumbled. "For god's sake—call her *mother.*"

Shooting the two of them a death glare, he was about to rise when Win caught his sleeve. "I saw Spencer..."

Jake, ashen, stared down at her. When he didn't respond, she peeled her face off the pillow, her lashes wet and sticky. "I saw him. He was standing over Olivia.... I think Vecula cursed him."

Jake's brow furrowed. "Vecula?"

"Evan's sister...a witch. She's buried under the oak out by the old church."

Grayson sucked in his breath. "It's her?"

"They hung her there...and then they buried her. She's always been here."

Before he left, Win caught the sleeve of Jake's robe, pulling him close. She needed to tell him what she'd learned. Jake eyed her with concern, but his lips curled when she said, "I don't think Spencer was responsible for Katie. I don't know for sure, but I think he was innocent."

"Then it was just an awful coincidence?" Jake said, and Win nodded, settling on the pillow.

"I think so," she said. "But...I hope it helps you. Maybe a little."

It suddenly struck Win why Mary whispered Katie's name in the first vision. She was meant to unravel the mystery, learn the truth, and in doing so, give Jake peace. His son never killed Katie, but it didn't mean he was innocent. Spencer had much to answer for.

Jake half smiled and squeezed her shoulder. "Go to sleep."

Even though glaring sunshine streamed through the open door, Win's eyes fluttered closed, unable to fight the pull any longer. Numb, she sagged on the pillow and let sleep wash over her. When she woke, Jake, Luke, and Grayson were gone, and sitting on the bed next to her was her mother.

The pad of Alice's thumb stroked the back of her hand, and the light, gentle touch sent a crawling chill across her skin. Win moaned. "You're in shock," Alice whispered. "Just sleep."

"I need to get up."

Alice rolled her eyes at her daughter's defiance. "It's too bad Evan is laid up. We could use her right now."

Win shifted, alarmed. "Is she okay?"

"She's exhausted...Rowan is with her." Alice shifted on the bed, running a hand over Win's hair. "I wish you had told me about this. This...*jumping*. For god sake. We're supposed to be there for you."

Win smiled weakly. "You were a little preoccupied. And now I know why."

Alice let a sigh drag through her lips, looking out of the window. "I'm sorry you found out like that. There is still a lot to talk about."

"Yeah, it'd have been *a lot* easier for me if you'd just told me..." Win joked, half-hearted and tired. "But I understand. We get to start over now, all of us."

Alice smiled and kissed her temple. "My little fixer."

A fat tear escaped her closed lid, leaking onto the pillow, her thoughts turning to Evan, laying in her hospital bed. "I can't fix everything."

Alice shushed her and stroked her hair, guessing her train of thought. "We can't do any more to help Evan right now. Everyone is here, waiting downstairs."

"I'm getting up," Win said, hardly able to bear it any longer.

Alice waved her hands in protest, as Win rolled and moved to her elbows. Pain sliced through her center as she sat. Something prodded her neck and with a start, she fingered the chains at her throat, both Iris and John's pendants, now melded together from the heat of the fire. They didn't even resemble the Wolf or the Hare, just a melted blob. Win peeled it off her neck and hollered as skin came with it. Alice gasped. "Win—no!"

"I'm getting up!"

Wobbling, she got to her feet, and the world spun, sending her careening towards the carpet as two hands caught her wrists. "Got you," Jake said, straightening her. Heavily, she leaned on his arm, unaware he'd been in the room.

"Jeez, you are almost as stealthy as Grayson," she quipped, as the room swayed. She took a step, her vision wobbled and she groped for the bedpost.

"If you're going to be so pig-headed, at least let us help you with the stairs—there's a lot."

Win dabbed at her dry lips with her tongue, in need of a drink and a toothbrush, her mouth felt like the inside of a litter box. Jake's arm wove around her back, lightly supporting her as she contemplated tackling the long, sweeping staircase. A marble hallway awaited her at the bottom and she imagined cracking her skull if she fell. No amount of Therian healing would bring her back from that. She tugged his shirt and he tossed her a wry smile, guessing her thoughts. "Back to bed?"

"No—a shower please."

Jake groaned, and before she could protest lifted her off her feet and carried her into a nearby bathroom, dumping her next to a deep, luxury tub. He shot Alice a look, rolling up his sleeves. "I'll leave you to it."

Alice tutted, and helped Win undress. The moment her clothes were off, she broke into goose bumps, hardly able to stand the feel of water on her skin. Alice gritted her teeth, her pained expression enough to convince Win she must look ghastly. Her mother gently lathered her hair, and Win whimpered in pain, clutching the wall as soap roiled down her body. But she felt better, lighter, and after Alice toweled her dry she was ready to face the stairs. Despite the clawing sensation of spiders under her skin, Alice's touch was comforting, and after a while she let her mother wrap her in her arms.

Jake waited outside the room with fresh clothes, slacks and a hoodie. "Carla's," he said. "Yours smell like bonfire—I threw them in the trash." She ducked back inside the room and changed.

To Win's dismay, he held open his arms, as if to carry her bridal style down the stairs, and her eyes flung to her mother. Alice shrugged helplessly. Jake noticed her confusion and said, "Win, it's this or a fireman's carry. You should go down and put your boyfriend out of his misery—he's stared a hole in the carpet."

When she refused, Jake threw his glare skyward and yelled Grayson's name over the banister. Within seconds, Grayson's blonde head appeared, his face pinched as he trotted up the stairs. Win held out her arms but Grayson scowled, refusing to meet her gaze. He was pissed with her for lying, for not telling him what she planned.

Win grunted and snuck an arm around his neck, letting him slip her off her feet. She winced as air hit the blistered soles of her feet. "Where's Dad?" she called over his shoulder as he lifted her down the winding staircase.

"He's staying with Rowan at the house—she needs him there. This is all such a mess." Alice followed closely behind, her wane smile not reaching her eyes. Overnight, she looked like she'd aged, flecks of grey tousling her strawberry blonde hair. At the bottom of the stairs, Jake led the way to the ornate family room. The fire crackled in the hearth and Win didn't think she could stand to sit too close. Luke and Ella sat together on the couch, and to her surprise, Cole was at the desk reading over a large book. Win's face cracked as she smiled. "Hey!"

Ella bolted from the couch and flung her arms around her, nearly knocking her to her backside. "Oh, Win—why did you do this?"

Win hugged her friend as tightly as she could manage without swaying, letting Ella lead her to the couch where she plopped beside Luke. Luke's eyes were watery, his hand found her nape. "Good to see you up—we were worried."

Grayson hovered over the three of them, thrusting a glass of water into her hand. "Whatever you found out better be worth nearly frying alive for, Win."

She didn't dare look at him. She knew he was angry, and something resembling disappointment lay in his eyes, reminding her of her father. Lying was something they promised they would never do. He was her rock and there was nothing she couldn't tell him, and yet she'd run the first chance she got, knowing he'd try and stop her.

"It was worth it, but I don't have the strength to keep going over it, so you better all listen."

Win waited for them to gather, Luke huddled next to her and Ella perched on the arm of the couch. Cole listened intently from the desk and Grayson stood in the door, arms folded. Win made quick work, relaying everything she'd seen in the brief, painful time, right from the moment Mary was speared with an arrow, to Vecula strung up from the tree.

"Those words, the final things she said as she died. Can you remember them?" Ella asked.

Win scrunched her nose. "I can try."

Ella dashed to the desk, where she prodded Cole to move aside and grabbed a notebook and pen, thrusting it into Win's hands. Ella grabbed Cole by the collar and pulled him towards the door. "See if you can write them down—Cole you're with me."

"Yes ma'am." He gave her a mock salute. "Where exactly are we going?"

"The museum—I think I know some books in the basement that might be useful, if I can convince my mom to let us in. Wolfric said his native tongue was still around, hidden in other languages. Win, see if you can remember anything and we'll be back soon!"

Luke, concerned he'd not been invited, rose from his seat and watched forlornly as the two of them trailed out the door. He muttered something under his breath as he hurried out a different door, pride dented. Win watched him leave but didn't say anything to inflame the situation. Jake and Alice were somewhere in the building, and for the moment, she was alone with Grayson, who was staring daggers at her across the room.

"Come here, *please*." She forced away the knot in her throat. Grayson grunted and kicked away from the wall with his boot.

"You've got homework." The door slammed behind him. Rather than chase him and demand his attention, which was her strategy when he got mad at her, she sat, notebook poised on her lap, and scrambled back through her foggy memory to recall Vecula's dying words.

Win's hand moved seamlessly as she scribbled them down. Fingers trailing to her throat, she fiddled with the chain, now a melted blob of silver. Her breath quickened as she recalled the way Vecula twirled on the rope, almost as if it were a game, one last macabre party, a way for everyone to remember her. Win shivered and put the book down, hopping off the couch and going to find him.

She wandered the hallway, pausing by the mantle as she spotted his hulking figure in the parlor. Hands shoved deeply in the wells of his pockets, if he heard her approach he didn't turn, jaw bunched and eyes fixed, as he stared at Callum's painting.

Win snuck up behind him, linking her arms under his and pressing her chin into his back. "Please don't be mad at me—you know why I had to do this."

Her chin moved as he let out a caged breath. "Win..."

"No." Her eyes were wet. "Don't you dare be angry with me. I had to go back. I can't stand this, Grayson, this waiting game...she's my family!"

Taking her wrist and pinning her to the wall, he kissed her as though he hadn't seen her for a week. Win wound her arms around his neck, wishing they were back in their motel, alone, only them. Her heart knocked under her shirt as he let out an anguished moan against her mouth before pulling away. He kissed her temple, resting his chin on her head. "I'm so *mad* at you."

She kissed his jaw, trailing around to his ear, all the while he pressed her against his chest in a tight hug. "I'd like to see you when we're really fighting."

He pulled back, forehead pressed to hers. "I mean it. You shouldn't have run. Haven't I proven I'd back you up, no matter what? You didn't need to hide what you were planning. *You* are my family, Win. I can't lose you."

"I'm sorry," she said, running her hand through his messy hair. She *was* sorry. After the night at the cabin, they'd promised each other no secrets. Grayson came back to her completely open, laid bare, hiding nothing, and she in turn asked so much from him. She'd asked him to shelter her and keep her safe, which he'd done without pause, facing the wrath of her family. "I won't lie to you again."

His eyes dragged to the chain at her neck, he flipped it over and frowned. "This got fried..." he hissed, as though imagining the heat causing the two pendants to meld into one. "It's a shame—can I have this?"

She let out a shaky laugh, then pulled the chain over her head, letting it drop into his open palm. She suddenly remembered he'd pinned her to the wall, his hips locking her in place, and blushed. "We ought to..."

"Yeah," he said gruffly, letting her go. "Shaggy and Velma will be back any minute."

They walked back to the family room, and she slapped his shoulder. "I thought you never watched cartoons as a kid?"

"I didn't." He looked embarrassed. "When you used to go out at five am at the motel, I couldn't sleep till you got back, so I watched the television, and that weird cartoon was on at that time of the morning." Grayson's face creased in mischief. "Ella reminds me of Velma."

Win sniggered. "Wait, does that make Luke, Fred—or Scooby?" She burst out laughing, as Luke entered from the other door, swigging from a coke can.

"I see you are feeling better," he fired with a sneer, flinging himself onto the couch, in a mood Win guessed had something to do with Ella taking off with Cole. Win let her arm trail from Grayson's shoulder and plopped down next to him.

"Did your dad talk to you?"

Luke folded his legs under him, batting the empty can back and forth between his two hands. "Yeah—I had a half-sister I never knew about. It makes me sick, what they must have gone through. But we talked—and..." He broke off, his eyes searching hers. "I know—where my mom is."

Win gasped. "Luke....that's great! He told you?"

"Well I kind of demanded to know. And finally he gave in, admitted he'd sent her away years ago because he was scared Spencer would hurt her. Win..." He shifted on the seat, nervously taking her hand. "When this is over...will you come with me to see her?"

Win's chest swelled, delighted he'd asked. "Oh, Luke, of course I would...but don't you think...maybe Ella might be the better one to go with you?"

Annoyed at the mention of her name, he dropped her hand. "I don't think she would."

"Of course she would! You should ask her—in fact I'm not taking no for an answer. I'm going to pretend you haven't even asked me."

A coy smile played on his lips, and she tilted her head to look at him. His nose *was* bigger without his glasses, but it suited him. "She isn't going to take me back, Win. Even if I got on my knees and begged."

Win's lips pursed, snorting out a laugh as she grasped his chin and popped a kiss on his forehead. "You should try it sometime, you might be surprised."

Ella and Cole arrived back at the house along with gusts of wind, and sheets of icy rain. They moved into Jake's library, hauled up on the couches, and tables with a crackling fire burning in the grate. Dutifully, Alice and Jake remained out of sight. Judy bought them snacks, drinks, fuel to keep them going while they poured over the old books Ella had stolen from the museum basement.

Books lay strewn over every available surface. There was a mix of language textbooks from ancient Egyptian and Mesoamerican to old Norse. Win even spotted *Tales of the Shaman*, the book Ella used the night they called Iris out of the spirit plane. Wolfric said their language was old, and hidden through time, so Win guessed Ella grabbed everything she could think of.

"We might be able to spot something that looks like what you heard," Ella chirped hopefully.

Win wondered how difficult this task might be, like looking for a needle in a haystack. On the floor Ella sat cross-legged, and Cole sat on the couch with a book splayed across his lap. The fire crackled, and Luke yawned. He was sitting with his back to the couch, right next to Grayson, who was frantically chewing at his short nail beds.

The morning lapsed into a sleepy afternoon, the weight of the book in her lap, made her drowsy, and Win struggled to focus on some of the language jumping and flickering on the page. The books Ella took from the museum, with her mother's key, were old textbooks, used for schools and colleges, and it seemed every flip of the page turned up nothing.

Win hobbled to the group, and sat across the table from Ella, who was nose-deep in text. She'd chewed her lower lip so hard it was bright red. "Anything?" Win asked.

Ella had the notepad of Win's random scribbles, and she'd copied it down for Cole and Luke to read.

Ella's eyes shot out of a daze, the whites of her eyeballs red. "No. Maybe you should try saying it aloud? It might help. What you heard and what you wrote could be two different things."

Cole stuffed his mouth full of a croissant and slid in next to Ella, leaning over her shoulder. He glanced at Win, licking his lips. "That could be an idea—we've got a lot of language here and some basic words."

Win threaded her fingers together on the tabletop, aware of the group's expectant gaze hot on her skin, and the burden of responsibility settled like a lead weight across her shoulders. They were waiting for her, her plan, her ideas, because somehow, as crazy as it felt, she'd wound up at the head of it all.

"Okay..." she took a gasp of breath and repeated the words aloud, as best she could remember. Cole stared hard, listening and then dove back into the text. Ella nudged him aside, trying to peer over his shoulder as they both tussled with the book.

Cole ground his teeth and relented, holding up his hands in defeat.

"She drives me crazy," he muttered. Win wondered at how close Cole and Ella had become in the last month, and she darted her eyes in Luke's direction, who was hovering hawkishly over the pair.

Grayson shot her a smile from the couch, she got up, throwing herself beside him. Win ran her hand up his arm, stopping at the dimple in his chin. "Are you still mad at me?"

Grayson attempted to look angry, his blonde brows drawing together, but he broke when she pouted. "Seething—can't you tell?" He gathered her closer. "Don't do that to me again, please."

His face pinched, running his hand along her thigh curled on his lap. "I want to keep you, Win Adler. We are here to help you—you should let us."

Win's silence signaled her understanding but not necessarily her agreement. How could they stand in her place when Wolfric chose her to bear this burden? How could she stand back when her sister was torn apart again and again, when she was the target? Guilt was a parasite alive in her muscle, shredding her decisions, making her doubt herself. The line was drawn, but only Win stood on the other side of it.

Win left him to wander to the table, where Cole and Ella still hogged the books. Cole looked miserable, and rubbed at his eyes, she didn't even need to ask if they'd found anything. He and Ella were sharing an old text on Mayan language.

"Say it again," Ella urged, flipping open the thick pages of the book. Above her, Luke sat on the desk, his legs folded under him. "But say it slower, this time."

Win flopped into a chair, the silence of the library oppressive, only the pattering of rain pelting the glass. She closed her eyes and called back the memory of the vision. Vecula's last words whispered on a frightened, tearful breath as the hangman tightened the noose around her neck. Win exhaled it out "I think...Kuxtal...Katan...does that make sense?"

Ella pointed her nose into the book, and ran her fingers along the old text. Luke smiled fondly and stroked the back of her neck, but like a fly she swatted him away. "I need to concentrate!"

"Fine," he grunted, rising to his feet, pacing the carpet. "Anything else you remember?"

Win forced back the vision. Vecula's tear streaked face, moments before her death, her words fluttering on the breeze, words that didn't sound right in her mouth. "Otoch....and, I think....Manik and Vinklii?" Win slapped the table, her cheeks burning. "It's useless! I can't remember."

"You're doing good." Ella smiled in encouragement. "This is ancient language...it's hard!"

Cole peered over Ella's shoulder. "Wait!" he cried, thrusting his finger under her nose and into the book. "*That!* There?"

Ella scowled, annoyed she'd missed it, and batted his hand away. Then she gasped. "Win...did you say Otoch...or Toch?"

Win held out her palms. "Otoch." She nodded. "It was Otoch."

"It means home," Luke breathed, glaring over Ella's shoulder. Win's skin prickled, as though a ball of wool unraveled before her eyes.

"And Manik...means to take over?" Ella said.

"So as in...*home* take over? That's creepy."

Cole grabbed the book out of Ella's hands and the brunette threw him a glare. "Hey!"

"You missed these," Cole protested when she tried to prise it out of his hands. "You aren't the only brain in the room, you know. I can read too!"

Ella sniffed, while Cole bumped her aside. Outside a clap of thunder shook the house and for a second the lights dimmed. Luke shuddered, his expression mirroring Win's as rain pounded the glass. Win rubbed her arms. "I don't like this at all." As if feeling the tension in the air, Grayson rose from his seat, stood behind her, placing his large hands on her shoulders. Win leaned into him and closed her eyes.

His silence was deafening, under the lamp light Cole was pale, and raked his hands through over his fuzzy head.

"Body!" Cole clapped the book shut, grinning from ear to ear. "Vinklii is *body!*"

"You solved the mystery, well done," Ella remarked, smartly, grabbing the book and thrusting it back into her lap. "Now let me do the rest."

There was a flash of lightning and Luke jumped off the desk. Win lifted her chin, her gaze drawn to the direction of the door and the shape of a man lurking there. On her feet, she shrieked, clapping her hands over her mouth. All of them froze, staring at the giant of a man, windswept and soaked in the door. "Wolfric?" Win gasped.

Wolfic Varga staggered through the door, hobbling and panting hard. He leaned on the frame and nearly toppled forward. Win dashed across the room, grabbing him under the arms. "What happened to you?" she asked, panicking, as Grayson took up the slack, dragging him to the couch. She hissed, pulling back his wool coat, revealing bloodied gouges across his torso. "You're hurt!"

"It's alright." He eased her away. "But he beat the hell out of me. I barely got away."

"You jumped?" Win spat. "You said..."

"Evan was in trouble...I could feel her through the thread binding us. I had to use the flame." His breathing sounded wheezy, and Luke shoved a pillow behind his back. "I wanted to kill him. I wish I could have—and spared you this."

Win stared at him with rounded eyes. "You said not to get involved. I *listened* to you. And you just did it anyway?"

"I love her!" Wolfric snapped, wiping grimy sweat off his brow. "She's my kid sister. I went—to give her hope. Surely you understand how you can love someone even though they drive you crazy?"

Win and Luke exchanged a brief glance over his head, before Wolfric finished. "I had to go."

"But you don't have any jumps left!"

"I've got one," Wolfric corrected her. "One, and I'm done."

Rain hit the glass and Win knelt at Wolfric's knees. "We've run out of time."

Wolfric gritted his teeth, shifting into a position that didn't cause him pain. "Spencer can't open the door without your blood, and now he knows it. It's Evan who is out of time. I can help you..." He nodded to Ella, who'd grabbed the book, and trotted across to the couch.

"Kuxtal Ka'tan...it means *live again*," Wolfric growled. "Vecula's last words on earth were a goddamn curse."

THIRTY-FIVE

"Who did she curse?" Cole asked.

No one else in the room needed to ask the question. The truth hung there for all to see, like Vecula swinging from the oak. Cole might have been a little slower to see it, but the rest remained worryingly silent, each trying to imagine if this could be true. Win's eyes darted to Luke, who'd gone ashen.

Vecula lived—inside someone else.

Ella closed the book, her complexion drained of color, and carefully she looked to Luke, then Win. "I think it means to take over...another person, a body. To live again."

A chill erupted on Win's neck. "Oh god. What does this mean?"

"It means I've been a fool—a goddamn idiot," Wolfic said. "It means in her last moments, my sister cast a curse before she died. It means...she never left."

"How is this possible?" Win asked. "I saw her die."

Wolfric sank into a chair. "I know, that's what I don't understand. I felt her go...her essence. And all these years I haven't sensed it. Not once."

"Essence?" Cole prodded, and Wolfric lifted a brow.

"Her soul," he offered. "We were bound by blood and magic, and there's an invisible thread that links us all, no matter the distance."

When nobody rushed to fill the silence, Wolfric continued, "When my brother Isaac died, his thread vanished. When Vecula was hung, hers did too. But now I see what she did. She was hiding."

"Inside who?"

"A body. An unwilling victim. Someone pliable, vulnerable, and young. Someone who wouldn't have been able to stop her." He laughed out loud at his own stupidity. "Seriously...can't you guess?"

Win and Ella locked eyes, but Ella was first on her feet. "Oh my god—Mary!"

"Mary Hickory—the unfriendly ghost," Wolfric confirmed.

"You saw Mary at the oak...it must have happened then," Ella reminded Win. As if she needed a visual reminder of Mary circling the great tree. It was ingrained into her memory.

Win's head swam, she stood and paced the floor. "This is starting to make sense...but Mary died during her failed Calling. What did Vecula stand to gain hiding inside Mary?

"My sister latched herself to Mary's soul because she was the *last* born Hickory."

Luke shifted, his lips an odd shade of gray in the dimly lit room. "So her blood would open the door, and close it?"

"My sister planned to use her to open the door, to *force* Mary's calling early, and use her blood to cross to Nassau...except that never happened, did it?"

"Spencer killed her," Luke chimed in, and Wolfric grinned savagely.

"No, he *didn't*, not the first time," Win butted in, her head swiveling to her boyfriend who had gone awfully quiet in the corner. "Originally, she was killed by a hunter."

Grayson's jaw bunched and he balled up his fists. "My ancestor."

Everyone looked at Win and her cheeks burned, but she reluctantly nodded in agreement. "She was murdered by a Riley."

"Right," Wolfric confirmed. "Whatever he did interrupted Vecula's plan. Instead of the door opening for her, Mary died by violence and the earth, the *stone* had no claim on her soul. It was a waste of effort and magic and Vecula's essence was expelled from Mary's dead body."

Win recalled the black mist, dust like particles floating on the air around her body as Mary died. She shuddered, realizing Vecula had left her unwilling host.

"This is so messed up," Cole groaned into his hands. "How do you know this?"

Wolfric flexed his shoulders, grimacing in pain. "I have a gift of being able to go back."

"So she's been hanging around out there," Luke was baffled. "All this time?"

"She would have gone into hiding, maybe sleep for a hundred years, two hundred, who knows?" Wolfric mused. "She would have tried again...who knows how many times she tried to connect...to find the *right* soul to partner with...she would have needed someone...."

"Strong?" Luke finished for him, but Wolfric shook his wild mane of hair.

"Actually, I was going to say vulnerable."

Win sat back on her heels, her mind swimming, frantically trying to focus. "The oak...she's there. She's always been there—waiting."

All three of them remained silent, locked in thought. Win's thoughts were scrambled, but slowly things started to float together. The vision, the small child waddling toward the tree. The woman who called out to Spencer. She remembered Jake and Alice in the woods, their fractious conversation. Something was wrong with his boy...something was wrong with...

"Mommy, there is a monster in the house."

"Spencer," Win said aloud, voicing her worst thoughts, meeting Luke's watery eyes. "She took Spencer. He was perfect, young, vulnerable...a good host."

"I'm sorry, what?" Cole looked about the group aghast. Luke paled, dropping down on the couch. He held up his hands.

"Spencer...is Vecula." He puffed, rubbed his eyes, and paced again. Win couldn't keep track of his movements, so frantic he made her dizzy.

"Luke...it's not that simple," Wolfric said, watching him pace up and down. "Vecula hid deep inside him, and I believe their souls fused. There is no way to know who controls who."

"It's like an infection," Cole said. It seemed like the perfect way to describe it. Win, baffled and appalled, fell to the couch.

Vecula, wearing Spencer like a boy-shaped costume. She'd hurt so many people...Rowan...Evan. All in pursuit of Win, killing her and using her to open the door. But, Win wondered about Rose. Why hurt her? What had Vecula to gain? Win rubbed her cold arms. Perhaps that was just a game for her, a way to amuse herself while she waited. Hurting Rose was just for fun.

"Listen," Wolfric puffed hotly, his breath shattered as he watched Luke pace back and forth. "My mistake was doubting Vecula. I didn't think she possessed the smarts to pull off something like this—the ultimate long con. Your entire life...your brother isn't who he should have been. Your *brother* never stood a chance."

"You mean...Spencer...is melded..."

"*Buried* under her," Wolfric confirmed. "And that's why I couldn't sense my sister. She has fused with him so deeply I wouldn't have found her. She's used him as a human shield."

"Can we save him?" Luke asked, his eyes wet. Win jolted at the question, the imploring tone in his voice. It was the question she guessed he might ask the moment he figured it out. "I mean...is there a chance? I never even knew my half-sister and now you tell me I've lost my brother. A brother who could still be in there."

Wolfric whistled, shaking his head. "It's a long shot, kid. If he's still in there, he'll be a shell. Can you imagine what it would be like for him?"

"Why did she choose him?" Grayson asked, his voice quiet in the corner. "Why not Win? If that's who he—*she*—really wanted?"

"Win would have repelled her, she's too strong. If she had tried to link with Win, or anyone else, she would have failed, and been expelled again. She needed the right soul, the right person to latch to, so she could get close to the last of the line. *Win*. Vecula hit the jackpot with Mary the first time around. A vulnerable child with hidden power, and bonus—she was able to open the door. Only Vecula was interrupted at the crucial moment."

Grayson wandered closer, a pensive expression taking over his features, Win already guessed what he was thinking. "So, if my ancestor hadn't killed Mary...Vecula would have crossed, gone home. This would be over...none of this would have happened. Rowan getting shot...hurting Evan..."

"It's not your fault!" Win snapped, annoyed he would dare blame himself. She was surprised when Luke jumped in.

"It's a stretch, Grayson. It's nothing to do with you...you can't blame yourself for what your crazy ancestors did. Jeez, have you met *mine?*"

"Why did Spencer kill Mary?" Ella asked, and all eyes turned in her direction, she was still holding Luke's arm. "When you sent him back, he killed her. If Vecula is inside him why would she let him?"

Win let her thoughts gather, the cold aftershock of their discovery made a shiver run down her body, and the reason was as chilly. "Because she wasn't of any use to him," she answered before Wolfric could. "Rowan stabbed him. When he went through he was wounded, and in a mutated body. Spencer isn't stupid. He knew he'd never be able to call the door by himself and Mary hadn't completed her Calling. She was useless to him."

"Right," Wolfric gritted out. "Survival would have been his first priority."

"Cursed blood is pretty tasty," Luke joked, and Ella immediately dropped his hand in disgust.

Cole was on his feet. "Can we just keep on track? What does *she* want?"

"What do you mean?" Win asked.

"Well, it seems like all Vecula really wants is to go home," Cole spluttered. "Is there any way we can just give her what she wants...and send her home?"

Thunder clapped outside, and Win flinched. She found Grayson's fingers with hers and squeezed them. Luke sat next to Ella at the table, and she absentmindedly rubbed his shoulder, a movement so natural, she didn't appear to be aware she'd done it.

"There's a problem with that...a huge one," Wolfric said, after a long beat of silence. "If we somehow send her home, number one, Spencer is gone for good. No take backs. Unless we can find a way to split them?"

"Then we have to find a way!" Luke cried. "We have to separate her from my brother. I'd do anything to get him back—even if I had to care for him for the rest of my life. He's my blood and he's been violated—for decades."

"Surely she'll be happy once she gets what she wants?" Ella said. Over the table, she linked fingers with Luke. He looked down at their joined hands in surprise. Ella blushed and ran her hand up his forearm.

"Yes, she'll be reunited with Nassau, our father," Wolfric agreed with a reluctant tone to his voice. "And then she'll be more powerful than ever. Once she goes through the door, what's stopping her from coming back? What's to stop her from bringing my father here? And that is something you don't want. You'd be toys to him."

"We have to think of something," Win said suddenly, alive with a seed of an idea. "If it worked we can't just hope and pray she won't come back."

A crack of thunder outside shook the room, and in the hearth, the fire sputtered, almost as if Vecula's ghost joined them. Wolfric sucked in a breath, his eyes darkened as though he pondered something dangerous. Win prodded him. "What are you thinking?"

"I have an idea...but it's sketchy...and dangerous."

"All our plans are sketchy and dangerous," Luke quipped, his voice lost in the unusually quiet room.

"We need to bring in Evan and Rowan," Wolfric said gravely. "To take down Vecula, we're going to need everyone. We're going to need an army."

THIRTY-SIX

Rowan shifted on the bed, unsettled and dry-mouthed as she sat up. Beside her, Evan slept deeply, her lovely face relaxed, and soft and her lips parted. Rowan pressed a kiss to her temple, and Evan's eyes fluttered open. Sleepily, she smiled and yawned.

"How long was I asleep?"

"A couple of hours," Rowan replied, pushing a hair out of Evan's eyes with her fingertips. "I'm only waking you because you've eaten nothing."

Evan sat, stretching her arms. She retracted them in a wince, clutching her ribs and Rowan's stomach flipped. Evan tried to wave her off but it was too late. She edged back the covers, where Evan was sleeping in her underwear. Her mouth worked in horror as a garish purple bruise spread over Evan's ribs, like paint running across a canvas, then suddenly it vanished. Rowan looked away before she burst into tears.

"Rowan...it's going to be okay."

"No, it's not," Rowan moaned, wiping her eyes. "He's hurting you."

Evan's fingers brushed through the ends of her red hair, a gesture that should have been soothing, but it hurt all the more. Rowan didn't think she'd live without her. Imagining her gone, dead, made it hurt to breathe like a knife wedged under her ribs. She could barely form any thoughts.

"Spencer needs me," Evan said. "And won't hurt me if he can't get what he wants."

"And when he gets what he wants? What then?"

Evan exhaled through her nose, helpless to answer the questions Rowan demanded. "Let's hope I don't give in—I'm stronger than I look, you know."

Rowan folded her arms around her, kissing her face, her own wet with tears. It struck her how much she'd bawled the last few days. Pulling back she stroked the pad of her thumb under Evan's cheekbone. "Don't leave me, okay? Don't. Leave me." She kissed her mouth. "I will never forgive you."

Evan smiled weakly. "I wish she knew she had you waiting for her in a couple of hundred years. You are so worth it, Rowan Adler."

Commotion from outside distracted them from the moment. Rowan, puzzled, lifted off the bed and dashed to the window. Gripping the ledge, she stared into the yard as Win's truck pulled in, followed by Ella's car and then lastly Jake's Mercedes. Frowning, she watched as they all piled out. Win glanced up, spotted her and waved.

Rowan's jaw dropped as an enormous man climbed out of Ella's car. She didn't have any idea how on earth he'd fit inside, the entire vehicle rocked as he disembarked. Monstrously tall with wiry black hair and an unkempt beard, he looked like he belonged in a dad's garage rock band, with his ripped jeans and faded Guns 'n' Roses shirt.

"Who the hell is that?" Rowan asked, but part of her already knew. She'd seen his picture on the Boston College website, not that he looked anything like any professor she'd ever seen. Evan sidled up beside her, pressing her face to the glass and she gave a sharp hiss.

"Oh...crap!"

Rowan laughed at the expression on Evan's face. "Is that...?"

"My big brother," Evan groaned.

Rowan moved like lead, stopping at the foot of the stairs. Their quiet, peaceful home was taken over by a group of tired-looking misfits. The front door burst open and in walked people, too many people for this one house. All talking, some arguing, spitting one-liners back and forth. Luke argued with Cole, the kid she'd seen at school. Win and Alice were in some kind of heated discussion and Jake trailed behind, closing the door after him.

Ben emerged from the kitchen, his mouth gaping. "What the hell is this?"

"Dad...it's okay..." Win began but Ben cut her off with a wild flick of his hand.

"Who is this?" He pointed at Wolfric, who looked like a bear from a scary child's bedtime story, completely out of place in the quaint floral decorated hallway. Then he stared bug-eyed at Jake. "What is he doing here?"

Jake groaned and rolled his eyes. "I said he wouldn't like this."

"Ben, enough!" Alice held up her hand, her eyes shimmering. "We don't have time for this."

Wolfric spotted a shadow, lurking behind Rowan on the stairs, and gruffly, he cleared his throat as Evan peered around her. "Hey, babe."

"Wolfric?" Evan ran down the stairs, throwing herself into his massive arms. Swept up in his embrace, Evan sobbed into his shirt. Wracked with grief, Wolfric hugged her hard, till she creaked.

"I'm sorry," he muttered, wiping at his eyes.

Evan beamed at him. "You've nothing to be sorry for."

He wagged a finger at her, trying to look annoyed even though his eyes shone with emotion. "You've been meddling Euelea. But this time, we get to put it right."

Rowan's heart tugged at the smile they shared, the way she playfully batted his cheek with her palm, like they had never been apart. He hugged her again but this time gently, then took her face in his hands and kissed her forehead. "I have an idea," he said. "But I need you. I need my clever little sister."

Over the top of her head, he locked eyes with Rowan, who remained on the stairs watching them with interest. They looked so alike it was unsettling, the same smile, same golden skin, the familiar way their lips curled.

You got the pretty one. Rowan looked up, spotting her mother watching from across the hall, with a sly smile on her lips. Rowan blushed when Win chuckled too, having heard Alice's remark.

"I think you might need to sit down," Win said, her face suddenly sober. "There is something big I have to tell you."

Win's hand settled on the base of her sister's spine. Rowan slumped on the couch, too stunned to speak as the room flooded with bodies. Win squeezed her shoulder, and Rowan lifted her chin after a long, gaping pause. "The *whole* time?"

Win bit her lip. "The whole time."

Rowan snapped her head in Win's direction. "Even when we were kids? Teenagers? In *school?*"

"Yes, and yes," Win said, wrapping her arms around Rowan's waist. "I'm sorry."

Wolfric, cleared his throat, clearly listening in. "Look—we don't know for sure where Vecula begins or Spencer ends, the two are *one.* Everything he ever did was because his thinking was altered—like whispers in his ear."

"It's like a parasite." Cole chose to impart some misguided words of wisdom, and Win held back a snort. "Like one of those amoeba things that eat your brain."

"Ew—Cole," Luke muttered. "That doesn't make it better."

"How do you think I feel?" Jake said, having slipped into John's old leather seat in the corner. "My son never existed—gone along with Katie."

Win deflated, hurting for him. Ben, who sat by the fire and made a face along with a causal, roll of his eyes. "Of course, you have to make it about you, Jake."

Luke clicked his tongue, impatiently, and Win tried to ignore the venomous glares tossed back and forth between the two men. Like two dogs fighting over a stick, their backbiting grated on her nerves.

"Wolfric seems to think we could separate them," Luke announced to the room and Rowan bounced out of her seat. Win didn't blame her, the prospect was daunting and terrifying. To have Spencer in the world, loose and free…. Who knew what he would be capable of?

"What? No. Are you crazy?"

Win was on her feet, grappling with her hand to pull her back. "Calm down. He wouldn't be the same person..."

Wolfric cleared his throat. "Right now I can't say for sure what parts are Spencer and what parts are my sister... it's blurry, confusing and the two of them have linked so deeply over the years, their personalities would have meshed."

"We have to try, Rowan," Luke begged, his eyes shining. "He's my brother. We could save him. Something *good* could come out of this mess."

Breathing shortly, Rowan agreed to sit, and Win grabbed her hand tightly. Finally, she said, "Then what's the plan?"

Evan, having remained silent the whole time, lifted her gaze, speaking to the room and everyone waiting to listen. "The Hatsik. It might work."

"And what's that?" Jake asked, with a dragged-out sigh. Win flipped him an eye roll, annoyed with his impatience and he clicked his mouth shut.

"It's a separation incantation; used when possession has occurred...to extract a ghost...or a spirit from another person, but it would need to be done by her blood kin. We would join hands and trap her within a circle...but..." her voice trailed off. "It's what we do with her *after*...if it even works. We can't let either of them free once they've been separated."

Win noticed the way Evan and Wolfric locked glances, something unspoken passing between them, the slight darkening of Wolfric's eyes made her stomach clench. After a long pause, Wolfric said, "I do have an idea."

"You do?" Win asked, wishing she could be privy to the private conversation, but whatever brief moment they'd shared, it was over. Evan eased from her seat and grabbed up an old notebook on the coffee table. Wolfric took it out of her hands and got on his knees in the middle of the floor, opening the book to a blank double-page spread.

Grabbing a pencil from a jar, he drew a shape, which crudely resembled a five-pointed star.

"Is that...a pentagram?" Ella leaned over his massive shoulder and he grinned, impressed.

"It's a pentacle. We're going to make one—from blood."

"Gross," Cole muttered.

"No—it's not what you think. We have the blood right here in this room. *Five* members of the same family."

Win stared around the room, locking eyes with Alice, pale and nervous as she leaned closer to get a better look. Evan pointed to each of them, taking the pencil out of Wolfric's hand and writing a name at the tip of each point. "Win, Luke, Rowan, Jake...and at the top sits the alpha."

"Me?" Alice gasped.

"Alice," Evan said and by her side, Rowan sucked air. Win shook her head, like light filtering through a closed drape, suddenly it was clear.

"This is why you brought back Mom? You knew this would happen?" Rowan said.

Evan's eyes darkened at the suggestion. "No. I didn't *know* this would happen. But I knew the time would come when we would have to trap him. A blood pentacle is powerful and binding and if the links remain in a place he wouldn't be able to escape. If your grandfather had lived, it would have been John sitting at the head. In the summer when you discovered you were all connected, that Iris was Jake's mother, then I got the idea. After John died...I knew I had to bring Alice back. Where she was needed."

"God, Evan..." Rowan chuckled. "You could have just said..."

Win pushed aside her growing frustration, annoyed they were steering off track. "Back to the plan!" She fell to her knees beside Wolfric. "I feel like we are overlooking a massive hurdle. How do we lure him here? We have no idea where he is."

"I know where he *was*," Wolfric said, cagily pressing the gauze on his torso. "He was in Cedar Wood, hauled up in the woods near the old tavern which used to sit on Battle Street. But that was two hours ago. I have to go back one last time. Go back and lure him here, somehow get Evan on that side to raise the door...."

"That won't work!" Win cried, frustrated. "You can't use another jump. And *blood* opens the door. It has to be me. I have to go."

"No way in hell!" Grayson, who'd listened the whole time stoic and silent, rose from his darkened corner of the Hickory family room. "You barely made it back the last time."

"There's no choice," Win ignored him, avoiding his glare, imploring her to see sense. "It has to be me. I'll make the jump, find him and get him to chase me *here*. If I take Evan he'll have to follow me. He needs her. If I can get her to raise the door...will she even be strong enough to raise it?"

"Oh, she will," Evan piped up. It was odd, to hear her talking about herself in the past. "She knows how to raise it. She's majorly holding out on him."

Win nodded. "Then let's hope she can hold on a little longer."

"No, *no*!" Grayson pushed his way across the circle. "What if you can't get back? What if we're not ready?"

Win's eyes flashed. "This is the plan, Grayson. You have to be ready. When I open the door, you have to be waiting on the other side."

"This is crazy," Ben whistled through his teeth. Win, buoyed by the strength her decision gave her, smiled, even though it was odd and no one else was. She could do this. This was what she was put here to do. Even if she burned to ash, she would try.

Timidly, Alice raised a narrow wrist in the air. "Can I ask a question? If this works, what do you plan to do with Vecula? Or Spencer? You can't just let them free."

A murmur went around the room, and Evan paled. Thunder rolled over the house, a storm building in momentum. "Leave Vecula to us," Evan said. "We're her family. We'll deal with her."

"How do you know she won't try and come back if she crosses the door?" Alice asked, unwilling to be brushed aside. "We can't risk everything—our lives and risk she might come back?"

Wolfric stared hard at the fire, it shone in the depths of his dark eyes, and Win shuddered. "Leave it with me. I have an idea."

Win's hairs stood to attention on her arms, and she rubbed them briskly. She didn't like the sound of that, and something prodded her mind, an errant thought demanding attention. An inkling of what he might have planned, but she shook it away. Win had enough to deal with.

"And you aren't going to share this idea?" Alice asked.

"Just worry about Spencer," Wolfric cut her off with a firm glare. "We don't know what kind of mental state he'll be in."

Wolfric made a noise in his throat, and all eyes fell upon him. "There might be a *tiny*...small detail...that could cause a problem. *Before* we can trap her, we have to separate them by performing the Hatsik."

Win blinked in confusion. "You said you could separate them?"

Evan and Wolfric shared a glance, and he stared at her as though waiting for her to realize her oversight. Evan visibly paled, remembering a detail she'd forgotten. She palmed her forehead. "I forgot. We need Isaac."

Luke raised his brows. "Your *dead* brother?"

"Yeah..." Wolfric scratched the back of his neck. "He is kind of important. The Hatsik is performed by kin of the spirit. Vecula's kin...so in a word, the three of us."

Win felt hope drain out of her, just when they'd been so close to forming a plan, something that could actually work. Isaac was dead, long forgotten centuries ago.

Ella edged around the circle, dropping to her knees beside Win. She looked awkward, worried, and was building to say something. Finally, she uttered, "What if...someone stood in for him?"

Win twisted to look at her, and Wolfric scratched at his scraggly beard. When he didn't speak Ella plowed on. "I mean...in the summer, we called to Win's dead Aunt Iris. We called her out of the spirit plane. Couldn't you do that with Isaac, and he hitches a lift with someone?"

Evan and Wolfric shared a glance, and Win couldn't tell what they were thinking, both coming to the same conclusions. Wolfric hooted and gave Ella's chin a playful pinch. "She's a little genius!"

Ella beamed and gazed hopefully around the group. "Then it could work! Who wants to body share with Isaac?"

"Ooh, pick me!" Cole's hand shot up, and Wolfric chuckled.

Luke cackled, rubbing at a mystery ache near his temples. "Jeez, Cole..."

Cole deflated, blushed, and snatched his hand back. Rowan rubbed his shoulder. "He's so cute."

"As gallant and heroic as your offer is," Evan said, giving him a sassy wink. "Isaac was a warrior, and he'll likely bond to someone of a similar ilk...someone he can sense and feel..." Her gaze wandered idly to Grayson, still tucked in his corner, and Win's cheeks went red hot, guessing to what she inferred. She shot to her feet, blocking Evan's eye with her body.

"Oh...no way in *hell* is he having him!"

The words were out before she could stop herself. Grayson shot her an understanding smile, despite her cheeks reddening with everyone looking at her, like she was some possessive girlfriend.

"What if something happens to him? What if Isaac likes him too much and won't pack up and leave?" she whined.

Grayson pushed her aside, but gently. "Win...if you're going to risk your life then you have to let me do something."

She fingered his shirt, pulling him into an embrace, not caring if anyone watched, even if her dad looked mildly uncomfortable. She pouted, like a four year old. "No, it's too dangerous."

"I hate to admit it Win, but Evan is right," Wolfric said. "Grayson and Isaac are *literally* perfect for one another. And as delightful as your boyfriend is, I'm sure Isaac will vacate when he's told to."

"Then it's settled," Grayson said, ignoring Win's splutters of protest. "I'm all...his."

A plan, of sorts, had taken shape around them. Win's heart lurched at the thought of the task ahead, her only mission was to find Spencer and lure him right back here to the Hickory yard.

"So it seems everyone has a role in this plan," Ben said, and eyes flung in his direction. He looked grey, his mouth pinched. "And what am I supposed to be doing while all this is going on? The goddamn crossword?"

Win laughed. "Dad..."

"I don't have a job either!" Ella piped up with a raise of a hand.

"You're moral support, Ella," Evan said with a smile, though Win guessed her friend wouldn't miss this for the world. Ella had been safely tucked up at home when they'd last faced Spencer. Win worried she could be hurt.

"What about me?" Cole asked, crushed his earlier offer of heroism had been laughed off. Wolfric started at him hard, then at Ben lingering on the arm of the couch.

"Didn't you get expelled once for blowing up the Principal's car?" Wolfric asked, but he already knew the answer. He cocked his head, thoughtfully. "Or was it setting a fire in Chemistry class? Or stealing...."

Cole's cheeks went pink. "How do you know that?"

"I know everything."

"Then yes...I may have....done all those things."

Wolfric shot him a pointed look. "Then you're on the distraction team. As in, you need to make sure the cops are kept busy. There's going to be quite a light show in the woods and the very last thing we need is the police turning up and Spencer going on a killing spree." His brow bar glinted as he arched it. "Think you can come up with something to keep them busy?"

Cole grinned but Ben didn't share his enthusiasm. "And have him slung in jail?"

Jake's hand shot up. "I'll bail him out—if he gets caught. But I have a feeling Cole can run pretty fast when he needs to."

"Wolfric can always use the *force* to get him out of jail," Luke joked, tapping his temple. Win didn't miss the wane smile on the older man's face, the way his eyes wrinkled. For a split second he looked sad, and it made her gut churn, her earlier thought coming back to grind her. Wolfric was planning something without them, and she had a feeling Evan was in on it.

Cole beamed with pride, his chest swelling like an over stuffed chicken. "This is awesome. Blowing stuff up is my jam."

Beside him Ben groaned, but Jake only chuckled. Wolfric snapped the book shut, with a sense of finality he looked at everyone, pointedly, and Win was filled with dread of what was to come.

"Well, then people," he said. "It seems we have a plan."

THIRTY-SEVEN

The rain died as night drew in. Win and Ella said goodbye, alone in the privacy of Win's bedroom. Ella caught her while she changed clothes, and Win couldn't help but feel like she was preparing for war, her stomach was one giant boulder of anxiety. Shakily, she pulled on a faded pair of jeans, running shoes and a sweater, pulling her hair off her neck in a bun.

Inside, she was terrified, the task ahead loomed, and prickles of fear coated her skin. What if something went wrong? What if Grayson was right and she couldn't get home? What if she burned up before re-entry?

Ella, who seemed to sense Win's dread, appeared behind her in the mirror and hugged her around the waist. "Be careful—I just got you back."

Swallowing down a sob, Win hugged her friend hard, then peeled away with a smile. It was easier to hide how she felt; the juddering mess that were her insides. "It'll be okay. You guys do your part and I'll do mine."

Ella sank her teeth into her lower lip. "Jake and Cole went to get the supplies for his plan."

Win made a face. "What is he planning?"

Ella smirked. "He said it's best he doesn't involve us. In case he gets taken alive."

"Grayson isn't back yet, either," Win said, worried. After Wolfric closed the book on the plan, Grayson mysteriously vanished, promising he'd be back within an hour, but at her last check, that was two hours ago. Jake and Cole had gone to visit one of Cole's friends, to hook him up with whatever equipment he planned to use to distract the entire police force of Cedar Wood. Ben tagged along with them in order to feel some kind of use, and Win sensed her father feeling like an outsider. He wasn't Therian, he didn't have any skills to bring to the fight, and Win worried he'd end up getting himself hurt. Nobody knew what to expect.

The house was quiet, apart from Luke, Rowan, and Evan, who were downstairs, but as night crawled in, Win sensed it was time.

Earlier, before everyone dispersed, Evan asked to be alone with Win. She made Win lay down and then laid her hands on her chest, breathing hard as shimmering violet light left her fingertips. Win closed her eyes, numb and relaxed, as the scolded muscle under her flesh healed and cooled. Energy surged through her body, and she felt like she could run for miles. When she opened her eyes, Evan's nose trickled with blood. Win gasped, horrified. "Evan!"

"It's okay." She shrugged her off. "You need it more than I do." Evan wiped her nose on the edge of her sweater, her skin clammy when Win took her hand. "You've got a jump to make."

"And you have a spell to cast," Win reminded her. "Evan...what if you're too weak...."

Evan's eyes flamed, a flash of blue crossing them, enough to startle Win, enough to drop her hand. "I'm not weak."

"What is Wolfric planning?" Win asked, now she had Evan alone. "I know there's something you aren't telling me."

"Let Wolfric keep his secrets. We'll deal with Vecula—for good this time."

A car pulled up in the driveway. The distraction team had arrived. Win's heart fluttered, she followed Ella downstairs as Jake popped the trunk on the car. As they jogged across the drive, he threw them a charming smile. "I do come in handy, sometimes," he joked. Win slapped his shoulder. She grimaced when she saw the contents sprawled in the trunk.

"Shoes, jewelry and half a trunk full of fireworks...the perfect man. I really don't get why you don't date more," she joked, though it didn't lighten the mood.

"My weird family puts them off," he deadpanned.

Luke appeared behind them, his arms folded. "I don't even want to know what Cole is planning."

On cue, Cole jumped from the back seat of the car, eyeing the box in the trunk. It was filled with a colorful variety of skyrockets, smoke bombs and snakes. Enough to produce one hell of a light show, and a lot of noise and chaos. "We're good. I'll put on a display big enough to distract them from anything going boom boom in the woods."

Win side hugged him. "Please don't blow up the town. Or any cops—or yourself!"

Alice's shape appeared on the porch steps, watching anxiously. She'd changed into a sweater and jeans, and rubbed her arms briskly. "Are we going to do this?" she called.

Win eyed the driveway leading to the road, her face pinched with worry. Where was Grayson? She didn't want to leave without saying goodbye to him. It was getting cold, the temperature dropping, and their breath fogged on the air. She bit her lip. "He isn't here!"

Luke followed the direction of her gaze, guessing her thoughts. "He'll be here. He said he'd only be gone for an hour."

Win's fists balled. "I can't leave without seeing him."

Evan and Rowan trudged out to the yard, Rowan's arm firmly under her ribs, supporting her every step. For the last hour, Evan had drained of color, and she'd hardly been able to stand, her legs wobbly. Rowan looked exhausted with worry.

"We can't wait Win," Wolfric said. Win wasn't sure where he'd been, but he appeared from the forest, his coat splattered with dew. "It's now."

"Okay...." Her eyes pricked with tears, and Ella squeezed her hand. Panic flooded her system, as they all walked into the woods, the entire Adler, Fraser and Varga family at her back. Win's knees shook, the mounting terror built in every step she took.

When they had reached a shadowy clearing, about a hundred yards in, Wolfric whistled for them to halt. "Here should be good." He placed his massive hands on Win's shoulders and her heels sank into the mud. "When you jump, really picture Evan, picture Spencer. Aim to get as near as you can—and then you need to draw them here. Do you recognize this part of the woods?"

Win's brow beaded with sweat, and her mouth dried up. "I mean, yes...it all looks the same to me."

"No it's not—concentrate!" Wolfric had his teacher's voice switched on. Roughly, he turned her in the direction of an old rotted cedar stump. "Remember *that.*" Then he spun her, and pointed to the upended roots of an oak, knotted and rotten on the ground. "Remember *this*. You have to lead him here. This is where we'll be."

"Right, right," she replied, nervously. God, she could barely take a full breath. Wolfric turned to the rest of the group gathered behind.

"Jake, Alice, Luke and Rowan, you four need to be ready to make the blood pentacle the moment Win gets back. But when Win opens the door from the past, myself, Evan and Grayson will be ready to perform the Hatsik—while you're gone Win, we'll get Grayson in place to stand in for Isaac. Where is Grayson?"

"Here!" a voice called, and Win's knees buckled with relief. He jogged through the clearing, crossbow strapped to his back, his eyes on her as he ran. She smiled, holding out her arms as he lifted her off her feet. She burst, covering her face as she wept into his shirt.

"I didn't think you were coming," she said. "I didn't think I'd get to say goodbye."

Grayson stared at the awkward audience over her head, and threw them a sheepish grin. "Have I got time to speak to her? Alone?"

Wolfric muttered something inaudible under his breath about wasting time, but Grayson paid no attention, dragging Win away into the forest out of sight. Stopping by a fallen log, she punched his shoulder. "Where were you?"

He grinned, opening his palm. "Take it easy. I wanted to get something done while I had the chance."

Sitting beside him on the log, she looked at his palm in confusion as he laid his gloved hand in her lap. Her pulse spiked, and heat exploded up her chest. "What's this?"

"I had it made. Hank knows a metal worker in Mickle-ford—that's where I was. I had your silver blob shaped into this."

Win's lungs juddered as she took the tiny silver ring between her fingertips. It wasn't a fancy design, but looked like woven threads melded together, like branches on a tree. Words stuck in her throat as she held it up to the light. It was dainty and simple, perfect. The two pendants, her grandfather and Iris melted together, just as they always should have been.

"Grayson..." Emotion welled in her voice. "I don't know what to say....wait...what finger is this going on?"

Grayson released a strained chuckle, guessing her train of thought, and he blushed. "Well, I thought this one...for now." He placed the ring on the index finger of her right hand, it slipped down easily over her knuckle, and she admired it with a brewing sigh of relief. She grinned up at him.

"Good plan...I like it on this hand," then she added with a mischievous twinkle in her eye, "for *now*."

"For now. Like after college, and when we can both afford more than a motel room by the sea," he said, closing his fingers over hers. "I'm yours, Win."

She kissed him, like it was possible she might not see him again. When she pulled back, he was as breathless and shaken as she was. "Come back to me, please," he choked out.

Hand in hand, they walked back to the group, and it was Luke's turn to pipe up. "Um...do you mind if I have a moment?"

"*Jesus!* Fine!" Wolfric growled, storming away in temper. Luke didn't take her far, only yards away where he could speak to her alone.

"Win, listen to me." Luke's fingers circled her wrist gently. "Don't die."

Her throat thickened, keenly aware of Rowan and Grayson watching them in the distance, the mist rolled and floated between their shapes. "Luke...."

"No, listen," he said, his throat bobbing. "Don't die. You have to promise me you'll come back."

Watery eyed, she lifted her gaze but could hardly look at him. "I want to promise that but...."

"No." His blue eyes, were like faded denim under the moon, he squeezed her hand. "If you die...I can't...I won't comprehend anything else. You just have to come back."

He took her shoulders and abruptly turned her to face the group, where Ella and Cole were in deep conversation. He pointed at them. "See that? I want that to still be us in twenty years...forty years...when we're one hundred. Not Cole, he'll likely be dead at forty from a smoking-related disease. But you, and me, and Ella...we have to be together when we're little, wrinkly, and old. You're my best friend."

Win chuckled, his words making her heart settle. "You really want to be stuck with me when we're one hundred?"

He took her hand and kissed the back of it. "Of course I do. I found out yesterday I lost a sister I didn't even know I had. I can't lose another one."

Breaking, she dissolved, laughing through tears as she snuck her arms under his and pressed her face into his shoulder. He kissed her forehead. "And another thing...I never said thank you. You saved my life."

She beamed. "You, are so welcome, Luke Fraser." Standing on tiptoe, she hugged him hard. "Don't let Grayson die...or Ella...or my dad."

Luke rolled his eyes. "I'll look out for your dumb boyfriend."

They walked hand in hand toward the group.

"Jeez, who died?" Win joked, which instantly fell flat. Rowan hugged her fiercely, and Win took her arms, squeezing her tight.

"Go save my girl," Rowan whispered into her hair. "You can do this, Win. We're right behind you."

Grayson could barely look at her as she said goodbye to her ashen mother and father, kissing and hugging, and pretending this was just temporary. That she would come back. She had to come back. She went to leave, to walk off into the distance like a hero, and no one stopped her.

Far enough away, she closed her eyes, praying, thinking of Evan, as a tear tracked down one cheek. Movement in the trees caught her eye, a shape standing in the thicket just beyond her family, who crowded to watch her jump. It moved, flitted between trees, and Win's chest swelled. The ghost of a wolf peered at her through the bush.

I love you...my little fire cracker.

"I've got this." She didn't need to whisper the words, only needed to think them before she felt her palms graze with fire. Then in a blaze of light, she was gone.

THIRTY-EIGHT

Win vanished into a ball of flame. Luke folded his arms, his heart thudding erratically in his chest. Alice sobbed into her cupped hands. Watching Win burn, wasn't nothing. Raking his hands through his hair, he stared at the charred circle she'd left behind, a hollow ache in his gut.

Beside him, Grayson cleared his throat for attention. "Can I say something?"

Irked, and his shoulders instantly stiffening, Luke rolled his eyes. "Sounds like you're going to anyway."

Grayson squared up to him, both equals in height and weight, though Luke had the edge, his shoulders ripped with muscle. "If you're still in love with her, tell me now."

Luke's jaw dropped. A flush crossed his cheeks. That wasn't what he'd been expecting and darting his eyes in Ella's direction, he prayed she'd not heard. "In love with her?"

Grayson swallowed hard, his eyes going skyward as if even the sight of him caused him pain. "If you are tell me. Please."

"It's over, Grayson. Win and I...she doesn't have any feelings for me like that."

"Maybe not like that." The statement left his mouth in a wearied breath, like he'd been waiting to release the truth for a long time. Luke's eyes went saucer wide.

"Excuse me?"

"If she was forced to choose—between you and me. She'd choose you."

Luke's heart whipped faster, blood draining from his face. "What?"

"You heard me. You didn't have to listen to her crying every night for the first two weeks we were in the motel. She adores you, she'd die for you—she nearly *did* die for you. So even if a tiny part of you still hopes for something to happen between you...tell me now. Because there'd be no contest. I'd lose."

Appalled, Luke staggered, hardly able to take in what he'd said. Luke and Win had forever. If tonight worked and they both lived through this, he had a lifetime ahead with her in it. Therians could live past one hundred, Win's old Uncle Willard was living proof.

"No," he said, openly and honest. "Grayson, it's over. I was dumb, and confused...."

"I don't blame you," Grayson said. "I would understand."

Luke's eyes widened in confusion. Grayson would walk. He would walk away from Win if she was unhappy, if he thought he would get in the way. The guy *really* did love her. He shook his head with finality. "I would never make her choose. It's over."

Grayson huffed through his nose, and for the first time Luke looked at him with grudging respect. He was decent, a good guy and made for Win. The conversation had taken a very dark, uncomfortable turn and Luke decided to lighten the mood.

"Besides, if anything happened to you tonight, she'd kill me. Like put me in the ground *Vecula* style. You forget... I was there when *you* went missing. She's so in love with you, she can't see straight half the time."

A smile, soft and weary crossed Grayson's lips. "Well...okay."

Luke cocked his eyes at Ella, his heart swelling. "It's not Win I want."

Grayson nudged his shoulder with his elbow. "She's crazy about you. Even I can see that."

"I've messed things up, badly," Luke admitted, feeling playful despite the impending battle of doom rapidly approaching. He batted Grayson's massive shoulder with his fist. "Look at you and me—talking about girls—like we're bros."

Grayson stared at him, confused. "I don't know what that means."

By this time, Rowan wandered across, arm in arm with Ella. Grayson, buoyed on by sudden confidence and camaraderie, asked her, "Rowan—what's the heat? Win told me to ask you."

Rowan gaped at him, then dissolved into a fit of hysterics. "Oh, man. I'm not sure you want to know."

"I want to know."

"So do I!" insisted Luke, his interest piqued. Having been a part of the family for a few months, he'd never heard this interesting Therianism. Rowan giggled and then whispered the gory details into his ear.

Okay, he'd definitely not heard *that* before. Learning Therian females hit a phase in their life where their bodies went into a reproductive meltdown, no matter how they felt about it was enough to make him uncomfortably warm. He was glad it wasn't going to happen to him. Already plagued by sudden, inexplicable bouts of horniness, he didn't need that as well. Luke howled with laughter.

"That's a thing?" Luke glared at Rowan in disbelief.

Rowan snorted. "It's a thing, Luke. Trust me, I went through it."

Grayson went beet red. "Just tell me what it is."

"Maybe you should ask my dad?" she suggested with a wink.

Grayson firmed his chin. "Fine, I'll ask him!" He went to stalk off, but she grabbed his hoodie, laughing.

"No, seriously don't. I was kidding."

Cole joined the group, keen to know what they were laughing about and when Luke whispered it to him, he broke out into a massive grin. "That sounds awesome."

"You would think so," Luke quipped, his smile curling at Grayson who looked as if steam could snort out of his nose. Pink cheeked and humiliated, Luke admired at how well he withstood Rowan's relentless takedowns. She loved giving the guy a hard time.

"Never mind, Cole," she said, throwing the shaven haired kid a brazen smile. "I'll go through mine again in four years. I'll look you up."

Cole beamed, and Luke snorted in disgust, batting his friend in the stomach. "Don't you have a light show to put on?" he deadpanned, and Cole dashed into action. He jogged away, quick to hug Ella before he left, promising he'd be back.

Wolfric stood behind the group, his jaw hanging in disbelief and a large stick in one hand. "What kind of conversation is this?" he snapped. "Can we focus? Get our minds out of the gutter for two seconds?"

The group manifested around him, Luke shuffled in next to Ella, and they shared a smile. He liked how wild-haired, and pretty she looked standing in the dark. Now errant thoughts were placed in his head, he was struggling to focus on anything other than how good she smelled. And how he'd like to chase her across the forest and what he might do if he caught her. A dull ache throbbed in one of his eye teeth, and he pushed on the sharpened point with his tongue, hoping no one noticed. Too late, he glanced up and caught his father staring at him, grinning. Luke stared at his shoes.

Wolfric demanded their attention by whacking the stick on a log, and he couldn't suppress a giggle determined to force its way out of his mouth. This felt like a school field trip.

"When Win gets Euelea—*Evan* to raise the door on her side, we'll be waiting here. I've drawn a pentacle in the mud." He pointed to a spot under a tree.

"In the mud?" Jake muttered, and Wolfric silenced him with a death stare. Next to him, Alice snorted.

"Still so concerned about your clothes? Nothing changes," she joked, earning a half-smile out of him.

The bumpy line in the mud was large enough for the five of them to sit with Wolfric, Evan, and Grayson sitting inside, and hopefully, if everything worked, enough room for Spencer when they trapped him.

"Jake, Rowan, Luke, and Win will sit at the points. It doesn't matter where as long as Alice sits at the head."

Alice attempted to smile, managed a shaky nod, and Ben rubbed her shoulders.

"Inside the pentacle, Evan, myself, and Grayson will perform the Hatsik, and we'll separate Spencer from Vecula. If the pentacle is formed, he or she won't be able to escape. But—the links can't be broken. The chain between the five of you must stay intact—no matter what happens. When you sit in place, reach out as if you can touch hands, you won't be able to, but focus, and I'll invoke the spell. Your blood will do the rest."

"Do not break the chain," Evan affirmed, her arm around Rowan's shoulders.

Jake frowned. "Why'd you say it like that?"

Evan exhaled as if contemplating the worse scenario in her head. "It isn't pretty—separating souls. Once Spencer is free of her, we won't know what kind of state he'll be in, so it's important you remain firm and don't break the link. Whatever you see."

Alice and Jake shared a glance, and she warned him with her eyes. Jake looked dismayed but dutifully rolled up his sleeves, which made her snort with laughter. "He gets it," she said. "He rolled up his sleeves—which means business."

"However," Wolfric brought them back to the present. "Before any of that can happen, we need our brother Isaac. Grayson—you're up."

Grayson's complexion drained but honorably took a heavy step forward. Wolfric gave him a solidarity pat on the shoulder, causing him to sway on his feet. "We'll perform the ritual and call Isaac from the spirit plane. I know you'll make him more than welcome—he's going to love you." With a weary sigh, the bear-like man glanced around the tense group. "Any questions?"

At his side, Ella nestled to Luke's hip. He didn't think she was even aware she'd inched toward him, but her hand shot up. "When we called Iris in the summer, we had to call to the elements, we needed rocks, feathers, candles...water..."

"A spirit shaker!" Luke added, to which Ella cocked a brow in amusement.

"You mean a spirit stick?"

"That's what I said," Luke offered with a shrug, picking up a loose twig by his cross-trainers and twirling it between his fingers. Ella chewed on her lip, trying not to laugh, as Wolfric stared at them hopelessly.

"No, we don't need rocks or water or...spirit shakers...Evan and I are the children of a *god*. Think we'll do fine with some regular abracadabra. Are you taking this seriously?"

"They are," Jake said through gritted teeth, flinging the group's younger members an acidic stare. Luke wasn't sure what prompted his sudden surge of playfulness. Maybe it was the oppressive task ahead, the crushing feeling of doom settling on his chest. Things were about to get serious fast, and Win was risking her life for them somewhere. And he was getting the giggles.

"Now, once Grayson and Isaac are all cozy and acquainted, and Win comes through the door, we have to be ready to bind Spencer in the pentacle. That's when the three of us will perform the Hatsik. If this works...once the two are separated, we'll let Vecula cross. I guess that's the first thing she'll try—to get back to our time." Wolfric's dark eyes flicked in the direction of his sister, who shrank under his gaze "Once she's crossed—then we'll do the rest."

Luke didn't like the way he said it, with finality, and feared there was a part of the plan he'd missed, something important. He ground his teeth. Win wouldn't have missed it, he wished she was here.

"All good?" Wolfric said, though he didn't look convinced. "Just remember—keep the link, focus, and don't make any movements to leave the pentacle. If the pentacle holds, they won't be able to get away. We do not want him getting away while we perform the Hatsik."

A pregnant hush went around the group, and Luke's thoughts wandered to Win, his gut-churning at the task she faced on the other side. Face to face with his brother, luring him to this very spot, it made his blood chill. He hated to imagine how she was feeling.

"Everyone take their places. It's time to call Isaac." Evan hobbled to her brother, her hand on his shoulder as he eased her to the ground. Grayson rubbed his temples, shaking his limbs like he was preparing for a run as he sat beside her and took her hand.

Ella and Luke stood to the side, pressed closely together and watching in fascination as the adults waited behind. Wolfric tossed them a glance. "As soon as Win opens the door—be ready to take your place in the pentacle."

"You've said that like five times," Luke remarked smartly. Wolfric puffed, and Luke wondered what kind of grumpy professor he'd make. Luke imagined his students must be terrified of him.

Evan, Grayson, and Wolfric sat cross-legged inside the massive five-pointed star drawn in the mud, and with a savage grin, Wolfric held out his calloused palm for Grayson to take.

"You ready?" he said. "It's time to meet your new roommate."

THIRTY-NINE

Win arrived in the dark, burning alive in the exact place she left. Except when she opened her eyes, it was wet, dark and cold. And she was alone. Whirling around the clearing, there was no sign of Luke, Grayson, Rowan, or her parents. She forced away the urge to cry, now wasn't the time to go to jelly. Relief flooded her system, thankful she'd made it in one piece this time, not caught in some horrendous burning nightmare like before. It still hurt, her skin raw and sensitive, and she guessed Evan's healing helped make this jump easier.

Shaking out her wrists, smoke still puffing from her sleeves, her cat eyes darted about, and she spotted the tree which in the future, was rotten and laying on its side, here it was upright, but Win recognized the markings on the bark. Mentally taking note, she scanned for Cedar stump and clocked it instantly.

Thank god. She had a reference point. With her fingers trembling, she pulled the tie out of her hair and fastened it to a branch, something to look for when she ran back here, hopefully with Spencer chasing her.

You can do this. Nerves built in the pit of her belly, glancing one more time around the clearing, committing it to memory. Evan had to raise the door here, so when she crossed, everyone would be waiting.

Why did this feel like a shot in the dark? Could they truly pull this off?

We have to. There was little other option. Spencer would continue to punish Evan until she gave him what he wanted. A thought occurred to Win as she lifted her nose to the air, tracking Evan's scent. She hoped in the eighteenth century, she would smell the same.

How did Win know she was going to walk through to the right point in time? Wolfric hadn't been clear. She hoped if she focussed, thought about where she wanted to end up, then, like jumping, she'd arrive at the correct point.

She walked, her feet squelching in thick mud, and then sniffed the air, her eyes straining in the inky darkness. There she was....

Evan's scent floated on the breeze, something woody and earthy about her smell, but it was unmistakably her. Win thought she smelled like coconut, like her shampoo, but the notes of her DNA sang in her blood, mixed with the smoky smell of campfire. Ears pricking back, she ducked behind a tree, pressing against the bark, as labored footsteps trudged in her direction. Holding her breath, she peered around the tree, hoping he wouldn't spot her hiding place—that he wouldn't sense her.

Spencer dragged Evan by her feet, her body making a track in the wet leaves and mud. Sweating and bloodied, he heaved the unconscious woman through the trees, his breath coming in short pants. Pausing, he stooped over her body, slapping her cheek. Evan's head rocked to one side, her eyes firmly shut, and Win winced.

He hit her again, harder this time, and Evan made a noise, a gentle whimper. Win's fists balled. Oh, she was going to enjoy watching him fry. Part of her wondered if Vecula was in the driving seat, if she pushed him, steered his actions. How much of Spencer still existed?

"Wake up," he nudged Evan sharply. Leaning over her, he pinched her chin between his clawed fingers. "Wake *up*!"

Evan wailed, throwing her arms over her head, and Win wanted to move right then. *Wait*, she told herself, *wait for the right time.* Crouching by the tree, she bit her lip as Spencer shook Evan's shoulders.

"I need water," Evan begged. "Please."

Spencer straightened, snorting with disgust and annoyance. Evan was waylaying him. At his full height, he was terrifying, morphed into a creature from a children's nightmare. His coat was singed and burnt, perhaps Wolfric's doing, and with his teeth, claws, and straggly hair, he looked nothing like the handsome boy her sister had introduced to her in the bar at Hardy's months ago.

Destroyed, mutated. Vecula's creation. Spencer didn't resemble the boy who'd come to her aid at the basketball game at school when Jack White cornered her by the lockers. With Luke's pouty mouth and Jake's long nose, he was a Fraser, through and through, and Win wondered what could have been. He would have been family. Could he be saved? If this worked and Spencer was free of Vecula's hold, what lay in the future for them?

Spencer yanked Evan's shoulders, giving her one last brutal shake, lifting half her body off the ground before he dropped her unceremoniously in the dirt. He stalked away, his coat flapping around his compact calves. Win knew of a brook nearby, Grayson's old camp, a place of many memories, and this could be where he was headed.

In her peripheral, Win watched him leave, waiting till he was safely out of earshot before bouncing from her hiding spot. Appalled, she dropped to her knees beside the woman, who barely resembled the Evan she knew. Her face was bloodied, bruised, and her right eye swollen to the point it welded shut. "Evan...Evan, wake up, please!"

At the sound of Win's voice, Evan's good eye flickered and opened. Her puffy lips twitched into a slow, painful smile. "Are you her? Are you Rowan?"

Win took Evan's hand, kissed it, and held it to her face. "Oh no, I'm sorry. Evan, I'm so, so sorry."

"Wolfric said you would come...an angel with red hair."

Win snorted a laugh through tears. "I'm not an angel. Evan...we have to get you up. Everything is riding on this. We *have* to move."

"I can't walk." Evan's voice faded to a wispy breath of air. "I can't run. I'm sorry."

Win looked down the length of her battered body, her thoughts chaotic and whirring. "Can you hold on to me? If I carried you?"

Evan attempted to lift her neck, hissing in pain. "How could you carry me?"

"Oh, trust me. I'm a lot stronger than I look." *And faster.* The thought occurred to her, a way she might be able to carry Evan across the forest at lightning speed. But she had never shifted in another time after a jump, she didn't know if she could.

Now was the time to test it out.

Gently, Win placed her hands on Evan's face, thumbs tracing the curve of her cheekbones, and Win hit her with her best, imploring stare. "Evan...listen to me. Can you summon the door?"

Weakly, she managed a nod. "Good," Win said. "When I get you to the right spot...you have to raise the door, and then I can open it. We have to get him to chase us. Can you help me?"

A tear tracked down Evan's cheek. "I'll try."

Win brushed back her lank hair. "Listen to me. I'm going to keep you safe, I'm not going to let him touch you again. When we open the door, you need to get away from here. Otherwise, I'll have a pissed sister in the future who won't ever get to meet you—and trust me, she's worth the wait."

Evan didn't reply, only stared at the trees above, and Win hoped what she'd said got through. She seemed dazed, confused, and pushing it aside, Win got up and stripped off her clothes, pressing them into Evan's hands. "Hold onto these for me. I don't want to jump into my family circle completely naked."

She caught sight of Grayson's ring glinting in the light, and she slipped it off, pressing it into Evan's palm. "Do *not* lose that!"

"What on earth are you doing?" Evan wailed as Win hauled her into a sitting position. Win's voice deepened, her canines lengthened, touching the tip of her tongue, and her eyes flashed a violent, bright yellow.

"Putting on my armor," she said, backing away, bare feet in the wet mud. "I'm going to look a little different in a moment. Climb on my back, and whatever you do—don't let go."

FORTY

The air crackled, and something shifted in the atmosphere. It happened the second Wolfric, Grayson and Evan joined hands. The two elder Vargas closed their eyes, and the sky parted, black swirling, chaotic mists enveloping their small triangle of blood, bone, and flesh.

Luke wound an arm protectively around Ella's waist, relieved when she didn't push him away. Her fingers wove into his back jean pocket, an old habit she used to have when they dated, and he gave her a squeeze. She smiled up at him, eyes wet and glossy. "This is terrifying, Luke. I'm scared Win won't get back here."

"Shush." He brushed loose hair off her forehead. "Win's got this. She'll come back to us."

"What's happening?" Jake cried from behind, and he cast his father a nervous look. All three adults watched in mounting terror as mini crackles of lightning buzzed and fizzed around the three people in the triangle. Grayson watched the whole thing unfold, his chin dimpled, and Luke imagined he must be grinding his teeth.

"It's okay, Jake," Rowan said, nodding to Evan, sitting cross-legged in the mud. "Trust them."

"Brother Nassau....father...we call to the air, earth, fire, and water...where we tread no one is above us, no one is below us...we ask you to allow our brother Itzma to cross...to bind with this mortal body..." Evan's voice took on an otherworldly quality, serene and firm, rooted in the earth.

The air fizzed, and black mist formed, swirling into an inhuman shape in the center of the triangle. "This is messed up," Luke muttered.

Grayson reared away from the mist, his shoulders drawn to his ears. Luke's stomach dropped. If this didn't work...if anything happened to the guy, he was going to be sharing roots with Vecula's skeleton. Win would kill him.

Wolfric spoke into the mist. "Father...Nassau, god of chaos and light, we beg you to allow Itzma to cross. Take this human body. We are of fire, water, air, and earth...no one is below you, no one is above...we ask you to let our brother cross realms..."

"Screw this," Jake said, tearing at his hair. Rowan moved beside him and tossed an arm around his shoulder.

"Dad, take it easy!" Luke warned, sounding more confident than he felt. "We've done this before—it'll work."

It's got to work...

The mist took shape. Curls of black particles merged and melted, forming a shadow, a large human shape hovering a foot above the dirt. Evan's hair blew back as the air shuddered and whipped into a lightning hazed frenzy. Ella burrowed her face in Luke's shoulder, and he held her tight.

The shape moved in a slow circle, arms and legs forming, then a torso. It was a man, too large to fully comprehend. With his jaw dipped to his chest, he had a mane of jet black hair cascading to his wide shoulders. Luke's eyes bugged as the full extent of his body was revealed. Dressed in a chainmail tunic and loose pants, he was barefoot, and every inch of his arms were inked in black tattoos, Aztec patterns snaked up his arms, his neck, and curled at his temples. Symbols, pictograms, and glyphs scrawled onto any area of exposed flesh, like war markings. Now he understood why Wolfric picked Grayson to be his partner. The man was massive, a warrior packed with muscle. Wordlessly, the warrior, Isaac, lifted his head, and his eyes glowed white.

Wolfric smiled. "We thank you, Nassau, for allowing Itzma to cross...Itzma...*brother*, take our human offering for the binding. Join with him and return to us."

Luke's mouth dried up. *Human offering.* He didn't like the sound of that. Luke felt a snap of sympathy for Grayson. It sounded a little permanent. Lightning struck the clearing, and Ella whimpered into his arm, hardly able to look. In one fluid motion, Isaac looked up and stared hard at Grayson. Then he lunged.

Alice cried out in horror, and Ella broke from his grip. Catching the ends of her fingers, he yanked her back. "What's happening? What's he doing to him?"

Grayson yelled in agony. Arms and legs wide, he rose from the ground, pulled in the center of the triangle, hovering with his feet dangling. A shock of black crossed his eyes. He went limp and dropped, every exposed inch of his face covered in the same black patterns stretching over Isaac's body. Grayson let out a sound akin to a growl, and Ella screamed.

"Please don't hurt him!"

"It's alright!" Evan called over the stormy air. "It's going to work."

Grayson howled. Alice ran forward, gripping Luke's shoulder. "I think something's wrong!"

His eyes glowed white, piercing, and he writhed on the ground. Muscles jumping in a chaotic, macabre dance, he flung left and right, growling and choking in pain. Blood dripped from the corner of his lips, and Ella flew to the outer edge of the triangle.

"Stop—Wolfric, please! He's killing him!"

"Ella, get back here!" Luke yelled. She was too close. Lightning danced dangerously close to where she stood.

"It's not working," Wolfric cried, real fear flashing in his eyes. "Why isn't this working?"

Grayson screamed as inside him, Issac, determined to get free, opened his flesh like a zipper. Luke's pulse spiked. This had gone downhill and fast, he was starting to share more of Ella's panic. With a sound like tearing paper, Isaac ripped free of Grayson's body, glowing as he floated into the circle. Alice and Rowan ran around the clearing. Rowan dropped to her knees, hauling Grayson's head into her lap. Her eyes went wide and flashed yellow with fury.

"What the hell have you done to him?" she yelled. Jake and Ben each took an arm and dragged him away right at the moment Grayson came to, blinking as he tried to sit up.

Sitting shakily, Grayson panted, bloodied and broken, the flesh of his arms ripped open. "He doesn't want me," he said, clutching at his beating chest. Something in his expression looked grim, and Luke sensed his feeling of failure. He'd been given a job and wasn't up to the task. "I'm not a match."

Isaac bowed his head, motionless as he floated in the triangle. Wolfric scrunched up his face, confused. "I don't understand....this should have worked."

Isaac lifted his chiseled jaw, immaculate sharp cheekbones, and glowing white eyes fixed at a point beyond the circle, and Luke swore he saw the warrior smile, a twitch of the lips as he gazed through the mist. Wolfric nodded in silent understanding, and Evan guessed his train of thought. "I understand, brother...I understand..."

Evan's eyes went wide, her mouth dropped open. "No, Wolfric...he can't..."

Isaac lifted his fingers, reaching into the swirling mist, opening his palm in an invitation.

Luke's blood froze in his veins. Everything primal and protective ignited in his body, every particle morphing into action, his teeth exploded, and his eyes darkened to those of an angry, dangerous predator.

"Oh...no," he growled, his voice dropping to an impossibly low octave. "He better not fucking *dare*...."

Isaac lifted his eyes and smiled. He was staring at Ella.

FORTY-ONE

Win ducked to the leaves, shivering. Hunching her spine, she shuddered, calling to the earth below her fingertips. Heat swelled through her center, and with a gush of relief, she shifted. Elation brought tears to her eyes. On the ground, Evan gaped at her wide-eyed. "Oh...my...."

Win shuffled nearer, nudged Evan with her snout, and dropped to her belly. Evan retracted her hand, then with growing bravery, her fingers inched to Win's fur, running her hand along the length of her body. Win rolled her shoulders, signaling with her eyes that she needed Evan to cling on. Gritting her teeth, Evan lifted off the dead leaves and straddled Win's back, all her clothes still tucked under her arm. Win rose onto her legs, and Evan grabbed her neck. "I don't think I can hang on."

Wrapping her arms around Win's neck, Evan shuffled to a leaning position, her fingers digging into her fur. Win tossed her a look across her shoulder. *Please, don't let go.*

With a shaky nod, Evan gripped harder, wobbling as Win moved around the clearing. She peered through the darkness, knowing the timing couldn't be off. Sniffing the air, she detected his scent. He was on his way back, expecting to find Evan in the dirt where he'd discarded her.

Win ran, and Evan wailed, her grip tightening around her neck. Through leaves and trees, Win sprinted, her paws licking the dirt, bounding over dead, fallen debris. Evan bounced painfully on her back, and she could sense the woman's fear, scrambling to keep hold as she ran, her face buried in Win's fur.

It's okay... she said, uselessly, knowing Evan couldn't understand. Yards behind, she heard a screech, a roar of anger, and her lungs pinched. Spencer was coming.

Win pounded harder, her breath coming in great chugs as she darted through trees and undergrowth, frantically scanning the dark, trying to spot the place she'd arrived. Win dashed in circles, out of breath, adrenaline spiking in her veins. Where was it? Was she lost? Behind, Evan whimpered, her nails digging into Win's flesh.

Puffing, Win glanced about, then stopped. She'd heard breathing. Soft, controlled, and deadly. Win shook Evan off her back, and the woman crumpled to a heap.

Where are you? She scanned the trees, spotting a shadow duck between them. He was playing, darting between the trunks like a child playing hide and seek, watching her.

Evan...get down...

Evan scrambled away to a safe distance, and for a second, Win wondered if she understood, or was she so used to Spencer she just cowered in terror. The jaguar opened her mouth, she licked her teeth. Now she was pissed. She didn't have time for his shit.

Come on, you asshole...come out.

Win got her wish. Yellow eyes pierced the dark, followed by a massive body as Spencer pounced, shifted into his panther form. A snarl erupted from her throat as he rolled her, the full impact of his head butting her torso, knocked the wind out of her lungs. She scrambled in the dirt, barely gaining a second before he attacked. Win was ready this time. She swiped sideways, batting him with a hind leg, her claws raking his underbelly. When he was down, she pounced, her jaws sinking into his scruff, the soft flesh tender as she tossed him away by the neck.

Spencer growled and cowered, humiliation only serving to make him angrier. Win panted, her jaw sagging as they prowled around one another.

Spencer...I know this isn't you.

Win thought maybe she might be insane, but she had to try. She'd take it if there was even a chance she could get through to him. She'd try for Luke, for Jake, and for Rowan. Spencer could come back from this, couldn't he? A second shot at life, a do over? He couldn't be blamed for the awful things he'd done. It wasn't his fault.

I know what happened to you...that you have Vecula inside your head. I know the things she's made you do.

Spencer snarled, almost like a laugh. *Really, you think you have me all figured out?*

We could help you. We can bring you back to your family. To Jake and Luke....it doesn't have to be like this.

Spencer paced, his claws tracking in the leaves. *What makes you think I want that?*

I know she made you do things...

His eyes flashed in the dark, deadly and predatory. *Well, aren't you smart—solving the mystery. My dark, little secret.*

She wants to go home...to cross realms...she could leave, and you'd be free. Free to start over and have a normal life, Win said.

Free to do what, Win? Play happy families? I'm too far gone.

No. She prowled closer, begging with her eyes. *You can come back from this...you have a family who loves you. Luke loves you.*

Win wondered if her words were falling on deaf ears. He gnashed his teeth, eyes black and empty, and hope he might come with her willingly slowly drifted away. Time was running short, her skin burned, and she couldn't risk being pulled back without getting Evan to the right place to open the door. She couldn't do this dance all day.

If she leaves...you think I'll be happy...you think I want to go back to that life...do you know how good it feels to have this power? Newsflash Win...I'm never going back.

Oh, well...I tried. Win leapt. Her head thumped his in a dizzying blow and Spencer staggered, momentarily knocked off balance. Win whacked him hard with her paw, again and again, enough to stupefy him into submission.

She dashed to Evan and dropped. Evan crawled onto her back and dug in her nails.

Win took off, with Spencer slowly gathering his senses. She left him in her wake, leaves and twigs flying in the air as she ran. She hoped to god her family were ready.

FORTY-TWO

The air crackled around Ella, as she stood motionless on the edge of the triangle, her dark hair whipping around her shoulders. Wolfric stood and held out his hand. "Please, Ella—help us."

Luke startled out of his daze, his temper flaring. Ella took a shaky step nearer, and he moved. But to his surprise, Ben closed the gap, his hand landing on Ella's narrow shoulder, yanking her into his arms. "No way!" he yelled. "No way in hell is that monster putting his hands on her—take me instead!"

With Ben's arm wrapped around her shoulders, Ella looked tiny, shaken, and disorientated. The air shimmered, and massive, leaden black clouds circled the small clearing. Luke's pulse rocketed, and time ticked away. He broke into a sweat, knowing they weren't ready and any moment Win would arrive.

Evan wobbled to her feet. "Ben—he isn't a monster. Isaac was kind and good."

Ben let out a pitiful laugh. "He doesn't look kind or good! He looks like he'd take my head off."

In the triangle, Isaac floated, dead-eyed. His feet hovered above the ground, trapped in the vortex of the spell cast by his siblings. Ella pushed out of Ben's arms. "It's okay...I'll do it!"

"No!" Luke flew to her side, grabbing her arm. "You can't." He turned to Wolfric, staring imploringly at Isaac. "He could have anyone he wants—any of us would take her place. Why does it have to be her?"

Luke wiped at his face, surprised to find it wet. Red faced, he caught Ella's eye, as she gazed up at him. "Why does it have to be you?"

"It's not about strength," Rowan said behind him. She supported Grayson, propping him up with his arm tossed over her shoulder. The guy had been ripped apart, the flesh of his forearms sliced open. Luke felt sick. "If it was, Grayson would have been his match."

"I got it wrong," Wolfric called to Ella over the wind. "I thought he would be perfect for Grayson. Isaac was a fighter and he died a warrior's death. But Isaac was the best of us—the kindest, the gentlest. It was never about physical strength...of course it has to be you."

Luke's blue eyes flashed to the ghost turning in slow circles, and he shook his head, panic making his voice tremble. "Don't do this, please...I don't want you to."

Ella pulled out of his embrace, angry he was trying to stop her. "Win is coming! We don't have *time*, Luke. You don't get to make this choice for me."

"What if he hurts you?" Luke batted back, desperate to convince her this was a crazy plan. He sought something to say, anything to stop her putting herself in danger. Ella stared at Isaac, still holding out his hand, and she shook her head.

"I'll be okay."

"You don't know that."

"I'm willing to risk it. I know I can do this."

Luke's fingers circled her wrist, and one by one he let go. There was nothing he could do to stop her. What right did he have? Any input he had once, he'd tossed aside like her love. If he tried to talk her out of this, convince her she couldn't, she wasn't strong enough...well, then he was no better than his brother. "Of course you can," he said, broken.

He wiped at his eyes again. Ella broke away and, jumped into the triangle before he could catch her. Giving Wolfric a short nod, she closed her eyes and slapped her palms together with them both. Isaac whirled in a circle.

"Isaac we offer you this human body...return to..."

Isaac didn't need a second invitation. He dove, smacking through Ella's torso, hard enough to make her eyes roll and the air to whoosh through her teeth. Ella arched, her neck snapping to expose the long column of her throat. Gently, her eyes opened, watery and hollow as they filled with piercing white light. Evan's hands tightened on her wrist as she writhed, her neck arching as though her head could meet the base of her spine. Tension flooded the clearing, and the adults looked on in anguish.

Slowly, black war tattoos appeared, crawling up Ella's neck curling around her face, and Luke's lungs caught. She looked wild, her black hair falling down her back, more beautiful than he'd ever seen. Around the triangle, air whipped, like a mini hurricane erupting between the trees, bathed in a blazing blue light. Twigs swept from the ground, dirt flew, and trees bent double.

"Is she okay? Did it work?" Alice cried. Luke caught Ben's shoulder and they stared at Ella in horror. Ben grasped at his hair.

"We shouldn't have let her do this," he rasped.

Luke shook him. "It had to be her." But he didn't sound convinced, even to his own ears. Isaac settled within Ella's body, and the light shining out of her eyes belonged to him. He possessed her intimately, and Luke was struck with terrible jealousy.

There was no time to dwell, no time to allow his errant thoughts and possessiveness to fester. If he had his way, he'd scoop her up and carry her out of this forest right now.

The ground shook. A slow tremor vibrated up his calves. Ben grabbed his arm.

"What's that? Is it happening?"

Wolfric stood, his coat flying behind him as a fine, blazing blue mist appeared, and with a grumble, the ground quaked. The door was rising. He grimaced revealing his infamous teeth.

"Places everyone! *Now!* She's coming."

FORTY-THREE

Win pounded into the clearing, fog swirled across the ground, rising in puffs of mist. She drew up, halting so fast Evan slid from her back into the mud.

Win dashed behind a log, bending and cracking into human form, her lungs full of cold, sharp air. Darting out, naked and shivering she snatched up the clothing Evan held, stuffing her arms and legs into the damp jeans and filthy sweater. Evan smiled grimly, holding out her palm, in the center sat Grayson's ring.

Win puffed a sigh of relief, slipping it over her knuckle where it fit snugly on her finger. "Thank you!"

"He isn't far behind," Evan panted, struggling to stand. Win eased an arm under her ribs and gently lifted her, she gave her a wooly smile, brushing damp, bloodied hair out of her face.

"You're up, Evan."

She choked, her dark eyes frantically scanning the clearing. Win's gut twanged in panic, real fear crawling up her neck. Spencer wasn't far behind. "Please—I've got you, okay? I won't let him touch you."

Tearfully, Evan got on her knees. Win spied her hair tie tangled in the tree, exactly where she'd left it. At least she knew she was in the right spot. Sweat gathered under her arms, watching helplessly, and Evan placed the palms of her hands on the ground, eyes tightly closed.

Come on, Evan...please.

Win staggered through the clearing, in the distance she heard the stamp of paws, and her heart spiked. Evan chanted something soft and inaudible under her breath. Win guessed she must be drained. Her back bowed, so low her brow touched the ground. The woman had been beaten and starved, her body shattered.

Come on...

Violet pooled from Evan's hands, bright sparks fizzing and whirling, as the air whipped into a frenzy. Win's hair tore away from her face, bracing herself as leaves and branches lifted from the ground. Evan arched her back, arms wide palms splayed, and her hair wild as she stared open-eyed at the inky sky. The ground shook.

Win spotted a shape moving quickly into the clearing, and with gritted teeth she grabbed up a log and ran to meet Spencer head-on. The panther roared as she sprang out of her hiding place, so fixed on Evan he didn't see her leap. Win thumped him hard across the muzzle, strings of saliva and blood flinging from his lips. Dazed, he staggered and she backed off, waiting for his next move. She needed him awake and angry. Alert enough to chase her through the door, but she had to buy Evan time.

The ground moved, shuddered, and trees bent in the wake of the hurricane winds whipping around the clearing. The stone was rising. "Yes!" Win shrieked. She was already on fire, the pull back about to happen any moment, the tell-tale stinging sensation erupting over her skin cells. "You did it, Evan!"

Evan climbed shakily to her feet, and Win dashed to help, holding her at arm's length. But her relief drained. Blood pooled from Evan's mouth and her tear ducts were claret red. As Win stared at her aghast, one blood-stained tear dripped down the side of her nose. Evan's hands shook, but she nodded towards the stone. "You have to open it. I can't help you."

Win snatched up a sharp-edged stone, and with a yelp, sliced her palm, a dull sting rocketing up her arm. The stone pulsed with familiar blue light, and she remembered where this nightmare had begun. With Luke dying in her arms and sending Spencer through time.

Closing her eyes she stepped close to the stone's light, as it crackled and fizzed, tickling her fingers. She held up her palm, letting the light taste her blood. It throbbed, and pulsed with force enough to knock her backward into Evan's arms. A swirling circlet, a vortex of light appeared, rushing and crashing like a freak ocean wave. It was loud, deafening but Win could see straight through it.

"It worked," she nearly sobbed. They were there, waiting for her, all of them. The rush of relief intensified as Rowan appeared standing right in the center of the vortex, her wild red mane like fire dancing around her head.

Win felt Evan's sharp hiss of breath. "Is that her?" she breathed, watery-eyed. "Is *that* Rowan?"

Win's face split in a crazy grin, wondering how she could feel elation right at this moment, with death breathing down her neck. "Yes." She hugged her hard. "Yes, that's her. But you have to leave. You've got to get far away from here. *Now*, Evan please!"

Rowan and Evan locked gazes, and the tall redhead grinned bashfully, mouthing to her through the bright vortex. "I'm waiting for you."

Rowan's eyes creased with her wane smile. She held fast in the deafening, swirling vortex, struggling to stand firm, battered by high winds. Evan or the woman she would come to love years later, stood staring at her, open-mouthed and wide-eyed.

Win, looked away, distracted by a groan and cracking noises behind her. "Evan...run! Now!"

Spencer, shifted into his human mutation, rose from the ground, wiping blood and spit from his mouth. His nose was smashed, an ugly purple mess sprawling over his face. A sharp growl left his body, and he smashed the ground with his paws, running straight at her.

Win shook Evan's shoulders, giving her an imploring stare. "Go—please!"

Evan gave her a kiss, right on the forehead and brushed back her hair, before she vanished into the bush. Win balled up her fists, standing firm as Spencer powered closer. Her skin fizzled and crackled, any second she would be sucked back through time. Spencer gained distance, snarling. His mutated hand flexed, nails inching closer. Reflexively, she sucked in her belly, but she held, closing her eyes waiting for the pull. She could smell the blood on his breath.

Win evaporated in flames, her body curling inward as she was sucked through the jump. Spencer ran straight through the blazing path she'd left. Win opened her eyes, as she landed fizzling and smoking on the other side of the door. Gasping, she ran to the pentacle, the crudely designed pointed star drawn in the mud.

Between Rowan and Luke, she slapped down in the dirt. There was no time to wonder why Grayson wasn't in the triangle. Why Ella was there instead and why her best friend was black-eyed, unresponsive and clutching hands with Wolfric and Evan. No time to think, breathe, or care as Spencer landed through the door and fell in a heap in the middle of the pentacle.

"Now!" Wolfric yelled. "Ka'ja'le *hatsik.*"

Win and Luke exchanged a terrified look, as bright piercing light burned between their palms. Win yelped, as a rope made from shimmering white light traveled around the star, from Luke, to her, to Rowan, to Jake and then finally...

Alice screamed, attached to both Luke and Jake on either side. Her features pulled into a grimace as light pooled from her eyes, and white, hot blazing light burned between the five of them, led by the alpha. A blood pentacle, a star of protection made from family. She stared skywards, her face split in a grin of triumph, tears of joy rolling down her face.

"No one let go," she ordered, and they all tightened their grip. "Not even for a second."

FORTY-FOUR

"Rowan...get in the pentacle!" Wolfric's voice surprised her, and with a jerk, she tumbled out of her daze. Feet rooted, she didn't want to lose sight of her, silently vowing she'd never let anyone hurt Evan again. Through the vortex, she watched, helpless, as the woman she'd love in years to come vanished into the night. Rowan dashed across the mud and threw herself between Luke and Jake, catching them both looking at her with concern.

Jake's usual, arrogant smirk was replaced by a smile more sincere. "She'll be okay...she's tough."

Rowan's lips curled, nearly made it to a smile, fleetingly thinking it was sweet of him, his loaned strength in that moment did mean something. Further along the star she spotted her mother, smiling. "He's right. Trust she'll be okay...."

Locked in the triangle with her brother and Ella, *her* Evan waned, head lolling on her shoulders, and Rowan fought a wave of panic. What if something happened to Evan on the other side? What if Spencer had hurt her so badly that she didn't survive? She squirmed, momentarily drawing her hand into her lap, and Luke fired her a glare. "Don't you even think about moving, Rowan. You heard what Wolfric said!"

It was too late to protest. Time ran to a close. A ball of fire burst into the clearing, and her sister walked free of it, flames sizzling to ash. Wolfric spotted Win's arrival. Slightly dazed, Win looked around, spotted the pentacle and dashed for it. Grass slid under her shoes as she threw herself into her spot and reached out hands between Luke and Rowan. Right at that split second, the stone shook, lit with blue fire as a shape hurtled through the center. Spencer landed with a thud, his chin hitting hard, cold ground right where he needed to be.

"Now!" Wolfric yelled. "Ka'ja'le *Hatsik!*"

A sting, like a deep itch, tickled Rowan's palm, and white-hot light spread from their outstretched fingers, turning the pentacle into a bright, searing star. The light formed into a knotted rope of light linking them all. It went from her to Luke, to Win, then to Alice. Her mother reared and yelled skyward, light boring from her open eyes.

"What's happening to her?" Win screamed. Wolfric gave a hearty, dizzy laugh.

"This is what an alpha is for!" he yelled but shot Rowan a warning glare. "Do not break the link!"

Rowan clung on, her hands welded in white, blazing light. Tears beaded her lashes. "Mom..."

Wolfric cackled a savage laugh as a pair of white speckled wings tore from Alice's back, and she screamed in agony. Giant wings beat the air, nearly lifting her clear of the dirt, with only Jake and Luke to hold her back. The light roped between them bound them together.

The falcon was back. The rightful alpha shimmered and settled on the ground.

Win and Rowan exchanged a look, horrified, helpless, and Win shook her head. "We have to see this through!"

Weakly, Rowan bobbed her head, and with her gaze drawn to Spencer, it appeared the pentacle was working. He stood, all massive height, intimidating and terrifying with his body coated in soft silver fur, his feet ending in long, clawed paws.

He lunged for freedom. With an explosion of crackling light, he landed belly up, his expression dazed as though he'd hit an invisible electric fence.

"I think this is working!" Luke cried. Rowan barely heard him, too busy watching everyone else. Ben looked on in horror, a helpless bystander, unable to do anything. Evan swayed as the color drained from her skin, and Wolfric's hand shot out to steady her. Whatever energy Evan was expelling in the triangle, she looked like she was about to run dry.

Angry and snarling, Spencer rose from the ground. He lunged again, flying backward in sparks of light sizzling his skin. Wolfric led a chant, words unearthly and ancient Rowan didn't recognize. Evan followed, her head lifted to the sky, an unfathomable incantation spilling from her lips. Lastly, Ella joined; her wide, black orbs stared up at the night as a hurricane stormed around them. She chanted in their ancient tongue. This wasn't Ella, sweet, kind, and shy. It was Isaac, a warrior, a killer, ruthless and stoic. It wasn't even her face. Her features, once soft and round, were hard, chiseled, and etched with those strange tattoos. This was it, the Hatsik, Rowan sensed the power of the words, as under her, the ground rumbled.

"Nassau..." Wolfric finally uttered something in words Rowan understood. "We ask you to split this soul...remove what doesn't belong...cast out evil...."

Spencer bent double, howling, clutching at his head, then his gut. On the ground, he writhed, and shook, his back arching and cracking in impossible angles. Tears streaked his face as he whimpered, blood pooling from his ducts. Rowan felt Jake's grip loosen, and when she looked up, he'd gone ashen. "Jake..." She dug her nails into the light, almost as if it were his skin. "This is what has to happen...."

"It's going to kill him," Jake cried.

"Nassau, free this soul of Vecula Varga...cast her out...free this soul of her hold..."

Spencer rolled in agony, crying, whimpering, his torso arching off the dirt. A black mist rose from his body, curling shapes like ash in the air as it billowed upward, taking the form of a woman. "Yes!" Win cried. "It's going to work."

Jake looked at Spencer laying on the ground, and Rowan held him fast. "He's alive, Jake! Do *not* break this link."

The chant grew feverish, boiling to a crescendo, dizzying, and deafening and the world pulled apart at the seams. Trees dislodged from their roots, rocks flew and leaves scattered all around the clearing. Spencer screamed, one last time and then went slack as Vecula left his body and hung suspended in the trap they'd set.

The spirit of Vecula hovered, her bare feet limp as she tried to free herself from the pentacle. Over and over, she tested the walls, like a rat in a lab, seeking freedom. With black hair hung limp and wearing a filthy white gown, Rowan stared into the face of the woman who'd been responsible for so much heartbreak. And there was nothing, Vecula stared back with as much contempt as she'd died with, hatred seething from every pore. Nothing. Black, empty...evil.

Words stuck in her throat. She wanted to ask this creature why. What had Rowan ever done to her? To Win? Twisting her neck, she spotted Jake's wide-eyed stare, and she wondered if he was thinking the same thing. Behind Vecula, the vortex blazed with red fire. A door opened to another time, and Rowan stared at it in horror. Fire, hot and unyielding, a different kind of hell. Vecula's home was right there waiting for her.

"Vecula..." Wolfric called to his sister, and at hearing his voice, the ghost turned, casting her black eyes upon him. "You've been a real little bitch."

She didn't react, her eyes cast behind to the open vortex swirling at her back.

"Release me, brother," she said. Her voice was deep, inhuman. "Let me cross...let me go home."

"No!" Jake yelled. "You can't just let her leave—she has to pay for what she did."

Win cocked a brow, bemused. "We can't lock her up, Jake."

Rowan understood. She felt the same indignation bubbling under her chest, meanwhile, Spencer lay on the ground unconscious, blood dripping from the corner of his mouth.

"Vecula destroyed my son—she destroyed my life, his life! Why the hell should she be allowed to leave?" Pain coated his voice, and Rowan felt the full force of his agony.

Years of torture, the blame, the guilt. Over and over, she'd berated herself. Why had she allowed Spencer to trap her, to push her down, keep her in line? When the creature who held the answers floated before her, unrelenting, unwavering, and cold.

"Release me, brother...all I want is to return home. It's all I ever wanted."

Spencer pushed up from the ground, his elbows shaking from his weight before he crashed into the dirt, exhausted, and gray. Rowan gripped Jake's arm, sensing his resolve waning.

"I want to know!" Jake bellowed. "Why?"

"Then ask," Vecula turned the full coolness of her stare upon him, and Jake visibly shrank, faced with the emptiness of her eyes. "Ask your questions."

A ripple of calm wafted through the clearing, and for a beat, the hurricane stilled, the pressure in the air dropped, and Rowan's ears rang from the aftermath of the rushing air, her spine so stiff she swore she'd crack if she attempted to stand. Vecula's lips pulled back to reveal an aged, yellow smile and two small eye teeth, long and blunt. "Ask me why...I won't lie..."

Jake's eyes were wet, and for a second, his chin dimpled, verging on breaking. "Why did you hurt Rose? You didn't have to hurt her. She didn't deserve it." He broke off, sobbing into his shoulder, and Rowan gripped the rope of light harder. He was broken, torn in half, and she met Luke's grim stare. No one moved. They couldn't. Locked in their binding, no one could risk breaking the chain.

On the ground, Spencer coughed up blood, staggering to his knees. Slowly his dark, black eyes scanned the clearing, falling on each one of them in turn, to Win, Luke, and Jake.

Spencer and Rowan's gazes met. When was the last time she'd looked him in the eyes? Intimately, unbroken and honest.

Eyes locked, she saw *him,* the boy or the man he was. Free of Vecula, free to make his own choices, walk his own path. Rowan suppressed a shudder as it rolled through her torso.

It hit her.

Nothing. There was nothing. Spencer's eyes were as black and empty as Vecula's. Soulless. Dead.

"Why did we hurt Rose?" Vecula looked down upon Jake, her smile twitching. "Ask your son. It was his idea."

FORTY-FIVE

Win's mind shattered. Heaving, she felt Rowan's length of rope go limp in her hand, and without thinking, she dug in her nails. Rowan's eyes were wide, mad, angrier than she'd ever seen her. But it was nothing compared to the dumbstruck look plastered on Luke's face or Jake's deadened expression.

It was his idea...

Fleetingly she glanced at Grayson, propped against a tree, panting and clutching his torso. He mouthed to her to hold on, and her grip on the rope tightened as she dragged her eyes reluctantly back to Spencer.

Spencer was the one in the driving seat. He always had been. Vecula certainly picked the right soul to partner with, they were a perfect match. With a juddering breath, Win realized her naivety, she'd hoped to bring Luke back a brother, one who he could live with. She'd *tried* to see the good, except there was none.

"You're lying," Jake spat.

"Why would I lie?" Vecula whirled at him, venomous. The dark holes of her eyes made Win's flesh creep. "All I've ever longed for was freedom. I don't care about you—any of you. I want to go home."

Rowan's hand tightened on the rope. "You controlled him," Jake accused.

Vecula's smile didn't reach her eyes. "If that's what you prefer to believe...if it makes it a little easier for you to rest...Why would you care if I've been trapped for twenty-two years?"

"Trapped?" Jake spat. "You defiled him. Ruined his life."

"At first, it felt like a union, two souls meeting, entwining. Finally, after Mary's death, I had a partner," Vecula's voice trailed into the wind, fully aware she had a captive and revolted audience, much like the one on the day of her hanging, no one could look away. "Someone like-minded, someone who craved blood as I did. Someone who could get me across...but it didn't take long for me to realize *I* was the one buried, deep, alone, betrayed..."

Wolfric stood, his face crushed. "It's why neither of us sensed you...all these years...he buried you."

Vecula's smile was human, but only for a moment. "Thank you for setting me free."

Win's jaw sagged, a wash of cold running over her skin. Her eyes scanned for Luke, his expression resigned, disappointed, any hope of bringing back his brother crushed to dust. Groggy, Spencer rose from the dirt, daring to meet their gaze. Still holding firm at the top of the pentacle, Alice's eyes flew in Jake's direction, and the air around her shimmered,

"Jake, *don't* you move," ordered the alpha, her voice dropping and Win's neck tensed. White glowing orbs fixed on the eldest Fraser in the pentacle, Alice's order had to be obeyed, much to Jake's chagrin. A muscle in his jaw tensed, and Win could only guess what he'd planned to do. "Do not break the link, Jake."

Behind them, the stone was alive with blue, crackling light, causing a shimmering wake in its path, and the vortex swelled. In the center, what was a path to the past, changed into something else entirely. Win saw a red, hellish light, and Vecula turned, drawn like a beacon to a flame. It was home. "Please..." she begged. "Just let me go."

Wolfric and Evan held fast. "You have to answer to us...to Isaac. Vecula, he died protecting you."

"I'm sorry..." her voice softened as a beat passed. "What more do you want? Haven't I known enough punishment?"

Wolfric howled with laughter. "If you call living inside a willing body for years punishment...?"

He broke off as Vecula turned slowly, regarding Spencer on the ground, her mouth a pinched line. She looked relieved, elated to be free of him, and Win wondered if it could be true. Had she been buried, pinned under Spencer for years, no better off than laying waiting in the oak?

"You have no idea the hell I've endured."

Spencer craned his neck to look at her, surprised, as though he were finally seeing through his own eyes. "Is it time for us to go?"

Vecula revealed her fangs when she laughed. "There's no hell that would want you. Where I go, you can't follow."

Spencer growled. "You promised me...."

Vecula didn't look sorry. Spencer's face creased in disbelief and disappointment. "You said I'd move on to a different life—the life I was promised?"

Vecula flew for him, and to Win's surprise, he cowered. She snarled. "Believing the deluded ramblings of your grandfather was your first mistake—but listening to me was your worst. You are no better than those you hold in such low regard. There's nothing *promised* for you, Spencer, only hell. But maybe that's better than this pitiful plane of existence?"

Win stared at the mutated man on the ground in disbelief. How could he be so twisted? Spencer was dead inside, there was no explanation, no understanding of him. What on earth were they going to do with him? Too late, Win sensed her sister, Rowan's forehead beaded with sweat.

She slipped free. Alice saw, but too late. "Rowan....don't you..."

Rowan snapped free of the pentacle, a noise emitting from her chest. A howl of pure rage, so deafening it drowned out any order Alice could give. Rowan wasn't about to take orders, not now. Not with Evan fading, only yards away, not after everything he'd done. The light beam traveling around the pentacle went dead, and Win gasped, zapped by electrical shocks.

Spencer didn't make it off his feet before Rowan careered into him, a grunt exploding from his lips as she barreled him into the stone's light. Straddling him, Rowan hauled him off the dirt by his throat, her knuckles slamming into his face, over and over, until bone crunched, all while he fixed her with a dazed stare. Blood spurted from his nose, and Rowan's skin split, jaw clenched and teeth bared, utterly feral.

"Rowan, *stop*!" Win cried over the frenzied, high winds. Trapped in the glare of the blue light, Rowan was unaware of what was happening to her body. Long soft feathers trailed down the arch of her back, and her feet elongated, ending in sharp eagle talons. Tears spilled down her face as she shook him, cracking his skull on the ground, oblivious as two magnificent golden flecked wings tore from her spine. Win and Luke stared at one another in shock, remembering how the stone transformed them, causing a mutation, a strange half version of their animal form. Rowan looked like a wild, red-haired angel.

"We've got to stop her," Win cried. "She'll kill him."

The sky exploded. Win ducked, and Luke cowered as high above them, the night sky pierced with glittering multi-colored streaks of light. Whizzing, banging rockets erupted over the town of Cedar Wood. Somewhere, Cole had put on a killer light show. It was distracting enough Vecula took her moment to leave. With a slither of black mist, she eyed the people staring up at the sky and gave her family a small nod before vanishing into the flames of the vortex. The hellfire vanished, sucking her in, welcoming her home, and Wolfric yelled in frustration.

Rowan stopped her onslaught, out of breath, and her shoulders slumped. Barely conscious, Spencer gazed up at her, and her hands fell to his chest, upturned as she looked at the blood on her palms. Almost as if life left her soul, she slumped, falling. Her forehead hit his chest and sobbed.

Grayson came closer, coming up behind Win. She turned, throwing her arms around his neck, kissing his face with relief. "Are you okay?"

"I'm okay...but Rowan is about to commit murder."

"We have to get her out of that light," Win said, pulling away from Grayson as she ran. Crackling light enveloped her, and she shifted, her cells morphing, flexing as fur tracked the length of her form and her clothing evaporated to fragments. Chasing through the stream of light, she caught Rowan's shoulder, yanking her sister off Spencer's limp body.

Rowan yelled, fired up and boiling with anger as Win hauled her away by her underarms. In a fluid motion, Rowan twisted from her grip and smacked her jaw so hard Win saw stars. Blood pooled on her lip, and she licked it in shock.

Rowan's face lit up with rage. "Don't you dare stop me. This isn't your fight!"

"You'll kill him, Rowan!"

"Don't interfere with this, Win."

"If you kill him—there's not a way back. It'll be over—and I can't lose you."

Win wiped more blood off her chin, running from the gash under her lip, while Rowan paced, inches from Spencer's feet. "It's not about you!" she yelled. "It's not about you and what *you* want. This is my fight. I won't let him hurt anyone else."

Win's eyes pricked with tears, both facing off, caught in the blue light, mutated and strong. Neither sister backing down. "Then he's already won."

"I don't care," Rowan's voice faltered, dropping to her knees. "I don't care anymore. This just has to be over, Win. I can't keep fighting him. I have to end this."

She stooped, her wings spreading as a demonic, empty glaze filled her green eyes, talons bared like five sharp daggers. Rowan dove, prepared right then to take his life with her hands.

Someone got in her way. Ben took the force of her hit, wrapping his arms around her as they both crashed to the dead leaves. Win watched as Ben gathered his eldest in his arms. How had he even managed to step into the light? His hair was singed, fizzling, and blue flames licked at his clothing, but he didn't seem to notice or care. He took Rowan's face, wiping away blood and tears with his shirt sleeve.

"Dad...."

"Stop now, baby. Please. This isn't you. You are better than this—than him."

"No...."

"Rowan...I'm here."

Sobbing, hollow, and raspy, she tried to shake him off, but he held her shoulders firm.

"You weren't there. You weren't there when I needed you." She beat at his shoulder. "Why did you leave me?"

Ben's face aged in the light. He didn't seem to feel his skin blistering. "I should have been. I'm so sorry. I'll say it till I'm one hundred, and I know you'll never accept it. I'm so proud of you—"

"Dad...."

"I love you, Rowan. Don't ever believe I didn't love you. Stop now, please. Let's go home."

Rowan relaxed, the fight leaving her body, and she let her head fall on his shoulder as she sobbed. Blue light fizzled and crackled around them.

"Rowan... he's right," Alice's voice echoed through the light, pulsing on the current. Both sisters turned to see their mother standing on the edge of light, holding out her hands. Both girls walked to her, powerless, like being trapped in a tractor beam. Alice's wings were lost once the pentacle's magic was broken.

Outside the light, Grayson stood watching, chewing his lip bloody. Win threw him a tired smile, taking Rowan's outstretched hand as they walked to their mother.

Win and Rowan stepped free of the light, and Alice took their hands. "It's over. We won. Everyone is safe. Vecula is gone. Everyone is alive...it's time to go home."

The pads of Alice's thumb traced Rowan's bloodied, split knuckles, and the cuts and grazes knitted, sealed shut. "We have a life to get on with, together. He won't hurt us anymore."

Sniffing, Rowan tried to agree, momentarily distracted by Wolfric carrying Evan to a safe distance. Win pulsed with energy, every nerve ending alight, and she leaned on her father, finding comfort in the warmth of his hand on her nape.

Luke yelled her name, and she flinched. Then he yelled again, on his feet, waving his hands. Startled out of her stupor, she turned, but too late. Spencer ran straight for her, his face twisted, demonic as he raised his claws.

Sharp nails raked her abdomen. Win went rigid, like wading through water, her feet caught in sand, the current determined to drag her out. She looked down as blood ran through her fingers. Luke tore through the light, mutating into a feral half man half wolf, and barreled into Spencer, knocking him clean off his feet.

Dazed, Win pressed her hands to the gash across her torso as blood dripped down her stomach and trickled down her legs. Win found Grayson's eyes across the clearing as she dropped to her knees.

FORTY-SIX

Luke winced as inside the blue light, Rowan smacked Win in the jaw. He watched in a daze as Win staggered and wiped her chin in shock. By their feet, Spencer was a groaning, gurgling mess.

Luke stood on the edge of the pool of light pulsing from the stone. *Yeah, no way I'm stepping in that thing again.* He remembered the agony the last time, how the light had ripped the wolf from his body, replacing his human form with a twisted, crazed man-wolf version of himself. He wanted to bury the memory.

Above the trees, somewhere in the main center of town, an endless stream of screeching, shimmering fireworks burst through the dark. Stepping away from the light, Luke spotted Grayson lifting Ella into his arms, her head lolled against his forearm, and he dashed across the clearing. "Hey, let me!"

The Adlers were having a family moment, Spencer was on the ground, and Ben didn't realize he was fizzing like a sparkler. Luke ducked away.

Grayson looked destroyed, his hoodie ripped, blood pooled from welts through the exposed skin, his complexion a waxy gray. Dropping to one knee, Grayson slid Ella into Luke's arms, happy to let him take her weight. He groaned as he stood and patted Luke on the shoulder. The two of them shared a smile, a truce grudgingly formed between them. It lasted ten seconds before Luke waved him away, too concerned with the girl in his arms.

"Hey, Ella." Luke shook her gently. "It's over. Wake up."

Ella tucked her head into his chest, the corner of her lip curling, and her lashes fluttered. "Did we win?"

Luke smirked. "Come on, sunshine."

He waited for her reaction. Her lashes opened upon hearing the term of endearment, something he called her privately when they were alone. He was always too mortified to say it aloud in front of Win or Rowan. It would stop now, he'd never be ashamed to say what he felt ever again. Memories of her waking next to him on the cot bed in John's old den tugged at his gut. Couldn't they go back in time? Luke's eyes filled up, and he cursed himself. He'd been such an idiot. "Is he gone? Isaac."

He didn't need an answer. Ella's eyes were her own, heavy-lidded, peering up at him through long, dark lashes. The tattoos were gone, leaving her unmarked and herself again. "What's with all the fireworks?"

Vivid pinks, oranges, and greens reflected in the dark pools of her eyes, and Luke released a weary chuckle. "Cole came through. I hope the cops don't catch him."

He took her hand and pressed a kiss on her palm; her fingers opened to touch his face. That's when he spotted the mark on her wrist. Alarmed, he turned her hand over. "What's that?"

Ella squinted at the faded black tattoo situated just above the pulse on her wrist. It resembled a crude letter Y with two triangles jutting out either side. Ella gritted her teeth, and Luke's chest rose in anger. Isaac hadn't left her unscathed. "I'd like to know what that means."

"My mother will *kill* me if she sees that. I hope I don't have any others."

Luke's brows rose playfully, his jealousy evaporating. "Want me to check you over?"

"Think you're jumping ahead of yourself there." She grinned up at him sleepily.

As Ella gazed at the colorful display firing overhead, he rushed to fill the silence, his heart thudding so hard, he swore it would tear free of his chest. "I'm sorry, Ella." Luke couldn't keep the heartbreak out of his voice. "I'm so stupid—so stupid." He cried and whispered in her ear, kissing her hair, her temples, her cheeks. "Please, for the love of God, take me back."

He kissed her like he hadn't seen her for a year. Her mouth was soft, surprised, but his chest knocked when she kissed him back, her fingers curled in his black hair. "Take me back, please, please, *please*..." he begged between kisses.

She sniggered against his lips, and they parted. "What took you so long to ask?"

"Uh." He cocked a brow. "I didn't think you'd ever want to be with me again. Not after what I did."

"Yes, you are pretty dumb," she agreed snarkily, wiping at the corners of her eyes.

Luke made a face. "And I kind of lost my mind when Isaac took over you."

A spark of memory crossed her face, and she shuddered in his arms. "I'm glad that's over."

"I'm not good at sharing."

"Since when did you get so possessive?"

"Since you tortured me all this time—flirting with Cole—letting some warrior in your head, roaming around doing god only knows what." He was joking but also deadly serious, and had an odd feeling this was permanent. She was entirely his. As old-fashioned as it sounded in his ears, it was right. Wherever she went, he'd follow faithfully. Even if they went on their own paths for a while, college, work, they'd always find one another.

Ella's blush traveled down her neck. "Are you doing that weird imprinting thing dogs do when they love their humans?"

Luke snorted. "Can you quit it with the dog jokes?"

Ella pushed up, her back wedged against his knee. "Cole and I have so many—we can't waste them."

"Say yes, Ella. Put me out of my misery."

She laughed and tugged him in for a kiss, "Yes, you moron," she said against his mouth. Luke kissed her greedily. He'd missed her taste and how soft her lips were. "Yes, forever."

Ella wiped at her eyes, leaving a trail of dirt. Her gaze caught momentarily to the commotion inside the blue light. She pulled on Luke's collar. "Luke...*look*!"

Luke was already looking, head snapped back, alert as he eased out from under Ella, coming to stand. "Crap...Win! *Win!*"

He ran to the edge of the light, waving and screaming her name. Behind her, Spencer lurched from the ground, fangs bared, and hurled straight for her. There was no time, time suspended to a crawl as Luke geared up and ran, hurtling into the light. He winced and bared his teeth as the blue flames licked at his flesh, his clothing disintegrating to shreds as black fur erupted all down his body.

With the sickening realization he was too late, Win turned and arched inward as Spencer slashed at her stomach. Luke saw Win drop, and he barrelled into his brother, his shoulder wedged under Spencer's ribs. They collided, bone and muscle smashing against the other. Luke grabbed him by the collar, hauling him off the ground, and headbutted him. Spencer's eyes rolled. Luke had enough time to fling him down and scream at Wolfric across his shoulder.

"Will someone please do something about this *goddamn door?*"

FORTY-SEVEN

The slash across her torso stung, and blood seeped through her fingers. She could feel the threads of her skin cells entwining, healing. When she opened her eyes, Evan's hand was on her stomach. Closing her eyes, blood dripped from Evan's nose, and when it started to heal, she left to go to Rowan. It itched, and Win longed to touch it if only to relieve it for a moment. She pushed out of Grayson's arms and was on her feet.

"Where are you going?" he demanded.

"I can't let Luke do this alone," she said, a sense of de-ja-vu clouding her head. They'd done this before but now it was different. Spencer couldn't escape this time. Grayson caught her arm, and she mentally prepared her rebuff, anger boiling under the surface of her skin. She opened her mouth, prepared to fight him on this, to defend herself. Instead, he grinned, pride shining in his eyes. Grayson tugged her up against his chest.

"Put him in the ground, Wildcat." Win's knees buckled as he dropped a kiss on her mouth, and she smiled at him dizzily. She mouthed the words, telling him she loved him, before charging back to the fight.

Spencer grappled Luke by the shoulders, forcing him to his knees, and with a raised foot belted a blow into his abdomen.

Air whooshed through Luke's teeth as he sailed backward, his spine cracking the dirt. Luke landed awkwardly, his head striking rock, and he went limp. Win launched over him, landing on her feet, sending Spencer sprawling sideways with a roundhouse kick. Adrenaline coursed through her blood. The slash across her stomach barely stung. Before he could clamber to his feet, Win pounced, both knees dug in his back. She grabbed a fistful of dirty blonde hair and smacked his face into the mud. "Why won't you just *stop?*"

Rowan whipped her wings, sending Win sprawling in the mud. Beating with a frantic velocity, Rowan lifted Spencer into the air, but he struggled in her grasp and struck her thigh with his claws. Yelling, she dropped him from a good height, enough to stun him for a moment's respite. She landed, wobbling, and Spencer lunged with a flurry of arms, legs and wings as they fought. He grabbed her wings with such force, it looked like he'd rip them clean off. Win growled, and jumped on his shoulders, closing her hands around his throat. Panting, Rowan staggered to a safer distance, with blood trickling from the wound on her leg.

Roughly, he threw Win, and she rolled, but not quick enough to escape his hand biting at her ankle. He dragged her underneath him, trapped between his muscular thighs. Win saw stars, pain exploding in her skull as he hauled her off the ground and struck the back of her head against hard rock below. Her vision swam, nausea flooded her system, and for a horrible moment, as she rode an aftershock of another strike, she thought she might throw up over herself. "Spencer stop...why can't you just stop?"

Eyes like pools of bitter chocolate focussed on her, his crazed half-smile dropping. Did he even know anymore? Win's heart thumped. She didn't want to die. Not here, in the woods with her father watching, her mother standing nearby. Ella screamed her name.

I'm not ready. Tears filled her ducts. *I don't want to die here.*

Spencer's grip loosened for one moment, and he yelled in fury. Ben was on him, gripping his shoulders, wrestling Spencer with what strength he had. But he was no match. Win saw her father fly through the air, and her mother screamed. In seconds Alice was by her side. Spencer lashed out with a back foot, swiping Alice's legs from under her. What brief gratitude Win felt diminished the second she saw her mother's skin fizzle. Alice contorted and writhed, the stone's light determined to rip the falcon out of her body. Jake grabbed her under the arms and pulled her free of the light, leaving Win alone.

She'd barely risen off the ground before he pinned her again, her flesh pinching as he pressed her into the cold ground. "Why can't you just stop?" she spluttered.

The question struck him, left him speechless with his hands around her neck, ready to choke the life out of her. He pressed harder on her windpipe, and Win's lungs squeezed, the terror of air loss made her hairs stand on end. Then to her horror, he leaned so close she smelled the blood on his breath, pushing back her hair to whisper in her ear.

"With you dead...it's over, Win. Vecula has promised me a new beginning."

Win struggled for air, but she rasped, "It may have escaped your notice...but she left already."

"Nassau will welcome me. You will never win, do you understand? Once I bring him here...you and your inferior race of Therian will be wiped clean...your sister...your parents...my weak brother...I will join a world of gods, monsters, and magic. Think I'll fit in?"

She was losing, everything was fading, and blackness crawled at the edges. "I hope you know...you could have been loved, Spencer..."

Somehow she raised her hand and a tear escaped under her lashes. With the stone's light pulsing at his back, he was a silhouette lined with blue. She traced his brow with her fingers tips. "You had a family."

"Family are only people who hold you back, Win. Lumps of skin, you're bound to for life. Blood isn't thicker than water. It's just blood, nothing special...we all have it. Chemicals and particles, flesh and bone...you hold them in such high regard, don't you? Your precious family? In the end, we all die alone. But when *you* die—I get to cross, and I'll never know death."

Out of the corner of her eye, she spotted Wolfric. He mouthed something to her, and somewhere she heard Grayson screaming her name. Pressure overwhelmed her lungs, like drowning, clawing to the surface toward the light, the last bid for freedom. Muffled noise in her ears reminded her of the ocean. Win imagined it was a month ago, and she saw them walking side by side in the sand, their motel room waiting for them, their own world. She wouldn't graduate. She wouldn't go to prom. She'd never see day again. Win closed her eyes.

Do not die... Luke begged her before this all started. *Do not die...I can't lose you again...*

Luke lay unconscious, bruised, and his right eye swollen. Win stretched her fingertips, close enough to brush his hand. *Luke...please wake up!* If she died and Spencer beat her, would Luke be next?

The shadow of a wolf passed by, helpless as he looked on. Even the strength of her grandfather wasn't going to save her now.

*Get up, firecracker...*John's voice echoed in her head. *Keep fighting...you are better than this.*

He beat me, Grandpa. Win had died before, she knew the thud of her heart was slowing to a steady, drum beat. Oxygen cut off, her mind spiraled, noise evaporated, save from the endless shrill ringing in her ears. Bloodied nails clawed the ground, grasping for rocks and stones, anything she could find to use as a weapon. Her hand touched something sharp and cold.

The Wolf's eyes flashed yellow. *Do it...you can do this! Don't stop fighting, Win!*

Numb, her hand closed around the smooth flat rock in her palm. Win stuck his temple with a sickening blow.

Spencer went wide-eyed, and let go, his expression a mixture of confusion and fear. Fresh oxygen rushed to her lungs, and she gasped, coughing. Rowan ran, her wings splayed as she pushed through the light, grabbing Win under the arms.

Spencer swayed, and his eyes went blank. He staggered, confusion clouding his twisted face. When he recovered enough to stare her down, his eyes were filmy, blood pouring from his temple. Win didn't think it was possible for him to look angrier. He rushed at them, and Win shoved her sister out of his path, bracing herself for impact as he barreled into her, his shoulder under her ribs, knocking the air out of her lungs.

Bent double, she winced and straightened, catching sight of Jake coming closer with a large log in his hand. God, she wasn't going to let him kill Spencer. Jake was irrevocably broken, like Rowan. She'd stopped Rowan from killing him, she'd stop Jake.

It has to be you. End the line. Right now. I can come back from this.

Win wiped spit off her chin. As they stared at one another, she gestured to the vortex, a rushing portal to whatever underworld Vecula fled into. "You think Vecula's hell is better than a life you could have here? Why don't you go there, Spencer?"

He smiled. "Not without you."

If I kill him, I will come back from this. It has to be me.

Win roared. "You're not ending my line. *Ever.* I will never stop fighting you."

Spencer swung for her, and her vision whited.

It has to end. I have to end the line. I can come back.

She spun with velocity and sent dust flying in her wake. He powered closer, but she met his throat with five splayed claws, five sharp knives severing an artery in his neck. Blood spurted from the deep gash at his jugular, and he sputtered and blindly clutched his throat.

Rowan scooped her up, her wings beating the air as she tried to yank Win away. "No, Win..."

Jake was standing directly behind Spencer, his hands trembling. Drunkenly, Spencer landed in his arms, and Jake sobbed, his hands slippery with blood. His voice was a choked, garbled mess as Spencer gripped the lapels of Jake's coat, sliding down to the ground, taking his father with him.

"It's over," Jake said, holding his son while he died. He kissed Spencer's forehead as blood filled his throat, dripping down his chin. "I'm sorry I failed you—you won't hurt anyone again." Spencer gasped and choked as he slipped away, death finally claiming him. His head lolled, and his entire body went limp.

Win stared at them, dumbfounded as blood dripped down her fingers and landed at her feet. *I'm sorry, Jake...I tried...I did try to stop him.*

Jake didn't look up, but she knew he'd heard. He rocked Spencer, sobbing against his blood-soaked hair.

"Everyone move—now!" yelled another voice. It was Wolfric. Time slowed, and Win shouted his name. The man gave her a smile, his teeth shining as he raised his fingers in a salute before he turned and walked straight into the vortex. Win screamed and screamed. This was the plan, the one she'd failed to see coming. It was how this was going to end.

Wolfric whispered something and went up in flames.

Suspended in fear, Wolfric watched, unable to do a thing to help. Across the clearing in the light, Spencer straddled Win. He willed his little warrior to fight back. She *had* to fight back.

Evan was a dead weight in his arms, her mind and body shattered. Heaving, he carried her to a safe distance, propping her against a tree. Evan's eyes fluttered open, panic-stricken as she gazed at the vortex, open, thunderous, and ripping the ground to shreds.

Wolfric took her hand. "Evan, I have to go now."

Weakly, she nodded, resigned, defeated. "I only just got you back."

"Hey!" he said with a pout. "Who said this was over? I'm a Pheonix after all, I might just rise again. Who knows where I might pop up?"

Evan's lips barely made a smile. "Then come and find me in another hundred years. K'a'ak'ate, brother."

Wolfric choked. "Goodbye," he said. "For now."

His laugh was hollow, half-hearted, and he faced the vortex. It was quite possibly game over, but straightening, he adjusted his coat, smoothed his hair, and prepared to face his death head-on, like a warrior. Like Win, and Isaac.

Like Louisa.

He blinked back tears. "I'm coming to see you," he whispered, praying the love of his life waited for him in whatever version of the afterlife he faced. A century was too long to be parted from the woman you loved.

As he walked across the woods, straight into the light, he caught sight of Spencer staggering away, blood pouring from his throat, and he huffed a laugh of relief. The kid did it. The vortex was open, roaring, and beckoned him inside. He turned, meeting Win's confused eyes across the clearing, and lifted his hand in a salute.

She knew what he was going to do. This was always the plan, a one-way ticket and sure-fire way to close the door for good. His last jump had to count for something.

Wolfric grinned, holding out his open arms as electric blue shocks attacked his body, deep in the vortex. He didn't save Louisa, but he'd lived long enough to see her ancestor make things right.

Wolfric bellowed a laugh and closed his eyes, the last word he would ever say leaving his lips before he used the flame for the final time.

"Ka-*boom*!"

Win screamed, "No—Wolfric *don't!*"

He wouldn't come back from this, he might not rise again. Who knew where on earth or in time he'd end up? Wolfric went up like a ball of kerosene-soaked cloth, and around him the light paled, fizzing and spitting. Then he burst into dust, the shockwave of the blast sending the light careering over the woods. The door crumbled and moaned, grumbling as it exploded to bits. Chunks of rock and debris flew across the ground.

Ben ran, sweat pouring down his neck, and Win yelled, trying to turn back for him, pushing against sharp, strong gusts of air. "Dad!" she screamed. Their eyes met, and she stretched for his hand, but he was out of reach.

The last thing she saw was her father fall before the blast swept her off her feet. Losing balance she sailed backward. Alice screamed his name, and Win fell face up in the mud, cracking her skull. Debris flew overhead, and Ben vanished in a flurry of rubble. "Dad...no!"

The next few seconds were a chaotic nightmare. The ground rumbled, and light from the stone streaked skyward as the explosion rocked through the forest. Rubble flew in all directions as the ancient relic exploded, loud, bone-shaking and the vortex sucked trees, logs, and anything in its wake. Like a twister careering its way across farmland, it enveloped everything in its path. Win staggered to her feet to see Ella running and Rowan throw herself over Grayson. Jake stared, a look of horror on his face as he abandoned Spencer and dragged Luke free of the blast.

Spencer's dead body was thrown like a doll into the cyclone, and then it was gone. On her knees, Win crawled for a rock deeply embedded in the ground. Nails digging in dirt, sweat trickled down her brow. She couldn't stand up. The force of the air was too strong, the muscles in her biceps tore as she clung on, while around her branches snapped free of trunks, and loose rubble flew past her head.

Win screamed, her eyes leaking water as her muscles burned out, and the bones of her fingers couldn't hang on another second.

FORTY-EIGHT

Rowan landed on something soft and warm. A groan let forth from between her teeth, and she lifted her chin, her face inches from Grayson's. She cried in mortification. The force of the explosion had sent them flying across the dirt.

"Oh, *god*!"

"You saved my life," he said, shocked. As if she would ever have let him die. Grayson lay still as a rock under her, flat on his back, terrified and embarrassed, mostly because she was stark naked. Rowan rubbed at the back of her head, where it throbbed wildly.

"Don't get used to it," she moaned, rushing to cover her nakedness with her arms, not sure what to protect first. A blush streaked her cheekbones, and she glanced up to find him stripped to a thin t-shirt, holding out his bloodied hoodie. She snatched it and grinned sheepishly. "You're such a gentleman." She pulled it over her head, where it dropped past her thighs, enough to cover her modesty. It drowned her, and it was holding his body heat. The temperature had fallen, and the ground was flaked with ice.

"When did he get back?" Grayson jerked his chin in the direction of Cole, who'd arrived in the clearing, sweaty, dirty, and dazed. Cole clapped his hands, about to make a joke, but his mouth dropped when he saw the carnage.

"I was going to ask if I missed anything exciting...but...."Cole waved his arms. "You destroyed the woods!"

Rowan waltzed past Grayson, who blushed furiously as she flicked her hair. "You *so* looked," she accused with a wicked smile, and he grunted in reply. Glancing around the clearing, she was relieved to see she wasn't the only one with the naked problem. Luke was hopping from tree to tree, yelling at Cole to loan him his sweater. The kid grinned, enjoying his friend's humiliation.

The air was silent, eerily quiet. Even the animals had fled, nothing stirred, and for a moment, it felt like all life had been stripped out of the woods. Like the aftermath of a tornado, rocks and stumps were overturned, and trees revealed their knotted roots, pulled free of the ground. Rowan spotted Evan, propped sleepily against a tree.

Evan's eyes lit up, holding her arms as Rowan lifted her off her feet. She kissed her over and over. "It worked..." Rowan babbled into her hair, relief burst like an adrenaline rush. "It goddamn worked."

Evan pulled away, taking Rowan's cold face between her hands. "I love you so much."

Rowan scooped her up, holding her tightly, Evan let out a contented sigh. "Shall we go on vacation?" Rowan laughed through her tears. "Take off like Grayson and Win and just be by ourselves for a month?"

Spencer was gone. Not just in a different time, *dead* and gone. In those final moments, while Rowan scraped herself off the ground, she saw the almighty death blow Win dealt. Not even Spencer Fraser could come back from that.

It should have been me. I should have killed him, she thought, a dull ache in her chest. Rowan admitted there had been a moment where she could have ended him, pounding her fists into his face. She'd battled away memories, good ones, where he'd made her happy, if only for a while.

But she'd seen Evan through the vortex, barely able to stand, bruised, swollen, and violated. The man she thought she knew was nothing but a carefully executed act—all a lie. He'd never existed. Casting her gaze across the clearing, she saw Jake scrubbing at his swollen face.

Spencer was finally gone.

Rowan wiped at her eyes. "I'm making you stay in bed for the rest of the week. You aren't moving a foot or an inch." She placed kisses on the backs of Evan's hands. "I'm never going to stop wanting to protect you."

Evan's smile slipped just for a moment, and clutched Rowan's arm, so she didn't fall. Rowan fought a wave of panic. "Evan—what's wrong?"

"I'm done," Evan said, shuffling into her arms. "I have a lot of healing to do and don't have your Therain capabilities. And my brother is gone."

Rowan's buoyant mood sank. "I'm sorry."

"Oh, he'll be back," she said shakily, and Rowan wasn't convinced. The energy from Wolfric's last jump destroyed the door the moment he went up in flames inside the vortex. Rowan wasn't sure anyone could come back from that. "I need to go back to the house and sleep for a week."

"I'll come with you," Rowan said, eager and keen never to be parted from Evan again. Jumbled thoughts and plans for the future with this woman were suddenly interrupted. Rowan's exhilaration was short-lived.

Alice screamed her name. Blood iced in her veins as she turned, her gaze settling on her mother, on her knees in the dirt. Alice sobbed over a lumpy shape on the ground. Rowan walked woodenly toward it, her feet like lead.

No...no...please...

"Dad..." Rowan's voice choked. She couldn't breathe, edging closer, her mind refusing to believe what she saw. "Dad...?"

Ben lay sprawled in the mud, the back of his head caved in, blood matted on his scalp and strands of grayed hair. Voices whispered to Rowan as she inched closer, she heard Luke talking, and Jake attempted to take her by the shoulder, but she shook him free as the world slowed to a crawl. Ben's face was turned sideways, in an odd, sharp direction, gazing with lifeless, open eyes.

Rowan stopped breathing, or so she thought.

You couldn't vomit if you weren't breathing. And she did, right there in the dirt, acidic bile rising up her gullet, leaving her spitting and sobbing, bent double. Hot tears blurred her eyes. "No..." she cried. "No, no..."

Sirens wailed in the distance. Someone swore under their breath. Rowan fell to her knees, hardly able to touch him, he was still warm, and she kissed the side of his face. "This isn't possible...." She stood, and found Evan with her hard stare. "We have to go back...change things. We need to go back and warn him."

The color drained from Evan's golden skin, her lips an odd bluish tinge. She reached for Rowan, and her fingers trembled. "Rowan...I can't..."

"Yes, you can!" Rowan screamed, and it was a horrible sound. Strained and hysterical. "I *know* what you can do. Go back and warn him. Find Wolfric...he can't die!"

She'd saved Evan but lost her father. Narrowing her gaze, her eyes flashed yellow, bitter, resentful, and angry. Evan could fix this. She had to. She was a witch, the daughter of a God. Did she expect Rowan to believe there was nothing to be done? Rowan nearly murdered a boy she once loved. She'd skirted so close to complete darkness to save this woman. Her father couldn't be gone.

"*Fix* this," she said through clenched teeth.

Evan shook. "Rowan...I can't bring back the dead."

Alice screamed and rocked over Ben's body. Rowan sucked in her ribs like she was going to implode inward. "He isn't...you could save him, please! Do *something*!"

Sirens filled the air, and Luke looked about in real fear. "The cops are coming! We have to leave...someone take him...we have to hide this!"

"No!" Alice sobbed. "I'm not leaving him."

"Luke, Cole—help me," Jake ordered, grabbing Ben's arm and dragging him off the ground.

"You have to go back!" Rowan wailed. "He can't die...he can't leave us."

Ben was dead. Her father was gone. A hollowness filled her insides, and she choked. "This isn't happening." She was never going to see her father again. She ran for Evan, grabbing her too hard. "There has to be a way." Her voice strangled, tears and snot running down her face. "Bring him back...open the door."

"We destroyed the door," Evan reminded her with a quiet sadness, lost for words.

"Evan..." Rowan stared at her, outraged and horrified. "Fix this, please."

"I—I can't!"

Wolfric was gone, burned up in a ball of flame. But Win...Win could jump. Win could go back, warn him, and he'd still be here. It wouldn't be a morning when her father was dead, and she couldn't talk to him ever again. It would be like it never happened.

"Win..."

Rowan whirled hopelessly, her heart knocking frantically against her chest wall. Hope ignited in her heart; she flew across the clearing, kicking away rubble in her path. If Win jumped, warned him to get free of the blast in time...then he'd be okay...he wouldn't die, not here in this woods face down in the mud, like he was nothing, expendable something to be thrown away.

He used to let her dance on his feet, swaying her around the room when she was a kid. Rowan bent double, the air sucked from her body.

"No..." she choked. "Win...where's Win?"

Luke and Jake hurried across the woods, dragging Ben's body. A blood trail followed them, as through the mist, the shrill wail of sirens came closer. Perhaps Cole's distraction wasn't enough? The door had exploded, and half the town would be awake.

Rowan whirled in a circle, feeling like she was standing on a cliff edge with no one to pull her back, with blood beating in her ears. The world was ending, and she couldn't breathe. Where was her sister?

"Where's Win?"

Her answer came from Grayson, who stood in the charred remains of rubble left from the shattered stone. They locked eyes, and he fell to his knees, like the fight had left his body.

"She's gone," he said.

EPILOGUE

Light streamed through a curtain. Foggy-brained and dry-mouthed, Win opened her eyes. The sunshine dazzled her, and she turned her face away from the blinding rays peeking through closed drapes, framing a small dirty window.

What the hell was she wearing? Win gazed down, not even able to see her feet as she was clothed in some kind of long, beige linen dress, possibly the ugliest thing she'd ever set eyes on, and as she twisted her nose to shoulder, it smelled like pigs. She gagged.

Wincing, a dull ache exploded up her neck. Smacking her lips, she longed for water, spying a porcelain sink in the corner of the ratty kitchen. Where the hell was she? Wriggling her shoulders, she discovered the source of the pain. Both arms were bound tightly behind her back, and she was tied to a chair. Win's heart fluttered with panic, her gaze dancing around the room she was held captive in.

Win's stomach turned. More like, *when* the hell was she? All she remembered was the dull heat of the explosion at her back, clinging to a rock while her lower body was lifted off the ground from the force of the vortex. And like a switch being flicked off, she was gone. And her father...Win closed her eyes as her breathing threatened to get out of control. He'd vanished in the debris. In that moment, she'd lost sight of him.

Okay...don't start freaking out...

The door slammed open, and a man filled the empty space. Win whimpered. *Okay...maybe a little freak-out won't hurt...*

The rope bit her skin, sliced welts stung when she tried to move. Win rocked the chair a little, and it wobbled, which only served to garner the interest of the man who'd walked in the door. He was followed by another man and then another. Last through the door was a small, mousy young woman in a long, checked dress with curly brown hair. She rested her hands on her stomach, and when she pulled up a chair, Win spotted an enormous pregnancy bump hidden under the gown.

"Who the hell are you?" she blurted, her skin flaming. "Untie me right now!"

The first man dragged out a chair, turning to sit on it backward. He peered at her under his wide-brimmed hat. He was tall, tanned with a massive, bearded jaw. His lips smacked together, chewing on something slick and black, as he studied her with pale, glassy eyes. Under the hat, Win spotted wisps of blonde hair. "You're a little forward, aren't you? Don't see it's right you making demands. Not when we found you out there left for dead."

Win swallowed back any retort she could think of, now wasn't the time for a smart Lukeish remark, she needed to reign in her temper. She was in a cabin, in the woods, tied to a chair, and she needed to get the hell out of these ropes. Win cursed herself, all she'd been through in the last twelve hours, and she ended up like this. The insufferable humiliation of hurtling through the vortex in her birthday suit made her cheeks flush.

"And...not to mention you was buck naked?" the other man cried from behind, chortling. He was similar in height, maybe a little younger but skinny, all sinew and bone, with glassy, bulbous eyes. Both deeply tanned, outdoorsy, sweaty, and grimy. Woodsmen.

Wait... Win looked about carefully. *A cabin...in the woods, and those eyes.* The second man held a rifle, leaning heavily on the butt of the gun, making her very aware of how vulnerable she was. He tapped the butt, drawing her attention; a warning should she try anything rash.

Win tried to move her fingers and gave a short sigh when she felt Grayson's ring still firmly in place. Boy, did she have a story to tell him when she got back.

Except you're trapped here... Wolfric blew up the door. Win's insides coiled. She couldn't jump, not forward, not to her time. Her mouth dried up as the third man stepped out of the shadows. Win squinted and then gasped. God, she was so stupid.

This one was blonde, young, maybe a year older than her, with a chipped front tooth. Tanned, wiry and lean, and with a sharp jaw and a nose which looked as though it'd been broken once. His arm was in a sling, and he cradled it as he stepped into the light to get a better look at her.

"Jack...this look like the one who mauled you?"

Win squirmed in the chair as the one called Jack pressed closer, peering into her face with those familiar glassy eyes. He had a dimple in his cheek, which deepened as he looked at her, and as he got closer, she smelled pine needles and dead leaves.

Jack swallowed after looking at her for a long time. "She's got the eyes like the other one...look!"

Without warning, he rocketed out of the chair and yanked open the curtain, spilling bright light into the room. Win cried out and squinted, her eyes struggling to adjust, and all three leaned in to get a better look, muttering with interest. The woman kept her eyes down, her hands fidgeting on top of her bump.

The eldest chewed his tobacco, smacking his lips. "She's one of them demon Hickorys alright...but I ain't seen her before. She doesn't live with them."

What little color she had, drained out of her skin. "I'm not a demon."

"Are you a witch?" the gunman asked, scratching at the greasy scruff on his jaw. "Jack says he rescued a witch, then one of your demon friends attacked him. Witches don't tend to survive long around here."

He made a grotesque face, pretending to choke as though he were on the end of a hangman's rope. His tongue poked out between his lips. The older one laughed and punched his shoulder. Win stared at them, bug-eyed. The heavily pregnant woman made a disgusted face. "Elias!" she hissed.

"I'm not a witch..." Win realized he meant Evan. Their paths must have crossed, with Spencer too. "My name is Winifred Adler...I'm seventeen years old...."

He cocked the gun at her, pointing it at her temple, chewing the inside of his mouth, and sweat gathered under her arms. The woman jerked in her seat. She'd avoided looking Win directly in the eye the whole time, but now she looked terrified. "Please..." Win begged.

"Why were you naked out there in the woods? Casting some sort of demonic ritual?" the one called Elias asked.

"No...."

"What about the brand?"

Win's eyes went saucer wide. Jack narrowed his eyes at her. "Brand?"

"The mark on your chest," Jack reminded her, with a curt nod to her breastbone. "We saw it. It's a witch's mark. A brand."

"No," she stammered, realizing they meant the burn in the shape of a bird. Wolfric's mark. Win thought quickly. "It's a birthmark."

"Perhaps we should call the good Reverend to take a look," the eldest threatened. "He knows his fair share about witches."

Win's skin went clammy, and her stomach knotted. *The Reverend?* She locked eyes with Jack, shooting him with an imploring gaze.

"N-no...please. I was traveling...." She babbled, buying time, trying to think of anything that came into her head. The ring dug into her finger. "My husband and I were attacked on the road...please, I don't remember anything else." With her hands bound, she wriggled, working the ring off the right hand and managing to stuff it down over her wedding finger. Not an easy task, her fingers were slick and clammy.

Jack frowned and nudged his brother, who lowered the gun. "She does have a ring on. I spotted it when we were carrying her in. What's his name?"

"Who?"

"Your *husband?*" Jack repeated with a roll of his eyes. "What's his name? Would we know him?"

Win's excuses flat-lined, her brain woolly. "Hank...we lived in Mickleford. His name is Hank...Adler."

Rileys...these men were Rileys. This spelled catastrophic trouble because a room with her dead ancestors inside was somewhere on their property. Win didn't know why she came up with Hank, Grayson's boss in Mickelford, the man who ran the lumber yard. She was dehydrated, her throat dry and parched, and she couldn't think straight. And she didn't want to give them any information they could use. With a snag in her gut, she realized there was no one they could find. Win was alone. Straining her neck, she saw a discarded newspaper laying on the dusty kitchen table. Narrowing her eyes she managed to read the date. *1807.*

Win's stomach plummeted. Mary was already dead. Vivienne had been dead for two years. Who could she go to? How could she walk up to Hickory house, knock on the door and introduce herself?

Evan...Evan is here somewhere. Hope ignited then dwindled like a spluttering match. *You told her to run for her life. She has to live. You can't drag her back here where she'd be in danger.*

Wolfric was gone, up in flames inside the vortex, and his words haunted her. Win couldn't alter the line. Anything she did here could drastically alter her family line and possibly lead to a future without Luke, Rowan, or her mother. She was trapped.

Jack leaned casually on the back of the chair, his lips twitching with interest, while Win's resolve broke, and she sobbed into her chest. Droplets of water fell and soaked into the scratchy material of her dress. What the hell was she going to do? How could she get back to Grayson? Her parents? Rowan and Luke? Win sniffed, her breath catching. Despair washed over her, and she bawled, not caring if they watched, which they were, with increasing intrigue.

"Here," Jack said, shoving a filthy handkerchief in her face. To her horror, he dabbed her face dry with a gentleness she wasn't expecting. Ducking her eyes, she could barely look at him and burst again.

Jack pinched her chin, forcing her to stop short, his fingers digging into her skin. "Stop crying. No one here is going to hurt you, *Mrs.* Adler..." The way he drawled out the *Mrs.* made her shudder. He wasn't buying it. "My name is Jack Riley, and these are my brothers, Abraham and Elias. I swear we won't lay a finger on you. We're hunters and not in the business of murdering women we find in the woods."

Win blinked at him through spiky, wet lashes. "Then why am I tied to a chair?"

He jerked his chin at the injured arm in a sling. "Had a run-in with a nasty character...we have a lot of strange folks out here in the woods. We had to make sure you weren't one of them."

"I have no idea what you're talking about," Win lied, meeting his gaze with slowly dissolving confidence. He smirked, and something in her heart snapped. God, she wished he didn't look so much like Grayson. It hurt.

I'm never going to see him again...we blew up that stupid door!

Casting her eyes around the group, she wondered which one had killed Mary. It *had* to be one of them. Win was acutely aware she was playing for her life; these were dangerous men and killers, and if they discovered what she was, she'd die here. And end up in a glass case.

"You'll be just fine here with us," Jack assured her, drawing closer, giving her a charming, crooked smile, and something in his tone told her that was a lie. She wasn't going to be fine. She wasn't safe here. Not with people who tried to murder her family.

"Now," he said slowly. "*Mrs*. Adler. How about you tell us *everything* there is to know about yourself?"

Acknowledgments

I would like to take a moment to thank some special people who have made writing this book a memorable experience, and who have shown me such love, support and encouragement.

Any writer will tell you that the craft can be lonely, and I think we all have a romantic notion that we writers are tucked away in cafe corners, toiling away over our work and suffering, tortured and alone. This isn't the case, and although it can be a lonely, sometimes, these guys keep me going. Alpha and Beta readers are essential, they keep you sane, point out glaring errors and plot chasms, and give you that boost of encouragement when you need it.

Bethany Votaw, Kent Shawn, Chris Kenny and Alex Wolf are all amazing writers and I'm so lucky to have found you. Kim Campbell, thank you so much for keeping me on track and for being a pillar of support. If you need a proofreader, check out Proofing the Pages over on Instagram!

Thank you Thea, my incredible cover designer. I promise its only two more books!

Finally, thank you Ian, my husband and my best friend Ian, and my two daughters Eva and Grace. Thank you, Ian, for being a good listener, even though I know half the time it goes over your head. You are my best friend and confidant, and I couldn't do this without you. Thank you girls, I will tell you stories forever.

About Victoria

Victoria lives in the UK, with her husband, two daughters, and a very needy Tabby cat. Since the age of thirteen, she has written short stories and novels for young adults, creating worlds she wished were real and characters dear to her soul. She is a huge fan of paranormal fiction, loves scaring the life out of her kids and anyone who wants to read her work. Victoria is the proud author of the Wild Spirit series and looks forward to publishing more books in the series next year.

Also by Victoria Wren

The Wild Spirit Series
The Curse of Win Adler
Huntress
The Last Hickory
The Pheonix (Coming 2023)

Other Titles
Nocturnal Creatures (coming 2024)

Evelyn Grace Romance Author
Breaking Nick (coming 2022)

Printed in Great Britain
by Amazon